Ken & Dorothy West
1730 Utah Avenue
Flint, Michigan
238-0136 48506

The Favor

NICHOLAS GUILD

The Favor

St. Martin's Press New York

For information, write: St. Martin's Press,
175 Fifth Avenue, New York, N.Y. 10010
Manufactured in the United States of America

Library of Congress Cataloging in Publication Data
Guild, Nicholas.
The favor.

I. Title.
PS3557.U357F38 813'.54 80-21817
ISBN 0-312-28512-4

Design by MARY A. BROWN

FOR *my Mother and Father,*
and about time too.

The Favor

1

The room by itself was a problem. Just a square little box, not an inch of which you couldn't take in the second you stepped across the threshold. The door of the john was even made out of glass, which was weird—the rippled kind, of course, presumably as a small concession to modesty, but the light inside worked off the main switch, so you'd be like a goldfish in a bowl. Not much point in trying to hide in there. Not much point in trying to hide anywhere. Guinness decided he wouldn't bother.

In the end he settled for simply removing all the bulbs from the overhead fixtures, even the one in the bathroom. What the hell, Harry Bateman wasn't exactly Public Enemy Number One; he wasn't the sort to duck and roll just because nothing happened when he walked in and flipped on the light switch. His mind probably wasn't much used to concerning itself with the basic tactics of survival, which was just going to be tough on him. And anyway, if the last few nights had been any indication, he'd probably be half-swacked in the bargain.

God, what a bore. Guinness wondered how in the world he'd sinned that they sent him after runaway file clerks. For three days he'd followed this clown around, in the afternoons through room after room of pink, fleshy Rubens nudes in the Alte Pinakothek, and from six o'clock on through every strip joint and brothel in Munich, with only a break for dinner and a nice big bottle of Ürziger Schwarzlay. Friend Bateman certainly was having himself a razzle on his ill-gotten gains.

It was nine-thirty, and the dining room downstairs would be closed after eleven. Allowing, say, an hour to take care of this business, he could still make it if Bateman would hurry up and show. Christ, he hadn't had anything to eat since noon—it wasn't the sort of job you much wanted to do on a full stomach.

Thank heaven for small mercies, though. Our little file clerk seemed to be a chap of regular habits—sitting down to his schnitzel and brown dumplings every evening at a quarter after eight, and then back home to preen himself for the whores. He'd be along directly.

And alone, unless Guinness had rather seriously misread the man. No little friends up for a quiet night of room service and heavy breathing; he seemed to prefer them in their natural habitat. Or perhaps he was just afraid of the house detective.

Did they still even have house detectives these days? Did hotels still worry about the state of your morals—at all? No, he didn't think so. But Bateman, after all, had until a few weeks ago been leading a sheltered existence in rural Nebraska with a wife and two perfectly obnoxious daughters, so he might still entertain all sorts of quaint notions about the guardianship of the public virtue.

Anyway, the odds were he wouldn't show up with any easy ladies on his arm. At least, he hadn't yet. That sort of thing was for later, after he'd brushed the powdered sugar out of his moustache and reapplied his Mennen Speedstik and was ready once again to face the bright world.

Come on and hurry it up, Harry. My guts are growling and it's time you paid your score. You won't make it any nicer by putting it off.

Guinness sat in an armchair in front of the only window, the drapes to which he had drawn closed twenty minutes ago, after he had first picked the lock on the inside door and let himself in. The Luger in his hand was threaded with a silencer, which he kept unscrewing a quarter of a turn and then tighening back on as he tried to make up his mind whether or not to bother with the stupid thing at all. He didn't like silencers; they struck him as faintly melodramatic and they always threw your shot off a little—although across the width of a hotel room that would hardly matter very much. Still, somehow it made you feel silly to kill someone with a gun that didn't make any more noise than a champagne cork. Bateman would probably prefer to go out with a bang.

Nonetheless, there were things like instructions to be considered. It would be nice if he spilled his guts before he died, but Harry Bateman had to die. Nobody wanted him arrested and brought back to the States for trial; nobody was interested in that kind of publicity. No slipups, nothing fancy—just kill him where he stands. The fix was in, so for the record it was going to be death by misadventure—a heart attack, a fall in the bathtub, something like that—and it wouldn't matter how many bullet holes. If there were going to be bullet holes, however, Guinness would rather make them without waking up the whole hotel, and it was one of the myths of television that you could always count on downing a man with the first shot.

But perhaps it wouldn't come to that. Perhaps Bateman would turn out to be the reasonable type and could be persuaded to leave a nice presentable cadaver that wouldn't constitute too much of a trauma for the chambermaid. One could hope.

The room was perfectly dark. Even the lamps were disconnected, all except the one on the table next to Guinness's chair. He took another look at his watch, a digital job he had bought for himself as a fortieth-birthday present; you pressed the stem for a reading and the numbers would pulse on like a heartbeat, counting off the seconds. It was nine thirty-four. Presumably Bateman was lingering over the last of his wine. It wouldn't be the first time.

What would he do when he came in? There were two doors, an arrangement you only seemed to find in Europe, with only a few inches of space between them. The first opened out into the corridor and the second into the room, and only the second had a lock on it. So Bateman would take out his key for that and stand with his back to the outside door, which was equipped with a heavy spring at the top hinge, to keep it from closing. Would he try turning on the overhead before locking himself in? Yes, probably. He would stay between the doors and see whether he could find the switch in the narrow little patch of dull light from the corridor, and when he discovered it wasn't working he would step across the threshold—it would be a reflex; he wouldn't even think about it—to get close enough to the dresser to pull the little cord on the lamp, and the outside door would then slam shut on its own. And by then our man would be well inside the trap.

The poor little slob. Of course, he wasn't thinking in terms of traps; in his mind he still lived in that nice, safe world where you didn't have to think. Doubtless all Bateman's anxieties were about policemen, about being dragged back to Nebraska in chains to face a jury of his peers. He probably didn't realize that he had left all that behind him, that the interests he had offended by runnning off with a briefcase full of other people's secrets hardly ever troubled themselves about due process. The verdict was already in, and there was only the sentence left to be carried out.

But Bateman didn't know that. He had a fake passport

and lots of money and probably felt pretty safe. Why should he imagine that there might be somebody waiting for him in his room? Why should he suspect that anything was wrong when the overhead light didn't go on? Probably it just meant that the bulb was blown. Sure it did.

It was nine forty-six when Guinness finally heard a key in the lock.

Bateman was humming to himself, if that was the right word for the erratic little honking sounds that became audible as the inside door swung open, a kind of private jumble of noise in which could be detected, almost as if by accident, some approximation of a Strauss waltz—you heard them all over town, all whipped cream and *Gemütlichkeit,* through the open doors of restaurants and cafés and over the canned music systems in department stores. And Bateman was humming one as he tried to negotiate the entrance to his hotel room. He was feeling just fine, it seemed—he didn't have a care in the world. Not one.

He stood between the inner and outer doors, perfectly visible in the yellow light from the corridor, and then he pulled the outer door closed behind him and disappeared again into the darkness of the room. He was still humming; the tune would break off every once in a while as he breathed in thickly through his nose.

The inside door wheezed shut. Guinness waited for the click of the light switch, but it didn't come right away. Instead, there was a heavy scratching sound as Bateman made a number of painstaking attempts to fit his key back into the lock. What the hell did Bateman care? *He* wasn't afraid of the dark.

Finally he made it, and the lock turned closed with a rattle. And then the light switch—click, click. Nothing. Bateman paused for a few seconds—the waltz tune got lost in a concentrated, ponderously thoughtful exhalation—and then he tried it again. Click, click, click. And then the flat sound of his hand, feeling around on the dresser top for the base of the lamp.

Enough was enough. Guinness reached up with his right hand and pulled the cord on the lamp beside him, the only one that was about to go on for anybody.

The room was flooded with light, or at least that was what it felt like after all this time sitting in the dark. For Bateman, too, the suddenness of it seemed a shock—it seemed to catch him like a hammerblow, just at the base of the spine. He pitched around, bracing his elbows against the dresser as if he expected to fall down.

"Good evening." Guinness's voice was marvelously even, considering. He tried not to blink as he brought his Luger up so that it was pointing at a spot just under the left side of Bateman's ribcage. "If you move before I give you permission, I'm going to kill you. I'm going to kill you anyway, but I'll do it right now instead of waiting. Do you understand that? Just nod your head."

Poor Bateman—it would have been possible to feel sorry for him if he hadn't looked so damned ridiculous, with his knees locked and his back pushed up against the dresser to keep himself from clattering to the floor as if somebody had severed his spine at the top joint. His mouth kept opening and closing, seemingly without any reference to the will, like a machine somebody had forgotten to turn off. Finally all this up-and-down motion managed to translate itself into a stiff nod. Well, good; the message had filtered through at last.

He wasn't any older than his late thirties—a few years younger than Guinness, who was hardly ready to class himself as an antique—but at that moment, as his pale blue eyes glistened in his thin, suddenly rather withered face, he might have been the mummy of Rameses, come back to life to die all over again. Even his little soup-strainer of a moustache looked comically too large for his shrunken mouth.

It happened that way sometimes, when you were, say, two-and-a-half sheets to the wind and all at once you had to sober up much too fast. It seemed to squeeze something out of you. Bateman looked half dead already, his bony hands dangling at his sides as if he didn't quite know what to do with them. The poor little bastard—he just wasn't ready for these kinds of games. And he wasn't going to have much more of a chance to get ready.

"Now I want you to sit down on the floor, with your feet straight out in front of you. Just there." Guinness gestured with the muzzle of his Luger to a spot just to one side of the center of the carpet, well clear of any furniture, where Bateman presumably would be less subject to bright ideas.

"And it might be well if you remember that for all I know, you're in deadly weapons up to your eyebrows, and you're not likely to persuade me into thinking otherwise. So if you reach into your pocket, or if either of your hands disappears from sight, even for a second, you get your ticket canceled on the spot." Guinness pulled back his lips to let his teeth show in a parody of a smile. "And don't imagine I'll be sorry if what I pry loose from your cold, dead fingers is a wad of kleenex—I'm not the compassionate type."

He pointed to the spot again, with a movement that suggested a certain impatience, and Bateman began his awkward descent. It was painful to watch him as he slid slowly down to the floor; his joints seemed to be stiff with age, and he gave the impression of a man crawling backward into a hole. But he kept his hands in plain view, and when finally he was still again, sitting with his back bent forward in what looked like exhaustion, he kept them flat on his thighs, the fingers widely spread.

Neither man spoke. For a long time they were like that, one of them sitting in a chair, the other on the floor, as they studied each other in the pale, pitiless light from the one lamp. Bateman didn't seem afraid anymore—but perhaps he had never been afraid. Perhaps it had only been the surprise. After all, Guinness didn't feel under any obligation to think badly of the man.

"What were you going to do?" he asked finally. "I mean, when the money ran out. What was supposed to happen then?"

Bateman didn't say anything, but after a moment he smiled thinly and shrugged his shoulders. And then the smile died and he was still again.

"Don't you know? Didn't you think about it?"

It was only a question—or, rather, two questions. There wasn't any tone of outrage or incredulity in Guinness's voice; he was just curious. More curious, apparently, than Bateman, who only smiled again and shook his head.

"I guess not. I guess that means I didn't care." He looked around the room for a few seconds, the way a man might trace the vagrant journey of a housefly, and then he looked down at his hands again, and then he looked into Guinness's face, squinting, as if he were having trouble pulling him into focus. There was a pair of glasses in the breast pocket of his jacket, but he made no attempt to reach for them. "Can I have a cigarette?"

"Where are they?"

"In the pocket of my shirt. I've got the matches there too."

"Then draw the lapel of your coat back with the tips of your fingers. Don't do anything except very, very slowly."

You might almost have thought he wasn't moving at all. It probably took him forty-five seconds to open his coat, to extract the pack of cigarettes from his pocket and set them down on his thigh, and then to shake one out and light it. When he had the thing going, he blew out the match with his first puff of smoke and then casually dropped it on the carpet beside him. The same with the ashes; as the cigarette burned its way down to the end, he would flick them off onto the floor. What the hell, he wasn't the one who was going to have to clean up.

"The money—how much of it have you got left?"

"About thirty-five hundred." Bateman seemed to consider that fact for a moment, terminating his reverie with a syllable of voiceless, ironic laughter. "I was going to pack off to Spain in a couple of days, in search of a better exchange rate."

Guinness only nodded. Thirty-five hundred left—that sounded about right. Bateman's wife had reported him missing a little under four weeks ago, and the way he had been living—reckoning in the women—would probably account for about two hundred fifty dollars a day. Figuring another few thousand for transportation and counterfeit papers, that would bring it up to about fifteen thousand dollars. Fifteen thousand was probably pretty close to current market value for the kind of intermediate-level classified material to which someone like Bateman would have had access—allowing, of course, for a substantial markup further along the line.

Bateman, after all, was just a wholesaler; the real money was all made by that handful of merchant princes, the entrepreneurs of the snatch-and-grab business who could put all the little pieces together into coherent wholes worth hundreds of thousands, sometimes millions of dollars. You couldn't begrudge them their profits. It couldn't be an easy thing to do, probably like reconstructing a wedding cake out of the crumbs stolen by fieldmice.

"I don't suppose there's any chance you and I could cut a deal?"

Bateman looked embarrassed, but he needn't have been. Guinness wasn't offended by the suggestion. Hell, why should he be offended? If a man has thirty-five hundred dollars, what should stop him from trying to buy his life with it? But he frowned anyway, shaking his head. He was sorry for Bateman, but that was the way things were.

"Then they'd be after two of us. You wouldn't last another week, and I'm not going to spend the rest of my life hiding from everybody, not for that kind of money. It just wouldn't be worth it. Sorry."

And that seemed to be that. It was astonishing how little Bateman seemed to mind; you might almost have thought he was relieved.

His cigarette was nearly finished now. He hadn't really paid much attention to it, just taking a shallow puff now and then and, for the rest, shaking the ashes off with an absent-minded spasm of his hand; but now it was almost down to the filter, and he pinched off the mouthpiece between first finger and thumb and started casting around with his eyes for something to do with it.

There was a small triangular ashtray made of white porcelain on the table at Guinness's elbow—a light little thing, thin as a sea shell and perfectly harmless—that he picked up and tossed onto Bateman's lap. Bateman nodded thanks, ground out the smoldering filter, set the ashtray down on the floor beside his right knee, and lit another cigarette. This time he took a deep drag, filling his lungs and then blowing smoke up at the ceiling. He laughed as he watched the white plumes curling in upon themselves as they rose through the stale, still, hotel room air.

"At least this way I won't live to regret it," he said, and laughed all over again. He seemed to think the whole thing was exquisitely funny.

Guinness, however, didn't laugh. He had seen all this business too many times before to think it was funny. The joke had worn thin for him.

Because, of course, Bateman wasn't really such an isolated case. The poor little slob at the end of his tether, schooled to resignation by a life lived in a tract house with an overweight wife suffering from varicose veins. The job that meant nothing, that seemed, over the years, to be gradually replacing the marrow in your bones with compressed air; the loud, hostile, sneering children, partaking of your substance but living a life as alien and incomprehensible as anything you could imagine on the planet Mars. The present and the future, a blind wall stretching into infinity.

And so Bateman had taken his chance, had jumped at it, seizing it in both hands. A month of pleasure and freedom, and what came after didn't matter worth a tinker's damn. Prison, poverty, exile, death—anything but going back. And now we sit on the floor and crack jokes with our murderer, becoming almost his accomplice, in a crime almost without a victim. We are washed in the blood of the lamb, oh Lord. Our sins are many, and we hope for nothing. Prison, poverty, exile, death. It's all the same.

"I can offer you one kind of a deal," Guinness murmured, shifting uncomfortably in his chair. "Not your life, but perhaps something else."

He didn't like this sort of thing. There was something distasteful and—yes—slightly vulgar about dickering with a man over the terms on which you would send him to the embalmers. If the boys back in Washington just wanted somebody snuffed, then fine; Guinness was their man for it. It was the work he had been doing for, it seemed, as long as he could remember, and he didn't mind it at all. He was good at it, maybe the best in the business; he even took a kind of pleasure in it. But all the qualified instructions that went with a job like this one—they just weren't his cup of tea.

"Find out who he tumbled for," Ernie had said. "We'd have more than a passing interest in knowing who corrupts our poor, innocent little file clerks with visions of pink champagne and friendly ladies in black lace underwear—the word is Bateman's having himself quite a time over there. See about that, would you? And we won't mind if there are a few bruises on the body." He had smiled that ratty little smile of his, the smile of the ex-field man suffering through an attack of nostalgia. "You see to it that the little runt comes clean before you tuck him in."

Ernie wasn't such a bad guy by the standards of the profession, but Guinness just thought that maybe next time he wanted all these kinds of embellishments he could damn well crawl out of his windowless office on G Street and see to them himself.

Guinness looked at the specimen in front of him, wondering about his probable tolerance for pain. Because that was what Ernie had had in mind, unimaginative clod that he was, what the Trade called "knuckle dusting."

Not that you were likely to get anywhere just tying somebody down to his chair and slapping him around some—that sort of thing only worked in Shirley Temple movies. You never get anything out of anybody that way, especially when he knows that the minute you stop hammering at him you're going to scatter the contents of his head all over the room. Torture, to be effective, has to be made to seem worse than death. If possible, much worse.

The mind, and not simply the nerve endings, is what you have to work on, and with the general run of humanity it wasn't too difficult to get the results you wanted, even when you had only a little time and were stuck in a hotel room with cardboard walls, where any amount of screaming would probably wake up the whole corridor. A couple of pieces of tape over the mouth and the eyes—they're able to concentrate so much better when they don't have as many distractions—and then you start crushing the joints of their fingers, one at a time, with a pair of pliers, telling them all about it while it's going on, keeping them reminded that we're not likely to run out of finger joints any time soon. Usually, by the time you've started to work on the second finger, they're ready to tell you whatever you want to know. Their brains have turned to jelly, and all they want in the world is for you to stop. On the average, it's about that simple.

Bateman, however, could just turn out to be a special case. Oh, he'd talk all right—Guinness didn't have any anxieties about that. He probably wasn't any more the high-principled, heroic type than the rest of us, and that was fine. Guinness didn't have much use for heroes.

So you might get him to talk—so what? There wasn't any guarantee that what he would have to say would be the truth.

You break a man down, really break him down, and he won't lie to you. You become God for him, the only god there is. The only one that counts. You have eyes that can see into the soul, and if he lies you'll know and there will be no release. So he won't lie—he won't dare.

But Bateman might dare. He might just remember that a pair of pliers doesn't make anybody God, and it might give him a kick to have that final little laugh on you just before you send him off to hell. Just for spite, the son of a bitch, he'd probably cook up some whopper that would cause no end of grief. What should stop him? He knew he was cold meat.

And knowing that, and that Guinness was only another fellow mortal, the same flesh as himself, he only smiled, flicking another ash to the carpet with that careless little twitch of his hand.

"You want me to play kiss-and-tell, I'll bet," he said, with the quiet voice of one who is in on the gag. "You're going to tell me how they set me up, those bad men who lured me away from the paths of virtue, how they knew it would come to this, how they're the ones who made all the real money while I took all the chances, how they're laughing their asses off at what a chump I was. You don't want me to let them get away with it; am I right?"

He took another slow, steady drag on his cigarette and watched the smoke drift upward. When it was gone he made a little flourish in the air with his hand, dismissing all such final vanities.

"You want me to die knowing that I'll be avenged. Was that the way it was going to go?"

Guinness refrained from congratulating himself on his shrewd insight into human nature. It could be that he liked Bateman that much better for not being the sort who would fall for all that guff, but liking Bateman wasn't going to make anything any easier.

"Something like that." Guinness spoke almost in a whisper, looking straight into the face of this man he was shortly going to have to kill. He wanted to be believed, so he was telling the truth. He wanted them to trust each other; it was necessary that they trust each other. And the only way they could do that was for Guinness to offer such terms as he was prepared to keep. "And perhaps there were one or two other things, but I don't suppose you'd be interested."

He leaned forward in his chair until his elbows rested on his knees. The gun in his hand pointed at the wall, at nothing that mattered. It wasn't a time for making threats.

"Tell me, Bateman—isn't there anything now that you've lived long enough to regret?"

"I'd do it again." His voice was a trifle louder than it needed to be, and it wasn't really that Guinness didn't believe him. It was just that the flicker in his eyes gave him away.

"Come on, Bateman. That isn't precisely the same thing."

Bateman didn't answer—he didn't have to. It was written all over him, in the way he held his hands together, in his very silence. He was a man like other men, of the same flesh. And Guinness, who had a daughter and a pair of wives in his own past, understood perfectly.

"If you make it come down that way, tomorrow morning, when they find you, the weapon will be in your own hand." Guinness leaned back into the padded chair. "Suicide. Nothing more reasonable than for a man in your position to blow his brains out—a man on the run, a man with no money left and nowhere to go.

"And think how pleased everyone will be. My employers will be satisfied because you'll be dead. And the police—well, it's always so much less trouble for them when there's nothing left to investigate. So it'll be written off as suicide, and that'll make the insurance companies happy because they don't have to pay off. By the time your family finishes shelling out to have you put underground they won't have two cents to rub together, and won't they be just tickled about that. Won't they just love your putrifying guts, and won't they be right."

He let it rest at that for the moment. You can overplay

these things, and he wanted Bateman to have time to think. He wanted him to imagine how his dead body would look lying on the carpet in a pool of curdled blood, with his eyes still open and a hole in the side of his head the size of your foot. He wanted Bateman to think about the wife and the teenage children back in Nebraska, whom he had wronged.

"On the other hand, if we could manage a nice heart attack . . ."

The ash on Bateman's cigarette was nearly an inch long. He seemed to have forgotten all about it, although he appeared to be looking right at it as he studied both his hands very carefully as they lay in his lap. You could hear his breathing, fast and shallow, and suddenly he swallowed painfully hard. There wasn't any mystery about it; he was suffering through that purely physical fear of death that doesn't give a damn about how there isn't anything left to live for, that just wants to live.

Then he looked up again, straight into Guinness's face, and the inner struggle seemed to be largely over.

"You can arrange that?" It almost wasn't a question at all. It was almost nothing more than a statement of fact, something to be borne with whatever limited stores of nerve a man might have left.

Guinness nodded, hating himself—hating Bateman for having brought it all down to this. "I have something right here in my pocket. It leaves no trace, and I'm told it doesn't even hurt. Fifteen, twenty seconds, and it's all over.

"But it's going to cost you."

When the thing was finished, Guinness stepped out into the empty corridor and closed the hotel room door quietly behind himself. No one would see him leave; no one would know what had happened. The whole thing would be nothing more than another shadow cast across the screen of memory, and, eventually, not even that.

"I can't tell you his name," Bateman had said. "I never heard it. I only met him the one time, but I don't imagine I'll forget him." He flicked the long ash from his cigarette, smiling at the absurdity of what, without really thinking, he had seemed to imply. As if he would have time now to forget anything.

"He was tall. Six-two, six-three, something like that. About my age, but he gave the impression that he took care of himself, and he looked a lot younger. Very thin, very tan—you know the type. A snazzy dresser. Short hair, almost white.

"It's not much, but it's all there is." Bateman lifted his palms from his thighs and turned them over, as if to show that they were empty. "I hope it's enough. Do you know who he is?"

Guinness's eyes narrowed as he remembered a man he had seen once in the lobby of a hotel in South Carolina. A tall, thin man with hair the color of bone. He remembered the photograph of a little girl, with a pattern like the cross hairs of a rifle sight traced around her head. He thought about the men he had had to kill to keep that little girl alive, about how one of them had looked with the back of his head shot away. He already had reasons enough of his own for wanting to close the file on this particular skinny, white-haired bastard, and now Bateman, who was shortly to join the other ghosts who haunted whatever little scraps of free time Guinness could spare for the consideration of his sins, now Bateman had given him one more.

"I don't know his name either," he almost whispered. Somehow he couldn't seem to bring himself to look Bateman in the face, so he looked at the carpet instead. "I'm not even sure he's got a regular name, but in his file they call him Flycatcher."

And so it was done. Bateman was dead, having settled his bill in the only way remaining to him, and Guinness left him behind in his room and took the stairs down to the main lobby. As he walked along he touched an envelope in the breast pocket of his coat; it was thick with hundred-dollar bills. Tomorrow he would wrap them in a couple of sheets of stationery, so that larcenous postal clerks wouldn't be able to tell what the envelope contained, and drop it in the mail. Within the week thirty-five hundred dollars, along with a little note of apology Bateman had somehow felt called upon to write, would arrive in Nebraska. That had been part of the deal, and Guinness was disposed to keep his word.

He checked his watch. The dining room was still open, but the appetite was gone. He thought perhaps he would simply go back to his own hotel and go to bed.

2

In the Nymphenburg Palace there was a gallery hung with the portraits of beautiful women—beautiful, at least, by the standards of the 1840s, by the standards, apparently, of Ludwig I, who had had an affair with Lola Montez and whose judgment in such matters ought therefore to carry some weight. Chubby pink faces with long noses, milk-white shoulders, hair done up in loose romantic clusters of curls, that sort of thing. There was one dressed in a Turkish jacket of cloth-of-gold, wearing a red fez with a long black tassel that reached all the way down to her bosom. She looked uncomfortable, and her half-closed eyes seemed to register a peculiar mingling of boredom and something that might, had she been only a few years older, have been interpreted as regret.

Guinness frowned at her, not really seeing anything, wondering what the hell he thought he was up to, stalking around from one room full of gaudy antique furniture to the next, like a goddamned tourist. He had already missed his flight out to Rome, where he was supposed to hole up and live the life of the quiet, unobtrusive, virtually invisible vacationing academician that was his cover, until the clever lads back home found him another mess to clean up. He didn't like hanging around like this after a job. It made him nervous.

And he didn't like palaces—big rooms gave him the creeps.

"Two this afternoon," Mehring had said. "There will be

no difficulty with the identification—you will know him at once."

Guinness disliked Mehring, as much as it was possible to dislike someone who was virtually a stranger. In Mehring's case, that turned out to be a great deal. Quite enough, in fact, for present purposes.

Aside from the enormous social disadvantage of being a policeman, Mehring was one of those people who try to create the impression that, really, they know everything there is to know about you, that of course it's perfectly pointless to imagine you could have any secrets from them. It was a bad habit, very annoying to other people and likely to bring one to grief.

Two o'clock. Guinness checked his watch and confirmed that he still had about ten minutes to wait. When he was finished here he would drive back to town and have his lunch; he had slept late that morning and breakfast, such as it was, had been around noon, so he wasn't particularly hungry. Lunch could wait a little longer.

And then, no later than this evening, it would have to be on to Rome. It wouldn't do to hang around for another day, for all that Mehring had practically given him a free pass.

Guinness would be sorry to leave; he liked Munich. This had been the first trip in nearly eleven years, and then only for four days. He liked the cooking, and particularly the desserts. You couldn't touch the Germans when it came to junk food.

In one corner of the Marienplatz, all the way across the square from the Town Hall so you had an unobstructed view of the revolving figures in the clock tower, there was a tiny restaurant that provided outdoor service when the weather permitted and seemed to specialize in desserts. You could sit at a little circular iron table, in a chair backed with colored plastic tubing, and watch the world go by as you drank your morning coffee and nibbled at pillow-shaped, brittle pastries, glazed with honey until they were brown as mahogany and filled to bursting with lemon curd, the consistency of library paste, or sweetened raspberries. Guinness had remembered the place from the days when he criss-crossed Europe in the service of MI-6, always stopping off in Munich for a day if he had the chance; it was still there, after all these years. Even the menu was the same.

It had rained early in the morning, and the streets were still wet when Guinness left his hotel. The awnings over the shop windows ran like rivers and forced him to step off the sidewalk to keep from getting wet; so, for all that the sun was out in force and already making the air gray with humidity, he was afraid he would have to eat inside. He needn't have worried—as he approached he could see one of the waiters, a fat blond walrus of a man in a white apron that reached almost to the tops of his shoes, wiping off the last of the chairs with a towel. He smiled when he saw Guinness, who was a big tipper and with whom he carried on short conversations in an almost unintelligible mixture of languages, and gave the chair one final flick with his towel as he pantomimed an invitation to sit down in it.

"Wvat vill you like *zu essen heute Morgen, mein Herr?*" he asked, showing his teeth, two of which were covered with gleaming gold crowns, in a ferocious grin. *"Etwas Kaffee, nicht wahr? Und* you vill like for to look *an dem Tablett mit Gebäck?"* He held out his arms, as if supporting a monstrous pastry tray, and the grin grew positively wolfish.

Guinness ordered a cup of coffee and took two plump turnovers from a huge plate covered with a paper doily.

"You vill like *ein* Herald-Tribune? *Über Amerikanischen Fussball zu lesen?"* The waiter pressed the tips of his plump fingers together and his eyebrows shot up almost into his hairline, but they didn't play football in the middle of June and, besides, Guinness wasn't a fan. He shook his head and smiled.

"Nein, eh?" You could feel the man's disappointment as he readjusted the carefully starched and folded napkin that was draped over his forearm and sauntered back inside the restaurant. Guinness's indifference to *"Amerikanischen Fussball"* was an unchanging mystery to him and seemed to rank as one of the major misfortunes of his professional life.

Guinness fished a paperback edition of *Mansfield Park* out of the pocket of his raincoat, but he didn't attempt to read it. Instead, he set it down next to the delicate white plate upon which his turnovers lay and watched the midday crowds beginning to form across the square in front of the Rathaus. They were very patient and would wait quietly until the clock in the tower struck noon and the mechanical figures began to move around and around through an elaborate double-tiered opening, almost like one theatrical proscenium on top of another, at about the roofline. Guinness had seen the spectacle every day for the past three. It had seemed to hold some inexplicable charm for Harry Bateman, and so the two of them had witnessed it together, dozens of yards apart in that silent crush of people, every day.

But Guinness didn't want to think about Harry Bateman, and so he didn't. He had slept fine last night and he felt just wonderful this morning. The thing was done and he had a little stretch of free time in front of him, to be spent in the Eternal City, where he could walk around the Forum counting the pulltabs from the Coca-Cola cans until his masters found something else for him to do, and so he pushed Harry Bateman from his mind.

An old woman shuffled by, stout as a beer barrel in her heavy cloth coat, carrying a net shopping bag that seemed to contain nothing except oranges. A couple of blond schoolgirls in their uniforms—skin like butter! A kid about twenty with a long, dark-brown beard, of the sort you would have called a hippie ten years ago but who went unnoticed today. Some clown of about fifty in a pair of *Lederhosen* and a green felt hunting cap with a brush in the band. Several Japanese tourists, all of approximately uniform height. The waiter stood by the entrance of his restaurant, pulling at the fringe of his moustache, his eyes vacant and dreamy.

Guinness picked up one of his turnovers and tasted it, discovering that it was pineapple. When he had lived in California with his late second wife, pineapples had been a dime a dozen, but in Europe, so he understood, they were considered distinctly luxurious and had to be imported from Africa. The turnover, therefore, qualified as something of a lucky hit. He took another bite, chewing it slowly and thinking about California and about how long ago all that seemed now. He discovered that his coffee had grown cold and signaled to the waiter to bring him another cup. It was five minutes until noon.

By the time the chimes in the clock tower had finished ringing, the second cup of coffee was already probably no more than lukewarm and still untasted. There was a wasp showing a marked interest in the half-eaten pineapple turnover, and Guinness kept perfectly still as it wavered about in the air and finally came to settle on his plate, allowing it to proceed unmolested with its agile reconnaissance of the pulpy, whitish-yellow filling. He had lost all appetite for breakfast himself and couldn't see much reason for begrudging the wasp.

A couple of dozen yards away, leaning against the stone fence around the memorial column to the Virgin that occupied the center of the square, a man was watching him. He didn't make any bones about it; he obviously didn't mind a bit if Guinness noticed. He was simply watching, with his hands shoved down into the pockets of his trousers.

There had been no tail that morning. There had been no tail at all, not since he had arrived from the States three days before; Guinness didn't have a doubt in the world about that. You were very careful about such things if you wanted to stay alive, and Guinness was a very careful fellow. They would have known he was in town, of course—the "they" encompassing a whole range of people with all sorts of unpleasant motives—you simply assumed that. They weren't stupid, and airport and train terminals were regularly watched. Probably the police had some sort of arrangement with the hotels, and probably they weren't the only ones. After a couple of years, you gradually abandoned the comforting illusion that somehow you were invisible. But nobody had been wandering around in Guinness's shadow while he had escorted friend Bateman on their tour of the city. Guinness had eyes in the back of his head for stuff like that, and there hadn't been a soul.

So here was this guy with his hands in his pockets, bold as brass. Guinness put him in his late forties—hair already beginning to turn a purplish gray and parted a little too close to the center to be quite fashionable, a heavy face with deep lines around the mouth. Weary, unintelligent eyes behind a pair of gold-framed glasses—something Guinness remembered from among the twenty-some-odd photographs he had been shown during his final afternoon of briefings; at this distance, of course, he couldn't even be sure that the eyes weren't simply painted on with watercolors. He couldn't be sure of a damn thing.

Guinness wondered if his onlooker was as heavy as the crumpled brown suit he was wearing made him look. What a slob, you thought to yourself; the type who could be counted on to fall over dead from a coronary occlusion in another eight or ten years—too much gooseliver and brown dumplings, too many happy hours at the *Bierstube.* But that, quite probably, was one of those carefully cultivated illusions that people in their line of work tended to foster about themselves. It was always a good idea to allow people to underestimate you, and the German Federal Police doubtless made their people stay in reasonably decent shape, even up to the level of major.

What was he waiting for, the son of a bitch? Why didn't he just trot right over and state his business, instead of being so insistently cutesy and conspiratorial about it? Perhaps he expected Guinness to go all sweaty with apprehension under that steely gaze, or perhaps he thought that the hint would be taken and the two of them could go off together to conduct their interview in greater privacy. Well, in that case he would have himself a long wait, because Guinness wasn't visiting any dark corners with anybody, not even with the third-ranking counterintelligence officer assigned to Munich—perhaps most especially not with him.

Fuck the bastard. He could stand there until his pension was due; if he wanted to chat he could come over and do it right here, right in the Marienplatz, right in front of God and everybody.

Guinness took a sip of his coffee—for form's sake more than anything, since it was stone cold. It was also pretty nasty, and he made a face as he set the cup back down. Hell, enough of that; it wasn't worth poisoning himself just to look properly nonchalant. After a while, the wasp lost interest in the pineapple turnover and flew away.

"Professor Guinness?" announced the Slob, having finally made up his mind to risk those few dozen yards and introduce himself. "I am Gustav Mehring—but of course you know that." He crinkled his eyes into a smile, the same eyes Guinness had remembered from the Company's album of family portraits. "May I sit down?"

Guinness didn't smile back but made a short little gesture

toward the other chair, which creaked ominously under Mehring's weight. He didn't speak; he would leave all that sort of thing to the guardian of the public safety here.

Mehring took out a small flat cardboard box of cigarettes, presumably English, and lit one, looking calmly around at the other tables and chairs, at the front of the restaurant and the little painted flowerbox that stood next to the door, at anything and everything, as if he didn't have a thing on his mind. It was a gambit Guinness had seen millions of times, in real life and on the late late show, and he was already bored with the discussion that must inevitably follow. He made a small bet with himself as to the precise phrasing of the opening question that was shaping itself in Mehring's head, and he was actually a little appalled at how close he had come.

"Do you hear much from your friend Mr. Bateman?" Mehring smiled again, the clever fellow, and waited patiently for Guinness's hands to start trembling uncontrollably. He waited quite a respectable while, and when it didn't happen his disappointment registered itself in the deepening of the lines around his mouth. Nowhere else, just there.

"I don't know you, Herr Mehring," Guinness answered finally, trying hard not to sound more annoyed than he really was—after all, who did this clown think he was talking to, Alice's White Rabbit? "And I don't have any friends named Bateman. So why don't you be a good boy and just push off—you're blocking the view."

Mehring laughed—yes, it was very funny—and used the hand that held his cigarette to indicate his dismissal of these preliminary maneuvers. It was a gesture very like the one Bateman had made while he sat on the carpet in his hotel room, bargaining about the terms upon which he would die, a little wave that almost wasn't any more than a spasm of the fingers.

"Come now, Professor Guinness. Your fame has preceeded you. We know of your government's displeasure with Mr. Bateman, and we assume that you were sent to our beautiful city expressly to—how shall I say it?—to communicate that displeasure to him, in the strongest possible terms."

The waiter came outside again, and Mehring signaled to him and ordered a cup of coffee for himself. When it was on the table in front of him, he stubbed out his cigarette in the metal ashtray about halfway between his place and Guinness's and lifted the cup to his lips. He seemed to like it, which wasn't very surprising; it looked like it was under about an inch and a half of whipped cream.

"We have a witness who saw you leaving Mr. Bateman's hotel late last evening," he went on, in a lowered voice since the waiter hadn't yet gone back inside. "And as it happens we found Mr. Bateman—the late Mr. Bateman—early this morning. The police surgeon estimates that he had been dead for approximately nine hours, which means that his passing must have taken place at very nearly the same moment you were seen in the lobby."

He was having such a wonderful time, was this one; he pressed the palms of his hands together and smiled tightly, apparently from sheer excess of smothered glee. It was funny that somehow counterespionage never seemed to bring out the best in people.

"A lovely hotel, the Bayerischer Hof—don't you agree? They were so shocked at the size of the bill Mr. Bateman was leaving unpaid, and by the fact that not so much as a ten-mark note was left in his wallet when the body was taken away—I rather suspect that was something they had established for themselves while they were waiting for us to arrive—so shocked, in fact, that we thought it best not to communicate to them any of our suspicions."

For a moment Herr Mehring fell perfectly silent; he

stared down at his coffee cup as if he had lost the thread of what he was saying and was waiting until it came back to him. Then all at once he looked up reproachfully at Guinness, pushing his eyebrows together as he frowned.

"And I ask you, Professor Guinness—this man is found dead and an assassin of your reputation is directly on the premises. What were we to think?"

Guinnness in his turn frowned, wondering why it was that the only time anyone ever seemed to call him "professor" was when they wanted to needle him.

"How did he die?"

It seemed an obvious enough question, considering the circumstances. But Mehring looked as if he had just been asked to guess the exact weight in grams of the entire Bundesrepublik, Volkswagens and all. For perhaps as long as five seconds the coffee cup, which he had been raising to his lips, hung perfectly motionless in the air.

"Come on, Mehring—did somebody shoot him, was he struck by a bolt of lightning? How did he die?" Separately, and with elaborate care, Guinness repronounced each of the four syllables of his question. It didn't seem to help, however; all he got was the same puzzled stare, as if Mehring couldn't understand why anyone would be interested in the sordid details, as if his policeman's brains were being turned into vanilla pudding by the effort of trying. It was then that Guinness himself understood that nobody could care less about Mr. Bateman, dead or alive, that the corpse over which some chambermaid had stumbled in the small hours of the morning was nothing more than a pretext.

The clock on the Rathaus tower said twenty minutes to one. In all likelihood they hadn't even done the preliminary autopsy yet, and, even if they knew what they were looking for—which, unless the people in Guinness's shop who provided him with these gizmos didn't know what they were talking about, they didn't—it would take them days and days of spinning down emulsified tissue samples before they found anything inconsistent with the theory that Bateman had died of cardiac arrest. So the police didn't have any hard evidence that there had even been a crime committed, let alone a case against Guinness. And God knows they wouldn't have come within shouting distance of him without at least that much, not if they meant business.

Guinness could feel himself beginning to relax—Mehring at least wasn't going to try anything as vulgar as arresting him. No, he was here on other business. Bateman simply provided him with a context, a plausible excuse for walking up to a known American agent, bold as brass, and sitting down for a spot of coffee and a little chin wag, something that might otherwise have raised a few eyebrows among the cognoscenti.

Fine. Wonderful. So what did he want?

Mehring allowed his cup to sink back into its saucer, and the lines grew deep again around his mouth. He wasn't ready to say yet, it was clear; he wasn't finished playing Dick Tracy.

"Doubtless you and others like you feel quite free to come here and murder one another at your leisure. The natives, of course, would not dare to object."

Possibly only the reappearance of the waiter at that moment kept Mehring from losing his temper; the force with which he pressed his flattened hand against the tabletop, as if this action somehow held him down as well, was enough to suggest how close they had come to something ugly.

Guinness signed to have his place cleared and took a twenty-mark note from his billfold, and the waiter, picking up the plate that held the two nearly untouched turnovers, frowned and inquired whether everything had been satisfactory. By the time he returned with Guinness's change on a little metal salver, everything seemed to have smoothed itself out.

"I keep telling you, I don't know any Batemans," Guinness said quietly, not even bothering to look up from counting out the tip he would leave behind; he wanted to see how far he could push Mehring. It wasn't purely malicious—it would be worth something to find out how badly everyone wanted to stay on their best behavior. When he knew that, he would be a good deal closer to knowing where he stood.

A woman walked by, carrying a tiny pearl-gray poodle under her arm like a handbag. She was a knockout—about thirty and wearing a knitted dress that stretched itself pleasingly over her can, which Mehring watched recede down the pedestrian mall exactly as if he didn't have another thing in the round world to hold his attention. Maybe he didn't.

"Yes, of course," he said finally, tearing himself away from that retreating vision. "But you have so many friends in Munich that we needn't talk about Mr. Bateman if the subject distresses you."

He got up out of his chair, looking as bulky and soft as an animated sleeping bag, and dropped a couple of silver coins on the table. The visit was apparently drawing to its conclusion.

"In fact, you have a friend who wishes to see you very much." The tight little smile returned to his face, but this time it registered a peculiar urgency, the urgency of a whispered entreaty. "It is not a trap of any kind—I am not stupid enough for that."

But Guinness wasn't taking any chances. He went back to his room and left a coded message where it would be found by certain interested parties if he didn't phone in within a day or so, just to prove he was alive. He wanted people to know, if he didn't happen to get back, just where he had gone, and at whose invitation. Mehring understood all this and, like a sensible man, wasn't interested in bringing down the wrath of God upon himself. It was such little arrangements and understandings that kept you alive in this business.

He turned away from the picture of the girl in the Turkish jacket, wondering if, after all, coming here hadn't been rather stupid. After all, he wasn't paid to respond to mysterious invitations from German policemen. All he was doing, really, was satisfying his curiosity, and the United States government didn't pay him to be curious. Uncovering secrets was what they had the CIA for—if, indeed, they had it for anything.

One minute to two—no, forty-five seconds. To hell with it, he would give whoever it was another five minutes and then he was clearing out.

There was a fireplace in the gallery, made of rust-colored marble flecked here and there with green. It was quite a production, with a fancy screen and andirons decorated with gold statuettes of the Sphinx. On the mantle was a gold clock with glass sides so you could watch the movement, except that the thing wasn't running. Probably nobody had bothered to wind it since the end of the last century.

As he walked back and forth on the hardwood floor, Guinness imagined that the sound of his footsteps could have awakened the dead.

When he turned around he noticed that there was someone else in the room. He was standing with his back turned, apparently admiring the portrait of a woman in a severe black dress and wearing a red flower over her ear. He was holding his hat in his left hand and he had lost most of his hair; what was left had obviously once been red but had grown sandy. Guinness couldn't imagine he was more than an inch or two over five feet—and he also couldn't imagine how he had gotten so far inside the door without being heard.

Mehring, you hypocritical bastard—Guinness smiled to himself at the scorn with which Munich's sworn protector regarded foreign assassins. Apparently, selling your services to the enemies of your country was quite another matter entirely. Mehring the messenger boy, the Herr Colonel's faithful dog.

It was him right enough, right on the button. Guinness retraced his steps, not worrying a bit about the noise, until the two of them were abreast, at opposite ends of the wall. Guinness didn't try to be cagey, didn't pretend he was interested in pictures; he just wanted to make sure that this was the right one—after all, lots of men are short with thinning red hair, and it had been a good fifteen years. But still, there was something . . .

There hadn't been any mistake. It was he. In profile you could still see the same blunt, Slavic features—the eyes were narrow, almost Oriental, as he studied the portrait of the girl with the red flower—the same copper moustache, long and thick and trimmed perfectly straight, even at the ends. Perhaps he dyed the moustache; probably it wouldn't have looked so imposing if it had been allowed to go gray with the rest.

Up until then he hadn't seemed to notice Guinness, but all at once he turned and smiled, exactly the way he had smiled fifteen years ago, when that smile had been something you needed if you wanted to think you might have a chance to stay healthy. Guinness had never known his name, but names hadn't been terribly important—the little silver symbols of rank on the shoulders of an officer's jacket had told you everything you needed to know about him. And anyway, this one wasn't anybody you were ever likely to forget.

He jerked his head a little to one side, apparently inviting Guinness to follow him to some less-exposed location, and as Guinness came along beside him, and they began walking together toward the doorway, he felt a small hand slip inside his elbow, precisely as if they were accustomed to taking little strolls like this every day of their lives.

"So, my young friend, I see you have grown quite middle-aged." He laughed and made a gesture toward one of the stairways leading to an apparently endless formal garden that stretched out behind the Palace. "Let us go along the canal to the King's little hunting lodge. It is very lovely through there, and very private, and when we have finished we can admire the silver moldings on the ceiling of His Majesty's rustic bedchamber—when I was a student, you know, I used to come here and stare open-mouthed, for hours together. I had never seen anything like it; I think that, more than anything, is what induced me to become a Communist. Come, just through here."

3

The train for Amsterdam left at a quarter to six in the evening, so there wouldn't be any time to sit down for dinner. Guinness made just one quick stop at his hotel to pick up his suitcase from the concierge and then took a taxi straight to the station. Maybe he could grab a bite there.

On the drive back to town, Colonel Kätzner had given him the ticket—"An impertinence," he had said, smiling; "of course, I could hardly be sure you would agree, but sometimes it is more important to be prepared for success than for failure"—and had apologized like crazy because he could only take him as far as the Lenbach Platz. "Doubtless they are watching your rooms, and it would not be well for either of us to be seen with the other, but you will have no difficulty from here."

And he hadn't. The sign at the end of his platform indicated another twenty-five minutes to departure time, so he hunted up a phone booth and put through a collect call to a certain number in Stuttgart.

"This is Soldier," he announced crisply, knowing from experience that nothing attracts attention like a whisper. "I leave from track four in. . . ." He checked his watch against the huge clock over one of the ticket windows and discovered that he was nearly two minutes fast. ". . . In twenty-four minutes. Tell Ernie to keep his shirt on—it's purely a personal matter. I'll let you know when the smoke clears."

He hung up, frowning at the receiver under his hand and wondering whether Ernie would be a good boy and take no for an answer. It didn't seem likely. They wanted to own you, those guys; it gave them hot flashes if you blew your nose without permission. Well, they'd know where to find him if it came to that. But would it come to that?

"It came to that a long time ago," he had told Kätzner, walking beside him down a meticulously maintained pathway that ran parallel to one of the canals in the Nymphenburg Gardens—not even a leaf had been allowed to settle on the flat, mahogany ground. "You know how they are with field men."

That had made Kätzner laugh. He had thrown back his head and almost brayed, because, of course, he knew all about how they were with field men. It amounted almost to a family joke.

"I shouldn't imagine they will give you very much trouble—I shouldn't imagine they would dare." And that was also, apparently, a family joke.

There were a pair of huge swans floating on the green water, weightless, exactly as if they had been spun out of the air. Kätzner stopped to look at them, and at the little blond boy and his mother who were perhaps eight or ten yards ahead of them along the pathway, just where the swans glided on their canal. He glanced at Guinness and smiled, as if he expected something interesting to happen.

The little boy couldn't have been more than two or three—Guinness was no judge of children's ages—with the kind of transparently fair skin that makes you imagine that if you poured warm water over him he would probably dissolve. His mother, if that was who she was, was a heavy, indolent-looking young woman, and she seemed not to be paying any attention when the boy ran down to the water's edge and bent forward at the waist, as if to pick up something. But the swans noticed. They were very close, and the one nearer the bank flared its wings in menace and darted its head this way and that on its long, serpentine neck, hissing like an adder. It was quite a spectacle—you tend to forget how huge they are—and the little boy backed quickly away, too frightened even to cry.

"You see?" Kätzner gestured with his flat, broad hand, evidently experiencing a certain satisfaction in the way it had all gone off. "You are just such a one, my friend, an object of terror. Your employers count on it; it is why they have kept your old code name from your days with the British. Everyone remembers the Soldier, and now he has come out of his long sleep to hunt for the Americans. When your face is better known, this fear will make it hard for you to stay alive, but for the moment they are in possession of a great weapon. So they will not make too loud a noise if occasionally you swerve from duty—I expect they are probably frightened of you themselves." And he laughed again. But quietly, as if they were both dead men together and could afford to be amused by the fears of the living.

Well, one was allowed to hope so. Guinness stared out through the glass wall of the phone booth, watching the porters dragging their carts of luggage back and forth and hoping that Ernie wouldn't throw a tantrum. He didn't want to be dodging Company hoods every step of the way. He would have enough problems without that.

With fifteen minutes until train time, he managed to scratch up a little stand where they were selling beer and paper plates bearing a sausage and a hard roll and a dab of the strongest mustard on God's earth. You touched the sausage to the mustard and took a bite, and then had a bite of the roll, and then washed it all down quick with a swallow of beer—such was the drill. It was better than nothing.

He stood with his right leg pressing lightly against the side of his suitcase, eating furtively as his eyes worked through the patternless, hectic crowd. It was just for the practice, really, and the police spotters were so easy to pick out it didn't seem quite fair to reckon them into your final score. They just stood around with their hands thrust deep into their raincoat pockets, looking as if they'd come to collect the rent. Five or six cigarette butts scattered on the concrete floor within inches of their highly polished shoes—why did cops always have such an obsession with keeping their shoes shiny?—without even so much as a briefcase for protective coloration. It was almost indecent.

But they weren't the only ones around, so a fellow could at least keep himself amused. Munich wasn't much of a town for spooks, but even here the half-dozen or so major players would all have someone who picked up a few extra Deutsche marks by looking out for the bad guys. Sometimes even the same someone—Guinness knew for a fact that the Americans' man at Kloten also skinned his eyes for the Israelis and God only knew who else. It was a canon of professional life; by the time you got into the big leagues, and they had your picture in the briefing files, you stopped being invisible.

Kätzner was right, of course. When you stopped being invisible, you became a target. It was a law of nature, like gravity.

How long had he been back in the Trade? Two years and a little, and most of that in the States; they had only just posted him back in Europe. Well, it wouldn't be very long before somebody snapped his picture as he stepped out of a cab or something, and then, when some other somebody did his homework and came up with a dossier to fit the face, he would be cold meat for the first hard guy who wanted to make himself look like a big man by knocking over the

Summer Soldier. And, after all, how far away could that day be when a clown like Mehring could read him off the way he had, like the writing on the back of an envelope?

But, of course, Mehring had had some help—Mehring had had Kätzner. And Kätzner was a man with quite a head start.

It had been one of those wet, muggy Augusts you get sometimes in that part of Central Europe, where every so often there would be gusts of rain that would soak you through to your underwear. The weather was warm, so they weren't anything more than just a nuisance; an hour later the streets would be dry and you could begin once again to think you were perfectly safe. Somehow it seemed ridiculous to carry an umbrella.

And then, out of nowhere, it would be like someone had turned on a shower. Even if you happened through happy accident to be wearing a raincoat, in the five or six seconds you might take to reach a shop awning or the cover of a doorway you would be drenched. Your trouser legs would be wrinkled and clinging limply, and your shoes would squeak, and the collar of your polyester sport jacket would cut the back of your neck like a bandsaw. And there wouldn't be a thing you could do about it.

So, under the circumstances, tailing Shevliskin hadn't been a lot of fun. In fact, the whole business had smelled bad, right from the start. There was just something wrong.

Guinness had been in Belgrade for three days, mapping out his hit and wondering why he couldn't seem to get over the impression that he didn't have the field entirely to himself. After all, on the face of it, he couldn't have asked for anything easier. His mark was a man of the most regular habits, a perfect pushover. Shevliskin ate all his bachelor meals in the same little restaurant half a mile from his work at the State Security Office, and he always took the same route—a brisk six minutes and twenty seconds in each direction—and our boy Janik was a small, spruce, heavyish man who seemed to think the walk back and forth kept him in the pink of condition. It was almost too easy; he liked to smoke a cigar as he strolled along, and he could never seem to keep the thing lit. On all three afternoons he had stopped in the middle of the same block to rekindle, conveniently across the square from a building that advertised that it had office space to let. At a distance of a hundred thirty to a hundred fifty feet, standing perfectly still for probably close to a quarter of a minute, he was easy. You could have done the job throwing a custard pie.

And it wasn't a custard pie Guinness had brought along with him. It was a beautiful thing, in its way—a handmade, one-of-a-kind, single-shot nine-millimeter rifle that looked like just so many aluminum tubes when it was disassembled; Guinness had smuggled it all the way across Europe in the side pocket of his suitcase. It had a special five-power hooded scope so it wouldn't glint in the sunlight, and at anything less than seventy-five yards you could use it to punctuate a sentence.

Still, he found it hard to ignore the feeling that all was not well.

For one thing, Shevliskin was scared. He kept studying the reflections in shop windows, as if he could sense he was being followed. He had been doing it from the first day—from the first hour. He was a worried man.

Guinness was reasonably certain that he hadn't been spotted, so he didn't think it was him. But there was something that played on our boy's nerves. He was like a man conscious of being under sentence of death, simply waiting for the thing to happen. He was waiting—that was it—and with a kind of unfocused dread.

And then there were the police. There were just too many of them. It wasn't that they stood around in pairs on every corner; there were plenty of uniforms in evidence, but that was true everywhere east of Berlin. The guys in the olive drab coats and the peaked caps were kind of reassuring, in fact—you could spot them. But there were too many others, too many big men lounging around under their hat brims. Maybe they were the reason Shevliskin wasn't feeling very jolly; he seemed to be swimming through an atmosphere of official surveillance.

Guinness had wanted just to forget the whole thing and go back to London, but he had been a lot younger in those days and a believer that orders were orders. MI-6 wanted this guy's ticket canceled, and the job was supposed to come first. Letting your woman's intuition get the better of you wasn't considered very good form.

So he had gone ahead with it. On the second afternoon, while Janik ate his minced pork and pickled cabbage, he had scouted the building with the "For rent" sign and had found an empty front office on the second floor, picking the lock almost as fast as if he had been provided with a key. The window faced directly across to the spot where, two days in a row now, Shevliskin had stopped to relight his cigar, and there was a stack of packing cases in one corner, so there wouldn't be any problem about concealing the rifle; he didn't want to be seen carrying around any funny-looking bundles on the big day.

There was an Alitalia office on the fourth floor, which would provide a suitable cover story if he should for some reason be called upon to explain what he was doing in that particular place. After all, he was a tourist. He walked up the two flights of stairs and asked for a flight schedule, involving the girl behind the counter in a long and grotesquely complicated conversation—Guinness only knew about three hundred words of Italian, most of them inconveniently Dantesque—about the customs regulations. The idea was to be remembered as absorbed in his travel plans.

For the rest there was precious little to do. While his target was working in the inaccessibility of the State Security Office, Guinness followed his guidebook around the streets of Belgrade, trying not to get lost. It wouldn't have been hard—the guidebook was in English, German, and French, but most of the signs, and all the street markers, were in the Cyrillic alphabet, which he had to figure out by analogy with Greek, with rather questionable results. Finally he gave up and found he could do fairly well navigating by triangulation from three or four of the more obvious public buildings. After all, if worst came to worst, he could always just strike west and he would have to run into the Sava River—from there he knew how to find the boarding house where he had a room.

On the morning of the fourth day, he waited until about twenty minutes after they opened the main doors, when he could be reasonably sure no one would notice him, and slipped up to his vacant office to wait. It would be over three hours before Shevliskin would start thinking about lunch, but there were preparations to be made and, besides, Guinness was simply too nervous to be anywhere else. It was always that way.

During a five-hour stopover in Paris, he had taken a taxi into town, to a department store on the Boulevard Haussmann, where he bought, along with a couple of silk neckties and a bottle of the foulest-smelling aftershave lotion you could imagine, a pair of thin leather driving gloves. The label indicated they had been made in Poland, and they were two sizes too small. He folded them neatly and laid them on the packing crate he had set up in front of the window for a shooting stand, where they would be found by the police.

You had to be prepared for getting caught, and policemen tended to be very big on clues; these would give them something to feel uneasy about. The gloves he actually had on were made of plastic and came in rolls of a hundred. There was a little closet of a bathroom in this particular office, and when he was ready to leave he would flush them down the toilet, one at a time.

The rifle was assembled and loaded, and the scope was calibrated against the approximate width of the square—Guinness had paced off the distance the afternoon before. The window was open, only about seven inches because anything more would be a dead giveaway, and there wasn't a thing in the world left to do. Every few minutes Guinness would take a quick look outside to check the wind, but the leaves on the elm trees across the street were perfectly still. The building had no air conditioning—or, if it had, it had been turned off in the unoccupied office suites—so by eleven-thirty, while he sat on the floor glancing at his watch two or three times a minute, he was uncomfortably warm.

These things were always the same—you waited through an eternity, it seemed, and then everything was over in an instant. Shevliskin turned the corner, walked perhaps eight or nine paces, stopped, took his stub of a cigar out of his mouth and looked at it disdainfully, and put his hand into his jacket pocket to retrieve his matches. The box was still in his hand when he died; it went skittering into the street as his arms flailed out like things trying to escape on their own and he collapsed grotesquely to the sidewalk. For years afterward, probably for as long as he could remember anything, Guinness would remember how Shevliskin's life had stopped, in a kind of nerveless, sinking pirouette that seemed to go on forever but probably took no more than three-quarters of a second. For an instant he seemed to be reaching, with both hands, for anything at all and in every direction, and then he just fell down. There should have been blood everywhere—a nine-millimeter bullet is a cruel thing—but there wasn't. He just died, as if all the life had gone out of him at once.

Guinness didn't hang around to gloat. He hadn't heard the shot—somehow you never did when it went home—but that didn't mean nobody else had. As soon as he saw Shevliskin lying on the sidewalk, and was sure the thing was done, he set the rifle down and got rid of his gloves in the toilet. Taking his handkerchief out of his pocket to put over the door handle, he let himself out into the corridor, where there wasn't a soul, and walked up the stairs to the Alitalia office, forcing himself not to hurry. Ten minutes later, with a ticket for Rome in his inside coat pocket, he left the building.

Or, more accurately, he tried. They arrested him at the door.

To be perfectly truthful, he didn't even make it that far. The column of police came through first, bursting in so suddenly that they almost ran right over him. There were five of them; the first one peeled off and backed him into a wall, pushing at him with the heel of his hand, and the others bulled up the stairwell—left, right, left, right—in step, by God.

"Hey, man—Jesus!"

What did the innocent traveling public sound like when all of a sudden they found themselves being muscled around by some uniformed goon with a nightstick the length of a fence pole? He tried to make it come out convincing, to give it the proper mixture of fear and startled indignation, and the fear, at least, was no problem. This one looked for all the world like a gorilla, grabbing him by the shoulder and spinning him around so that he had to catch the wall with both hands to keep from cracking his forehead. "Now look, fella . . ."

It was a calculated move, part of the impersonation of harmless American outrage, but he knew what the result would be when he tried to turn around and confront this . . . hell, he could have been anybody, a bus driver, for all Raymond Guinness, who was an inoffensive tourist—who, after all, had rights—had any idea. The trick was not to look like you saw it coming when, just to teach you the customs of the country, our friend brought the handle of his baton down across your cheekbone in the manner of someone striking a gong.

From then on everything was easy. You just curled up on the floor, like a good boy, trying to hold your eyes in until somebody turned down the voltage enough so that you could breathe again.

Three hours later, while he waited with eleven other detainees in a white-tiled containment cell with only a single plank bed upon which to sit, his face still hurt. If he forgot and happened to touch the welt that extended from his right temple down to about the middle of his chin, he would experience a wave of nausea that almost wouldn't allow him to stay upright. He would have liked to pound on the door and holler in a loud voice, demanding to see someone from his embassy—it was the sort of gesture you imagined they would expect—but the sound of his own voice at anything louder than a whisper, or just about any sound at all, made his whole body throb. The guy who had hit him had known what he was doing.

Guinness sat on the far left side of the bare plank bed, where he was able to lean against the chain that ran diagonally down from the wall behind him and attached itself to his corner with a heavy iron plate. The cell was so narrow you couldn't have lain down widthwise on the floor, and you wouldn't have wanted to in any case because it was covered with cigarette butts and streaks of mud and suspicious-looking stains. There was a toilet bowl, the seat of which had been removed for some reason, and it was occupied on a more or less permanent basis by a scrawny, stone-hard, elderly peasant with yellowish white hair and terrible diarrhea; the old man crouched there with his trousers down around his ankles and his head in his hands, the nails of which were blackened and clawlike, in a perfection of physical misery that left no room for shame. There were four others besides Guinness on the bed, and the rest stood around, leaning against the walls and looking at nothing. No one spoke except for a small, balding man in a dirty blue shirt and coveralls who seemed to know about four different languages, including English, and who was so obviously a police spy that everyone ignored him until he too fell silent.

Guinness had never been in jail before and was astonished at how quickly he was getting used to it. Of course, for most of the first afternoon his face bothered him too much to allow him any great leisure to consider anything else. They hadn't killed him, or even questioned him yet, and at least three of the other men in the cell had been picked up in the same sweep of the area in which he had been arrested, so perhaps he wasn't the only suspect. Perhaps he wasn't a suspect at all—maybe they just wanted to question him to find out if he had seen anything. At any rate, the next move was theirs and he could wait. He had been careful, so they didn't have a thing on him. They couldn't have. He kept reminding himself of that consoling fact, over and over. For the rest, he thought about how much his face hurt, so by the time he was ready to pay anything like attention to his surroundings they had lost their novelty.

The cell was without a window, and they had confiscated Guinness's watch, so he had no way of knowing with any certainty what time it was when they came to get him. One assumed night—it had been some time ago that a trustee, in a heavy gray outfit that looked like a suit of pajamas, had brought them little tin trays of a purplish stew that smelled bad enough to overcome any curiosity you might have had about how it would taste; Guinness had given his to the old peasant, who seemed to need fortifying after his ordeal. Anyway, he was beginning to figure out that time meant very little in a prison. All he knew for sure was that it was late enough to make him wish they would just let him curl up somewhere and get some sleep. He hadn't closed his eyes the night before—he never could before a job.

"Mr. Guinness? Please sit down."

The interrogation room was tiny, perhaps only half the size of his cell, and there were six uniformed policemen. Only one of them was seated; he smiled and motioned for Guinness to take the only other chair, across the table from himself.

But Guinness remained on his feet. He looked around at the faces of his captors, from one to the next, trying to read them, to discover what they wanted, how much they knew, what they might have guessed. But they all seemed to be wearing masks, even the one seated at the table, whose smile might have been painted on for the occasion—perhaps his most of all.

"I want to talk to someone from my embassy. And I want a doctor."

He brought his fingertips up to the huge oblong welt which, among other things, had nearly closed his eye for him. "I don't know what this is all about, but that thug of yours could have killed me."

And then he sat down. He folded his hands together and

rested his forearms on the tabletop, allowing himself to hate them. He was exhausted and—yes—frightened, and the inside of his head felt like it might come leaking out of his ears, but to hell with them. They had gotten all they were getting.

After a few hours, they figured that out for themselves and had him taken back to the cells.

This time he had one all to himself—but he had been expecting that. Two years before, when he had been going through his training up in Scotland, they had told him how these sorts of things were done. "When they want you to think," they had said, "they let you be by yourself. They aren't being nice—they just don't want you to get distracted while you're imagining what a fix you're in. It's harder to be a hero in a vacuum, and they know it."

Was it the same cell? It could have been—the same plank bed, the same toilet with the seat removed, the same white tile walls. He lay down on the bed and glanced casually around, the back of his head resting on his right hand, trying to see if he could find anything different, but the light was too dim. Perhaps that was something different right there.

They had said they had him cold—that was what they said. But they wouldn't even tell him why he'd been arrested. To hell with them; they were bluffing. They had spent the whole three hours trying to trick him into betraying himself. They didn't have anybody cold.

"What is your real identity, Mr. Guinness?"

"You have my passport—you can read."

"Why did you leave the gloves behind?"

"What gloves?"

"Who paid you?"

"For what?"

"Who sent you here?"

"I'm a tourist."

"What were you doing in that particular building?"

"You have the ticket. Talk to the Alitalia people—ask *them* what I was doing."

He didn't know anything, he was a tourist buying space on the flight to Rome, he wanted to see someone from his embassy, he didn't know anything about any damn gloves. Over and over and over. And now they wanted him to sit in his cell and conjure up all the terrible things they were going to do to him if he didn't break down in big salty tears and confess everything. To hell with them.

After a couple of minutes, the light went out. Well, that was about par—they would let him go to sleep now so they could wake him up in three or four hours and drag him back, groggy and startled, for another round. Fine. He wouldn't disappoint them for the world. He rolled over on his left side, cradling his head on his elbow, and closed his eyes.

As they hauled him down the corridor, a man on either side holding him up by the arms, he almost had to laugh. It was like a parody—these guys had been watching too many World War II movies. What was next, electric cattle prods and the Death of a Thousand Cuts? Strong lights? Rubber hoses and bamboo slivers under the fingernails? It was all too incredibly corny for words.

But it wasn't like that at all. They just sat him down and questioned him. This time there was no table, merely a couple of chairs, and his interrogators—there were three of them this time—took turns. The questions were the same—always the same—but the three of them would take turns sitting in the other chair to ask them.

"Why were you in that building?"

"To get a plane ticket, to go to Rome—haven't you noticed? Belgrade isn't very lively."

"Why were you in that building?"

"To get a ticket."

"Why did you leave the gloves behind?"

"It's August. What would I be doing with gloves?"

That was how it went, for three days. Every few hours they would bring him back, and the questions would start all over again. In between he would sleep or eat his meals—the purple stew, which he discovered himself just able to tolerate, although he never could figure out what it was made of—or try to keep his mind under control.

They were doing their best to screw him up, and it was working. Sometimes, when he was returned to his cell, the light would be on; sometimes it wouldn't, and he would have to find his bed in the dark. Sometimes, for no apparent reason, they would turn it on while he was sleeping, let it burn for a while—for half an hour, or for five minutes, or until they came to fetch him again—and then let the room sink back into darkness. They would bring him something to eat and then wait until he fell asleep again and wake him to eat something else. A few times they didn't give him anything for what seemed like weeks. They just wanted to turn him around.

And it was working. He got so he was afraid of closing his eyes—he didn't want to lose track of the time. He began to think he had been under arrest forever. And he was beginning to become seriously frightened.

How the hell long were they going to keep this shit up?

At one point, the famous gloves were brought in, and Guinness was told to put them on. He couldn't—they were too small. He peeled them from his fingers and threw them on the floor, grinning wolfishly.

"They aren't mine," he said. "They must belong to somebody else."

So he was staying even, at least. They weren't getting anything. He would lie on the plank bed and think to himself, they haven't got anything. Not a thing, not a fucking thing. And then he would be seized with fear, wondering whether he had been talking out loud.

And then one day—or night, or whatever—there had been somebody new to play Twenty Questions. A new face, somebody different. Well, that would be fun. Except that he was tired—dead sick of this. And his brains felt like bruised taffy.

Except that the colonel wasn't playing. He simply stood with his back against the wall, watching Guinness over the interrogator's head.

The uniform declared he was an East German, a colonel in the military police—but that could mean anything. What was he doing there? What would he care about who got knocked off in Yugoslavia?

And the rules had changed. The man sitting in the other chair—the first one who had questioned him, on the very first day—leaned forward, his hands resting on his knees, the eyebrows in his neat little face raised up almost into his patent leather hair.

"We wish to question you concerning the death—the assassination—of one Janik Shevliskin, an employee of the People's Government. We wish you to confess. Now, without further delay. We have all the evidence we require to convict you in the People's Courts, and you will be sentenced to death."

Guinness was listening, but his eyes were on the colonel, whose upper lip was covered by a pair of perfectly straight, coppery moustaches. He was a small man, perhaps only an inch or two over five feet, and as the interrogator spoke, issuing his demand for an immediate confession, the colonel smiled and, almost imperceptibly, shook his head. It was a sign meant for him alone.

"I haven't killed a soul," Guinness heard himself saying. "I never heard of this guy, and I insist upon seeing somebody from my embassy."

4

"Why? You must have had a reason—what was it?"

They were standing next to the fountain behind the Nymphenburg Palace, listening to the water splash, with only a couple of pale, languid goldfish, about the size of small trout, drifting here and there beneath the cloudy strands of algae, to keep them company. Guinness had his foot up on the rim of the pool and was retying his shoelace, frowning with concentration.

"I suppose you must know I've always wondered. What made you do it?"

Kätzner's hands were in his trouser pockets, which pushed his shoulders up and accented the faintly military cut of his tweed jacket. He shrugged, somehow managing to confine the gesture to his eyebrows.

"Are you really curious about such things? Is that part of your price?"

When Guinness didn't answer, even after the shoelace had relinquished its hold upon his attention and he had straightened up and was smoothing down his trouser leg, then Kätzner too began peering down at the fish as they hung, almost immobile, in the gloomy water.

"I was about to arrest Shevliskin—that was why I was there. That was why we were able to arrest *you* so quickly. The British must have known; that must have been why they sent you. He was one of theirs, and doubtless they didn't wish him to fall into unsympathetic hands." He smiled then, but not at Guinness. At some reflection of his own, perhaps—in the water or elsewhere. Or perhaps at nothing so specific. Under any circumstances, he did smile. "I shouldn't have liked to appear a poor loser."

Obviously, he didn't even expect Guinness to believe him—oh, about the arrest, yes. But not about the motive. At least, not entirely.

"And then . . . Well, a distaste for amateur productions, probably. Those fools were never going to get anything from you—they even seemed to be laboring under the childish delusion that you might actually have been innocent."

"And, of course, you never . . ."

"No."

It wouldn't have occurred to Guinness not to believe him. It seemed so self-evident, but apparently Kätzner felt some need to explain. He pointed to the crowd of people who were coming down the palace stairway into the gardens; there were probably fifteen of them, and they were obviously part of a tour—the women were in front, listening to the guide, while the men all seemed to be loitering behind, apparently bored by furniture and plasterwork and the Baroque formality of trimmed hedges and gray gravel walkways. It was to them that Kätzner was pointing.

"You see those safe citizens?" he said, and took his hand down as if he were dismissing the whole group from existence. "A few of them look old enough to have been in the War—perhaps they were very brave. Let us hope so. I doubt if any have ever come into a foreign city, quite alone, and killed a man to whom they had never spoken a word. So let us hope that they are innocent as well as brave, and carry that armor on their souls.

"I have interrogated scores of innocent men, my friend, and they are always afraid; they can't help themselves, because they discover that being brave has nothing whatsoever to do with it. Courage, they find, is nothing but an encumbering respectability, so many of them confess because they cannot tolerate the moral solitude. Prison or ruin or even death—they are not afraid of these things, perhaps. But the other terrifies them."

He glanced at his watch, and his face registered something like faint surprise, and they began walking back, toward the archways that led to the front of the palace and the parking lot. Kätzner once again slipped his hand inside his companion's elbow.

"The man who used that astonishing rifle to snuff out the life of Janik Shevliskin would not have been frightened in that way. Perhaps he is no braver than other men, but he is unlikely to have been dismayed by solitude. Fear of oneself—that is what he would lack. That is how you betrayed yourself, my friend. You had no such fear."

Hadn't he? He seemed somehow to recall a certain sensation of paralyzed relief when, finally, they had let him go. They had returned his passport and his money—had even reimbursed him for the flight ticket they had prevented him from using, making something of a production of it, as if they were doing him the greatest kindness in the world—and had given him exactly twenty-four hours to get the hell out of the country.

He remembered the sunshine, too—as a stab of real physical pain, like a pair of fingers trying to see how far back into his head they could push his eyeballs, when he passed through the open front doors of the police station. Actually, it had been rather overcast, but how much did that mean when you hadn't seen anything stronger than a lightbulb for better than three days? It had been enough to make him feel slightly sick, and only the sheerest exercise of will had kept him on his feet until he felt himself far enough out of official reach to find somewhere to sit down.

A cup of hot soup in a little outdoor café, a quick stop to

pick up his suitcase from his bewildered landlady, and then on to the airport for the first flight out—to anywhere; he didn't give a damn, so long as the direction was more or less west. On the plane, he had to sit with his raincoat wrapped around his hands, they were shaking so badly.

Anywhere turned out to be Zürich, where he checked into the first hotel he could find and ordered breakfast—it was ten o'clock at night, but that wasn't going to be allowed to make any difference. He huddled on the floor in the middle of the room, as far away from the walls as he could manage, and ate the whole basket of rolls and drank every drop of the tea, and then wrapped the big fluffy feather comforter around himself and went promptly to sleep. On the floor, in the middle of the room. Granted, he might have been a trifle overanxious, but at least that way he *could* sleep.

Two days later, when he had the impression he might have put himself back together enough to risk it, he returned to London to make his report. Yugoslavia was definitely off his list, he said; Belgrade didn't agree with him. They didn't argue about it and they didn't ask him why he was overdue, and he didn't volunteer any explanations—he didn't mind admitting to himself that his nerves weren't made of piano wire, but he didn't see much point in confiding the secret to MI-6.

No fear? That wasn't the way he remembered it, but perhaps Kätzner had had something else in mind besides simple garden-variety survival anguish. Kätzner was a subtle creature who saw further into these matters than the rest of us, and Guinness was prepared to take his word.

Stuffing the greasy and mustard-stained paper plate into a trash barrel, Guinness picked up his suitcase, balancing himself against the weight, and headed for the platform. By the time he was settled into his seat, the last stragglers were already rushing past his window, as if they expected that any time now the train would slip away from them forever.

The little tug that meant they were on their way reminded him that he hadn't thought to pick himself up anything to read. There was, of course, the copy of *Mansfield Park* he had been dragging around with him for the last week and a half, but that was in among the dirty shirts in his suitcase and, besides, he found it impossible to manage anything that required serious attention while he was traveling—there was just something about all the jiggling around. A nice out-of-date issue of *U.S. News & World Report,* or any one of those interchangeable German magazines with a picture of a naked girl on the cover and articles inside about the idyllic marriages of rock stars and cheap family vacations in Portugal.

But, of course, he had forgotten.

The only other people in the compartment were an elderly Swiss couple, who talked only in whispers and only to each other, looking at him, if at all, with furtive hostility. The woman, who was seventy if she was a second, kept readjusting the raincoat she held on her lap, as if harboring some suspicion that Guinness might want to peek up her dress. Guinness crossed his arms, sliding down in his seat and closing his eyes, and pretended to nap; it amused him to listen to those two talking about him—in their native dialect, which, probably, they imagined would be as impenetrable to this "*Usländer*" as Linear B.

He awoke with a start when the train pulled into Würzburg—the name was on a large sign attached to the station wall. He looked at his watch, discovered that there were only a few seconds lacking from eight-thirty, and concluded he was hungry. The sausage and roll hadn't done the trick after all, it seemed.

"Is the dining car open?"

The conductor, who was young and swarthy and whose face was badly scarred by acne, simply smiled and looked perplexed; so Guinness asked his question again, this time in

German, and received an affirmative nod. Five cars ahead, he was told—they would be serving until nine.

Looking back through the glass door into his compartment, he wondered whether the old couple would be tempted to go through his luggage while he was gone. The suitcase wasn't even locked, and they were welcome. They seemed to be under the impression that he was a runaway husband—either that or a drug trafficker. Why else would anyone be wearing ready-made American clothes and traveling through the middle of Europe by himself? Why, indeed?

Outside, the black landscape slipped past them. You couldn't see anything, nothing except a sense of movement in the darkness. Once, he thought, he saw a glimmer, a kind of murky sparkle. A river, maybe. Or maybe just a little cow pond magnified into something larger by its own vagueness. After Mainz, they would be traveling along the Rhine, which they wouldn't be able to see either. Maybe that was to be part of his punishment—the runaway husband doesn't get to see the Rhine.

Had Bateman? Perhaps it hadn't been on his itinerary; perhaps he'd only been interested in brown dumplings and the ladies. Had Kätzner?

Of course, his flight from the nest had been back in the early sixties, and there had been plenty of time since if he had been so inclined. And perhaps you got a break if you could plead extenuating circumstances.

"It was a question of freedom versus extinction, you see," he had explained, smiling the way one does when called upon to apologize for some breach of etiquette. "I was sufficiently compromised that the Dutch police were within a few hours of arresting me—it was the accumulation of all the tiny mistakes one commits over so many years—and so it was necessary for me to disappear. On my side of the wall, one's masters tend to assume the worst if you have allowed yourself to fall into enemy hands. I didn't even pack a bag. I simply hired a car and drove over the border into Germany. Within twelve hours I was back in uniform, making my report in East Berlin. So, you see, the question of desertion hardly comes up—I could scarcely have taken them with me."

He was right, of course. He could scarcely have done that.

Guinness was a specialist, a technician. He killed people; he didn't break into security installations and rifle the safe—intelligence gathering was out of his line.

So he had never had to think in terms of maintaining a cover for years at a time, while of necessity the face grows to fit the mask. It struck him as an unnatural proceeding, and apparently he wasn't alone. Apparently it had struck Kätzner the same way.

"You have no concept of the strain," he had said, the memory of it pulling at the corners of his mouth as they walked back toward the car. "I was in Amsterdam for six years—one either comes to believe in the role or, eventually, one begins to crack around the edges." He looked up at Guinness and smiled, as if to recognize that the joke was entirely on himself.

"And, I suppose, I began to feel very Dutch. I suppose I thought I would stay on there forever, and so it seemed safe enough to marry. It was madness, of course—I told myself it would enhance the cover, if you can imagine. But Margot was a sweet woman, and we all tell ourselves lies. So I did it. I married, and pretty soon we had the child. Somehow I never really supposed I would have to go, never have to leave them, but, as you see, it became necessary."

And Guinness had understood perfectly. He had made the same mistake himself, twice. You imagined you could live like everyone else, that the Little Woman would never find out and you could have it both ways. But the first Mrs. Guinness had left him, precisely because she had found out, and the second had ended up dead on his kitchen floor because she hadn't. And Guinness too had a daughter who was growing up somewhere without a father, whom he had only seen a single time since infancy. Kathleen had been right to pack her traps and disappear, because there was too much blood on his hands and because, if she hadn't, it would have been her name on the little steel plate in the mausoleum at Colma. So Guinness understood, both the desire for something like normal happiness and the magnitude of its folly.

The dining car was nearly empty, and the waiter, who was sitting at a table near the galley smoking a cigarette and sharing a pot of coffee with the cook, appeared less than pleased when Guinness came in and looked like he expected to be fed.

He was directed to a table very near the end of the car, as if they wanted him as far away from them as they could manage, and the waiter brought him a menu and then told him they were out of nearly everything.

"Then, whatever you do have—I leave it to you."

For some reason, that seemed to have shifted the balance in his favor. The waiter smiled, apparently having forgiven him for prolonging his workday, and they talked for several minutes about all the wonderful things that could be done with what was left around in the pantry. It didn't look like anyone was going to starve.

Would he care for a bottle of wine? Sure, why not? It would be six hours or so before they reached Amsterdam, and he would need his wits about him then, but six hours was six hours. He could go back to his compartment and sleep—he would do that anyway—so it didn't make any difference.

The waiter retired to his galley, walking with that peculiar splay-footed gait that reminded you so forcefully of a duck but that was, on a moving train, the absolute precondition of maintaining one's balance.

The tablecloth was white and heavily starched, and, on its own little plate, with a pat of butter, was a hard roll of the kind you simply couldn't seem to find in the States. There was even a little yellow flower in a weighted holder in the center of the table—the Europeans knew how to do these things right.

The first course was a cream of asparagus soup, served with about half a dozen croutons bobbing around in it, obviously there just for the aesthetic effect. The waiter brought it and then retired to the other end of the car, where he could watch Guinness's progress with the discriminating eye of a connoisseur. He didn't try to hurry him; there was all the time in the world. He seemed to take a vicarious satisfaction in the whole process, and maybe he did.

And the main course—well, what more could you have asked for? A veal steak in clarified butter and lemon sauce, a little rice, a little creamed spinach, and a grilled tomato topped with toasted breadcrumbs. There was even a salad, with an oil and vinegar dressing and sprinkled over with finely chopped egg, the sort of thing that made you think you wouldn't mind if you never saw another head of iceberg lettuce again. Guinness cracked open his roll and made his slow, gratified way through it all, helped along by a bottle of delicious topaz-colored wine.

The train stopped in Frankfurt for about six minutes, and Guinness noticed that the Swiss couple got off. They went past his window before they were met at the end of the platform by a stout, fortyish, unhappy-looking woman whom their manner betrayed as the prodigal daughter. She was wearing a heavy raincoat, and her drab, dark yellow hair hung in thin little strands down to the collar. The reunion didn't seem very cordial, and parents and child disappeared beyond Guinness's field of vision. In a few moments, the platform was all but empty again.

When they were once more underway, the waiter brought out a cup and a silver teapot clutched awkwardly in one hand and a bowl of vanilla ice cream, with two peach halves sliding slowly away from each other toward the sides, under a covering of raspberry syrup, in the other.

"Peach Melba," he announced, grinning like a gargoyle.

Guinness had nearly finished it, and was sipping on a second cup of very strong tea, when a man who looked to be in his very early thirties, wearing a short camel-hair coat that was belted around the waist and a brown hat with a brush sticking out of the band, came in and sat down three tables in front of him, with his back turned. The waiter approached to inform him that dinner was no longer being served, but he shook his head and asked for a cup of coffee—"*Etwas Kaffee, bitte*"—and the waiter shrugged and brought it to him. He barely touched it. Guinness called for his bill, paid it, counted out the tip, and got up to leave. The other man was very scrupulous about not turning around, but even through the back of his heavy coat he seemed tense, as if he would jump if someone happened to touch him on the shoulder.

Etwas Kaffee, bitte. The clothes were German, but the accent wasn't. Guinness wondered whom he could have been working for, and why these guys never learned to relax and act like the rest of the human race. He had just boarded—hell, he hadn't even thought to take off his hat yet—and who got on a train and immediately went to the dining car for coffee? Probably he could have ordered it in the station and paid a third of the price. They never seemed to learn.

What to do. What to do, what to do. What did the stupid son of a bitch want? Well, the only way to find out was to ask him.

Of course, trains had certain obvious disadvantages in

that respect; they tended to be a little public, and there weren't very many corners you could jump out from behind. Trains—let's face it—were distressingly straightforward. One would simply have to make the best of it.

What *did* the guy want? Guinness checked his watch—it was a few minutes after ten. The next stop was Mainz, but not for at least another half-hour, so the chances that our friend in the brown hat would simply pull a gun and start shooting were at least diminished. You didn't want to have him surprising you between cars, where he could chuck your corpse out into the pitch black at forty miles an hour and nobody would be the wiser, and for the same reasons it might be just as well to stay away from easy access to windows; but otherwise, if you could keep the game in your own court, you were reasonably safe from murderous attack. People didn't do that sort of thing, not on a moving train, not if they weren't complete morons.

The problem was getting away afterward—it was only in the movies that you made a leap for freedom and went rolling dramatically through the underbrush as the Orient Express steamed off into the distance, and you sure as hell didn't do it in the middle of the fucking night; you might as well just take a head-first run at a brick wall.

No, if you wanted to kill somebody, you waited until two or three minutes before the next station, when everybody was busy with their luggage, and then you slipped away before anybody spotted your victim slumped to the floor. Otherwise, you might find yourself walking right into the arms of the law. After all, trains were equipped with radios—they could always call ahead.

So, assuming the worst case, that Brown Hat was a thug and that whoever gave him his orders meant business, we were reasonably safe for a while. There were limits, but the risks were manageable. But we also had to do something about him pretty quick, because the free pass wasn't going to last forever. Twenty minutes—no more. He had to be in the bag in twenty minutes.

Another thing Guinness had always admired about the dining facilities on European trains was the wonderful cutlery. They didn't expect you to go after a piece of meat with a butter spreader; you got a real knife, with a scalloped edge, and a point that would go through something tougher than a potato skin. Guinness palmed it, slipping it up inside his shirtsleeve, under his watchband to keep it from falling out, and he left an extra twenty marks with the tip so the waiter wouldn't think to come after him when he noticed it was missing—never in his life had Guinness had any trouble with an overtipped waiter.

Well, it wasn't an act of thievery that would rest very heavily on his conscience. He needed the damn thing a lot worse than The Trans European Express did. It wasn't considered good form to carry a weapon when you were traveling—customs officers were touchy about that sort of thing these days, and you never knew who was likely to end up going through your pockets; it just wasn't worth the risk. But he didn't particularly feel like stepping into this particular dance contest without so much as a darning needle. This guy could be anybody—somebody's harmless little gumshoe, Jack the Ripper, anybody—but taking chances wasn't the way to grow hoary with age in this business.

The doors between carriages were pneumatic—you pressed a little plate near the latch and it would slide open of its own accord, with a very audible thud. So Guinness had no trouble keeping track of the gentleman's progress; he tried to maintain a car's length between them, and all he had to do was to listen for the sound of the door. Brown Hat was making slow work of it, but of course that was to be expected. He had to check all the compartments along the way to make sure Guinness didn't manage to double-back behind him.

Almost the whole train was dark. Here and there a few souls still had their reading lamps on, but for the most part everyone was trying to get a little sleep, or at least to rest their eyes—most of them, probably, were going at least as far as Bonn, which was a good two hours away, so there wasn't anything to keep alert for. That was fine. Provided nobody had to go to the can suddenly, he and Brown Hat would pretty much have the place to themselves.

He went by his own compartment and found that the Swiss couple had been replaced by a pair of middle-aged men in hiking clothes—jeans, flannel shirts, high-laced lumberjack boots, the works. They seemed to be in very earnest conversation, their heads almost touching, like a pair of newlyweds. Guinness didn't disturb them. He never even slowed down.

It was a long train; Guinness and his little friend could play hide-and-seek almost indefinitely. But these matters required the nicest sense of timing. The trick, of course, was to string your man along just far enough to allow him to get careless, to begin to feel a certain impatience, or a nagging suspicion that perhaps he'd lost you somewhere, but not far enough that he begins entertaining any inconvenient suspicions that perhaps up ahead something is being prepared against his arrival. You have to have some sense of whom you're dealing with—if Brown Hat had looked like an old hand, Guinness would have jumped him after the second car; but that kind of paranoia only comes with experience, and this one didn't strike him as a terribly accomplished heavy. No, better to let him wait awhile.

Car after car, Guinness trailed him along. At each of the carriage doors, he would wait, straining his ears as he listened for the door at the other end to wheeze open behind him, keeping a rough check on what kind of progress his tail was making. And the poor slob was speeding up—a healthy sign. He was getting restless. Well, good for him.

Finally, when he wasn't more than three cars from the end, Guinness decided to set his trap. He waited, just inside the door, just beyond where the corridor turned a sharp little angle, as if elbowed aside by the compartments. He waited and he listened, and when Brown Hat came through, in the second or two after the door opened and he stepped inside, while he was still in that blind corner, while the noise of the door closing behind him blotted out everything else, then Guinness would rush him and try to take him down before he had any idea what had happened.

He fished the dinner knife out of his sleeve, wiping it off on his handkerchief. For just a moment he allowed himself to weigh the thing in his hand, and then he put it out of sight in his jacket pocket. There would be plenty of time if it came to that, but there wasn't any point in killing someone just because he was tailing you. The point was to find out what he wanted, and whose side he was on. There wasn't anything to be gained by being hasty.

Guinness could hear his heart pounding—loud enough, it seemed, to render it a little astonishing that the whole corridor wasn't out to see where all the racket was coming from. Why didn't the guy hurry up?—he seemed to be taking forever.

And then, in the car ahead, there was the sound of a door sliding open. It closed, and the next door opened almost immediately. Guinness held his breath . . . one, two . . . he wanted to meet him just at the corner, maintaining his forward momentum. Three, four . . . As the second door slid closed, Guinness started to move, keeping his eyes on the thickening shadow that was pressing toward him from around the corner.

At the moment of impact, he wasn't aware of anything except the texture of the camel-hair coat under his hand; Brown Hat might have been a roll of carpet as he stumbled back against the wall, and, without looking up into the face in which nothing seemed to register except astonishment, Guinness drove the points of his fingers, pressed together and held rigid, into the soft spot under the breastbone. Brown Hat let out a sudden gasp and doubled forward, to get caught on the side of the face by Guinness's knee.

After that it was easy—some of it. There was no fight left in the nearly unconscious body Guinness dragged back to the narrow space between the two carriage doors, where there was hardly room for both of them to stand. The games were over; Guinness undid the man's coat and took the dinner knife out of his own jacket pocket. He wrapped his handkerchief around the blade, so that only about an inch and a half of the point was showing, and clutched it tightly in his hand to keep it from slipping.

Then he allowed himself a deep breath—this part of it was never easy—and plunged the knifepoint through the exposed shirt front, just a thumb's width under the ribcage. Brown Hat hadn't seemed to realize that he was even alive, but the impact opened his eyes with a snap. He didn't move. He didn't cry out. He didn't even look down. He merely stared into Guinness's face with an expression of pathetic terror.

"Don't worry, pal," Guinness murmured—he even smiled, as if they were intimate friends. "It's only a little blade. But you'd better make the right noises, or I'm going to pull it straight across, from one side to the other, and suddenly you'll find your guts hanging down around your knees."

5

"My God! Mr. Guinness—I never . . . please, I'm just a courier. Mr. Tuttle said . . . please take that thing . . ."

Guinness could feel the blood beginning to trickle down over his fingers. It wasn't a bad wound, hardly deep enough to pierce the abdominal wall; a couple of stitches and everything would be good as new. This guy wasn't much of a hard case—he could hardly talk he was panting so fast.

"What did Ernie say? Let me know quick, before I start to lean on this thing and push it right through to your kidney."

"Mr. Tuttle said . . ." He seemed to forget, for a few seconds, what, exactly, Mr. Tuttle had said; he swallowed hard, with a kind of gasp, as if the effort had brought him close to strangling. "Mr. Tuttle said to ask if the 'personal matter' could have to do with the gentleman you knew from South Carolina, if you thought you'd have better luck than in Mexico. He said you'd understand."

Guinness understood, just fine. Slowly, being sure not to let anything tear, he pulled the knife blade free. The courier's hand stole down and held Guinness's handkerchief, which by then was almost soaked through, against that side of his belly. He looked down, probably unable to see a thing, and by then the terror was beginning to subside. His lips pursed in what was probably astonishment, and perhaps the beginnings of resentment—that always seemed to come next.

"Shit," he whispered, drawing out the syllable. Apparently the novelty of the experience was still what impressed him most.

"Tell me about Flycatcher . . . Stop it, you're not likely to die any time soon—tell me about the gentleman from South Carolina."

Guinness's voice took on a feverish insistence, but he had to grasp Ernie Tuttle's messenger boy by the coat collar and shake him for two or three seconds before he managed to dislodge his attention from the fact that his intestines weren't squirting out like tomato paste.

And then, slowly, the courier raised his eyes and began studying Guinness's face, clearly appalled, as if some terrible secret had been revealed to him.

"I was only . . . Jesus, you must be . . ."

"Worse even than that, pal—now tell me about Flycatcher. Where is he?"

"I don't know. I don't even know who this Flycatcher is; all I was told was that you were to phone when you arrived—Mr. Tuttle will be waiting for your call." He shook his head, apparently wishing very badly to make it understood that this was as far as anyone had taken him into their confidence.

"You're sure? That was it?"

"Yes—just that you were to phone."

It was just boneheaded enough to be true. It was just like Ernie to go to all the trouble to find out what train left Munich at that particular time, and then to get a man on board just to tell one of his errant shooters not to lose touch with home. It was Ernie's style, right down the line, even to the teasing allusion to the unfinished business with friend Flycatcher. Ernie was a romantic; he loved the cloak-and-dagger stuff.

Without releasing his hold on the man's collar, Guinness opened the window behind them, threw the dinner knife out into the darkness, and closed the window again.

"We'll be in Mainz in about ten minutes," he said. "You get off there. Tell Ernie to keep his people out from underfoot. Tell him I'm not on anybody's caper, but the rules aren't any different. I'm not going to waste any more time trying to pick out the good guys from the heavies, and it'll just be a little hard on the next poor soul who gets in the way."

"I didn't notice you were so easy on me."

There was an edge in his voice, as if—silly boy—he expected Guinness to feel guilty, or maybe even to ask his pardon. It made you wonder what he thought the world was like.

"You're alive, aren't you?" Guinness let go of him with contemptuous roughness, a little surprised at his own anger. "You'll find yourself a doctor and have a few stitches put in—a jolt of penicillin if you want to make a big deal out of it. You'll live. It'll give you a scar to show to the doxies; you can make up all sorts of dramatic lies about how you got it. Just get off in Mainz. And don't forget to deliver *my* message."

They were still standing together in the connecting passage when the train drew to a stop. There weren't many people out on the platform—it was after ten-thirty at night, so you couldn't blame them—and nobody paid any attention when Guinness unlatched the door and the messenger, whose face he was only now to see out of shadow, disembarked and, after an oddly questioning backward look, disappeared.

There was an overhead lamp outside; it threw a slanting beam of light across Guinness's lower body, and he glanced down to see that there was a wide smear of blood across his thumb and the back of his hand. It was already nearly dry; he made a fist and a few flakes popped off and fell twinkling to the floor, like the crushed fragments of a Christmas tree ornament.

There was a lavatory in the next carriage. He washed his hands and checked his cuffs and trouser legs for stains and, finding nothing, patted a little water against his cheeks and forehead and pulled a couple of paper towels out of the wall dispenser with which to dry himself off.

The face that watched him so speculatively from the mirror didn't look at all happy. He was beginning to acquire a network of lines around the corners of his eyes, emphasizing their cruelty, and his hair was beginning to go gray—just in threads so far, but the future was clear. Age had deepened the hollows, sharpened the ridges. He was beginning to look like one of those carved stone faces on Easter Island. No wonder people thought he was a monster.

Come to think of it, he had been a trifle casual about sticking that blade into Ernie's courier. It happened to people in his line of work—they lost all sense of their own humanity, as if they had gradually evolved into some separate life form. Only their own survival mattered. Only their own survival had any reality, as their victims flattened out into the two-dimensional characters in a badly cast melodrama, just images flickering on a screen. You might as well be dead as feel like that. You were dead.

Well, perhaps it hadn't quite come to that yet. He wasn't the blue-eyed, auburn-haired boy he'd been at twenty-three, but at twenty-three he had stepped into this business with his eyes wide open, had fulfilled a contract on one Peter W. Hornbeck in return for one thousand pounds sterling and the everlasting gratitude of Her Majesty's Government. So perhaps he hadn't been such a model citizen, even then.

And once in, you don't get out. You lose volition—it's like throwing yourself over a cliff. He had tried to get out once. A new life—he had made it work for seven years and then, suddenly, it hadn't worked at all. So now he no longer tried. He had surrendered the idea that there would ever be anything more than hotel rooms and train rides, and the work itself. How many more Batemans would there be before his own retribution? Eventually he would begin to slow down, or he would make a mistake, and someone would kill him. They had tried often enough, and Guinness didn't have any illusions about being immortal. One of these days they would make it good. And there would be precious little point in claiming a foul.

He pushed the idea from his mind—that sort of thing wasn't going to help—and checked his watch to give himself something else to think about. It was quarter to eleven. The train would reach Amsterdam in another four and a half hours. Starting then, there would be plenty of other things to think about besides the state of his soul.

The two men in his compartment turned out to be a couple of vacationing high school teachers from Portland, Oregon. They were both in their thirties, and this was apparently their first trip away from home. Like Guinness, they were on their way to Amsterdam; the shorter of the two, an individual of placid appearance, with dreamy blue eyes and a rather tangled-looking reddish beard, asked if he had ever been there before and if he knew anything about the prices, which were rumored to be among the highest in Europe.

"Not in nearly eleven years—things were cheap enough then, but that was before everybody went so crazy."

They talked about traveling, and, when Guinness mentioned that he was an English professor, the three of them started trading horror stories about the appalling ignorance and stupidity of their students.

They had a long hike into the depot, most of the length of the train, and then down in a steel elevator about the size of someone's living room to a dank underground passage that smelled strongly of excrement. Guinness carried his own bag, much to the vexation of the porter, a diminutive, gray-skinned lad whose dish-water blond hair was all the way down to his thin shoulders and who moved with dreamlike slowness and didn't look like he could pick up a dime.

The two history teachers stayed with him most of the way—they only had their backpacks, so the porter didn't much like them either—and even asked if he'd be interested in splitting a cab into town with them. They seemed like nice guys, but Guinness smiled and lied and shook his head.

"Sorry. I've got a friend who's driving in to pick me up."

He waited until they were safely off and then found himself a phone.

"I got your message, tough guy."

Ernie Tuttle's voice, even over the thousands of miles of cable from his office on G Street, sounded familiar and pleasant at three-twenty in the morning. It amused him, apparently, that his messenger boy had had the scare of his young life.

Tuttle was the closest thing in the world Raymond Guinness had to a friend—it wasn't a relationship upon which he would be prepared to stake a great deal, but in their line of work you couldn't be choosy. Another time they could laugh about the clown with the hole in his side, but not now. He didn't want to get sucked into all that now.

"Where's Flycatcher? Tell me about that, Ernie."

At the other end of the line, there was what novelists describe as a pregnant pause. Guinness waited, looking around the depot, which was by then virtually deserted, assuring himself for perhaps the fortieth time that there was no good reason on earth to assume that anyone had spotted him yet—it was just a feeling he couldn't seem to shake . . .

"Guinness—you are in Amsterdam, aren't you?" The tiny glint of anxiety in his voice probably should have told Guinness something already, but he just wasn't interested. He just wanted Tuttle to get on with it. He wanted to hear about Flycatcher.

"Of course I'm in Amsterdam, you fathead. And you

know it. I'll bet you've got the train schedule spread out on the desk in front of you, so why ask?"

"Then you're not alone, pal. Your good friend with the white hair has been spotted on four separate occasions over the last three months—something's up with him. I thought you knew. I thought that was why you were there."

"No. I didn't know."

There was a kind of fatality to the business, he thought. For two years, ever since South Carolina, it had been the sole permanent ambition of Guinness's life to kill Flycatcher.

Flycatcher had a favorite tactic, to intimidate people through their children, to impress upon them how easily little throats could yield to the knife, little heads shatter under the impact of a sniper's bullet, and he had always found it a very convincing line of argument. But in South Carolina the child he had threatened had been Guinness's own. He hadn't succeeded—at the cost of several lives, Guinness had redeemed her and returned her home safe—but from that moment on, Flycatcher had acquired the distinction of his own very personal Nemesis.

Revenge had very little to do with it, although there was plenty of motive for revenge. No, it was nothing so vulgarly personal. And Guinness drew no moral judgment—he was the last one who had any right to do that—but somehow it had settled into a fixed conviction that Flycatcher's mere existence made the ground ache, as if the very globe itself was oppressed by his presence. Life was simply insupportable as long as that man was breathing.

And now, once again, Flycatcher had been delivered into his grasp.

"Are you there, Guinness?"

He looked at the receiver in his hand with what amounted to surprise. "Yes—of course I'm here. Where else would I be? What's the matter with you, Ernie? You getting deaf?"

"Don't you worry about me, pal—you just worry about Flycatcher. They say you nearly got him last time, that after Mexico he was holed up in some private sanatorium in Costa Rica for four months just making up his mind whether or not he was going to keep breathing. But a miss doesn't pay the bills, pal. You nail him this time. And for God's sake don't show yourself until you absolutely have to—the word is he's so spooked about you he'll bury himself underground if he so much as knows you're in the same country."

Guinness frowned, at nothing in particular, and remembered that in the normal world it was the middle of the night and people had been sound asleep forever. In three hours, maybe even two and a half, the sun would be up.

"I don't need a pep talk, Ernie."

From the other side of the broad Atlantic came an odd, gurgling laugh. Ernie really ought to go back into the field, Guinness confided to himself—he was getting kinky with boredom.

"I know you don't. Given half a chance, you'll take the son of a bitch's skull apart, won't you. I just thought you'd like to know, if by some miracle you didn't already, that he was within reach.

"Now, you'll need a contact—someone to run your errands for you. We've got a good, reliable local agent in place. You'll love this . . ."

The last time Guinness had been in Holland was in 1970. He and his first wife had come for the week, just to get away from London for a while, and had spent most of their little holiday taking bus tours to the cheese markets in Alkmaar and the mile upon mile of tulip fields along the road to Leiden. They had eaten raw herring and admired all the picturesque little fishing villages, and had spent a whole day in Delft, where Kathleen had purchased a set of dishes that somehow managed to get itself lost in the mails. It had been a happy week, one of the nicest times he could remember, and, as a result, Guinness had never felt the slightest inclination to return.

"Grand Hotel Krasnapolsky," he said to the taxi driver, an immensely fat man whom he found sleeping soundly, his arms wrapped around the steering wheel, in a parking space in front of the train station. He didn't wake up until Guinness had climbed into the back seat and slammed the door shut behind him.

Everything was dark on the way in—you had the sense, however, that you weren't being taken through precisely the nicest parts of town, so perhaps it didn't matter. Anyway, no one was wasting any money on street lamps.

The hotel itself was a gaudy, modern structure, right across the square from the floodlit façade of the Royal Palace, which Guinness remembered vaguely—the tour buses used to mass almost next door. Somewhere, out of sight in the darkness, what sounded like perhaps as many as ten or a dozen youthful voices were singing popular songs, accompanying themselves on probably a nearly equal number of guitars. After a moment, he realized they were singing in English, although he couldn't make out more than the occasional word. They were pretty terrible.

A uniformed doorman came down the front steps of the hotel and opened the taxi door for him and took his bag from the front seat. He gave the impression he was glad of the company.

"Doesn't all that racket keep the Queen awake?" Guinness asked, retrieving his suitcase from him and holding out a tip. The man smiled and curled his hand quickly around the money, as if it were something nasty he was trying to keep out of sight.

"Oh, the Queen does not stay there," he said. "She lives somewhere else."

"I'm not surprised."

Guinness had found the hotel's name in the phone book. He had never heard of it before and didn't care anything about it now, but the sight of the lobby depressed him unutterably. You might as well have been checking into a motel in Alpena, Michigan. He didn't like it any better when the desk clerk told him there weren't any rooms.

"Look again," he said, allowing the corner of a twenty-mark note to stick out between the middle and index fingers of his right hand.

"A single room was what you wanted?" The desk clerk was a suave creature with carefully combed black hair who seemed just a size too small for his clothes. "Yes, it seems I was mistaken—for a week, you said?"

The name on his passport was Charles W. Reilly, and he signed the registration form as such and was handed his key. A bellman took his suitcase and led him through the bar, past the entrance to the dining room—which for some reason was screened off—around a couple of corners to an elevator. They rode up to the third floor with a hamper full of dirty laundry, and Guinness was shown down a corridor to his room. He tipped the bellman, who merely grunted, and threw the suitcase on the bed.

The room was very small, and unbelievably hot. The walls were a pale green and the carpet green and yellow in a bizarre pattern probably intended to suggest the ripples on the surface of a fishpond. He stepped into the bathroom and rinsed off his face, which made him feel a little less groggy, and then opened his suitcase and hung up the extra sport jacket and pair of trousers it contained and dumped the rest into a drawer. The bed was more of a problem—he took off the spread and pulled down the counterpane and tried to rumple the sheets, putting in a few creases that he hoped might look somewhat more convincing after a few hours of being pressed into place by the blanket. Then he took off his shirt and went into the bathroom for the luxury of a shave—

there wasn't any point in calling attention to oneself with a day's growth of beard, and who knew when he would have a chance tomorrow to pick up another razor? When he was finished, he checked his watch.

Four-fifteen—plenty of time.

If anyone came nosing around before tomorrow evening, they would have every reason to believe the room was occupied. If he had been spotted, it would give them someplace to stake out, someplace to come looking for him, a nice diversion upon which they could waste their time. In the meanwhile, he would have a chance to get himself good and lost.

He put his shirt back on, retied his tie, picked up his jacket from the back of a chair, and felt around in the inside pocket for the streetmap he had taken from a rack at the front desk. On the way up he had noticed there was a side entrance—apparently the hotel wasn't very worried about their guests shooting the moon. At that hour, with some luck, he should be able to get clear without anyone seeing him. After all, even if someone was watching, they would hardly be so crass as to post a guard. He slipped his arms into the sleeves of his jacket, took a last look around to make sure everything appeared properly untidy, and stole out, closing the door behind himself as quietly as possible. He had an appointment, it seemed.

6

You wondered how many innocent American tourists, after unpacking their bags and filling out handfuls of postcards for all the relatives back home in Sioux Falls, after a nice heavy dinner in the hotel restaurant, after tasting for perhaps the first time in their lives wine that hadn't been bottled in California, how many of these had taken the wife out for a little evening stroll through all those interesting-looking side streets behind the Voorbrugwal Canal, which, perhaps, if they happened to have been given a room in the rear, they had seen from their window. Probably thousands of such happy couples had crossed over the quaint wooden bridges and admired the beautiful, efficient, peculiarly Dutch architecture, some of it dating quite clearly from the boom years of the Seventeenth Century, when Holland had controlled trade with the treasure-laden East and her navy had been the envy of Europe. Many of the buildings, as it happened, had large plate glass windows on the ground floor—presumably installed sometime after the days of Rembrandt and De Ruyter—and behind any one of these, seated on a bar stool, with her legs crossed provocatively and her skirt hiked up past the tops of her nylons, was a lady whose lewd smile the car salesman from Indiana would feel all the way down to his elasticized socks.

But there were no errant husbands flitting about at a quarter to five in the morning—all of those were safely asleep long ago, having left the field clear for more hardened lechers of which, even at this hour, there was no discernible shortage. Like conspirators assembling to plan acts of desperate terrorism, they slipped furtively in and out of the doorway to a dark little basement from which issued the sound of pinball machines and the dull thud of rock music, a sign on the outside advising you in Dutch, English, and German that for five florins were available within the widest selection of pornographic films in the city, which apparently was saying something.

Guinness checked his map and tried to locate a street number, and discovered himself under the eyes of a pretty negress whose rouged nipples were clearly visible over the top of her pink babydoll nightie. She had just taken up her position, pushing aside the curtain that had covered the plate glass window and climbing up on her stool, and she looked at him as if he had come to answer her most impassioned yearnings.

But he had already been through that phase, in San Francisco, after the death of his second wife, when he had imagined himself to be wearing the mark of Cain and felt sometimes he might die of loneliness. The whores chattering among themselves in Vietnamese as you lay on a mattress in a tiny room, waiting. No, he had discovered soon enough that that sort of thing wasn't at all to his taste, so he smiled and shook his head and moved away. In any case, she wasn't the one he was looking for.

On the front stoop, just about at eye level, a little congregation of teenaged waifs, no more than children really, were lounging back against their rolled up sleeping bags and passing around a briar pipe that certainly was filled with something besides shag. One of the girls stared at Guinness vacantly as he walked past—her long blonde hair had gone so long unwashed that it looked as if it had been coated with candle wax, and she was wearing a thin cotton dress that stopped just short of her bare feet, which even in the dark he could see were incredibly dirty. It was a cool night for the time of year, but she didn't seem to notice. Guinness wondered how long it had been since she had noticed anything.

Finally he found the street—really, not much more than an alley; you could almost have stretched your arms out and touched the buildings on either side—and kept going right on past. He didn't want to make his approach until he was a little clearer about what he would come up against down there. After all, he couldn't even be sure he'd find anybody home. Another two blocks, and he would double-back and have a look from the other side.

When he got that far, he discovered himself in what, anywhere else, probably would have been called "Chinatown," except that the few yellowish-brown faces in evidence looked more Polynesian than Chinese—in all likelihood they were Moluccans, political refugees from the Dutch surrender of the Spice Islands. Guinness went into an open food shop occupying one corner of his street; the walls in front and to the outside were simply notched out, so he had an unobscured view. He sat down at the tiny five-chair counter and ordered a plate of something, which turned out to be mainly saffron rice with a few pieces of unidentifiable meat on top, and pretended to listen to a couple of ancient gentlemen who were arguing violently in a language that sounded like nothing he had ever heard before. They paid no attention to him. Even the proprietor seemed to be deliberately ignoring him. That was fine.

The food shop had a "46" painted in yellow overhead on the side street, so Number 23 would be across. A couple of women were standing in the middle of the passage, their arms folded across their breasts, talking. Only one window on that side showed any illumination, and it was approximately where he would have expected Number 23 to be. The woman with her back to it was small, almost frail-looking, and her hair was cut very short, forming a little cap around her head. At that distance, and in the decidedly poor light, there was no more you could say with any conviction. The other one was taller, but even more obscured.

Guinness discovered that he had finished his rice and what was apparently chicken. He ordered a glass of tea, poured a teaspoon of sugar into it, and drank it off. The food had been a mistake—he was beginning to feel sleepy again.

He paid, counting out the amount from his slender supply of florins, and took a final look around to prove to himself for perhaps the twentieth time since leaving the hotel that there were no familiar faces in evidence. He stepped into the side street and started walking slowly toward the small woman with the pixie haircut. No one seemed to pay any attention.

"Yes?" She came up to him as he stood in front of her doorway, staring up at the yellow numbers painted on the brickwork overhead. "I can help you, maybe?"

He diverted his attention to her, curious about her rather nasal accent and the fact that she had thought to address him in English, and noticed that she didn't automatically smile the moment his eyes touched her. He regarded that as a point in her favor and smiled himself.

"I hope so. Is this your place?"

"Yes. Would you like to come inside?"

She opened the door for him, and he stepped into a tiny room that was nicer than he had expected. There was a carpet on the floor, a chest of drawers, a mirror, and a small bed covered with a bright Madras spread. Another door led to a bathroom, hardly larger than a phone booth—there were even a few chairs. Perhaps this was something else that the Europeans did better. He stood by the chest of drawers while the woman drew an outside pair of drapes; the big picture window and the bar stool were, in any case, hidden behind a curtain, so they didn't demand to be acknowledged. There was no sense of one's privacy being in danger, almost no sense that outside there was a world to intrude. It was an atmosphere that just missed being intimate, like part of an estranged past.

"You are American, yes?"

She really was a small woman, and her hair was a pale, pale brown that looked as if it might have been frosted with silver. Her eyes were large and green and worried as she smiled at him—but one imagined that her kind of work was burden enough. Guinness would have put her age at thirty-one or two.

"The clothes, yes? But it is very fashionable to look like an American now, so perhaps you are not. You are English, yes?"

She began taking off her sweater, rolling it up over her shoulders, and it was then that Guinness noticed how white her skin was, almost bloodless. Perhaps she was cold—as soon as the sweater was off, she reached down and turned on an electric heater. The flesh on her breasts looked tight and drawn-up.

"You are English, yes?"

"I'm the Soldier, Janine."

It was a perfectly instinctive reaction, but the first thing she did was recoil, drawing in her breath and clutching a corner of her sweater to her bosom as if she had been startled in the bathroom by a spider. Guinness turned his eyes away, giving her a moment of privacy, and found himself wondering why it was that he hated his life so much. When he looked at her again, she had put the sweater back on.

"I was not expecting anyone," she said calmly, the way any woman might who finds herself encumbered with an unwelcome and bothersome guest, someone whom she cannot simply dismiss.

"But I know who you are—everyone has heard of the Soldier."

Guinness said nothing, and the woman's faint, mocking smile slowly died. He wasn't angry, precisely; he was merely disappointed—*Everyone has heard of the Soldier.* It made him feel like a freak.

"I need a place to stay, somewhere I can get some sleep and not worry about who has a key. I'll probably have to have a car."

She shrugged her narrow shoulders, suddenly all business, and Guinness experienced a little flicker of sympathy. It was probably like this all the time for her, men who knew just what they wanted. But clearly, standing alone in this tiny room with Raymond Guinness, celebrated killer of men, she felt no need for compassion from anybody. In her dark green turtleneck sweater and her boots and her heavy brown skirt, she looked very self-reliant, very tough—he liked her, although he perceived that it would be a mistake to show it. And maybe she really was tough.

"Anything else?"

"Yes. As you say, the clothes are American—get me some new ones, and a razor, that sort of thing. I had to leave all that, to buy some time. Can you manage everything?"

Outside, on the street, there was a woman's laughter. Apparently one of Janine's neighbors had found herself a live one. But that might have been on another planet for all it mattered now. This one, whom Ernie had called "Janine," whose customers, if they knew her by any name, probably called her something else, who might really be anybody, regarded Guinness with dispassionate, appraising eyes. It was very possible she was trying to decide what size suit he would need to blend in with the shipping clerks and the cheese merchants.

"Yes, I can manage everything. Tomorrow morning? Is this soon enough?" It was a real question, and he nodded.

Yes, this would be soon enough. She had only perhaps five hours, and that seemed all the time in the world.

"My friend Aimé has gone to Spain for two weeks with her boyfriend. He is very rich and not so young anymore, so perhaps he will marry her now and then she will never come back. She left me the key to her flat. You will not have any disturbance there—this one has been her boyfriend for a long time now, and she never brings her other boyfriends there. Two weeks—you will not stay so long as that, I think."

She gave him the key and smiled.

"You go now. It is only a dozen blocks from here. I will follow, but it would seem odd if we left together."

The sky was already beginning to change from black to slate gray when he found the place, up two flights of stairs on a building that faced one of the canals. Apparently, from the mailboxes, there were only three other apartments in the building, and one of those seemed to be vacant. That was fine—he didn't want to attract anybody's attention. But with only a few other people to worry about, he could time his departures and arrivals so no one would be likely even to know that he was there. The place immediately beneath him seemed to be the one that was empty, so no one would even hear his footsteps.

It wasn't much, just a bedroom, a bathroom off the hall, and a little kitchen that was like an annex to the front sitting room. Guinness made a quick tour, just to prove to himself there weren't any boobie traps, and then went back into the bedroom, sat down on the bed, and kicked off his shoes. He was tired. He looked around the room with stupid, incurious eyes, hardly seeing anything at all.

He wondered if Aimé was having a good time down in Spain, and if her elderly boyfriend had taken her to the seaside, where they could sleep with the windows open and listen to the waves breaking. But, of course, you didn't listen to anything while you were asleep—unless you were Raymond Guinness, celebrated killer of men, and then you listened to the wallpaper peel because there were people in the world who didn't like you. You were famous. *Everyone has heard of the Soldier.* You didn't dare relax because somewhere along the line you had become a celebrity, and people stood around in train stations waiting for a glimpse of you so they could earn a little extra money by phoning somebody with an interest in spattering your brains all over the bathroom tiles. Aimé was asleep down there in Spain, and in her bedroom in Amsterdam Raymond Guinness was trying to work up the nerve to lie down and close his eyes. It seemed a remote enough possibility.

He had a headache, a knocking sensation. He was about to get up and go into the bathroom to look for some aspirin when he realized that the knocking was coming from the front door. He assumed it was Janine, and she must have been trying to raise him for a long time, because the sound was beginning to take on a certain urgency. He got up, slipping his shoes back on simply as a precaution, and went to the door.

In certain lines of work, if you wanted to live to enjoy your troubled conscience, you didn't proceed merely on the basis of an assumption. Guinness flattened himself out beside the door, gripping a small glass ashtray in his left hand, and reached over with his right to throw the bolt open. Nothing happened—there weren't any sprays of automatic weapons fire or anything like that. The knocking just stopped.

"Soldier?"

It was a perfectly familiar feminine voice and, feeling like a chump, he pushed himself away from the wall and opened the door for her.

"Soldier, are you . . ."

She stood in the hallway, looking at him—or, more specifically, at the ashtray in his hand—aware, apparently, that he had intended to beat her skull in. Well, not hers, but whoever else's it might have been at that unholy hour. For some reason she seemed to resent what struck Guinness as a perfectly reasonable precaution, but he was tired of worrying about whether people liked and understood him. He set the ashtray back down on the table from which it had come and went back into the bedroom to lie down, kicking off his shoes again. What the hell.

"You would like some tea, yes?"

She had followed him and was sitting on the corner of the bed, holding onto the strap of her shoulder bag with both hands, as if it would brace her against falling to the floor. When he shook his head, she reached into the bag and brought out a small, nickle-plated automatic pistol, letting it rest in the palm of her hand, an offering rather than a threat. When he didn't take it, she set it down on the bedspread.

"It was all I had right now—later, when you know what you will need, I will find it for you."

For a long moment, they both looked at her ludicrous little toy popgun—you might almost have imagined it to be a piece of wedding silver someone had given them and they couldn't quite figure out what to do with it. And then he realized, with a certain amount of surprise at his own dimwittedness, that she had been trying, after a fashion, to apologize. He picked the thing up and set it on the night table, next to his head.

"Thank you."

"I will need your trousers," she said abruptly, without seeming even to notice the change in subject—perhaps it hadn't changed.

Guinness was startled enough to laugh, but if it had been a joke she was hanging onto it. She seemed very composed, her hands folded together in her lap, and he noticed that her green eyes had lost their worried look.

"I need them if I am to get you new clothes—at least, I

need to measure them. And the jacket and the shirt. The shoes as well," she went on, pointing down at where Guinness's scuffed loafers were tipped over on the floor, like beached canoes. "Although perhaps you are not so worried about them, yes? A European would not wear such shoes, but perhaps no one will think to look at your feet."

"No, perhaps not."

He swung up to a sitting position and started to unbutton his shirt. When he took it off and handed it to her, she went over to the chair on the back of which he had hung his coat, turning her back while he undid his trousers. When she had them, she took a tape measure from her pocket and measured the waist and the inside seam of the right leg, always with her back to him, while he pulled away the bedcovers and crawled inside. The sheets were like ice.

"While you're at it, my wallet's in the inside jacket pocket; almost everything I have is in dollars and marks—can you get it changed for me?"

"Yes."

"Thanks."

When she turned around she was holding his wallet in her hand. She watched him with an odd, speculative expression for a moment, and then she took the money out, counted it, and returned the wallet to his jacket pocket.

"The stores will be open at eight—I will be back here at nine. Is there anything else you need?"

"No."

"Would you like me to stay until the morning?"

He shook his head, wondering whether common politeness didn't require him to offer some explanation, but apparently it wasn't expected. She picked up her shoulder bag and left, without another word, without giving him any chance to do anything more than wonder. As the door closed behind her, he had a second in which he remembered that he really ought to get up and see about the bolt, but somehow it no longer seemed to matter—let the Bad Guys come if they felt like it; they were welcome. And then, suddenly, he was asleep, dreaming of Cornwall and the thundering sea.

There was an outdoor café on the Leisestraat. If you took one of the outside tables, close to the sidewalk, you could look up the street to a cobbled bridge that arched massively over the canal, like a restraining hand. Several people stood at the railing, including a number of children whose voices Guinness was able to distinguish, even over the noise from the street, at a distance of close to forty yards. One old man in a dark gray overcoat was throwing small handfuls of what were probably breadcrumbs down onto the water, so probably there were ducks in the canal and they were what caused the children to laugh.

Guinness sat leaning back on one of the café chairs, moodily staring at his shoes. Janine was right; they were a dead giveaway. All morning long, he hadn't seen another man wearing anything like them. Later in the day, when he had a chance, he would see whether he couldn't find a shoe store and get himself a nice, sturdy pair of brown lace-ups.

"It is a good fit," she had said, smoothing out the material with her hands as he sat at Aimé's dressing table, which had the only mirror in the room, trying to knot his tie—he could see her hands in the glass, working slowly and carefully, as if she wanted to force the jacket into place over his shoulders. "But I do not think someone with eyes would take you for a Dutchman. You are too big—you spread out too much. You move like someone who is used to plenty of space, and Amsterdam is too small and crowded."

She had stopped kneading him, but her hands still rested on his shoulders in the easy intimacy of a man and a woman alone together at nine-thirty in the morning. They might have known each other for years.

"Have you eaten your breakfast yet?" she asked, stepping

back to let him get up from the little velvet-covered bench where he had been sitting amidst the bottles of perfume and the cold-cream jars; it had almost been like sitting on the floor.

"No." He smiled, shaking his head. "I'd just gotten out of the shower when you came."

"You would like some, yes?"

"Yes. Thank you."

Aimé apparently worried a lot about the state of her waistline—"She is this thin," Janine had said, holding up a finger—so there hadn't been much to choose from in the refrigerator. Some vegetable juice and a few rye crackers, not even an egg. The tea was English, a blend Guinness hadn't tasted in nine years, so that made up for a little bit—except that there wasn't any milk.

"Ah, you take milk!" she had said, laughing, clapping her hands in front of her face and pretending to be astonished. "How ver-r-r-ry Br-r-r-ritish."

He smiled and raised his cup as if to offer a toast, thinking it was nice to have a woman find you amusing, even if it was only because of the way you drank your tea. It was perfectly ridiculous, he was aware, but he felt almost as if he had been given a present.

All of which subtracted nothing from his present problem. That was what happened when, even for the odd half-hour with a pretty woman, you forgot that you hadn't come all this way to spend the time making daisy chains.

He had left the apartment at around a quarter to ten; he could have walked to where he wanted to go in twenty minutes, but in his profession that would have been considered the most drastic lapse of technique. So he had spent a sensationally boring two hours window-shopping—picking up a cab for half-a-dozen blocks and then circling back on foot, sneaking out the rear exits of buildings, zig-zagging all over the place just to make triple sure he wasn't being followed. By five minutes to noon, he was satisfied. Either they had an Olympic track team on him, or he was clean; he would have run them pretty hard, and not even two or three men could have stayed with him and kept from being spotted.

So everything was fine, except that he hadn't thought to ask Janine about what people did in this country for lunch—he had been far too busy feeling all warm and runny and masculine inside.

In Switzerland it was easy. The stores simply closed up between the hours of twelve and two and everybody went home for a veal chop and noodles and an hour's nap. You didn't have to worry about any conscientious file clerks staying behind to tidy up, and nobody hung around in the employee's lounge to gab about last Sunday's soccer match. You didn't do that; you went home and listened to the radio while your wife dished up mounds of steaming food and retailed her grievances. There were rules—it was as if the whole damn country were unionized.

But, like an idiot, Guinness hadn't inquired. You had to know the quaint native customs, you understand, or you could be in for no end of trouble. So, naturally, there wasn't a thing you could do except to sit in the sunshine, drinking a bottle of Heinekin and pretending to read the newspaper, while you waited across the street from a foreign-language bookshop staffed for the moment by a white-haired old lady who looked brittle enough to shatter like glass if somebody opened the door suddenly enough to blow her off her chair, poor darling.

It was a nice bookstore. They had a whole wall of Penguin paperbacks—you wondered how many copies of the Venerable Bede they sold in a decade—and magazines from all over. Guinness had purchased his copy of the *Times* there, somewhat astonished to find that it was only a day old. The grandmother behind the cash register had made change for him and smiled and tried out a few words of English, glad at that hour, it seemed, for the diversion.

Kätzner had told him about the bookstore, and almost nothing else. "I can provide the necessary addresses," he had said, hunching his shoulders in a shrug as they strolled through the Amalienburg, the sound of their shoes on the hardwood floors echoing like pistol shots.

"But you must understand that I have not been back in nearly twenty years now. I am too well known now—I would be arrested at once, although probably they would not connect me with the Heer Maarten Huygens who was the East German spy they never quite managed to apprehend in 1962. And, of course, my own people are involved in this matter—somehow, I am far from certain quite how. My appearance in Amsterdam just at present would undoubtedly have catastrophic consequences. No, my friend, it is you who must go in my place."

He had made it sound so simple, like waltzing down to the corner grocery for a can of creamed corn. But, of course, that was part of what had made him such a success—you believed him. You saw the world through his eyes. You could know perfectly well that, in all probability, you were going to get your ass shot off, but you went anyway. Somehow all difficulties evaporated in the presence of that amiable clarity of purpose.

Guinness tried not to think about it, so he stared morosely at his shoes and thought about Janine, wondering if she had forgiven him yet for not taking her up on her offer of a little heavy breathing. She had been friendly enough over breakfast; she hadn't given any signs of harboring resentment—apparently it was just part of the service and, after all, she was a pro in that particular line of endeavor and probably wouldn't take a refusal personally. What the hell, though—she hadn't exactly tried to present him with a bill. Women were funny about that sort of thing—you never knew what was going on inside them.

Well, he'd make it up to her. If there was time tonight, he'd take her out to dinner and make a pass at her. If she went for it, fine; she was a pretty woman and Guinness wasn't made of balsa. If she turned him down, then at least she'd have whatever satisfaction that could afford her. Under any circumstances, he didn't want to hurt her feelings.

He wouldn't mind getting laid—it had been a while.

But first, he thought, he would get rid of the shoes. The first principle of surveillance: don't do anything that might make anybody curious. The shoes had to go.

He looked at his watch—it was almost two o'clock; if people hurried up, he could have this phase of the business over with by four, and that would leave plenty of time. How long could it take to buy a pair of nice, heavy-soled Dutch booties?

About three minutes later, a small, attractive woman of about twenty-three or four—shoulder-length brown hair swept back to half-cover her ears, bare slender arms coming out of the sleeveholes of a strikingly pretty cotton print dress—turned the corner into the Leisestraat, crossed over the bridge, and proceeded to the door of the bookstore. Guinness waited until she was inside and then folded his newspaper, finished his beer, and fished around in his pocket for some tip money.

Fine—he was delighted. Now that she had returned to work he could take a leisurely stroll back down along the Amstel and toss her apartment.

7

"I know nothing about her," he had said, his attention absorbed, it seemed, by the rococo cherubs that kept threatening to slide down from the ceiling of the king's hunting lodge. He stood with his hands clasped behind his back, his face unreadable. "Nothing significant."

A crowd of tourists flooded in through the open double doors, and Kätzner glanced at them with distaste, signaling to Guinness with a slight movement of his head that it would be necessary for the two of them to retreat. When they were outside again, on one of the wooded paths that led back to the much more regal formality of the gardens, he stopped and turned around for a moment, contemplating the elegant little jewel-box of a building, lost, apparently, in undemocratic satisfaction. Suddenly he turned to Guinness and smiled.

"My little Amalia of the Amalienburg—I took the name from that temple to decadence. It is a perfectly respectable Dutch name; one hears it all the time. It was my little joke."

So little Amalia grew up, apparently. Kätzner's wife had remarried, a man named Brouwer, who adopted the child. Mrs. Brouwer died of cancer in 1973, and what domestic life between Amalia and her stepfather had been like was something about which Kätzner hadn't a clue. He had kept a discreet eye on her over the years—she attended the University of Rotterdam briefly, just long enough to put her in contact with radical politics—but concerning the quality of her life, what she was like, how she felt about herself, he understood nothing.

"It is an odd condition of existence, is it not, to feel your own child a stranger to you. I haven't even a photograph to know her by, and thus she always is to me as she was when I left—four years old, with curly hair and dimples in her knees. One would think I should have grown indifferent by now—after all, what is she but a shadow?—but somehow she draws closer to me as that time recedes further and further into the past. Perhaps as one grows old one becomes . . . what? I should like to say, 'more human,' but I am not sure. Certainly more sensitive to what one has discarded along the way. Did you ever marry and beget children, my young friend? Can you have any conception of what I mean?"

Guinness thought it prudent not to answer, and the two men walked on back over the canal. By then it was late afternoon, and the wind had begun to turn cold. They spoke very little.

And so, as Guinness stood in the living room of the tiny apartment, contemplating the objects on a small round table in front of the curtained window—a wooden cigarette box, two little ceramic statuettes of Dresden shepherdesses, a colored pencil, half-a-dozen copies of an English magazine called *Women's Own*—he tried to form some sort of impression of Amalia Brouwer, almost as if it were something that could be carried back to her father, whom Guinness didn't imagine he would ever meet again. But he felt an obligation of sorts to try seeing her through Kätzner's eyes. Kätzner couldn't be the one, and so it was up to Guinness to concern himself with whatever it was that could be found out from statuettes and colored pencils.

He looked around him, noting the dried flowers in a pot next to the gas fireplace, and the tiny stain, the approximate shape of Australia, where someone sitting on the left side of the sofa had probably spilled a drink over the beige carpet, and he thought about his own daughter, who was eleven now and probably wore black patent leather shoes and worshipped John Travolta with all the passion of her young heart. Two years ago, in South Carolina, on the one and only occasion he had seen her since infancy, it had been Old Maid and science fiction novels, but nothing was constant. Now, probably, she wouldn't even remember him, and that might be for the better.

"We must bear the consequences of the ways we have chosen for ourselves," Kätzner had said. "There is very little point in pretending to be the victims of circumstance, because what is that but the sum of what we have done with our lives? Has it not been so with you, my friend?"

Guinness decided he would be systematic and save the bedroom for last. He knew he would be much more likely to find whatever it was he wanted—and what that was he really couldn't have said—whatever it was that would untangle Amalia Brouwer's peculiar trouble, in the bedroom. Bedrooms are where women really live their lives; two marriages had been enough to teach him that much. But he would wait, and thus miss nothing.

The kitchen was hardly large enough to fall down in. There was almost nothing in the refrigerator except half-a-dozen cartons of strawberry yogurt—you didn't have the sense this was someone who ate most of her meals at home. In the cupboard he found several bottles of liquor, most of them with the seals still unbroken—cognac, British gin, a half-empty fifth of unblended whiskey—not the things a woman drank. And too expensive a collection to manage on what you earned selling paperback copies of Balzac. The little lady had a friend, it seemed.

The hall closet yielded nothing. There was a woman's umbrella dangling from a hook, a wine-red cloth coat hung up in a paper dry-cleaner's bag, and a rather mannish raincoat. Guinness searched the pockets, but they were empty.

The bathroom medicine chest, he was happy to note, was uncluttered by fingernail files and night cream and old pots of lip rouge. He took down a plastic squeeze bottle of sun screen, unscrewed the top, and smelled it—it smelled like nothing except sun screen. A little yellow box of laxative pills, a tube of Chap Stik—"You're a long way from home"—two or three drugstore cartons with undecipherable Dutch names but with the sort of packaging design that suggested the contents were useful against the customary feminine complaints. Amalia had struck him, in the glimpse he had had of her, as a healthy out-of-doors specimen, and nothing so far contradicted that impression.

Guinness shut the cabinet and frowned, feeling very much at sea. He had always hated the beginnings of a job, the sense that he was feeling his way in the dark, and this one was rather out of his line anyway. Nobody had given him a contract on Amalia Brouwer—quite the contrary, he was supposed to save her life. But he was an assassin by training, not a bodyguard. He didn't even know what, precisely, he was supposed to be guarding this body against. But, then, neither had Kätzner. It was all a great muddle.

"Somehow," he had said, taking off his hat and rubbing the back of his hand over his nearly bald crown, although the gardens of the Nymphenburg were far from warm, "somehow she has managed to put herself in some terrible danger. It hangs around her like an atmosphere—real, but as undefined as that. She is nothing more than a pawn; they will sacrifice her readily enough. It seems they plan to kill her in the name of the great socialist revolution."

He pursed his lips and made a contemptuous face—the Marxist policeman apparently had little sympathy with the imperatives of amateur conspiracy.

The bathtub took up the whole far end of the room.

There was a hand-held shower fixed to the wall with a bracket. Guinness swept aside the curtain and ran his hand along the inside of the worn porcelain basin. It had a gritty feel, as if it hadn't been scoured out in several days. He tried peering into the drain, but it was too dark, so he probed tentatively with his index finger until he found the trap, a coarse mesh basket, like the bell of a sherry glass, that came out without difficulty. The bottom was matted with hair and soap scum, probably two or three weeks' worth.

The hair came clean enough with a little rinsing; Guinness wrapped it in a couple of thicknesses of facial tissue and patted it dry. There wasn't enough light in the bathroom, so he took his little discovery back to the kitchen where the sunshine streamed in through a window over the sink.

It sorted out into three categories—the girl's, not surprisingly, longish and a medium brown, made up the bulk. But in with it were several strands of black, wavy hair, short enough to suggest a man. The whiskey drinker?

And then there was a third kind, which Guinness couldn't have given his oath was human at all. Very fine, very short, somewhere between white and gray. You might have taken it for cat hair, except that not many people took their cats into the shower with them, and there was no evidence of an animal anywhere in the apartment. So one presumed it was human, and one hoped it was male—otherwise Amalia had an awfully butch girlfriend, and there was no evidence of that either.

So, two men. One dark, the other . . . what? The dark one was the more frequent visitor—either that or Whitey didn't much care for using the shower.

Whitey. Were the unopened bottles for him? Was he a cognac drinker?

Short whitish hair, short whitish hair . . . Guinness decided he could think about it later and folded up the whole loose fluffy wad in a paper towel and slipped it into his wallet. He wouldn't let it gnaw at him now—no point in jumping to conclusions.

Curly met him as he walked into the bedroom. He was right there, staring out of a picture frame on Amalia's night table; you couldn't miss him.

Guinness picked up the frame and examined the photograph of a smiling young man whose black hair was only partially covered by a military cap—the insignia on his shoulders indicated a captain. It was a broad face, the sort of face a lot of women might find appealing. A strong face, if you ignored the faintly pleading expression of the eyes. The writing in the lower-right corner had been done with a broad-tipped pen—*"Pour Amalia, avec mon amour, Jean."* Not a very imaginative sentiment, but one that would serve. So now he had a name—or, at least, a given name. Jean.

The cognomen was on the flyleaf of a volume of poetry, an anthology of the type used by schoolboys. Jean Rênal. Had he lent the book to Amalia? Given it to her? Tried to use it at some point in his wooing and left it behind? Under any circumstances, it was there, on a little shelf over the dresser, along with a two-volume edition of *Madame Bovary*, the essays of Montaigne, and *Hard Times* in English.

Jean Rênal.

So, a military officer—not French, the uniform was wrong; Belgian?—a captain. Amalia's lover—one of them. A name, a rank, a face. What was he in all this? Did he matter, or was he just a bystander, a probable casualty—a victim? Did he know he was sharing his girlfriend with another guy? What in hell was a Jean Rênal anyway?

He would get in touch with Ernie. Ernie was good at placing people—all those computer data banks in Washington could use the exercise.

During the next hour, Guinness went through everything—drawers, the contents of spare handbags, the wastepaper basket, everything. And he concluded that Amalia Brouwer probably wasn't a very happy young woman.

Someday he would announce it to the world, Guinness's first law of frilly knickers. The clothes they wear out on the street were a promise, a declaration—a dare sometimes. And there was no truth in advertising. If you wanted to know how a woman really felt about herself, you took a look at her dainty unmentionables. Amalia Brouwer was a very practical soul, all white bras and cotton panties, and her nightdresses were about as interesting as so many hospital gowns. She was a pretty girl; she should have been up to her eyebrows in silk and peek-a-boo lace, but she wasn't. It was all function and utility and no nonsense with her—you could see that in the bareness of her apartment. She just seemed to be camping out, poor little thing.

And then there was the absence of personal mementos. Usually, at that age, they have boxes and boxes of letters on pretty notepaper and photographs of school friends and maiden aunts and long-dead pet poodles. Even Louise, his second wife, that practical girl—even into her thirties she had kept invitations to fraternity dances and college yearbooks and funny hats from New Year's Eve parties. Women were like that.

But all Amalia Brouwer had to prove she hadn't come into existence the day before yesterday was her large framed photograph of Jean Rênal, *"Pour Amalia, avec mon amour, Jean."* And she couldn't very well throw that away—a man capable of such astonishing originality of expression would miss it if it were gone when he came back to get his rocks off and take his shower, and no doubt he would be sure to ask what she had done with it.

"She is nothing," Kätzner had said. "She runs errands, she takes messages over the telephone—the sort of thing that is hardly even illegal. She is one of those who are sympathetic to the people's struggle." His short syllable of laughter might almost have managed to be cruel if it hadn't carried such obvious desperation.

"You see? I doubt if the police even have a dossier on her—she could escape free of it all; she is not yet entangled so completely as that. But now she is in something where they will forfeit her life as casually as you or I might relinquish the scrap of torn rag upon which we have wiped our hands. You cannot conceive of what these people are like."

You could see that it haunted him, this danger to his faceless child. You could hear his breathing as he walked along and watch the muscles of his neck thicken. Kätzner had been around. He had seen such things many times before this, and it would have required no great feat of the imagination for him to picture to himself the fate of this highly expendable little Dutch girl who just happened to have his blood in her veins.

You cannot conceive . . . The words of a Communist secret policeman to a professional assassin—dear God, what could they be like?

"I know no details," he had continued, almost to himself. "I simply saw her name on one sheet of an operations report, lying on a colleague's desk in Berlin, and, believe me, it was not possible to inquire further. That was two days ago—perhaps I was intended to see it; I do not know. I do not even care, really. All I care for is that she was marked down as '*bevollmächtigte Auslage*,' an authorized expense. Whatever happens, they mean for her to die. It is part of their plan."

These people . . . What "people"? Kätzner must have had some ideas about the cast of characters, but he hadn't elaborated. One wondered why.

One wondered about a lot of things. Kätzner was no fool—what was he suppressing, and for what ends? What was it, just reflex party loyalty? Or was there something else, something that might have made Guinness tell him that he would just have to pass, thanks, that he had a plane to Rome leaving in a couple of hours and the boys in Washington didn't like him moonlighting.

Well, that was Kätzner's business. Guinness didn't really mind not knowing—he didn't frighten particularly easily and, at bottom, he didn't want a reason to back away. It wasn't simply that he owed the guy—he did owe him, his life in fact, but there was more to it than that. They understood each other, these two; they belonged to the same species of man, which made the sympathy between them immediate and compelling. That was why Kätzner had saved his neck all those years ago in Belgrade, and that was why Guinness had come to Amsterdam.

So he would play it on Kätzner's terms and hope for the best. The cast of characters didn't matter.

And it wouldn't have done him any real good to know what was up, even if Kätzner had known—and it was possible he hadn't. Things came to you; Guinness would find out soon enough. And at this stage it didn't make any difference; he could hardly just walk up to Amalia Brouwer in the street and tell her to take a long vacation somewhere, that the bad guys were after her. She wouldn't believe him—she believed in The Cause. She would think he was nuts, or something worse. No, he would have to wait until he could rub her nose in the treachery of her friends, and to do that he would have to find out more than Kätzner could ever have told him. It was better if he came to his own understanding of the thing.

Little girls, playing Mata Hari. It was pathetic; it made you want never to see another James Bond movie for as long as you lived. What did they think, that it was all just some mildly entertaining indoor sport?

Guinness sat on the edge of Amalia Brouwer's bed, wondering what the world was coming to.

Because, of course, Amalia Brouwer had done just about the dumbest thing it was possible to do in the spy business—she had written something down. He hadn't the faintest idea what it was, just a six-number sequence: 230987. A four-number combination, a passport number, possibly even an address. If it was coded, it could be anything. 230987.

But there it was, made hideously conspicuous by the pains that had been taken to hide it—the poor little twit had written it out on a tiny slip of paper and taped that to the underside of the drawer in her night table, as if the undersides of drawers weren't the most obvious places on God's earth to look for people's little secrets. Probably it referred to something or someone she had been instructed to use or contact only under certain specific circumstances, or probably only once, or perhaps never. And she had been afraid she would forget, so she had lapsed into the habits of the ordinary world and written the thing down.

Well, maybe Guinness could figure out what it meant, and maybe this time Amalia Brouwer would get lucky, and her *faux pas* would go some of the distance toward saving her life. One assumed it was possible.

230987.

He traced through the apartment in his mind, trying to discover whether there had been anywhere he might have given himself away. No, she wouldn't know anything had been disturbed, not unless she had been setting little traps—threads across the doorsill, that business—and probably not even then. After all, his very expensive education at MI-6's boy scout camp up in the Hebrides was supposed to be fairly exhaustive about such matters, and Amalia Brouwer didn't strike him as the cagey type anyway—the cagey type didn't leave numbers taped to the undersides of drawers.

And as to touching things . . . well, that went without saying. You never knew—if it blew up on him, and little Amalia ended up the object of a murder investigation, Guinness didn't want any of his fingerprints ending up mounted on police slides. He had been a very careful boy.

He smoothed the bedspread back into place—even an amateur might notice the outline of a strange man's ass on her cotton counterpane—took a last look out the living room window to make absolutely sure there weren't any interested observers down on the pavement, and let himself out through the front door. In five minutes he was nearly a quarter of a mile away.

"A man must necessarily be mad to father his first child when he is over forty. They say that is the age when we commit our greatest follies, when we begin to feel the hot breath of mortality on our necks, but one would imagine that one such as I, who was in the resistance movement as early as 1936, that I might have come to terms with the prospect of death. So I do not think that was it—I think it was the illusion of safety."

They had been driving back into Munich, and the rain had started up again. There were small pools of water on the asphalt roadway, and Kätzner had put on his glasses because, apparently, the glare through the windscreen was bothering him. He looked older with his glasses, as if he might actually be in his middle sixties. He looked tired, and sick of living.

"Did you know that I attended the university here?" he asked, turning to Guinness and smiling. "I came up from Sigmaringen when I was eighteen—my mother wanted me to be a priest, but my father was a lawyer, so . . . At any rate, I stayed only a year. Hitler and *Das Kapital* saw to that—I was young and believed I was witnessing the twilight of the world."

Had he expected some kind of response? Guinness merely stared out at the road, hoping Kätzner would shut up. He didn't want to be bothered with this man's disillusionment; he didn't want to hear any sad, sad stories about how life was a snickering harlot. You catch any field man in just the right mood and it's always the same thing—the world was a bad dog, sure to bite you if you tried to scratch it behind the ear. Everybody had his favorite metaphor for lost innocence and the corrupting power of service to wickedness.

But he understood. He liked Kätzner, even admired him—God knew, Kätzner was a better specimen than himself. It was just that each man's portion of misery was sufficient for his own needs; it did you no good to pity anyone.

Still, he did understand. Kätzner had been studying jurisprudence and Karl Marx when the Spanish Civil War seemed to demand that he choose sides, and 1936 had found him on a train to Barcelona, to join the Communist militia there and lay down his life, if necessary, in the struggle against the forces of reaction. The acolyte had found his new god, and he rushed to his baptism, his confirmation in the mysteries of hopelessness.

And that was how it had begun. After the fall of Madrid, he and a few other die-hards made their way over the border into France, and from there Kätzner was routed to the Soviet Union for training as an agent for the by-then inevitable war against his homeland. By 1941 he was a captain in the Russian army and their man in the East Prussian city of Königsburg. In 1942 he was in Dresden, in 1943 in Waldenburg and Gleiwitz, and from 1944 through the Russian conquest in Berlin itself. Apparently it had been a pretty gaudy career.

"I was even arrested by the Gestapo once," he said, the way someone else might mention their reception by the Queen. "That was just after the retreat from Stalingrad—excuse me, Leningrad—and they were excessively nervous.

But I escaped. And then, in forty-five, the Russians nearly shot me before I could convince them to confirm my identity with the NKVD offices in Moscow. I never in all those years felt like a traitor, not until I found myself in that detention camp outside of Potsdam—we had won, we had defeated Hitler, and I felt like a criminal and longed for death. It is odd, isn't it."

Maybe so. Maybe that was the disadvantage of having a moral sense, without which Kätzner would probably have stayed in Munich to finish up his degree and settle for a wife, five children, and a fat law practice in this imperfect world. Maybe he saw the folly now of running off to fight in Cataluña—maybe he had seen it then and hadn't cared. Apparently he cared now.

And Guinness—who had begun with no sense of anything except his own purposes, who had taken a British contract on a man he had never even seen from no higher motive than a certain sum of ready money, and thus had set the pattern of his whole adult life, Guinness understood perfectly well. You begin at opposite ends and meet at the hollow center. All illusions are betrayed—belief in causes, belief in righteousness, belief in self. Nothing is left except the work and, since every man has to have something, the work itself, the integrity of that, becomes its own search for the Grail.

So you don't imagine you can win; you merely hope to discover the terms on which you could be prepared to lose.

And thus he knew what Kätzner had meant when he had said of his daugher, "She is nothing." Let her stay with her illusions, he was pleading—at least, so many of them as might not kill her. There was no knowledge of good and evil, only of evil. Let her marry some harmless man and have babies and die in bed, never dreaming of dark truths.

Guinness stood leaning against the embankment that ran

along the great Amstel Canal, just below the bridge of the Sarphatistraat. The wad of paper towel containing the hair from Amalia Brouwer's bathtub drain was clutched in his fist—he didn't look at it now; there wasn't any need. The short threads of pale gray, he knew whose they were now. Suspicion had hardened into certainty. And he knew that Kätzner had known and why he had kept it to himself. He had wanted Guinness to see the girl first, and then to discover her danger. He had wanted Guinness to make good on his promise—the girl had to come first.

And he would—he would try to keep her well out of it. But the man with the bone-white hair was known for the brutality of his methods. It wasn't going to be easy.

Oh God—oh God, oh God. He closed his eyes and tried not to see Kätzner's child. Not that way, not with her throat cut or the side of her head a ragged crater. How many times had he thought of his own daughter, his own baby, his Rocky, whom probably he would never see again—how many times had she come to him in his dreams, just that way. It hadn't happened, but it might have, and it couldn't happen now. He just couldn't let it happen.

In a sudden and, for him, inexplicable moment of fury, he crushed the little package of loose hair in his fist and threw it at the water sweeping past his feet. As if to mock him, his angry missile floated down to disappear under the bridge, as gently as a snowflake.

8

"A telephone number," she said—so much for that mystery. Janine looked up from the slip of notepad paper upon which Guinness had written out the six-digit sequence he had found on the underside of the drawer in Amalia Brouwer's night table. "Without the prefix. I would think it must be here in Amsterdam."

"Can you find out the address?"

"Yes—but not today. Tomorrow. Is that all right?"

"That's fine."

They were sitting in the kitchen of her apartment—hers, not Aimé's, although there was little enough to choose between them. They were drinking tea at a square table not much bigger than a chessboard, and the tea came in clumsy earthenware mugs that you could warm your hands around. In the artificial light Janine's eyes had taken on the color of emeralds, as if they had been illuminated from behind. They made her look even paler, and more vulnerable. Guinness shifted uncomfortably in his chair, wishing he had caught his plane to Rome and the brutal logic of his existence had been left alone. He didn't want to take responsibility for anyone.

"This is private, you know," he said slowly, staring down at the table, giving the impression he might have wanted to bore a hole through it with his gaze. "I think there's a connection with the man they want me to nail here, but he's not my object. It doesn't have to do with Ernie Tuttle; it's not any interest of his, so maybe you'd better just back out of it. Get the phone number for me in the morning, and then just pretend you've never heard of me. Nobody's going to pin any medals on you for this one."

"But you do think it touches Flycatcher, yes?"

Except for a slight tightening around one side of his mouth, he didn't register any surprise. But certainly he was surprised, and he didn't like it. He hated these little unexpected turns—they almost always meant trouble.

So he forced himself to smile, the way you might smile at a precocious child.

"Who's been telling you about that?"

"Everybody—nobody." She held her hands apart, shooting her eyebrows into the little fringe of bang that came about halfway down her forehead. "He has been seen here, and now you are here. One draws a conclusion—there are not many who have not heard of your quarrel, that you have made it your object to kill him. You will kill him, yes?"

"Yes—if I get the chance."

"Then it is not private." And then she smiled—it was a nicer smile than his. "Flycatcher is on the list, yes? Then it is *not* private."

How could he explain it? To go for Flycatcher was chancy enough, but to try working around him to the girl was increasing the risk geometrically. At least when you wanted to kill somebody, you knew where you were. But this—it was going to be like sticking your hand into an anthill. But you could never make that clear to anyone. They just didn't believe you.

"Do you know anything about him?"

"What everyone knows—that he is a bad man."

"So am I."

She shook her head, as if he were talking the most arrant nonsense, and covered one of his hands with both of hers.

"Not like him. Some men are like terrible diseases; they murder with no logic. They say he is like that—like a small child who wants to leave a mess."

"See to it you don't end up a part of the mess," he said, getting up from the table. It was after eight o'clock, and this conversation wasn't getting him anywhere. He decided he was hungry.

"How do you like the shoes?"

He turned around suddenly to face her and pulled up his trouser legs three or four inches to display a pair of high-topped brown walking shoes, like cut-down infantry boots. Janine put her hands up to her mouth and began to laugh.

"Oh, yes," she was able to sputter out. "Yes, very elegant." And then she started to laugh again—she couldn't help it, apparently. And it was a pretty laugh. Oddly girlish, if that word meant anything.

"Well, hell. I was planning to take you out to dinner, but if you feel that way . . ."

"No." She waved a hand at him, the fingers a little spread apart, and then had to put it back over her mouth to smother another hilarious collapse. "No, they are very good. The disguise is perfect—you could be a big farm boy, in the town for a holiday. I see a hundred pairs just like them every day."

And then, of course, both of them were perfectly silent again, because they had both understood what she had meant. She was without embarrassment and didn't even look away, and Guinness, realizing that it was his problem, tried to think of something to say to indicate that he didn't care about all those other pairs of shoes—he didn't care, really, and he didn't want to seem to be passing judgment.

"Good. Then the big farm boy wants to know where we should have something to eat—our young lady doesn't show any signs of having plans for the evening and, anyway, I don't want to have her tumble to anything just yet. We can give it a rest until tomorrow."

He smiled, trying to look persuasively eager, and it seemed to work.

"I will just change then, yes?"

The door to Janine's bedroom had been left ajar. Living alone, perhaps she had gotten out of the habit of closing it, or perhaps she simply didn't care. It was by far the largest room in the apartment and was even equipped with a pair of sliding glass doors to a small veranda—she had the top floor, so it afforded a good view over several smaller buildings to the trees and serpentine waterways of the Vondelpark—but apparently it still wasn't large enough for comfort. In any case, the door was standing open.

Guinness sat at the tiny square table at which, one assumed, Janine ate most of her meals in solitude—there was nothing about the place to suggest she entertained many visitors—nursing his second cup of tea and wondering if he shouldn't move over to one of the uncomfortable-looking beanbag chairs by the opposite wall, where he wouldn't enjoy quite so unobstructed a view inside. Most of the bedroom, of course, was out of his direct line of vision, but right across from the entranceway was one of those peculiarly European oddities, a huge, ornately carved armoire, infinitely more suggestive of a bank vault than of anything in which to hang one's clothes, and the door to that too, into which was set a large mirror, had been left slightly ajar.

Janine had come out of her bathroom and was sitting on the edge of her bed, smoothing on a pair of nylons. She had her back to him—or, more accurately, to the mirror—and she looked perfectly delicious in her underwear, which wasn't the least little bit nunlike or self-effacing. Guinness's second law: a woman who goes in for pink garterbelts can't be all bad. He felt a slight tightening in his chest and realized that it had been a very long time since he had sat watching any such performance.

Was that what it was? Women weren't stupid, most of them—the view was there to be enjoyed. So fine, she wanted to remind him that neither of them had their insides stuffed with rose petals. He was reminded.

And then she glanced over her bare shoulder at him, and her expression suggested nothing at all. She knew he was watching her; she seemed to take that for granted. There was nothing in her eyes—not surprise, not amusement, nothing. And Guinness discovered that, quite unaccountably, he was deeply stirred.

"There—that was not long, was it?" She stood in front of him in a green silk dress that, without being vulgar about it, managed to suggest quite forcefully the outlines of her body, holding a small, shiny white-leather handbag. There was just the faintest trace of pale pink on her lips, making her smile look wet and enticing—no doubt about it, the lady was coming on to him. It was nice to deal with people who knew their own minds.

"Not long at all."

They settled on an Indonesian restaurant, not a hundred yards from Amalia Brouwer's bookstore. The drill was that you ate about five dozen different courses, all served on tiny earthenware dishes about the size of ashtrays—just a taste of saffron-stained vegetables and little piles of shredded meat and strange onionlike things that reminded you somehow of grapes, all managed with the fingers so that pretty quickly, if you weren't careful, your place setting started to look like Miss Havisham's wedding feast.

But the waiter, who wore a loose red-and-black patterned turban and a white mess jacket, would come along every once in a while and gather up the empty dishes, sweeping away the debris. He spoke neither English nor German, and precious little Dutch, but he seemed to know through some special sympathy just exactly what you wanted and so it didn't matter. If he had a fault, it appeared to be an absolute intolerance for empty beer glasses; he kept refilling them when you weren't looking, and Guinness discovered that he had put away three bottles before he caught on in time to wave the fourth one away.

"The food is very hot, yes?" She leaned across the table toward him, just as if she were explaining a local joke. "And besides, in Holland the men drink much more beer—do not be angry with him."

"I'm not angry; I'm just afraid I could drown, is all. Why? Do I look angry?"

"No."

"Is Janine your real name, or did Ernie dream it up for you?"

"No, it is my name. My mother wished me to be an actress and imagined that a French name would help somehow."

"Did it work?"

She smiled, and all at once Guinness felt like a monster, as if he had made a coarse joke.

"No, I was never an actress—no more than my profession demands."

"I'm sorry."

Fortunately, the waiter chose that moment to bring them a couple of steaming, jasmine-scented towels on a wicker tray, and Guinness made himself very busy wiping off the tips of his fingers, feeling profoundly uncomfortable in the silence. When he felt there was a chance the wretched moment might have passed away and risked a glance at her, he was astonished to discover that the expression playing over her face was one of amusement, as if it were his sensibilities that were at issue.

"You are an unaccountable man," she said, smiling again. "You are nothing like what I would have expected."

"What did you expect?"

She shrugged her shoulders.

"One would not have imagined the Soldier—or very many men—to experience much delicacy about the feelings of a whore." And she shrugged her shoulders again, dismissing, it seemed, any "delicacy" about the simple truth of her self-description. She wasn't asking for displays of chivalry; she was just stating a neutral fact. And he liked her enormously for that, so he frowned.

"Don't kid yourself—the Soldier's a real son of a bitch during business hours. I'm just off duty right now."

"And so am I," she said.

"Are you?"

"Yes."

It was a warm evening, and Janine wanted to walk back. Her apartment wasn't more than three-quarters of a mile from the restaurant and, with the streets clogged with tourists, Guinness didn't object. What the hell, he could risk it; if they were tailing him—and there wasn't a reason in the world to imagine they were—they wouldn't be likely to risk a massacre. That sort of thing was bad for trade.

So they would have a stroll. They would give dinner a chance to digest and they would hold hands and talk about whether his name was really Charles Reilly.

"Is it? I am sorry, but last night I saw your passport in your wallet. Is that your name?"

"No."

"Then what shall I call you? I cannot call you Soldier, can I? It would sound so odd to go on calling a man that."

"Then call me Charlie. I've always wanted to be a Charlie, and now I have my big chance."

She laughed at that and stopped for a moment, pressing her hands against the front of his jacket as she enjoyed the joke. And all the time her eyes searched the crowd behind them, even while her fingers pressed against his ribcage and her tongue moistened her lips. He leaned down and kissed her, just touching her lightly.

"Do you see any familiar faces?"

She smiled and laughed again and shook her head, almost imperceptibly. She was very good.

"No—but how could they know you were even here?"

She took his arm and they continued on, passing the outdoor café where Guinness had waited for Amalia Brouwer to come back from her lunch break. The street was narrow there and they were squeezed by the crowds, as if somehow they had happened into the midway of a carnival.

"They know. I've felt it ever since I arrived—you get a tightness in the back of your scalp, like you can feel the eyes. They may not have caught up with me yet, but they know I'm here. Flycatcher's too smart to let me just walk up and tap him on the shoulder."

"Yes? And is he so formidable?"

He glanced down at her, just to see if she wasn't making fun of him, and, sure enough, she was. You could see the amusement tugging at the corners of her mouth.

"If you're asking whether I'm afraid of him, the answer is yes. I'm not an idiot."

"I thought it was rather he who is afraid of you—at least, that is the gossip, that he dreads you more than death itself."

They stopped for a moment at the foot of one of the larger canal bridges where, for some reason, there was almost not another soul in sight. You could hear the waves lapping against the stone embankments and, from underneath the bridge itself, the clucking of the pigeons who apparently built their nests in behind the pillars. Guinness listened, not so much to them as to the pulse of things around him, trying to pick out some discordant rhythm in the sounds of a warm evening in a picturesque little city where people came to admire the tulip gardens and the paintings of Vermeer, but there was nothing. He and Janine might have been anybody as they stood looking down at the lifeless, opaque water, but they weren't. They carried their taint with them.

"I've rubbed up against him three times in the last couple of years—the last time I nearly killed him. I thought I had killed him. We can't go on like this forever. He knows that and so do I, so one of us will have to go and there aren't any guarantees involved. I'll get him if I can, this time or the next, or the time after that, and if I don't it'll probably be because he got me first."

He let his eyes roam back the way they had come and, when he was satisfied, put his arm over her shoulders. She seemed to melt into him; he could feel her cheek against the corner of his chest.

"It's like a bad dream, isn't it." She nodded slowly and he bent down and kissed her hair. "Then let's forget it for now—come on, I'll take you home."

Janine slept in the proverbial big brass bed, a spectacular, old-fashioned arrangement that creaked like a bullfrog under them while they made love. But Guinness couldn't hear it most of the time, not over the passionate, breathy, pleading nonsense that she whispered, almost gasped into his ear while she wrapped her legs with a kind of desperate force around his waist.

Of course, an intelligent whore is always the mistress of illusion.

Or perhaps it was that something else he had encountered more than once in women whom the practice of his profession had thrown in his way. Some of them simply wanted to be near something menacing. Like the groupies who hung around rock stars, they were fascinated by the aura; that was how they got their kicks, by feeling a murderer between their thighs. It always made Guinness angry, and perhaps a little brutal in his lovemaking, which was perhaps just exactly what they wanted. If they wanted to be used and tossed aside—well, that was their business. But he had never liked it. He had never cared for the trouble of living up to a fantasy.

Was that what it was with Janine? Certainly she had been interested enough in that side of things—*Everyone has heard of the Soldier.*

Certainly there had been no sweet reluctant amorous delay when they returned to her apartment—she simply turned to him and reached behind her back to pull her zipper down, letting him push the dress from her shoulders with his hands, like something to be brushed aside. It was an unaffected yielding, a submission automatic enough to make her seem to stand outside the thing, trusting or perhaps merely indifferent.

And when it was over, and she clung to him while they lay there together, as if she were afraid he might leave her more abruptly than she could bear, he could feel the wetness of her tears along the inside of his arm and wondered if she always cried, if that too was part of the performance—or if, somehow, he had wronged her. If, perhaps, she didn't like being treated like a technical problem to be solved and dismissed. Perhaps it was both. Or perhaps, somewhere along the line, her own expectations had collided and the business had gotten out of hand. It was one of those things you were never going to know; probably she didn't even know herself. Or perhaps she did. Perhaps she was smarter about such matters than he was—after all, how much would it take?

And so, because neither of them knew what to say, they said nothing. He brought his hand up to touch the side of her face and wished that somehow it might be possible not to have to live one's life this way, in little discontinuous fragments, as a succession of terminal moments. It would be nice if there could be a few tomorrows, but of course that was impossible.

"You cannot stay the night," she whispered finally—it wasn't a statement of the house rules, but a kind of apology. "I have to be a very good girl or my landlady will think the worst and evict me. I have always been the best of tenants, but she does not much care for having a whore under her roof. Do you see, yes? I am sorry. Soldier, I am sorry."

He laughed and kissed her, perhaps a little carelessly. None of it meant anything. "I thought we'd settled that I was going to be Charlie. What happened to that?"

"Nothing happened to that. You are the Soldier, and I am a whore named Janine."

"Are you angry?"

"No."

"Do I have to leave now?"

"No, not if you do not wish to. As a rule, they cannot leave fast enough."

"I thought we were off duty now. Do you want me to leave?"

"No. No—I do not want you to leave."

She rolled a little away from him, perhaps so as not to seem to commit herself to anything, and he reached across himself to touch her arm, resting his thumb in the cleft it made against her body, surprised at her smallness all over again.

"I don't like my line of work either, so can't we just forget it?"

"Can we?"

"We can try. At least, we don't have to give ourselves a hard time about it."

"All right."

"Fine."

The glass doors out to the veranda were open, allowing the gauze curtains to stir uneasily in the tentative, inconstant breeze. He wanted to get out of bed and check that there was no one standing behind them—except that that would have been ridiculous and, besides, Janine's bed was warm and the pressure of her body against his own was enough of a pleasure by itself to make him reluctant to move. So Guinness lay there, listening to her breathing and wondering if she had fallen asleep, and watched the ghostly presence as it quickened and died away, lit from behind by the pale glow from a distant and heedless night sky.

"Does it disturb you?" she whispered, twisting around to bring her face close to his.

"The wind—are you cold? In the summer I like to leave them open to the outside; it makes me feel less alone. But if you are cold I can close them."

"No. I'm not cold."

She smiled at him—it was almost too dark to see her face at all, but he was sure she was smiling—and her lips searched over his chin and jaw.

"You were just so alert. I could feel it pointing to the balcony—a tension. You do not relax, do you."

"I try not to. It's a bad habit. I'm sorry."

She kissed him hard, her arms snaking around his neck and along the curve of his back.

"You must not be sorry," she said. "We must neither of us be sorry."

"No."

The curtains smoothed down again, as if they had suddenly become vastly heavy, and at once there was a pressure of quietness in the room. Janine rose up, swinging her legs over the side of the bed, making the sheets whisper, and he watched her hunch in concentration as she felt for her slippers. The digital clock radio on her night table said one twenty-seven. It was almost time for him to go.

"Would you like a cup of tea?"

In the doorway, on her way into the kitchen, she was dimly framed for just a second in the gray light, a slim, almost boyish figure. You expected her to vanish, to dissolve in the dark air. And when she came back, the cups of smoking tea she carried in either hand seemed more solid than she.

They sat together in bed, and Guinness tried not to hurry. There was nothing waiting for him in Aimé's apartment, nothing he wanted—nothing that couldn't wait. He tried not to think any further than the next few moments, but, of course, the effort by itself was a reminder that little periods of refuge end and are not what make the difference. So he waited for his tea to cool and then drank it off. First one thing, and then the next.

"I want you to check on that phone number tomorrow." He put his hand on her bare thigh, just allowing it to rest there lightly, and smiled; it struck him almost as an act of betrayal. "And tag along with our little friend; find out what she does with those long lunch hours, would you? I'll make a few inquiries of my own, and we'll see what we find—okay?"

And she smiled and made agreeing sounds, and he knew he had to get out of there. So he rose out of bed, putting his empty cup down on the glass top of her dressing table, and started sorting out his clothes from the pile on the chair.

As a rule, they cannot get away fast enough. Well, perhaps he understood why, and perhaps it wasn't always from so unworthy a motive as Janine imagined.

"Doesn't your landlady watch the front door? Or should I scale down the outside of the building like a lizard?"

"No—you are allowed to use the front door." And she laughed, which was good. She laughed, he could permit himself to think, not because his joke was funny, but because he had made it.

"Do I ever get to come back?"

"I hope so."

And then he left, telling Janine to wait ten minutes before she turned out the lamp next to her bed—it was just a precaution. In the streets, no black sedans came whizzing by to spray him with machine-gun fire, and very quickly it became apparent that no one was following him. He listened all the way, doubling back on himself two or three times, but there was no one.

It didn't matter, this illusion of solitude. He might be on the other side of town, sound asleep—or in the next block, or pulled away for a few days on other business—but Flycatcher was there. And he would be just as awake to Guinness's presence. He would feel it; like a pair of magnets, they would twist around, trying to rush in or feint away, until they snapped together in a surge of ugly fear that, from the outside, would look like an embrace. Mexico had been a fluke, the accident that defined the inevitable. This time, one of them would have to die.

He had to stop and wait at one of the canals, where the bridge was raised, broken in two, to allow a sailboat to pass underneath. It was no more than a footbridge, hardly wide enough for a bicycle, and the lights at either end flashed red, on and off, on and off, making the pavement seem to bleed in pulses.

9

It had been the rainy season in Puerto Vallarta. In late November, between two-thirty and four in the afternoon, the rain came driving down straight as a plumb line, so that you could be sitting right at the edge of an open gallery, sipping on your margarita, and not run the slightest chance of getting wet. Guinness loved it. He had found himself a cantina down by the beach, far away from the big luxury hotels frequented by the rich Americans in their suntan oil and their gold jewelry, where the storm on the sheet-metal roof sounded like a marimba band. It was the perfect time and place to put your feet up and puzzle out the details; Flycatcher's boys all seemed to be terrific snobs and never ventured this far from the cocktail lounge at the Hilton—not without direct orders—and in weather like this you could hardly see across the street.

Ten days before, he had crossed the border at Laredo, Texas, with a modified twelve-gauge shotgun in the tire well of his dusty-brown, six-year-old Ford station wagon—Ernie had given his bond that it was precisely the car you saw all over Mexico, that nobody would even look at it except to steal the hubcaps. The roads had been lousy, and it had taken him three days to make the drive, sleeping off the road, curled up in a sleeping bag on the front seat with the doors locked and a .357 resting within easy reach, on the open lid of the glove compartment.

"He's down there," Ernie had assured him. "Apparently

he's had a house there for years, under the name of Baker—a cast-off mistress, one of the ones he didn't find it convenient to leave stuffed into a garbage can, told us all about it.

"She's what you might call a sorehead—no sense of humor. What the hell, they had some kind of a falling-out, it seems, and all Flycatcher did was whip up on her until her face looked like a checkered tablecloth and then drop her off in Mazatlan without the price of an enchilada. By relative standards, it was a fond farewell, but I guess she didn't see it that way—you know how women are.

"You'll have to check for yourself, but our people have the impression her information is on the level. She's pretty pissed at your pal. She says he's got a regular hilltop fortress down there—he lives like a rajah, but it's not going to be any holiday trying to get at him. Well, that's your specialty, not mine."

So on his first afternoon in town, after checking into one of the three rooms for rent over a feed store well away from the resort district, Guinness took a long walk, with a pair of field glasses slung over his shoulder, and tried to form some sort of impression of Flycatcher's defenses. It really was a hilltop fortress—the compound covered a good five or six acres, with a chain-link fence around the perimeter, and if the sentries were on their toes you wouldn't be able to get within half a mile without being spotted, the surrounding country was that even. It was going to be a problem.

And there wasn't a chance of luring the bastard outside, where you could get a clear shot at him. It wasn't as if he had a taste for sea bathing, or anything like that. No, according to his former paramour, he never left the grounds; if he wanted something, one of his goons came down from the mountain to see about it for him. This was going to be like trying to sneak into Windsor Castle to pinch the Queen's ass.

But it could be done. These things could always be done;

it was only a question of not turning pale when it came time to settle the check. No man is invulnerable—just providing his enemies hate him enough.

Ernie, always the understanding friend, had raised his despairing eyes to the soundproofing panels on his office ceiling, leaning back in his leather-upholstered desk chair and pressing his fingertips together as he prayed to his bureaucrat's Kali for guidance.

"Well, I suppose it's just as well," he said finally. "I suppose otherwise we'd have to send an army out after the guy—God knows, there haven't been very many volunteers—but I'm gonna miss you, Ray. You'll probably come back in a body bag; you know that, don't you? I mean, Texas was one thing, but down there he'll have all the home court advantages. And he does have an army. I don't give you one chance in fifty."

Guinness, of course, had figured the odds for himself already. His own estimates were nearly as bleak, but that didn't mean he enjoyed having them confirmed. So he had merely frowned, wishing Ernie would sign his equipment requisition forms so he could be on his way.

"I assume nobody's passed an Act of Oblivion around here—you still want him put away, I take it. Or have we all kissed and made up?"

No, we hadn't. For which reason Guinness was sitting in the meagre shade of a yucca tree, hoping the shadow would make him less visible as he scanned across the valley, perhaps three-quarters of a mile wide, trying to puzzle out some line of attack against that chain-link fence, which his field glasses had revealed to be topped with three strands of angled wire.

Well, yes. At night, if you were careful and took your time, you might make it that far. It was all a question of how frequently the patrols went around—a distance like that couldn't be covered in any less than, say, an hour and twenty minutes, and they would have a good three hundred fifty yards of perimeter to check. If they attended to business, they could manage that in, say, fifteen minutes. Five chances to spot somebody trying to crash the party. All right, he could risk that; as he got closer they'd be more likely to notice something, but he'd have a better shot at gauging their rhythm.

Of course, that all assumed a single patrol. If Flycatcher was sufficiently paranoid to mount several—and perhaps to have them going in opposite directions around the wire, so the time intervals became irregular—then Guinness might as well just drive up to the front gate and announce himself.

And he could see almost nothing. Inside the fence there were stands of low trees, screening off the inside of the compound. If there were men on duty, they were keeping out of sight, which was what you would expect them to do, and once he got inside—if he got inside—he would just have to play it by ear.

The sun was beginning to go down—if you looked west, toward the Pacific, you could see how, by some trick, the red sun had painted the waves a flashing silver. In an hour it would be dark, and Guinness was beginning to entertain certain abject thoughts about curling up somewhere with a pretty girl and a couple of bottles of the local white lightning and simply forgetting the whole business. He wanted to cry. To have come all this way and find himself stymied by a fucking fence was almost more than he could stand.

The necessities of the trade aside, Guinness was not a particularly vengeful type. He killed because that was his profession—malice played very little part in it. And at the same time, he had probably never wanted anything in his life as much as he wanted to kill this man who was known to him only by the codename of "Flycatcher," whom he had seen only twice, and each time only for a few seconds, to whom he had never in his life spoken a word.

"This isn't smart," Ernie had warned. "You know that, don't you? You start getting personal about these things and it blurs the judgment. Don't think I don't understand—if it'd been my kid, I'd be pretty mad too. But you tell me that Rocky and her mother came through it all right. He's not going to launch a manhunt, you know. Why should he care? So forget it, Ray. He doesn't even know that they were your kid and ex-wife. Just forget all about it, before you wind up dead."

"You never had a family, Ernie—don't tell me how you 'understand.' "

But it was getting cold—anybody could understand that. The ground was slick with mud from that afternoon's deluge; in places, where the undergrowth was thinner, you were up to your ankles. Guinness thought about the walk back to his rented room—blessedly downhill, but with the wind in his face—and again experienced a wave of despair. He raised his glasses, for one more sweep of the fence, knowing it was a perfect waste of time . . .

And then, with the glasses to his eyes, he started to laugh. It was a low cackling sound; he wasn't even aware he was making it. He was much too interested in the pair of black, pointed ears and the liver-colored throat that were so clearly visible behind the wire mesh. The son of a bitch had himself a kennel full of guard dogs.

Of course, he thought to himself as he picked his way down the steep cobbled streets, past the little houses that were rented by the month every summer by the *gringo* processed-foods executives and their wives; of course he had to admit that it was perfectly in character.

He worked it out for himself over dinner. After he had

changed out of his grimy, mud-caked jeans and had taken a hot shower and had put on the cream-colored sport jacket that rendered him invisible among the other Americans seeking native charm in the restaurant his landlord, the feed store owner, had recommended to him, after the indispensable first margarita, while he lingered over the sea-turtle soup—you could see the empty shells lying everywhere around the docks, great big mothers, some of them three and four feet across—while he squeezed out a chunk of lemon over his swordfish steak, he put the whole operation together in his mind. It wasn't going to be so very ghastly. Ridiculous as the idea sounded, he might actually even somehow manage to live through it.

The damn dogs, of course—that was Flycatcher's style all over. A man patroling with a rifle, all he can do to you is put a bullet in your head, but give the job to three or four Doberman pinschers and they can tear you to pieces. You'd end up looking like a butchered steer. They'd have to check your fingerprints just to make sure you were human. That last little touch of urbane brutality—it was what Flycatcher had never been able to resist. It constituted his besetting weakness.

Dessert consisted of chocolate ice cream, Mexican-style. It tasted like burnt-up old milk cartons, and Guinness spent the whole remainder of the evening wondering whether or not he was going to come down with dysentery. They had meant very well, but he thought that perhaps next time he'd just stick to the flaming tequila *babas.*

By about eleven-thirty the following night, he had managed to get within thirty yards of the perimeter without anyone shooting at him. He hadn't even seen a light. So he waited, crouched in a shallow depression behind a clump of mesquite, straining to detect some flicker of movement from behind the fence, but there was nothing. No symptom of human presence. There were the dogs, who would bark occasionally as, probably, they turned up a frog or the scent of some long-since-departed jack rabbit, but otherwise you could have imagined the place to be deserted.

So, there were no patrols, no armed men out to check if things were as quiet as they seemed. And that was to be expected too. You didn't turn your grounds over to a pack of snarling guard dogs and then hire yourself so-and-so-many additional thugs to walk around with carbines slung over their shoulders. The two simply didn't go together. The dogs, growing accustomed to the company of men, lose their effectiveness—they're not supposed to be house pets, after all—and if they don't, if they maintain that razor-sharp, undiscriminating savageness, it could get a little awkward for the men. So the dogs would have the place to themselves, which for Guinness's purposes was just fine.

In his youth in Ohio, in the apartment he had shared with his mother, there had been no room for a dog. His mother hadn't liked dogs—she hadn't liked her son, either; it had always been a little difficult for him to imagine what could have sparked any affection in that particular bosom—so Guinness had been thrown back on the occasional stray whom he would meet on the sidewalk somewhere and who, for a pat on the head or the corner of the sandwich he might be carrying along to school with him in his lunchbox, might condescend to follow him for a couple of blocks. As a result of these experiences, he had learned the importance, when dealing with animals, of soft words and bribery. A realist from his tenderest years, and never having been blinded by any one individual abiding love, he had learned that with animals, as distinct from men, practical considerations are what matter. The meanest cur, growling in a cold alleyway, can be bought off, can be converted into your friend for life, with a slice of canned Spam.

And Guinness, who didn't believe in doing these things by halves, had five pounds of raw steak along with him in a canvas knapsack. What the hell, the United States government was paying for it, and he didn't want Flycatcher's Praetorian Guard to think he wasn't a high roller.

"Nice puppy, good puppy, yes yes yes, that's a nice little doggy, yes it is . . ."

There were three of them, each one with a set of dental work that obviously hadn't been designed for service against moist Ken-L Ration. But you didn't kill your meal ticket, so by the fifth night, when Guinness had finally worked himself up to joining them on the other side of the chain-link fence, they stood around him, cringing and whimpering like poodle whelps, licking the beef juice from his fingers while he cooed sweet words into their pointed ears and tried to persuade himself that they really weren't going to have him for a hot midnight snack.

He hadn't even brought a butter knife. He hadn't wanted to tempt himself; the idea was just to have a look around—to make sure of the dogs and see how Flycatcher's domain was laid out. Tomorrow—or the next night—when he wouldn't have to stumble around blind, was plenty of time. For the moment, it was enough simply to have breached the walls.

In the beginning, he stuck to the protected borders, a dark fringe of palm trees and broad-leafed plants with loose, gaudy clusters of flowers. It was good cover, and at one point it came very near the house, which was a single-story affair, probably large enough to accomodate half-a-dozen people quite comfortably—well, it hardly figured that Flycatcher would stay up here by himself. He would need his bodyguards to make him feel important and secure.

The area behind the house consisted of three contiguous areas: a stone patio, a large rectangular swimming pool—the lights of which were off but that still glistened dimly in the lamplight from over the rear door—and the lawn, very well cared for, that stretched into the darkness for a couple of hundred yards in every direction. There were arc lights on two places on the roof, and atop poles at the very back of the lawn; they weren't turned on, but all anyone would have to do was touch a switch and that whole open area could be made bright as day. It was a little reminder—these people weren't fooling either.

The dogs followed him around for a while, sniffing tentatively at the cuffs of his trousers, but when they figured out that he wasn't carrying any more goodies they lost interest and wandered away to look for intruders, a category into which, it appeared, Guinness no longer fitted.

Everything was dark, except for the single light over the back door. Apparently Flycatcher didn't keep late hours—or perhaps he wasn't even in residence, a thought that had been gnawing at Guinness ever since his arrival in Puerto Vallarta. After all, Ernie's best information was already close to two weeks old. There weren't any guarantees that Flycatcher had intended a long stay, and men in his line of work were prone to sudden emergencies that called them away from their hours of leisure.

The house, of course, was where he was going to find out. He edged along through the border until he came to a spot where the dark corner of what was probably a bedroom jutted out to within twenty-five feet of him. He crossed over, disentangling himself as quietly as possible from the undergrowth, half-expecting the floodlights to go on the second his foot touched the lawn. They didn't, but somehow he doubted he would have felt much more exposed if they had.

Apparently Flycatcher supposed that his chain-link fence and his man-eating dogs were enough, because the house was a very ordinary structure, not at all designed to withstand siege. The walls were stucco and the windows were enormous—it might have been lifted bodily out of some poshy housing development in the States and transported here by magic. If Flycatcher hadn't bought it from some other owner, and perhaps even if he had, it revealed an unexpectedly middle-class side of his character; perhaps all he really wanted in the world was the life of a retired stockbroker in Scarsdale, complete with Olympic-size swimming pool.

And then, just when he was beginning to be comfortably contemptuous, Guinness noticed the alarm system. There was a little knob sticking unobtrusively out from one corner of the back wall; he nearly put his hand over it before he saw the shielding around the photoelectric cell. Doubtless the windows were also wired—probably double-wired, so you couldn't jimmy them open and you couldn't break them without setting off the end of the world. Leave it to Flycatcher.

All the curtains were drawn tight, so there wasn't a chance of getting a look inside. In all likelihood, there were a dozen men sitting around in the front room playing gin rummy, with Thompsons at the ready. Obviously, these people simply weren't prepared to cooperate at all.

In front, parked out in the open, were three cars, one of them a large black Mercedes that Guinness was willing to stake almost anything on was Flycatcher's personal chariot—the side and rear windows were smoked glass, and probably half an inch thick, and it wouldn't have surprised him to hear that the doors were reenforced with armor plating. The thing had that low-to-the-ground look of a car upon which certain "security modifications" have been made; it probably weighed seven or eight hundred pounds more now than on the day it had come out of the factory.

There was no garage, so perhaps Flycatcher hadn't gotten around to having one put up. It had been careless of him; it meant he had to cross about forty feet of open ground to get from the house to his car.

It was time to leave. Guinness knew he wasn't going to find out anything more, and every minute he spent hanging around there increased the chances of somebody casually glancing out a window and seeing a bush move.

And, besides, the dogs were back—they were still friendly, reasonably friendly, but he imagined there were limits to how long his welcome would last now that he was out of grade-A choice sirloin. It wasn't something he wanted to put to the test.

They followed him back to the fence, their huge red tongues rolling out over the teeth they seemed to be displaying for his particular benefit. They watched him climb up the fence, tensing expectantly, as if they were waiting for him to fall back to the ground—as if they were hoping that would happen so they could repair any recent derelictions of duty by tearing his throat out, with no hard feelings, of course. Probably, Guinness reflected, he was merely yielding to unjust suspicion, but he didn't like the way they kept making tentative little jumps at him, as if they were nerving themselves up for something more than just a goodbye kiss. He made a point of coming down well clear of the fence on the other side. It wasn't a world in which friendship counted for much.

So, back in his cantina, listening to the rain on the tin roof, Guinness tried to ponder the thing out. And it all came down to that forty feet between Flycatcher's car and his front door. You either got him right there, or you didn't get him.

The waiter, an amiable, brown-faced man of about fifty, brought over a small plate of smoked tuna, the local *hors d'oeuvre,* and withdrew himself, showing his large square teeth in a smile as he backed away. He had been particularly attentive on each of the three previous occasions Guinness had come there to wait out the afternoon rain—perhaps he entertained hopes that his place was beginning to catch on with the Americans, although there didn't seem to be any others around. Perhaps he was just a nice, friendly Mexican who took pity on middle-aged men who sat by themselves drinking margaritas on his veranda. It could even have been that he liked Guinness because Guinness was a big tipper. In any case, the smoked tuna was good enough to eat by the handful, and it constituted the only invasion of one's privacy. For the rest, you were left alone to watch the water stream down from the awning and to consider your sins.

By four-fifteen—rather later than usual—the rain had ceased, and Guinness got out of his chair and dropped three or four hundred-peso notes down next to his empty cocktail glass. Regardless of how things turned out that night, he doubted he would ever be back, and if things turned out so that he would never be back anywhere, he would just as soon leave the waiter rich as have Flycatcher's goons find all that money when they went through his pockets.

Distinct as that possibility was, Guinness felt pretty good as he went back to his room to get ready for dinner. After all, even if they sent him to perdition, there was at least an even chance he could manage to take Flycatcher along for the ride. Under any circumstances, it was nice to have a plan.

At three-fifteen the next morning, he discovered that the dogs were no longer quite sure how they felt about him. They seemed to be having trouble making up their minds—they didn't bark, which Guinness took as a positive sign, but they pressed their noses against the fence, growling if he approached any closer than they absolutely fancied.

The sight of them like that, their bodies rigid as springs and their noses wrinkled slightly to reveal their glistening front teeth, made him glad all over again that he had taken certain precautions. In a very short time there was going to be a great deal of noise and excitement—and probably considerable quantities of blood on the ground—and it would be just as well if the Praetorian Guard weren't in a position to feel the discomforts of conflicting loyalties. Probably another sackful of meat would cement their friendship. Maybe.

Part of regular United States government issue to all agents in Guinness's category was a small flat leather case containing a hypodermic syringe and four little numbered vials of clear fluid. Number Four was guaranteed to ensure that you never opened your eyes again, but Number Two, from which Guinness had extracted the full dose, only put you down for about five hours. Number Two was injected into the meat that Guinness began throwing over the fence in thick strips, spreading the bounty so that each dog got his fair share. He figured on about ten ounces apiece—he didn't want them getting sated. He wanted them to eat every bite.

When they had finished everything, including their quarrels over a few disputed chunks, all three dogs came back to the fence in expectation of more. They whined and wagged their stubby tails and jumped up on the chain-link with their front paws in a perfect ecstasy of welcoming affection. And while they waited for more goodies, Guinness waited for Number Two to begin taking hold, not even sure that it would—after all, it was supposed to be given intravenously; he had never tried it this way.

And, indeed, it was close to four minutes before the first dog folded up. He simply lay down, stretched out his muzzle on the ground, and closed his eyes with a weary sigh. The others followed within a few seconds.

Fine. Guinness unrolled his heavy Mexican blanket, leaving it double, and tossed it up over the angled top of the fence so that it fell just exactly over one of the poles—he didn't know why people bothered with those three strands of barbed wire; they were so easy to get past, it hardly seemed worth the trouble of putting them up. When he had climbed to the top of the fence and was perched uneasily on his blanket, he hauled the rest of his equipment up after him—his canvas pack, secured by a length of rope around both shoulder straps, with his shotgun tied to the rope's other end. First he brought up the pack, and then the shotgun, and then he lowered them both down on the other side and jumped down himself.

He pressed his fingers into one of the dogs' throats, feeling for the carotid artery. Its pulse was still strong and steady, although the poor beast was so out of it that you could pry open its jaws and its tongue merely lolled out at the corner of its mouth, like a dead snake. It would probably be morning before any of these particular beasties woke up—and then they would feel like hell for the rest of the day—but they would, in fact, wake up. No matter who else died there that night, at least the dogs wouldn't. Guinness was glad it hadn't proved necessary to kill them. They were savage enough creatures—as was he, as were the men he hunted—but they were also innocent. Only men, it seemed, were capable of evil.

He had no way of knowing how many men were inside with Flycatcher—or even if Flycatcher was there at all, although the presence of so many cars in front of the house suggested that he probably would be—and he had no idea how they would be armed. Probably pretty well; Flycatcher was hardly anybody's idea of a pacifist. Guinness knew that his only chance of success and survival was surprise, and so he had come equipped with the instruments of confusion.

His .357—a single-action revolver that, for this sort of

guerilla warfare, he regarded as more dependable than any automatic—was wrapped in a towel in his knapsack; he took it out and stuck it in his belt, just over his left kidney, where he could get at it easily but where it wouldn't get in the way. His shotgun was an automatic feed with the magazine block removed, so that it would hold about eight shells. He loaded it and distributed another half-dozen shells through the pockets of his windbreaker.

But all you could do with guns was kill people, what he was counting on were the gallon and a half of gasoline and the five empty tequila bottles with the rag stoppers, the makings of his Molotov cocktails. Surprise and terror, and there was something about fire that scared the hell out of everybody. Especially at four o'clock in the morning.

The black Mercedes was parked just where it had been the night before, and Guinness found a place where he could lie down behind the cover of some bushes—when the fireworks started, those rubber-plant leaves wouldn't offer him much protection, but at least the bad guys wouldn't spot him the second they stepped out the door. The ground was reasonably flat there; he could lie prone, making as small a target as possible. It was about seventy feet from the car, a bad distance for the shotgun, even with the choke tightened to full. He wished to hell he had a good old-fashioned 30-06 hunting rifle, but it was too late now; there had been no way of knowing how the setup would look inside Flycatcher's compound, and a shotgun was better if you had to go up against several men at once. Anyway, seventy feet was a bad distance for pistols too—he supposed he was permitted to hope there wouldn't be much in the way of automatic weapons to contend with.

Forty feet from the front door to the car. How fast could a man cover that distance, running for his life? So there wasn't going to be much time, either. Wonderful—better and better.

For a brief while, sitting over his smoked tuna, he had considered taking some electrical wire and twisting it around the two door handles to anchor them together. That would have slowed down anybody trying to climb inside to safety and would have ensured him of all the time he needed—it would have been like having them at the end of a target range. But he had finally discarded the idea. It was one more chance to get caught; the risks were simply unreasonable. And even in the hoped-for confusion they might spot it.

Guinness laid his shotgun down on the ground, careful to find a spot where he wouldn't have to worry about dirt jamming the mechanism, and circled around again to the back of the house.

Now, of course, the idea was to get everybody out, and to prevent them from using the back door. As he sat squatting in the undergrowth, filling up his tequila bottles with gasoline, he thought about how he was going to manage to do that without spending so much time back there that he would miss the main show up front. And manage not to get himself killed in the bargain—he would have to be standing right out there in the open, all the time he was trying to con Flycatcher into believing there was a regular posse assembled in the bushes beyond his swimming pool.

And how the hell long was the burn time on a gasoline bomb anyway? He didn't much relish the prospect of having one of them blow up in his hand and turn him into a six-foot candle.

Five was too many, too chancy. He would settle for three. One at the back door, where the flames would lick up over the tip of the shingle roof and set it going, turning the whole area, hopefully, into an inferno; one through the window of what looked like the front room; and the last right through Flycatcher's bedroom window—at least, he hoped it was Flycatcher's bedroom. Three bottles, and a fourth one with just the gas-soaked rag stopper that he could use to light the others—that might save a few seconds' fumbling with the damn cigarette lighter, and seconds were what mattered. It was all he had—the moment, or two, of paralyzed distraction, the brief few instants while they tried to sort out what was being done to them.

He carried the bottles with him, setting them down at intervals as he made his careful way across the stone patio, keeping almost to the edge of the swimming pool, along a line that ran parallel to the back of the house and about thirty-five feet away. When he stood opposite the back door, with the last of the gasoline bombs on the ground between his feet, he took out his small, bright red, plastic butane cigarette lighter and applied its half-inch of flame to the rag stopper of the fourth bottle. His heart was pounding as he watched it kindle, and he kept wondering why the floodlights hadn't gone on yet, why he wasn't already lying on the stones with six or seven bullet holes in him—surely they could hear the racket his heart was making. Surely they could hear his breathing. These two seemed to him the loudest sounds in the world.

He put the lighter back in his pocket, picked up the gasoline bomb in his left hand—his throwing arm—and lit it against the orangish-yellow flash of the burning rag. Glancing back the way he had come, he could see the two other bottles, just catching a trace of reflected light from somewhere, just barely visible. Then he caught his breath, concentrating all his attention on the back door, as if it were the only object in the universe, and threw.

The bottle sailed dimly through the dark air, just a sputtering little point of flame, and then, in an explosion that shattered the quiet night, turning it in an instant into such a murky dawn as the world might know on its final day, that whole part of the building was suddenly a sheet of fire.

Guinness stood watching, transfixed for some fraction of a second, and then started running toward the next bottle. Sweeping it up, he lit it, fixed himself to the ground, and threw again. This time he didn't wait—he could hear the crash of the window shattering and, out of the corner of his eye, the ball of white fire. He could even hear the alarm ringing. By then he had the last bottle. He lit it, threw, and ran for the cover of the undergrowth. He didn't have to see now—he knew it had gone home.

As an afterthought, an idea out of nowhere, he took the revolver from his belt and fired a couple of rounds through the broken bedroom window, through the smoke that was pouring out of it now, not even hoping to hit anyone. He just wanted to make more noise. He just wanted to rattle the sons of bitches.

"FLYCATCHER!!" It was his own voice, but he could barely believe the sound of it. "COME OUT AND DIE, YOU BASTARD . . . FLYCAT-CHERRR!"

He didn't wait around. The house was an inferno—it must have been bedlam in there. They wouldn't have much time to think, and they couldn't stay inside more than another quarter of a minute or so, not if they wanted to leave alive, so Guinness ran around through the protected border toward the front. They would have to come out through the front. The whole rear of the house was going up like a funeral pyre, and they would have to assume the attack was coming from that direction. No, it would have to be the front for them. They would have to see that as their best chance. They would have to.

And so he waited, flat on the ground with the shotgun brought up against his shoulder; he waited through what seemed like the rest of the decade. He lay there, trying to will the door to open.

Come on, you sons of bitches, come to papa.

And then it did open, swinging wide as if of its own weight. They weren't going to just come rushing out; they weren't that dumb. They would expect an ambush.

And then one man, moving with his head down, as low to the ground as he could manage, started to make a dash for the black Mercedes—they would go for the Mercedes; it was the closest, and those armored doors would beckon to them like their mothers' arms. Guinness took aim, and then let him go. The man scrambled for the front door on the passenger's side, pulling it open and diving out of sight behind it in what seemed like a single movement. That was all right. Guinness could wait. He wanted Flycatcher, not just some faceless foot soldier. There was no point in giving his position away. He could wait.

Come on, baby—what's keeping you?

They did it the right way. Guinness was almost caught off-guard when the rest of them—one, two, three, four of them, with Flycatcher right in the middle, protected by the bodies of his minions—the whole mob made their run for the open car door. Guinness let them get about fifteen feet, as close as he dared, before he opened fire.

It was too far—it was just too far. It didn't allow you to make sure of them, not at that range. You couldn't be absolutely sure of your kill.

The first shot caught the lead man in the abdomen. He didn't even have time to scream; he just dropped to the ground as if some giant hand had swatted him down like an insect—whether he was dead or not there was no saying. The others almost fell over him, but Flycatcher never even broke stride.

There he was, looking tall even while he ran hunched over. All Guinness could see was the white hair, nothing of the face. He just kept on running, closing on the car door, running because he knew he was the only target. The poor sucker was still in his pajamas.

The head? Should he go for the head? No, too much chance of missing at that distance. Guinness fired once more, at the middle of what he could see, taking in everything from the knees to the middle of the chest, and there was a little explosion just at Flycatcher's hip as the cloth of his drawers went flying away and a long red smear instantly appeared halfway down his thigh.

And then once more, but it was too fast and the shot was wild. It seemed to catch him somewhere in the chest, and there was more blood, and Flycatcher stumbled and looked up. And the expression on his face said that he believed he was already a dead man.

But somehow, in the instant before Guinness could bring the shotgun back down to aim again, Flycatcher had made it to the car. Maybe he did it on his own, maybe one of his men helped him—Guinness would never know. In either case, the door slammed shut, and the car started backing away, like a frantic animal. And then it whipped around, faster than you would have thought such a big car could turn, and then it was gone.

"No. NO!"

There was one man they had left behind, and he raised his hands in supplication, looking around in front of him to find where the shots had come from, searching for someone with whom to plead for his life.

Sorry, pal. Not a chance. Guinness stood up and stepped from behind the cover of his rubber-plant leaves. The man watched him, his face blank, and then his eyes widened with horror as Guinness raised the shotgun. Probably he never heard the explosion.

No one else came out of the house. If there had been any

more inside, they were dead. Guinness looked at the two still corpses on the ground, and then at the bloody tiretrack that made a dark smear glistening in the light from the burning house. It was Flycatcher's blood, and there was a lot of it, so maybe he had been dead even then, even as somehow he managed to get inside the car. If not, then he would die quickly enough. Maybe he would die. Maybe the earth would be free of that encumbrance.

Guinness wiped off the shotgun and left it behind, wedged under the arm of one of the two dead men who lay twisted there before him, their faces to the asphalt. In a few minutes, no more than that, the house would be a smouldering ruin, and by then he would be gone, swallowed up again by the darkness like a damned soul.

10

But, of course, Flycatcher hadn't died, although for a while it had looked that way. For several months there had been no word of him. No one had spotted him—he seemed to have fallen off the face of the earth—and the Company had just about made up its collective mind to transfer his dossier to the inactive file. But Guinness wouldn't hear of it.

"He's just gone to ground," he would say. "He's nursing his wounds somewhere, but he's alive. I know when I've killed a man, and I haven't killed that one—he'll be back."

And, if asked, he could give you good enough reasons to suppose he was right. After all, Flycatcher had always employed a lot of very heavy talent—had there been any sudden glut on the thug market? You didn't see a lot of guys standing around on street corners, idly cleaning their AK-47s while they waited for offers of employment. People like that tend to make themselves highly visible when they want something, and the rumor mill was quiet. The organization was holding together, Guinness would tell them. The troops were just waiting for their captain to mend.

That was what he would say, and there was every reason to suppose he believed it. But it wasn't the real reason he kept going down to the film room to comb through the archives for every ten-second cutting of every goon said to have taken Flycatcher's shilling. It was a feeling, almost a superstition, that he would have known if this particular

Nemesis had really bled to death on the front seat of his armor-plated Mercedes. They were like Siamese twins, Flycatcher and he, and he would have felt some change within himself if the world had been relieved of that burden.

And he felt nothing. There was no release. So Flycatcher was alive.

And then, of course, it was confirmed.

"He's back," Tuttle had said over lunch in a seafood restaurant in Baltimore, whither he had driven, on his own time, apparently for no other reason than to break the bad news to his friend Guinness. "He was spotted the day before yesterday in Montreal—we almost managed to collar him, but he got away. I'm sorry, Ray, but I don't think it comes as much of a surprise."

"No. It's no surprise."

And then, when they had finished their softshell crabs and were walking out to the parking lot, just as Ernie Tuttle was about to open the door of his car and drive off to resume his life in the vast bureaucracy of the United States intelligence establishment, Guinness took him by the arm, holding him just firmly enough to command his friend's undivided attention.

"I want him, Ernie—you understand me? When you've got even half a lead, he's got to be all mine. I won't take no for an answer."

So the hunt had continued. A dozen times, in Madrid and Belfast and Tunis and the mountain resorts of the Swiss Alps, over and over and for months, Guinness would find himself a week, or a day, or sometimes just a few hours behind his quarry. The trail was always just cold enough, as if Flycatcher knew he was there and was trying to tease him.

And he was—at least, he knew Guinness was there. It was becoming Flycatcher's cross, apparently, the knowledge that there was always someone behind him.

"He knows it was you in Mexico, Ray. He's spooky as hell."

Ernie was in Europe—just to tell him that? He said no, that there was something going in Vienna and he had just stopped off for a moment between planes, but the truth was a vague thing in their world, even between friends.

"Last month in Marseille you almost had him—at least, so we hear. He pulled out and left his people holding the bag, left the whole operation, whatever it was, to go to pieces. He does that a few more times, and he'll be out of business; the gentlemen who pay the freight won't trust him anymore, and that'll be that. It seems you make him nervous."

Big deal.

Guinness sat in a tiny coffee shop in Amsterdam, making breakfast out of a cup of tea and a buttered roll that tasted for all the world like an onion bagel. Ernie Tuttle was across the water in his wood-paneled Washington office, typing up memos and planning the ultimate coup that would land him in the Directorship, and Janine, presumably, was out seeing about the telephone numbers that young girls kept hidden under their night-table drawers.

And Flycatcher—where was he? Had he done a flit again, or had he finally decided that the inevitable had arrived and it was time to stand his ground? It would be interesting to know.

But it was seven o'clock in the morning, an hour at which the tangled threads of fear and revenge all seem a trifle insubstantial, like the trailings of a cobweb. Guinness had managed about five hours of dreamless sleep, which, under the circumstances, could be counted as an unlooked-for blessing. He had a not-unpleasant ache in his groin, another blessing, and Janine would be meeting him sometime before noon to tell him all about her discoveries. Maybe somewhere before this thing was settled they would find the chance for a few more fast falls; it wouldn't be as good as the first time—when was it ever that?—but what the hell. After the first flush of youth, pleasure becomes a serious matter, not to be disdained. And he liked Janine.

The coffee shop was in the basement of one of the downtown office buildings and was uncomfortably cold. Guinness had a seat at the counter, from which he could watch the door, and he perched discontentedly in his chair, stirring his tea in a vain effort to disperse the milky film that kept forming on the surface.

He had done everything it was possible to do up to that moment. He had dispatched Janine on her errands and he had phoned Ernie to have a background check done on one Jean Rênal. In another two hours he would take up his seat at the outdoor café to watch Amalia Brouwer show up for work, but until then all he could do was keep out of trouble and wait. Ernie, who had sounded as if the telephone had called him out of a deep and restful sleep, had said he would have everything in hand by lunchtime—lunchtime on the Potomac, presumably, which meant there wouldn't be much point in calling back before around six that evening. So there was nothing to look forward to just immediately. Guinness would spend the time walking, trying to convince himself all over again that no one, absolutely no one, was on his tail. It was becoming a ritual.

When finally he could get the waitress to notice him, he paid his check and went back upstairs into the sunshine, which was dazzling after the neon twilight of breakfast. The only places open were other restaurants; the shops wouldn't start business until nine. He found a bakery, however—one assumed that the housewives of Holland had to have their morning sweet rolls—so he went inside and bought a half-dozen sticky, cinnamon-covered pastries that would have been called bearclaws in the States. Twenty minutes after breakfast and he was hungry all over again. One assumed it was just nerves.

He struck out in the direction of the Rembrandt House, which had the advantage of being away from anywhere anyone could conceivably imagine he would want to go—what the hell, he wouldn't have time to have much of a look at the place, but if there were somebody behind him he didn't want to appear to be wandering aimlessly—tearing off pieces of pastry and stuffing them mechanically into his mouth as he walked.

At the appointed hour he was sitting with his prop glass of beer at one of the outdoor tables across the street from the bookshop. The little old lady was already there—they weren't open for business yet, but she had let herself in with a key and was running a busy featherduster over the magazine racks. Amalia was not yet in evidence, but it was still early.

Of course, that morning's significant fact was the gentleman who was in evidence, seated over a cup of coffee and a sweet roll two or three tables away from Guinness. He was pretending to read a newspaper, much as Guinness himself had only the afternoon before; he had it folded down to a strip about nine inches wide and was holding it up in front of his face like a screen, but his fingers were dug so deeply into the newsprint that the knuckles had turned white. He had been frozen in that posture for about the last ten minutes—ever since the waiter had brought him his order and, while he counted out the tip, he had seen Guinness in the act of returning from the little boy's room. There had been just a flicker of recognition in his eyes, but it had been enough. Guinness remembered him too.

Stuck in the waistband of his trousers was the tiny nickle-plated automatic that Janine had given him the night of his arrival. It wasn't much of a weapon, but at close range it would probably serve its turn. Fortunately it was small enough to palm, and he slipped it into his jacket pocket under cover of shifting uncomfortably in his chair.

"Keep holding onto your newspaper," he said, his voice low and even, almost friendly, as he sat down at the other man's table. He was holding his beer glass in his right hand, and the other was in his jacket pocket. "A wrong move buys you a hole in the face, so be nice. We wouldn't want to disturb anybody."

He smiled and took a sip of his beer, which for some reason seemed unnaturally bitter, and his companion peered cautiously over the top of his paper at him, obviously less than easy in his mind.

"Try to look a little happier, would you? That's it—give us a big grin to please the paying customers. Now let's take a walk."

Guinness made an almost imperceptible gesture with the point of his chin, and they both started to rise out of their seats. Very carefully, the other man folded his newspaper once more and set it down on the table next to his half-finished cup of coffee, and Guinness nodded approvingly. As they walked out between the other tables to the street, Guinness was behind, and he was glad to see he wasn't dealing with the reckless type—the object of the morning's exercise let his hands fall limply to his sides, as if they were simply so much nerveless weight.

Of course, he would be a pro. He was one of Flycatcher's people, and they grew up fast. Guinness recalled this one, sprinting toward the black Mercedes with his head pulled down.

They went on for about half a block together, until they came to the sheltered stairway to a group of second-floor apartments—you could see the shiny brass mailboxes inside on the narrow porch. It would offer a few seconds of privacy; they wouldn't need more than that. Guinness gave him an amicable little shove—between professionals, the hint was enough; there wasn't any call to get hostile about these things—and when they were off the street he leaned the man against the brick wall and patted him down, finding nothing more sinister than a small snubnose .32 caliber revolver in a holster clipped to his belt on the right side. Under the circumstances, almost nothing.

There was also a wallet, with a Canadian passport in the pocket behind the folding money, made out in the name of James K. Lind. In this business, one supposed, one name was as good as another. The color photograph was of a withered, dark-haired, worried-looking man in his middle forties, a man who had come to the conclusion that he was past this sort of thing, who, on the whole, would have preferred packing it in to start life over as a shoe salesman but who knew that from now on there was only a one-way corridor. The eyes told you all that, and the way he had turned his face just slightly away, as if the camera were something else it might not do to meet too directly.

Guinness put the passport back and returned the wallet to its place in the inside jacket pocket. When they found him, it would save everyone just infinite amounts of trouble if he still had his papers on him. So long as there was no suggestion of robbery, the police were generally willing enough not to push their investigations too hard. The odd death by misadventure wouldn't be allowed to muddy up their tranquil little routines, especially when they discovered, as doubtless they would, that the passport was a forgery.

"Come on, Mr. Lind," he said, pulling him around by the shoulder. "Let's you and I take a little walk."

And they went on together down the street, Guinness just a half-step behind, not even bothering about either of the guns he carried—they both knew he could have either of them out and ready before "Mr. Lind" had managed five yards, so why make a production?

"It was you in Mexico, wasn't it." The words came floating back over the other man's shoulder, and Guinness nodded, perfectly aware that the gesture would have been unseen.

"Sure. You were the first one to go for the car—your boss doesn't pay you enough."

"Can we make a deal? It was one thing down there; he was the one standing behind me with a gun then. Just name your terms—I don't owe him a fucking thing."

It was hopeless, of course. You couldn't believe a man under threat of death, and this one had seen him sitting across the street from the bookstore. No doubt he had made the connection; it was the sort of news that would buy his way back into Flycatcher's good graces, no matter what he might have had to do or say to keep alive. And then Amalia Brouwer's life wouldn't be worth an hour's purchase—Flycatcher was a very cautious man.

And, of course, Mr. Lind knew all that. He knew Guinness couldn't afford to let him go—he was just deluding himself, giving himself a little license to hope. Why take it away from him?

"We'll see."

Even in Amsterdam there are alleyways, narrow spaces upon which the surrounding buildings have turned their backs. Most of the time they end in a cement stairway down to some basement door.

"After you."

Mr. Lind started down, holding on to the iron railings as if he were afraid his legs might give out beneath him. When he stood on the last step, he reached out and took hold of the door handle, pulling it toward him.

"It's locked," he said, turning around to look back at Guinness, who was already clutching the revolver, the butt turned around, and raising his arm—he didn't care what all the karate champions said; if he was going to hit a man, he wanted to hit him with something a little harder than the side of his horny hand.

"It's locked."

Guinness gave it everything he had, and the blow caught Mr. Lind just on the temple and he fell down as if he had been swept off his feet. Lying on the stairs, he tried to turn himself a little, as if he wanted to see up to where Guinness was standing; the expression on his face was almost reproachful and his mouth opened, perhaps to say something. And then, very suddenly, he went limp. That was the way it happened—Guinness had been hit on the head often enough himself to know that you didn't go out all at once.

He reached down and felt the carotid artery. The poor clown was still alive, so apparently this one wasn't going to be easy on either of them. Sometimes, if you hit hard enough, you could kill them with a single blow, but apparently this wasn't one of those times.

He took the head between his hands, pressing his palms into the temples, and brought it down with a sharp crack against the edge of one of the cement steps, and this time it did the job. Mr. Lind stiffened slightly—that was just the nervous system protesting its extinction—and then he was very decidedly dead. His eyes were already beginning to dilate when Guinness clipped the revolver and its holster back into his belt.

And then he left, careful not to hurry, leaving the late Mr. Lind in undisputed possession.

Janine found him standing around with the tour bus crowds across the square from the Royal Palace. They had settled on that as their fallback, and he couldn't have gone again to the café—he didn't want to be remembered as the gentleman who had left with another gentleman and who had then come back alone to finish his beer. So he had spent the last hour milling around, leafing through a pamphlet that described the various excursions and trying to avoid getting captured by any of the guides.

Janine stood by herself, near the tour company office, and waited for him to notice her.

"The telephone number is assigned to a warehouse near the harbor. I took a taxi down to see and there is a sign up advertising the building for lease . . . Soldier, are you not well?"

"Let's get out of here—I haven't had my lunch yet."

Guinness took her arm just above the wrist, and they walked quickly away. The casual observer, had he felt compelled to account to himself for the abruptness of their withdrawal, might have guessed they were on the lookout for some private place in which to have a subdued little lovers' spat. Or he might not have thought anything about it at all, since Guinness had hardly dragged her off by the hair.

And yet there had been something. It had been enough to persuade Janine to keep her own questions to herself, even after the two of them were well away and were sitting together in the dark interior of a restaurant across the street from what one assumed was the main post office. The waiter had brought a smoking plate of veal chops and mashed potatoes and set it before Guinness, who hardly seemed to know it was there. He remained crouched in his chair, apparently lost in some private vision, his face a dark and impenetrable mask, as if it had been cast in bronze.

And then, quite suddenly, he leaned forward and picked up his fork. You could have thought he hadn't taken a mouthful of food in days.

"Tell me again," he said. Just as suddenly as he had started, he seemed to lose interest and pushed the plate away from him. "About the warehouse—tell me again. Did you go inside?"

Janine, who hadn't touched the cup of coffee that had been placed in front of her, shook her head.

"No? Good. That was the right move." And he smiled. "What did you do?"

What had she done? Just coasted by, telling the driver that there must have been some mistake about the address. He had dropped her about half a mile farther on, and then she had doubled-back on foot to see what could be seen from the sidewalk.

"There was nothing." She hugged her arms across her chest and shrugged, as if surprised that she hadn't found the place crawling with guys in numbered sweatshirts with 'Flycatcher's Goonsquad' written in big letters across the shoulderblades. "The windows were dark—there was no one near. So I came back to look for you."

"I'll have a look for myself," he said. "You go back to your apartment and sit on your hands." He smiled—it was a joke. He would call her, and she was to wait where he could reach her. She would wait.

What he wanted, really, was simply to be by himself until he shook off the peculiar feeling that was, he knew from experience, nothing more than a visceral reaction to the events of the morning. No one, not even Raymond Guinness, the celebrated killer of men, could do it with perfect impunity. There was always, at the very least—unless one had become so hardened as to have no feeling at all—there was always the self-imposed retribution of a few hours' jangled nerves. Guilt, he supposed, refined to the purely physical.

For Guinness it took the form of a kind of claustrophobia, a sensation of being buried inside his own body. He couldn't get out, he couldn't breathe, he would never be able to talk to anyone again. He was covered over with something that was merely himself, his own vileness, and he would never, never get free of it. The effect was in a range between panic and shame, and there wasn't anything he could do about it except to wait until it went away.

Walking helped. If you simply sat around in your hotel room, it might last all day—at night it could be a perfect horror—but five or six miles of crowded sidewalk would usually turn the trick.

The locked closet of the mind. A professional hazard, like hemorrhoids for truck drivers. And a safeguard. A reminder that, after all, human life meant something and should not be destroyed wantonly. The worst thing in the world would be to be able to kill and suffer nothing. Perhaps even to enjoy it. Better to lose life than one's simple humanity.

Sometimes Guinness wondered whether he wasn't conning himself, trying to invent some fragile little shelter for his conception of himself as a moral being. After all, perhaps it was too fine a line he was drawing between his own slender claims to something like integrity and . . . What? Who?

I do evil and know it to be evil and this fact makes me better than someone like Flycatcher—was that the line? The unrelinquished possession of his tattered conscience? A damned soul but mine own? Maybe it was all just self-deception. Maybe there weren't any lines to be drawn.

Janine's warehouse faced one of the piers of what his map referred to as the Oosterdok. There was a stone embankment at the edge of the roadway, a drop of perhaps as much as thirty feet, and then the harbor complex. Guinness found himself almost parallel with the roof—the billboard that advertised that these premises were available for lease was just at the apex of the front wall, almost exactly at eye level. Here and there, along the other end of the wharf, men in heavy dark work clothes moved around, but there was no one near the warehouse, which seemed perfectly lifeless.

He didn't expect he would burst in to surprise Flycatcher and all his fellow evil-doers—he would hardly want to; all he had with him was that silly little nickle-plated automatic of Janine's—but he supposed it might be worth something to have a look inside. You never knew. You might learn something, although the odds weren't very good that Flycatcher would leave much in the way of useful information lying around in a deserted warehouse.

There was a stairway leading down to the stone quay. Guinness decided it would attract less attention if he simply walked down in broad daylight and tried the door—there wasn't any point in making a big sneaky production of it, after all.

The door was fastened with a heavy padlock of the kind you could open with a nail file in about fifteen seconds; with the government-issue lockpick he was carrying, it took even less time. He closed the door behind him and stepped inside onto a board floor that sounded like a drumhead with each footfall. No one had been inside for some time, he felt sure of that.

There was an office; the door was standing open. And inside, on a plank shelf, was the famous telephone. Guinness picked up the receiver—there was no dial tone. So much for little Amalia's lifeline in case the sky should fall. He wondered whether Flycatcher had also found that slip of paper taped to the underside of her night-table drawer and had decided to cut his losses. After all, people who wrote them down couldn't be trusted with secrets. Or perhaps it was simply that this particular plan was so close to fruition that lifelines were no longer considered either necessary or advisable. That was possible too—and perhaps more dangerous.

There was a bare little table in one corner, in the center of which was a paper coffee cup with perhaps as much as a quarter-inch left at the bottom. Dark stains along the sides indicated that it had probably been about half-full when someone had set it down there and then walked off and forgotten its existence. How long would that take? Even in the cool, moisture-laden atmosphere of a dockside warehouse, no more than a couple of days.

In a wastepaper basket, Guinness found several sheets of notepaper covered over with figures arranged in columns of three. He thought for a moment he might have stumbled on something until he realized the numbers were gin rummy scores. About thirty games—someone must have been awfully bored. He wondered whose writing it was, if perhaps this hadn't been how Mr. Lind had whiled away his time as he waited for his marching orders.

Guinness tried not to think about Mr. Lind, who, after all, had had to take his chances with the rest of them. There was no way in the world he could have left him alive—from the moment Flycatcher knew that he had any interest in Amalia Brouwer, her life was forfeit. He hadn't come to Amsterdam to be kind to thugs, but to keep his word to Kätzner. Kätzner wouldn't care how many of Flycatcher's troops ended up with their skulls bashed in. Kätzner didn't approve of Flycatcher.

You cannot conceive of what these people are like, he had said.

Well, actually—yes, Colonel, perhaps we can. Perhaps they aren't so different from the man you sent to stop them.

11

"He's a Belgian major, assigned to the NATO command there, and he seems to have taken a walk."

Guinness had gone to the public telephone in a hotel about six blocks from Janine's apartment; it was a huge place and seemed to cater mainly to tours, so the lobby was frantic. No one could have asked for anywhere more private, especially at that hour; half the human race seemed to be coming back from excursions to the Rijksmuseum and the pottery shops, and the remnant were collected around the elevator banks and the main entrance, trying to figure out where to go for dinner. There wasn't a soul to care about one more body stuffed into a phone booth.

"When?—how long has he been gone?" He covered his other ear with the heel of his right hand, trying to screen out some of the noise from the busload of tourists who had just arrived and seemed to be intent on battering down the front doors with their suitcases. But even then all he could hear was the crackle of the long-distance lines. "How *long,* Ernie?"

"Since this morning, apparently." Ernie's voice had acquired that confidential quality that always went along with the disclosure of the world's darkest secrets. He had a weakness for inside information; it was something you learned to put up with.

Which, of course, presupposed that there was inside information—Guinness wondered what kind of mess he would be walking into now.

"So what makes one day away from work such a great issue? Maybe he's home sick with the flu."

"No chance, pal. He's skipped; they can't find him anywhere. I'm told he's been under surveillance for some time—the best guess is he took himself off to avoid arrest."

Rênal? It was a myth that the camera didn't lie, but the man in the photograph that Amalia Brouwer kept on her night table hardly looked like a menace to the Western Way of Life. Or was he another one like Bateman, just a poor little schlub who had gotten in way over his head?

But perhaps that wasn't being quite fair to Bateman—Bateman, in his own suicidal fashion, had at least known what he wanted, had had the imagination to know when he was taking a wild leap into the abyss. It would be necessary to reserve judgment on Major Rênal, but he had hardly impressed Guinness as a paragon of originality.

"And, Raymond—our employers wish me to remind you that we are not in the business of playing housemother to the European allies. Our inquiries about this matter sparked a good deal of interest in Brussels—I'm sure they'd just love it if they could have their boy back—but I hope I don't have to remind you that we have no interest in wandering NATO officers. Just remember what we pay you for. Your concern is Flycatcher, not Rênal."

Guinness hung up without replying. He didn't feel sure he could trust himself, really. For the moment, at least, he wasn't Washington's man—he was Kätzner's. There was no way he could explain that to Ernie, so perhaps it was simply better not to try.

G Street could think what it wanted, and if it worked out that Flycatcher came within range then everything would be fine. But Guinness knew perfectly well that, bloodcurdling threats notwithstanding, if Ernie got any idea his man wasn't on the square with him, Amsterdam would be hip-deep in American agents before tomorrow lunchtime.

Across the street, on the corner of a bank building, was a sign that flashed the time and the temperature. In the old days Europe had been free of such monstrosities, but now it seemed that every city on the Continent wanted to be mistaken for Cleveland, Ohio. A month before, Guinness had been in England on a six-hour layover between flights and, having decided to kill the time with a little local sight-seeing, had discovered a Baskin-Robbins ice cream store almost directly on the other side of the road from Windsor Castle. There was no safety anymore.

He checked his watch against the bank building and confirmed that it really was only a quarter after six. In a little more than an hour he was supposed to show up at Janine's apartment, where the two of them would press their knees together under her tiny kitchen table while they pretended to eat dinner, but he wasn't sure they would have a chance for any of that now. There wasn't going to be any time for romantic dalliance—Jean Rênal, who would probably be arriving at his own lady love's front doorstep any moment now, was going to bring anything of that kind to an abrupt halt.

But he would have to make time—not for Janine, for himself. He had to have a moment in which to think, to fit all the pieces together, or he wouldn't have even a clue about what the next move should be.

Rênal, the Belgian soldier *cum* greeting-card heart-throb, NATO's bad boy, location uncertain, immediate destination a dead cinch. Amalia Brouwer, book merchant and part-time laborer in the People's Struggle, second-generation idealist. Flycatcher, terrorist, criminal, fashion plate, recent casualty of the Battle of Puerto Vallarta. These three, the lady and her lovers. Where did the one begin and the next end? What had they cooked up among them?

The main point was that Rênal had done a flit and was in transit to whatever rewards had been promised to him in exchange for whatever minor secrets the people in Brussels had been stupid enough to put within his reach. He was on his way to the arms of his beloved Amalia—and, presumably, some unspecified place of safety and comfort. At least, that would be his treasured assumption.

He could hardly have been expected this early on to appreciate the fact, of course, but Major Rênal was a dead man, a walking corpse. That was going to be the real payoff. It was such a foregone conclusion that Guinness had already counted him out of the game. From the moment he arrived in Amsterdam, he was simply no longer a factor.

Rênal was a defector. Unless he happened to have bounded off with the transcripts of the last ministerial council in his wallet, he wasn't of any further use to anyone—and probably not then either. He could come bearing the battle plans for World War III, and Flycatcher would express his thanks by ordering him shot in the ear. Rênal was going to end up fertilizing the tulips somewhere, since no one had ever accused Flycatcher of entertaining any sentimental fondness for keeping his word.

And, directly or indirectly, whether he was aware of it or not, Rênal was Flycatcher's agent. That was his problem and was shortly to be his fate. Flycatcher owned him. With Flycatcher in the game at all, there just wasn't any other way to figure it.

The question was—granted that he was Flycatcher's tool—who was his handler? The ardent Miss Brouwer of the white cotton underwear? She was the obvious candidate and, provided that the sexual inclinations matched up, it was more or less standard operating procedure for a lot of handlers to sleep with their foot soldiers. Sometimes it helped to keep them in line.

But somehow it didn't quite ring right—which was not to say that Amalia wouldn't see herself as the puppet master. She just didn't strike Guinness as the type. It was just too hard to imagine Flycatcher putting her in a position that would require that kind of long-range cynicism.

Amalia, after all, was an idealist, a believer in causes—we had her father's word for that—which condition of existence was only a kind of laughable weakness in the eyes of someone like Flycatcher. And Flycatcher, we had all long ago agreed, was a man with a keen eye for weakness. After all, you had to trust your sergeants, trust their judgment as well as their loyalty, and trusting Amalia Brouwer wasn't the sort of mistake you would have expected Flycatcher to make.

So what had he set up between these two, our accomplished villain? What, precisely, had he arranged for the maiden and the major, and toward what end?

The wind had shifted and was blowing in now from the sea. Guinness found himself wishing that, when he had made his escape from the Grand Hotel Krasnapolsky, he had thought to take his raincoat with him; he wasn't particularly enjoying how all the merry little breezes found their way down the back of his neck. He tried staying close to the sheltered side of buildings as he walked along, but it really didn't help much. It was as if the evening cold and the not-quite-unpleasant smell from the canals and the pressure of sound that the wind carried with it had somehow found their way into the very fiber of his soul.

It was just uneasiness; he knew that. He was merely blaming his apprehension on the weather. Because, whatever else Rênal's flight might mean, it would certainly accelerate matters. Whatever obscure danger Kätzner had perceived for his child was upon her now, because if Flycatcher meant to strike her down he would do it within the next twenty-four hours. If little Amalia had been Rênal's handler, then he wasn't the only one who had outlived his usefulness. Flycatcher would decide quickly enough to cut his losses, and they would both be killed. That was the way he worked—he didn't like loose ends, and Amalia, who wrote little notes to herself and hid them under her night-table drawer, whose bathtub had collected samples of his bone-white hair, Amalia would be too much of a hazard to leave behind.

"One's domestic sins are merely points in a line of consequences, nothing more. You see what a good Marxist I am? I believe in historical inevitability, even as it applies to the mysteries of private life."

Kätzner had been narrating the history of his marriage, squinting out through his rain-streaked windshield as they drove back to Munich. Like the drowning man who sees his life passing before him, he seemed so preoccupied with the steps by which he had made his way back full circle to the gardens of the Nymphenburg and this city where he had parted company with his innocence that it would have been unspeakably rude to do anything except listen. So Guinness had listened.

Perhaps that was the point—perhaps Kätzner was simply sucking him in, allowing him to commit himself more and more as with each succeeding word the subtle dialectician enforced his own reality and that of the child he had left behind him in Amsterdam back in the first beginnings of the fallen world.

"I am guilty of a vast dereliction in persuading you to this thing; my government's interests are involved, one presumes, and doubtless I betray them—it would be the first time in my life I have put anything above that duty. In 1962, the choice seemed simpler, and I left behind wife and child and returned to Berlin. Perhaps I could have done something else, taken them with me to some third country or asked for political asylum with the Dutch—I suppose I could have bought my freedom with a few well-chosen pieces of political gossip—but such a course simply never crossed my mind. And now, to preserve my child, I reverse myself. One hopes that somehow the two come into some kind of balance. I would like to believe that now I have paid all debts and nothing more is required of me, but I don't really imagine it is so."

And he smiled his sad smile, as if the inescapable tragedy of life were something so well understood between them that it hardly needed to be mentioned at all. The veteran of Madrid, who had prevailed over Franco and Himmler and even the NKVD, the East German colonel who had perhaps saved Raymond Guinness's young life out of, as much as anything, a sense of aesthetic fitness looked tired and old and disenchanted even with the range of his own self-contempt. And still he could talk of debts and balance and the keeping and breaking of faiths, as if all that could possibly still mean something in whatever was left to have survived the final twilight. It made you marvel at the resilience of dead illusions.

One wondered what sorts of illusions he must have been harboring in the winter of 1962, when the February snow had become packed down to ice along the sidewalks and the canals were frozen into obscure gray mirrors that reflected nothing. In Amsterdam, between October and March, the sea winds drench you with a wet, penetrating cold that seems to amount almost to a personal affront, making it hard to support very strenuously any exalted ideas of yourself.

Humanity, with its chapped fingertips and its splintering feet and its headcolds and its sad weariness under layer upon layer of sweaters and woolen scarves and heavy, sodden overcoats, is reduced by winter to some semblance of the truth about itself, is revealed as feckless and woeful and spiritually puny, mere vermin clinging to a speck of frosty mud.

Emil Kätzner, who for the next forty-eight hours, until the morning after his return to Berlin, would remain unaware that four months before he had been promoted to the rank of lieutenant colonel in the Army of the German Democratic Republic, had stamped his galoshes against the paving stones in front of his office door, trying to establish whether his toes could really be as numb as they felt. For six years he had been telling himself that he loathed the Netherlands, that it was worse even than the mud-filled trenches in Cataluña, a purgatory from which, apparently, nothing could release him. And now, on the brink of escape, he felt like a banished angel looking back for the last time on the green hills of Paradise.

It was eleven-thirty in the morning. He never came home for lunch, so his wife wouldn't be expecting him for hours—probably by the time she missed him he would already be in Hannover. When she woke up tomorrow morning, her husband of five years would have ceased to exist.

Her husband of five years. Maarten Huygens, the little man who worked as an insurance broker and was the father of the three-and-a-half-year-old Amalia—at that moment, as he weighed the door key in his hand, he was being murdered by the Emil Kätzner who was struggling to be reborn.

Margot—what would she think when finally it sunk in on her that she was alone? She was still in her early thirties, a good ten years younger than Heer Huygens, and not unattractive if you liked them a little *saftig*. Emil—for he was already Emil, and viewed her with the disinterested compassion of someone who had somehow stumbled into the anonymous tragedy of strangers—Emil, the Communist spy, remembered as if the recollection were years distant from him that Margot did, however, have a certain tendency towards moroseness, and he wondered if the disappearance of the mythical Maarten would sour her life forever.

He went inside, and the door rattled as he closed it behind him. There were one or two things he wished to retrieve from his office safe, documents that, if of no great importance, might cause some embarrassment in Berlin if they were discovered. Kätzner was a thorough man, and there was time. His usefulness here was at an end—certainly the police were no more than a few days away from making an arrest—but there was no particular reason why they should have the satisfaction of announcing his activities to the newspapers as another instance of "Iron Curtain" treachery. What they might suspect was their concern entirely.

There was a photograph on his desk, a color snapshot, in a small brass frame, of Margot and the baby. He hesitated for a moment and then decided to leave it behind. All of that was no part of his life now—it never had been; it had belonged to Maarten Huygens, and he was dead and buried now—it was better to make as clean a break as possible.

What would happen to them? The rather strained-looking woman and the little girl with the bright curly hair, what would become of them now? It was a question he could ask, even at that moment, with a certain detachment, since their fates were well distant from Emil Kätzner's sphere of concern. He had been exonerated from responsibility—that, again, belonged to Maarten Huygens.

Because, of course, the ethics of his profession exonerated him. The ideology of the class struggle, for which he had killed many times, in the open warfare of Spain and in secret ever since, for which he was willing, should it come to that, to allow himself to be killed, his faith that the movement of history rendered insignificant the sufferings of individuals rendered him guiltless. Not unmoved—after all, he was not a monster or a saint, to be entirely consumed by the egotism of his own dedication—but guiltless. He was fond of his wife, and he adored little Amalia, but he discovered that, even at the moment of departure, he could maintain a certain detachment from them, and from the sorrow of the man he had been even the day before.

So he didn't take the photograph. On the whole, it was better not to nurture the remembrance.

"You see? Do you see the error? I hadn't yet learned—the zealot had not yet learned that, after all, flesh is mere flesh and must, one time or another, have its way.

"But, after all, there is a fatality in all commitment. To love anything, from a child to an ideal of social justice, is to step into a trap. They fail, causes and people—or they blind us, or maim our souls, or force us to give over some version of ourselves."

And the rain streamed down the windshield, and the throbbing wiper blades beat it away, and Kätzner smiled, looking straight ahead, as if at some point in the far distance.

"What lured you into this business? Did they give you the big pitch about saving Western civilization from the forces of darkness?"

She merely shrugged her tiny shoulders, suggesting that, if they had, they had failed to make much of an impression. "I am a whore—it is a tiresome existence."

"More tiresome than this? I can't imagine."

Janine's car was parked across an intersection and three-quarters of a block away from Amalia Brouwer's apartment building. From behind the wheel, Guinness had an unobstructed view; with the Leica field glasses his companion had thought to bring along he could even count the leaves on the tree that stood out next to the sidewalk in front of the living room windows and reached almost that high.

Janine had made a thermos flask of tea, which she held between her thighs as they passed the cup back and forth, taking tentative sips because the stuff was still blindingly hot. She sat flush up against him, and he had his arm over her shoulder—not simply because it was more fun that way but for protective coloration; the Dutch were a very tolerant people, and nobody had to invent any reasons why a man and a woman might be sitting in a parked car together at one-fifteen in the morning. Besides, it was more fun that way.

"Do you believe he will come?" she asked, letting her hand nestle in his lap like a small animal.

"He'll come. I'm not worried about that—I just want to see how he's received."

Amalia's window was dark, but of course it would be. She had come home immediately after work and, as far as they could determine, she was up there by herself. Probably she'd been asleep for hours.

All the houses in both directions were dark. Apparently it wasn't a very lively neighborhood. Guinness wished he could get out and walk around for a few minutes; he had been sitting for hours and his ass was killing him.

"Would you like to spend the night tonight?"

Guinness smiled, not looking at her, not taking his eyes off Amalia Brouwer's front door, and let his hand slide down Janine's arm until the fingers came to rest on the curve of her elbow.

"You mean, what there is left of it? I thought you had to worry about your landlady."

"This once, we will take the risk."

Well, it was nice to be asked. Guinness simply hoped

that Rênal would make it sometime before dawn—tomorrow was likely to be a busy day and, passion aside, it might be nice to get a little sleep first.

He moved his hand around to the inside of her arm and, as he felt for her breast, she moved closer to him, pressing her shoulder against his ribcage. As usual, there was no brassiere in the way—even through the rough wool knit of the sweater, he could feel her nipple hardening under his thumb.

"Did you do this sort of thing when you were a kid?" he asked. "Did all the little Dutch boys and girls sit around in cars and play slap-and-tickle?"

In the pause before she answered, Guinness realized that, once again, he had probably put his foot in it. The lady made her living by entertaining men in a little room she rented by the hour and, not very remarkably, she seemed to suffer from a certain sensitivity about the topic—about any topic, in fact, that even came close. So why couldn't he just remember that and learn to keep his big mouth shut? It seemed little enough to ask.

"No. The boys did not like me at that stage."

"They must have been out of their minds."

Women were unaccountable creatures—her face, as usual, betrayed no emotion whatever, but she picked up the hem of her sweater and guided him underneath. He could feel her heart beating under his fingers and the warm smell of her hair was in his nostrils, and, naturally, it made him feel like a seducer of children.

All he would have had to do was to push her back against the seat and she would have slipped down her corduroy trousers and given herself up to him, for whatever reasons of her own, without a murmur. It was what she wanted him to do, and it would have been impossible.

After a moment, she realized it herself, and she brought her hand up and covered the outline of his beneath her sweater, pressing him against her breast as if she wanted to crush it flat under his palm.

"And you?" There was a hint of mockery in her murmuring voice. "Did you take the girls out in your car and make love to them in shadowed places?"

"I didn't even own a car until I was twenty-six, and by then it was too late."

And they could both laugh.

About half a block away, some kids were coming up the cross-street. There were three couples, and they were noisy and young, and Guinness saw through the field glasses that at least two of the fellows were carrying open liquor bottles in crumpled brown paper bags. On the evidence of the loping way they walked, it had been a long night for some of them. Guinness wondered why they couldn't be home gang-banging—they annoyed him. Anyone who was out on the street and wasn't Jean Rênal annoyed him. They went over the intersection and were gone, although it was still possible to hear them for several seconds after they had disappeared from sight.

According to his watch, it was nearly two o'clock.

"I'll give him another hour, and then we'll call it a night. He might not come—he might check into a hotel somewhere and try contacting her tomorrow morning."

Even as he said it, he knew he didn't believe it. Rênal wasn't going to bother with any hotels. *Avec mon amour, Jean.* He wouldn't have the imagination to be that cagey. If they hadn't arrested him yet, he'd come right to his little love nest, straight as any arrow.

And then what? The problem would remain what it had been all along, persuading Miss Brouwer that her friends were not the sterling characters they seemed. Really, from the first, there had been only two options—to move her out of harm's way, kicking and screaming if absolutely necessary, or to kill Flycatcher and thus render his little scheme, whatever it might have been, a thing of purely academic interest. Of course, Guinness would have vastly preferred the second.

But, as he had discovered long ago, life wasn't organized around his preferences. So it would probably work out that he would have to drag Colonel Kätzner's little baby girl off by the hair—and then what? Put an announcement in the papers daring Flycatcher to come out of hiding and settle up, man to man? Fat chance.

Well, he'd think of something.

"I do not understand why you should care," Janine said wearily. Her head was resting against Guinness's chest; it was obviously way past her bedtime, and she seemed ready to slide down into his lap and go to sleep. "If Flycatcher is as clever as you say, he will not let this Rênal come near him. So why do we wait?"

"We wait, my dear, because Flycatcher is not our target—not the main one, anyway. I'm thinking of the girl. I want to know how she hails the conquering hero. I want to know which way she'll jump when I light a fire under her."

But it was obvious that she had already lost interest in her own question. He could hear her breathing; in a few minutes, if he left her alone, she would be alseep. She had clamped her arm over his, as if the presence of his hand on her breast was something she didn't want disturbed. So be it.

At two twenty-seven, with her head nestled on his thigh, Janine was conked out. At one point she reached up to scratch her nose, but otherwise she hardly stirred. So Guinness didn't trouble her when the man in the black raincoat came into view at the corner and turned the street toward the apartment building. His back was turned—you couldn't see the face—but Guinness didn't have a doubt in the world.

And then the black figure stopped, directly in front of

Amalia Brouwer's front door, and turned around. It was Rênal, right enough. Guinness picked up the field glasses for a look, just to be sure, and the handsome, rather meaty face was unmistakable. The eternal amateur, he was craning his neck to see if anyone had followed him, probably not even noticing the gray Opel parked perhaps only seventy or eighty yards away—no, that wouldn't be obvious enough.

He disappeared into the doorway and, a few seconds later, the light was visible from behind the living room window. It went dark after about five minutes.

"Come on, Sweetpea. Rise and shine. You missed the big show—lover boy's come and gone."

Janine stirred, opened her eyes, and looked at him with a mixture of curiosity and resentment. He smiled and kissed her on the eyebrow.

"She was expecting him, Toots, and if she knows, Flycatcher knows. The poor suckers, I'll bet he's already got their graves dug."

12

Guinness was already awake when the alarm went off—he had been waiting, with one eye open, for about four minutes and managed to smother the fierce metallic buzz almost at once. It was a quarter after six.

Three hours of sleep. When this was over he would go to bed for about three days. He would check into a hotel and have his meals sent up so he wouldn't have to change out of his pajamas. He would go to London and find a room that looked out over a garden, where the loudest sound you could hear would be the chit-chit-chit of a sprinkler turning on the lawn.

He rolled over so the clock face couldn't taunt him and pressed his nose against Janine's shoulderblade. She didn't stir, and her skin was warm and smelled of bed; he knew if he didn't get up right that instant he would fall asleep again, but somehow it was difficult to care.

Maybe he would take Janine with him when he went off for his rest cure. Hell, it couldn't last forever—they weren't by any stretch of the imagination "in love," and he had learned through the bitterest experience that his profession did not allow him to form any but the most ephemeral of attachments—but they could string it out a little longer. Just a little longer.

But, of course, she might not want to come. There would

be all kinds of reasons why she might prefer to quit while they were ahead.

Under any circumstances, it wouldn't do any harm to ask. But not until this business was over—it wouldn't be fair until then.

Out of the corner of his eye, he could watch the curtains stirring in the light morning breeze. The sky was still a dull gray, but they weren't more than ten or fifteen minutes from bright sunshine. He could see why Janine liked to keep the door to her balcony open when she was home; the floating curtains did afford a certain measure of solace.

She turned toward him, draping an arm up over his shoulder. Their faces were almost touching, and she opened her eyes and smiled.

"Are you awake?" she asked. He drew the covers up over her bare back and allowed his hand to linger for a moment, just touching her soft, silvery brown hair where it brushed against her neck.

"Yes. Did I disturb you? I'm sorry."

"No."

Which, of course, rendered him without excuse. He didn't have any choice now; he had to get up.

Janine made them some breakfast while he was in the shower; she brought it in on a little wooden tray and set it down on the bed and waited for him until he had put on his shirt and combed his hair. Just a little basket of hard rolls and a pot of tea—the plates were tiny and he had a lot of trouble to keep from scattering pieces of crust all over everything. But it was very pleasant to be sitting together on the edge of the bed and smiling at each other, and they ate in cheerful silence as the street noises began to filter up through the open balcony door. They didn't want to say anything for fear of breaking the spell.

But even that couldn't last forever.

"I want you to go back to where we were parked last night," Guinness said finally, looking back at her through the mirror in which he was tying his tie. "When she comes out, tail her—they won't be looking for you, but stay cagey; I wouldn't be surprised if we aren't the only ones who might be keeping a casual eye on things this morning. Whatever else she does, she'll probably go to work just to keep anyone from checking up on her. If she does, meet me at the Rijksmuseum at ten o'clock. If she doesn't, phone me at Aimé's apartment at eleven."

"Where in the musuem?—it is a big place."

He smiled at her, thinking she was a bright girl and a good trooper, thinking how much he liked her and how much fun a couple of weeks on neutral ground with her could be.

"You'll find me at the *Royal Charles*—just ask a guard."

"And what will you do? Will you follow the other one?"

"Rênal?" Guinness shook his head. "No, he won't show his face. He's not very good, but I don't suppose he's retarded enough to go sightseeing—too many people are mad at him."

> *That pleasure-boat of war, in whose dear side*
> *Secure so oft he had this foe defi'd,*
> *Now a cheap spoil and the mean victor's slave,*
> *Taught the Dutch colors from its top to wave—*

Not very good poetry, really—it hardly even scanned—but then nobody could be a genius all the time.

On June 12, 1667, in the last year of the Second Dutch War, Admiral De Ruyter sailed up the Thames estuary to sink many ships and capture the *Royal Charles,* which had carried the King home from exile in 1660. It was the most humiliating defeat in British naval history, and Andrew Marvell, about whom Guinness had written some humiliatingly boring monographs before the facts of life pulled him out of academia and returned him to his old profession, Andrew Marvell had written a verse satire about the business, "The Last Instructions of the Painter," which had been good fun back in its day but required an almost encyclopedic knowledge of mid-Seventeenth Century political and social history to be read with anything like real pleasure today.

In any case, the Dutch had preserved the prow of the *Royal Charles;* it was on display at the Rijksmuseum, where a series of maps, rusty artifacts, and multilingual explanatory notices recounted the story of De Ruyter's triumph. Guinness had seen it all in 1970, on his last visit, but he studied all of it over again with methodical seriousness—these, apparently, were not a people who neglected the memories of their heroes. Well, good for them.

He paced around on the hardwood floors, conscious that his feet were beginning to hurt—it always happened to him in museums; he could feel the weariness creeping up his Achilles tendons—peripherally aware of the murmuring crowds that surged behind him, crackling their guidebooks and coughing impatiently as they did their cultural duty and chaperoned the children through the national attic. He tried to ignore them, to pretend there was nothing in the universe except himself and the Grand Admiral, but it was a losing battle.

The wall clock said it was six minutes after ten. He would give Janine nine more minutes, and then he would go back to Aimé's apartment and wait by the phone. If she didn't show up it would mean that Amalia Brouwer was on the move, and that was a possibility he didn't want to think about until he had to. So he tried to think about the *Royal Charles* instead, except that it was impossible.

He seemed fated to pass through all the great museums

of the world, waiting for the man with a rose in his lapel and a folded copy of the *Manchester Guardian* sticking out of his jacket pocket. Sometimes the work seemed on the point of absorbing him totally, leaving him no identity at all except that of Raymond Guinness, celebrated killer of men—the Soldier.

When this business was cleared up, he would go to the British Museum and spend an entire afternoon staring at the Elgin Marbles; he would stand in rapt attention before the Sutton Hoo exhibit until the guards concluded that he had become rooted to the floor. He would go to plays in the West End, and if anyone approached him it would merely be to inquire the time. Sure.

An hour after leaving Janine's apartment, he had gone back to the huge, noisy hotel perhaps half-a-dozen blocks away and had put in another call to Ernie Tuttle. It had probably been about one in the morning in Washington, and the low, feminine voice and the slamming door he had heard in the background suggested that Ernie was probably entertaining—he hadn't seemed too terribly pleased about the interruption.

"Jesus, Ray—give me a break, will you? Haven't you got any idea what time it is?"

"You're smothering me in guilt. Tell me what Rênal is supposed to have done."

It was at this point that a muffled conversation took place, only one side of which Guinness could hear distinctly enough to make out the words but which was of a sufficiently acrimonious tone, especially on the lady's part, to suggest that the phone had rung at an awkward moment. The exchange was terminated by the sound of what was probably Ernie's bedroom door being closed with excessive force.

"Okay, pal," he answered wearily. "What about him?"

"What did he do? What's he supposed to have ripped off that the people in Brussels are in such a lather? I want to know, Ernie."

But Ernie hadn't been terribly forthcoming—it seemed that someone, either Brussels or Ernie himself, was playing it coy.

"How long has it been since NATO sprang its leak? Can you tell me that, at least?"

"About seven months—they've been certain for seven months, so it's been at least that long. Why, Ray? What are you building?"

"I don't know."

"Hang on a second."

What happened during the next several seconds, whether Ernie went into the next room to soothe someone's ruffled feelings or simply wanted to make sure the door was closed, Guinness would probably never know. But when Mr. Tuttle came back, he was the Company's man.

"I just want to remind you again," he said, his voice harsh and flat and only this side of menacing. "Nobody here has any interest in Rênal. He's Brussels' problem, not ours. You just close the account on Flycatcher and everyone will be thrilled to death. But don't amuse yourself with stirring up the mud at the bottom of any quiet pools. Leave them alone. I mean it, Ray—leave Rênal to his fate."

Well, there it was. The cross every field man, no matter what his allegiance or political complexion, had to bear—"Stay out of it, it's none of your business." It was a hedge against capture and defection, to tell a man the absolute minimum he needed to know in order to carry out his assignment. You weren't so much of a loss that way if you happened to fall into bad company. The Sacred Principle of Compartmentalization.

They never let you see how your piece of the puzzle fit in

with the rest, and they always assured you that what you didn't see wasn't there. It was always all right, because the Powers That Be had everything well in hand and you really didn't have to worry about a thing. Except that sometimes their highnesses made a mistake—or decided that, too bad, you'd just have to be a casualty to the grand design—and the little insignificant detail they just couldn't bring themselves to share with you was what got you killed. It wasn't as if that sort of thing had never happened.

So, if you were smart and wanted to live to collect your retirement benefits, you stayed curious. It wasn't something they encouraged, but that was just too damn bad. There had to be a limit to team spirit.

And he didn't like this one. *He's Brussels' problem, not ours.* It just didn't smell right—for one thing, Ernie hadn't even asked him if he knew where Rênal was. Guinness wouldn't have told him, but what was there to lose in asking? Washington might not have any interest (although how much was there, really, in which Washington had no interest?), but it was the sort of information that would be worth having for a trade. It never hurt if someone in Brussels owed you a favor. But Ernie hadn't even asked.

And why was Flycatcher being so terribly, terribly ostentatious about the flight of his little pet NATO snitch? First he runs him through Amalia Brouwer, an amateur, a child who still thinks it's safe to write things down—the sort of person who'll attract attention like a red flag.

And then, when the lads back home finally tumble to the fact that Major Rênal isn't exactly squeaky clean, Flycatcher allows him to run away on his own, all the way up to Amsterdam, to the arms of the beloved Amalia. Why not just pick him up on a streetcorner in Brussels and spirit him off? Why let a bumbler like that leave a nice untidy trail behind him? No matter what his ultimate plans for those two, why would Flycatcher leave so much of the execution of their retreat in the hands of a thick-witted army officer and a schoolgirl?

Pour Amalia, avec mon amour, Jean. Holy Jesus.

Seven months. Had Ernie really said seven months? Rênal? NATO was one of the world's most sensitive and difficult intelligence assignments; it would take a very good man to keep from getting caught for three months, let alone seven. And seven months was the minimum—God knew how long they had had a leak before that. And one was asked to believe that Jean Rênal, the man who gawked nervously over his shoulder, looking up and down the street to see if anyone was following him, that this clown had managed to hang on at the military nerve center of Europe for seven months without getting caught. It simply wasn't credible.

So Guinness felt he could be excused for thinking that he might have stepped into something that wasn't just precisely what it seemed. And if they had their little secrets, so had he—Amalia Brouwer was his little secret, his and Kätzner's, and she was going to stay that way, at least for the time being. God knows what Ernie would make of her. Fishbait, probably.

"Forgive me for being late. She did not go to her shop until a quarter to ten, and I thought you would wish me to make certain she planned to stay."

Reflexively, he looked back up at the wall clock—it was eleven minutes after ten. Janine had gotten as close as his elbow without his having so much as noticed her. He was going to have to start watching himself.

She touched him on the arm, and it made him smile.

"Why was she late? What was she up to?"

"She went to the bank. I stood at the next window but

one and she withdrew all her money, some four or five thousand florins. She put the money in her purse and went directly to the bookshop, so she must still have it."

"And she didn't spot you?"

"No, she didn't spot me. She was far too preoccupied to notice anyone—she seemed excited, and happy. What does it mean, Soldier?"

He let his hand rest on her shoulder and smiled again, but it was a painful smile.

"I imagine she thinks she's about to set out on her honeymoon."

And then a curious thing happened. Guinness turned around, for no particular reason, and saw that someone was waving at him from the other side of the room. Before he knew it, he discovered that he had raised his own hand in a tentative greeting, and the two high school teachers from Portland were coming toward them through the crowds.

"Well, how are you enjoying Amsterdam?" he asked, slightly appalled by the triteness of his own question—he simply couldn't seem to think of anything else to say. The shorter of the two men, the one who had done most of the talking for them on the train, looked up at him from a frankly appraising inspection of Janine and grinned through his tangled beard.

"Very much. It's awfully expensive, though—we think we'll probably have to leave in a couple of days."

The other one, who seemed a little embarrassed and kept glancing down at the floor, grunted in agreement.

"Pardon me—this is Mrs. de Witt. Beatrix, these are two gentlemen I met on the train coming in." He turned to them and made an apologetic gesture and smiled. "I'm sorry, I've forgotten your names."

The short one let his eyes drift over to Janine's face, and

the wolfish grin reasserted itself. Guinness decided he didn't like either one of them—the intrusion came at a bad time, but he didn't like them anyway. He didn't care for the way this guy kept looking at Janine as if she were a piece of meat.

"Painter, Jeff Painter. And this is my friend, Hal Dietrich. Pleased to meet you, ma'am." Janine smiled in that bright, graceful, only slightly artificial manner that all women seem to have as a birthright, putting out her hand first to the one and then to the other—it was a Continental mania, shaking hands, and it always struck Guinness, upon whom an eight-year residence in Britain had left its indelible mark, as rather too hearty, appropriate perhaps to spinsterish Girl Guide leaders but not to a pretty woman greeting a couple of perfect strangers. But Painter, who obviously wasn't so squeamish, grabbed hold eagerly enough. While he talked to Janine, holding her hand perhaps a little longer than absolutely necessary, he kept dropping into a faint Border States drawl, a half-cajoling, half-intimidating cadence that some men seem to imagine absolutely devastating and that had been entirely absent before. Guinness's mind was made up. He really didn't like the guy.

They talked for a few minutes, exchanging observations about traveling, and Janine was solicited for her opinion concerning what was most worth seeing in Holland over the few days before Messrs. Painter and Dietrich were driven to Spain by their dwindling resources. And then Guinness reminded her that "Willem" was probably waiting for them, and they made their escape.

" 'Willem?' " she asked as they clattered down the cavernous main stairway toward the street.

"Your husband, Mrs. de Witt—don't you remember?" He showed his teeth in something approaching a smile. "I had to think of something to get us away from those two cowboys."

Outside, in the harsh morning sunshine, there were orderly lines of schoolchildren being readied by their teachers for the onslaught, and crowds of tourists, mostly clustered around the several stainless-steel vending carts manned by elderly, dark-faced women who might have been gypsies. Once again, Guinness was oppressed by the feeling that he was being watched, that somehow he had forfeited his anonymity and was under the gaze of someone with an unhealthy interest in his every move. That, or perhaps only the change of light, made him narrow his eyes and frown.

"Are you angry, Soldier?" Janine took his arm and looked around into his face with placid curiosity. "I thought they were rather nice."

"Who?"

"Those two men—your friends from the train."

Yes, of course that was who she would mean. He had almost forgotten them. His friends from the train.

"They seemed to think you were rather nice too," he said, smiling. "No, I'm not angry."

Her car was parked on a side street only a few blocks away. They walked there together, preserving the silence between them while Guinness tried to blank out his mind, to not listen to or look for anything so that he could see and hear whatever dissonance it was that seemed to be trailing along behind them. It was back there somewhere, just out of reach. Or perhaps it was just that he was tired and beginning to imagine things. That happened too.

Janine had been right, though. *I do not think someone with eyes would take you for a Dutchman. You are too big—you spread out too much.* It wasn't a congenial city for him; he felt crowded and strangely accessible. He was probably easy to spot. Flycatcher's people, if they were looking for him with any concentration, had probably stumbled over him half-a-dozen times—just like the late Mr. Lind of blessed memory, for all the good it had done him. Guinness had done his best to be hard to follow and, if they had found him, he was reasonably sure he had always been able to shake them off. But nobody was invisible.

So there was nothing to do but to keep shaking them off. They weren't dangerous unless they found out where you nested, unless you gave them a chance to organize something unpleasant in some nice quiet place where you wouldn't be looking for trouble and you wouldn't have anywhere to hide. Guinness didn't imagine they would try for him in the middle of the public sidewalk, not unless they had the traditional black sedan with four or five guys with shotguns all primed and ready. No simple garden-variety thug, unless he was an idiot and as a consequence reasonably harmless anyway, was going to try gunning him down just on inspiration, just on the spur of the moment. In a way, his reputation protected him from that; he was considered simply too formidable. There was something to be said for casting a long shadow.

But there might be something in getting Janine away from him, at least for a little while, until things were a little more under control. It might be true that he personally was possessed of nine lives, but that hadn't always helped the people who stood too close to him. Enough of them had died to keep him from thinking that he was necessarily the best thing that could happen to someone.

When they reached the car, Guinness took the keys out of Janine's hand.

"There's a man in the consulate in Düsseldorf, Teddy MacKaye; he's one of ours. I want you to go back to your apartment—on foot, I'll be taking the car—and pack a bag. Not much, not enough to get in the way. When I come back I'll have Amalia Brouwer with me, and I'll want you to get her the hell out of here. When you find MacKaye, tell him that the two of you are to be tucked up somewhere safe until I come in person to fetch you—if I don't come within a week, then Miss Brouwer should be shipped to the States, and you can come back to Amsterdam. I don't suppose anyone will bother you, but just to be on the safe side I'd stay out of the cloak-and-dagger business for a nice long time—forever, if you've got any sense."

She took his hand, the one that was holding the keys, and squeezed it, and peered up at him out of her enormous eyes, to which a worried look had returned for the first time since he had announced himself in her little rented room up an alley in the red-light district. Since there wasn't anything else he could do, he smiled, as if it were all a big joke.

"Tell them to squeeze her good when they get her to Washington; she probably knows a lot she's not even aware of. After, if they feel like it, they can keep a check on her for a while, but I don't think she'll ever present a menace to anybody's national security ever again, not after she's found out what a sucker Flycatcher has made of her. And then they can damn well give her a new identity and let her bury herself somewhere—she can marry a toaster salesman and sit in a semidetached house in Teaneck, reading Lenin."

"Where will you be if you don't come?" she asked, her voice calm, not from indifference but from the fatalism that already knows the answer to such questions.

"Silly girl—I'll be dead. What did you think?"

13

Amalia Brouwer had drawn all her money out of the bank, and Jean Rênal, so far as anybody knew, was waiting for her back at her apartment. It was just as clear as day what they had in mind, the poor foolish babies—they were getting ready to shoot the moon, to seek refuge in foreign parts, doubtless under the kind protection of friend Flycatcher.

Of course, at some point in the proceedings their expectations would begin to diverge. What did the major look forward to? Life with Amalia in a rose-covered cottage somewhere within easy commuting distance of the Kremlin? The silly fool—but, naturally, he didn't know that he wasn't the only one clogging up the drain in his lady love's bathtub.

And the fair Miss Brouwer, what was on her agenda? Tying the knot with the handsome, silver-haired stranger? An exciting life as a socialist Mata Hari, tempting the Enemies of Progress to their dooms? Some such piffle, surely.

"Why do you care so much about her?" Janine had asked. "What is she to you that you risk your life for her?"

It wasn't the implied rebuke, or even jealousy—Janine wasn't staking any claims, God knows—just a simple question. So he had kissed the inside of her hand and smiled.

"Not a thing, sweetheart. Not a thing. I'm doing it as a favor for a friend—just to oblige a friend."

And, as it turned out, it was almost that simple. Guinness discovered that, as a matter of fact, he really didn't much like

Amalia Brouwer. Possibly, if you could separate out the claims of parental love, neither did her own father. Maybe she would improve with age, once she'd had her eyes opened, but at the moment she struck Guinness as a puritanical, doctrinaire little pain in the ass.

But there were compensations. There was Janine, for instance, who had turned out to be quite another matter altogether.

"When this is finished up," he had said to her, still holding her hand between both of his own while they stood together in the middle of the sidewalk, "what do you say to the two of us going over to London for a couple of weeks? We could have a good roll in the hay—put on ten pounds apiece, get twelve hours of sleep every night, find out how the rest of the world lives when it's at home. It could be like one long Sunday afternoon."

He hadn't meant to ask her, not until they were both well clear of this mess, but what the hell. In a few hours Janine would be on her way out of the country—she was almost clear—and now seemed as good a time as any.

But perhaps he had made a mistake. Perhaps he had misread the whole thing between them, because there was something like an accusation in her eyes as she withdrew her hand.

"What did you think—that you could carry the little whore off with you, like a part of the luggage?"

"No. I thought perhaps it could be after working hours for both of us. We could make a pact—you wouldn't have to turn any tricks and I wouldn't have to kill anybody. We could try being human, at least for a little while."

They stood facing each other for a moment, like weary enemies, and Guinness had almost made up his mind to the idea that it had all been a ghastly miscalculation when, quite suddenly, she threw her arms around him, pressing her cheek against his ribcage. And then, just as suddenly, she released him and hurried away. He didn't try to stop her, hoping that was the right thing and that now, finally, they might have come to an understanding. He watched her until she turned the corner and was out of sight.

There was no future in it, none at all. And it didn't have anything to do with Janine, who was no fool and knew the sort of man he was and the sort of work he did and who wouldn't expect—probably wouldn't want—anything more than a couple of weeks of pretending that things like futures didn't matter. "We laughed when we met,/ And we laughed when we parted" was the way they would play it. Things didn't really work like that, but you had to have something. Nobody could be asked to live out his life as if he were alone on the planet, so you settled for the short-term loan at high interest and you took your lumps. You left the future to take care of itself.

And you tried to buy a future for Amalia Brouwer, because the one she had in mind wasn't going to lead anywhere except to the butcher's block.

The detail that kept sticking in Guinness's mind was the seven months. You had a Belgian major who seemed to have nothing but meat between his ears and who was run by a teeniebopper, and you were asked to believe that this winning combination could keep itself out of the slammer for seven months? It just wasn't in the cards.

The whole thing—Rênal rushing to his lady's arms, the big escape, everything—was just too damn theatrical to be real. You wondered why Flycatcher didn't put out a big flashing neon sign and charge admission. You wondered what the son of a bitch was staging, and for whose entertainment.

Don't amuse yourself with stirring up the mud at the bottom of any quiet pools. Leave it alone. So goeth the gospel according to

Ernie. Turn a blind eye, Raymond—we wouldn't want you to disturb anyone's illusions; anything but that.

It sounded like a goddamned love match. It made you wonder just exactly who was conning whom.

It was one of the abiding prejudices of Guinness's professional life that the people who gave him his orders were simply not to be trusted. He was not an Emil Kätzner—he hadn't joined up out of enthusiasm for any causes. In those days, his only cause had been himself. It still was.

To be sure, one developed a sense of fidelity to the work itself. If it became absolutely unavoidable, if there wasn't a way in the world he could get out of it, he might allow himself to be killed rather than blow a job. Even a mercenary had to find his integrity somewhere.

But that, basically, was what he was. He had worked for the British because they had paid the bills and, after a while, because they hadn't given him a choice; and now he worked for the Americans for much the same reasons. You didn't get to retire—he had tried, and it simply hadn't worked out. They kept their hooks in you; they expected you to die in their service and were prepared, if necessary, to see that things worked out that way.

And there was that in his own nature that bound the cobbler to his last. Guinness needed this life, he needed it to remind him that he wasn't simply a piece of the dead earth. Evil, be thou my good.

But one of the necessary conditions of the work, he had found, was that he trust no one, so Guinness didn't take it as an absolute article of faith that Major Rênal wasn't a matter with which he had to concern himself. That conclusion was being drawn just a shade too emphatically for his taste—he didn't like the idea that people were playing games behind his back.

And, of course, there was the awkward fact that he still

hadn't hit upon any instrument whereby to convince Amalia Brouwer that she would be well advised to accept his kind offer and let him get her the hell out of Amsterdam before Flycatcher used her for landfill. She was in up to her righteous little socialist eyebrows, it seemed, and would probably take some persuading beyond simply his solemn assurances. He would need something in the way of evidence. Something she would believe.

In all fairness, Guinness did suppose it would have been a bit much to ask her to take him at his unsupported word. After all, he wasn't even clear in his own mind yet what was happening. If it was Flycatcher's show it was going to be nasty—after all, a rattlesnake bite wasn't ever the kiss of peace—but he and Amalia Brouwer evidently didn't understand that gentleman in the same terms.

No, he didn't know precisely what was up. But Rênal might. At least, he might be in possession of those few stray pieces necessary to make the thing fit together, even if he himself didn't know what they meant. Rênal could very easily turn out to be a goldmine.

And there was only one way to find out, and that was to ask him.

So, much as it would grieve his conscience, Guinness decided that he was just going to have to ignore the wishes of his superiors and stir up a few quiet pools. Rênal, he had decided, was very much his business.

Janine's Opel was a jerky little thing—the clutch popped you into gear about a half-inch off the floor—but it had a full tank of gas and, according to the odometer, had managed somehow to go 34,567 kilometers without breaking down entirely. So maybe it could be trusted to get him around the city of Amsterdam—and Janine and Amalia Brouwer to Düsseldorf—before anything dire happened. It seemed at least even money.

He hadn't gone very many blocks before it occurred to him that he no longer had any sense of being followed. They just weren't there anymore.

Well, maybe they had never been there at all. Maybe he had just been suffering from an overheated imagination and the world was filled with anonymous strangers, or maybe whoever had been lurking in the shadows hadn't been able to hot-wire some poor innocent tourist's parked car fast enough to follow him. Anyway, he seemed to have the place all to himself now.

Still, there wasn't any point in taking chances. He tried a couple of long boulevard stretches, changing lanes every so often and letting his signal lights flash to see if anybody reacted. Then there were a couple of abrupt right-hand turns—out of the inside lane, right across the line of traffic—but nobody seemed to be making any Herculean efforts to keep up. He got a couple of dirty looks, but that was all.

Finally, Guinness pulled into a parking space along a nice, busy stretch of the Amstelveense and just waited. He studied the rearview mirror and, after a moment, got out of the car and took a quick walk around the block. When he got back he felt a lot better; he was as clean as a newborn baby's conscience and could go on his merry way without more than the customary misgivings.

So now, he thought, he would just pay Major Rênal a little unexpected visit and see if perhaps he couldn't catch him in a communicative mood.

It was close to eleven o'clock by the time Guinness drove past Amalia Brouwer's apartment. Everything looked perfectly orderly and suburban, although one would hardly have expected the bad guys to be doing sentry duty behind sandbag barricades, so he coasted on for another two blocks and then pulled into a side street.

He set the handbrake and dropped the car keys into his

jacket pocket, wondering if he wasn't making a mistake to bother with Rênal, if perhaps he shouldn't go right to the bookstore and simply drag Kätzner's daughter out in a gunny sack. It wouldn't be a very difficult operation to fill her full of sleepy juice and stuff her in the glove compartment until he could wheel her to Düsseldorf himself and put her in the custody of some nice men who would babysit with her and teach her how to cut out paper dolls until it was safe to allow her to return to Amsterdam.

Except, when would that be? Unless Flycatcher was dead—and that was about as uncertain a prospect as Guinness could imagine—it would never be safe. He would always assume that Amalia had crossed him, and he had a long memory for things like that; all they would have succeeded in doing was in putting off her execution for maybe a few months. It wasn't enough. Kätzner had wanted his little curly-haired girl definitely and permanently out. He had wanted her out of harm's way and cured for life, so that she would realize once and for all that messing about with terrorists and spies could be hazardous to one's health, that the toaster salesman and the semidetached house in New Jersey really were a better idea than trying to reform the world out of the muzzle of a gun.

So it would have to be Rênal. Rênal, or something else—and right at the moment Rênal was about the only game in town.

The morning sunlight came through the windshield as a bright smear; as soon as he opened the car door, Guinness could hear birds chirping from the insides of the compact little trees that stood every several dozen yards along the curb—it threatened to be a very pleasant day.

Across the street a mob of small children were gathered on a tiny patch of lawn to play some incomprehensible game that seemed to involve a lot of screeching. That was fine; it constituted a perfectly suitable cover noise, since there was nothing that attracted so much attention as the sound of a man's shoes on a concrete sidewalk if he happened to be the only human being in sight.

There was a problem about apartment buildings—they were generally provided with back doors. The rear staircase at Miss Brouwer's was accessible through a door in her tiny kitchen, if memory served, and it wouldn't take anyone more than a second or two to slip out into the alley and be gone forever if he were to imagine himself under siege.

And, complicating matters even further, the lady had been inconsiderate enough to install a chain on her front door. If Rênal was inside, and feeling anything like as spooky as he looked, he would have it up. So there wasn't any point in trying to pick the lock; the quicker, better, more efficient way was just to kick the whole goddamned thing right off its hinges.

Guinness walked down between the rows of houses, trying to pretend to himself that he lived there. He stopped once or twice to examine the dandelions on people's lawns and noticed that, here and there, the sidewalk was in need of repair—it was probably one of his more convincing imitations.

What, after all, was to be gained by making a big production out of sneaking up on the place? All Rênal had to do was to look out the window and he would see whoever was outside. And if he saw him, he saw him—so what? Rênal had, so far as he was aware, no reason to know what a Raymond Guinness was. He probably wasn't a frequent enough visitor to have much of an idea who belonged in the neighborhood and who didn't; the more you looked like part of the furniture, the better.

That window was right there on the second floor—Guinness tried not to look up when he turned toward the front entrance. He reached into his jacket pocket and took out Janine's car keys, just as if he planned to use them to let himself in. There was, in fact, a main door, but the lock was old-fashioned and childishly simple and Guinness could pick it so fast that a casual observer might have supposed he was actually using a key.

The inside stairway was carpeted and, in the tiny foyer, there was a small wicker table supporting a vase full of dried flowers. An intensely domestic atmosphere enveloped you the instant you closed the door behind yourself; it hardly seemed a place for breaking down doors and threats and violence and death. It was difficult to believe that such things could encroach on this tidy privacy. Guinness took out his small, nickle-plated automatic, snicked off the safety catch, and tucked it back into the waistline of his trousers.

Fortunately, the stairway seemed to be cement under the carpeting; the steps didn't creak and it was possible to proceed as quietly as a shadow. When he reached the second floor, he took out his automatic again. It looked as if he might need it—Amalia Brouwer's front door was standing open about three inches.

Well, he could have spared himself any anxiety about the stealthiness of his approach. He could have come galumphing up the stairwell at the head of the brass section of the Concertgebouw—Rênal wouldn't have minded. For all the startled expression on his face as he sat on the floor, his back resting in the angle between the wall and the end of Amalia Brouwer's much-loved bed, Rênal was well beyond any such considerations.

But he did look surprised. *I wasn't expecting you,* he seemed to be saying. Although what he probably hadn't been expecting wasn't Guinness but the rather garish bullet hole in his left cheekbone, just under the eye.

Somebody hadn't been kidding around—a fair share of the back of Rênal's head was decorating the room. There was blood everywhere, all over the bedspread and the carpet and in a long ugly smear down the wall, running into where the major lay crumpled like a discarded doll. A fair quantity had even run out through the bullet hole and down over his nose and mouth to collect in a pool on his shirtfront. It was like a slaughterhouse; you could smell it in every room in the apartment.

One assumed something on the order of a nine-millimeter. That kind of damage hadn't been achieved with a .22.

Guinness squatted down and peered into Rênal's dead eyes. They were pretty badly blackened from the impact of the bullet—there weren't any pretty gunshot victims—but the pupils were just beginning to cloud over. He probably hadn't been dead for much more than half an hour.

It figured. At that time of the day, almost everyone would be at work or out amusing themselves in the warm summer sunshine. The building was probably deserted; no one would have heard the shot, and if they had they wouldn't have bothered to investigate a single sharp puff of sound.

And then the killer would have slipped out, leaving the door slightly ajar so that it wouldn't take five or six days for them to discover the body. Probably as early as this evening someone in the house would realize that something was wrong—people just didn't leave their doors open in Europe, and in the middle of the summer a corpse ripens fairly fast.

It wasn't a very pleasant task, but Guinness set himself to looking through the dead man's pockets. You never knew—it might be worth something to know what they wanted found on the poor son of a bitch.

There wasn't much. Some change in the right-hand jacket pocket, a handkerchief, a black plastic comb, a slender gold-filled ballpoint pen in the pocket of his shirt.

His wallet was lying in plain sight on top of the chest of drawers, and Guinness went through that as well. It contained a passport, a driver's license, a few credit cards, a receipt for a couple of shirts bought in a department store in Brussels the week before, and close to fifteen thousand francs in large bills. Obviously, the murderer hadn't been interested in robbery.

It was painfully apparent that little Amalia was being set up to take the fall for this—God knows, she hadn't killed Rênal; she had been out of the building for hours, and Rênal was still very fresh meat. But she was going to take the fall. Her dead lover, in her apartment—his picture still stood on the night table—and doubtless she herself was slated for a precipitous disappearance. It wouldn't matter to her, of course, because Flycatcher was going to arrange things so she wouldn't be alive to be embarrassed by the police inquiries, but this particular homicide was going to be laid right at her pretty little feet.

One wondered why, though. Probably Flycatcher had set it up this way from the beginning—we run a snitch through an inexperienced girl so we can blow him away in her apartment and hang it on her—but what the hell for? Why do we want to draw so much attention to the disappearance and death of Major Jean Rênal? Why don't we just snatch him off the sidewalk some dark night and drop him in the Atlantic with enough scrap iron tied around his neck so that he'll stay down and never bother anybody again?

"Why didn't they do that, hey, Rênal?" he murmured, crouched down once again to look into the dead man's face. "What are you doing here, pal? Hmmmm?" But Rênal didn't have any answers; he merely continued to stare straight ahead, his face a mask of astonishment. *Isn't it amazing. I'm dead, the last thing in the world I expected.*

And all that money—they wanted to be sure that the

investigating authorities knew Rênal was doing a flit and wasn't just up for a weekend of muff diving. You didn't leave fifteen thousand francs behind unless you meant to, and they meant to make the major look just as guilty as they could manage. It was certainly an odd way to treat your employees, but then working for Flycatcher wasn't like being in the Civil Service.

Guinness rose and went into the bathroom to wash his hands. He hadn't been in the apartment more than two or three minutes and he didn't like to stay any longer than necessary—he wouldn't care to have someone walk in and find him there and, after all, how long would it be before whoever killed Rênal would pay a little visit to the bookstore and invite Amalia out for a drive in the country?—but handling corpses wasn't the sort of thing he really much enjoyed and he thought he could possibly spare the few seconds it would take to wash the blood from his fingers.

He took Rênal's passport and all but about four hundred francs of the money with him, stuffing them into his coat pocket.

He stopped in the corridor for a moment and looked around. It was a pokey little place, very much like the apartment in which his second wife had been living when he had leaned over the counter in the typing pool that first afternoon and asked her for a date. They had gone to a movie and then come back to the walk-up over a jewelry store she called home to crease the sheets a little and spend the hours between one and two in the morning polishing off about four boxes of frozen waffles.

Louise had grown tired of clerking in an insurance company and had gone back to school for an MA—she had some vague idea about teaching Jane Austen in some rustic junior college—and Guinness, who was in that long hiatus between employers when he thought maybe he would be able to stay out of the headhunter business, was a brand spanking new assistant professor of English literature. They managed to hold it together for about five years before the inevitable happened and somebody with a grudge from the old days had looked Guinness up and, not finding him in, had left Louise on her kitchen floor with an icepick sticking out of her ear. So much for happy times and the illusion of safety.

How old had she been when Guinness had come along to invite her to come out to dinner with him and attach a time fuse to her life? Twenty-six or seven, certainly no more. And Amalia Brouwer, what was she? Even younger—perhaps twenty-three. He went into the bathroom and, after a little hunting, found a thin wafer of soap perfectly camouflaged against one of the white porcelain corners of the famous bathtub. He ran a thin stream of warm water into the basin and, when he had rinsed off the soap film, dried his hands very carefully on a small towel that was draped over a ring next to the mirror.

Amalia Brouwer's nightie was hanging from a hook on the inside of the bathroom door; it was a little yellow cotton thing with a bit of fake lace trim around the hem, the sort of item you could pick up for ten dollars in any department store in the civilized world. Guinness was still holding the towel when he happened to turn around and see it there, and its effect on him would have been difficult for him to explain.

"My God—they're going to kill that girl," he found himself whispering, startled that something he had known from the beginning should suddenly strike him with the force of a revelation.

That was what they were going to do, and they probably weren't going to wait around about it much longer. It was the obvious play, to deal with Rênal and his girlfriend separately—they would hardly wish to drag her screaming from her apartment after they had shot him in front of her eyes—but there would be no reason for them to linger now.

Rênal was dead, but not for more than a few minutes. So what was Raymond Guinness, champion of the innocent, protector of damsels in distress, doing standing around drying his hands? Quite obviously, there just wasn't any more time to waste with sentimental gestures.

He threw the towel into the bathtub and within a few minutes was closing the apartment door behind him. He twisted the handle gently to make sure it had locked—there wasn't any point in drawing attention to the fact that there was a dead man in Amalia Brouwer's bedroom; she would have quite enough on her plate for the next several hours without having to fret about the police. When he reached the street, he tried to walk as fast as he could without giving the impression, should anyone happen to be watching, that he was in a hurry. His car driving away was the only sound in the quiet neighborhood.

14

The street on which the bookstore was located was closed to automobile traffic—it was too narrow, for one thing, and probably the city fathers worried about what the vibration from all those cars would do to their four-hundred-year-old footbridge, which was only half a block away. So that particular little stretch of cobblestone was a pedestrian mall; a fine idea if you leave out of consideration the needs of cloak-and-dagger types, who might feel a little nervy about trying to make a quick getaway on nothing but their shoe leather.

But there were other streets, and one of them, the next over, faced onto an alley that led back to an open courtyard not more than thirty feet square where the bookstore had its rear entrance. After all, you could hardly expect the delivery men to carry crates in balanced on their heads.

Guinness parked his car at the mouth of the alley. He might get a traffic ticket, but at least no one would be able to block off the entrance. The alley and the courtyard were too open to permit an ambush, so his escape, at least as far as the car, would be reasonably safe. That was as much as you could ask for.

He didn't even try the back door but walked around the block to the front. It was an enormous relief to look in through the main window and see Amalia Brouwer quietly reading a magazine as she sat behind the cash register. At least Flycatcher wasn't making a big hurry-hurry production out of it—apparently he still thought he had the wind at his back.

It was clear from the way she looked up, smiled, and then went back to her magazine that the man coming through the door didn't mean anything special to her—he was just another customer who would poke around through the shelves for a while, buy something, grunt when she gave him his change and said thank you, and then leave. Her face had registered nothing but the indifference of a shopgirl's greeting, and he doubted she was so consummate an actress that she could have concealed it from him if she had recognized him as anyone significant.

And that was fine. He had been giving her a wide berth ever since his arrival in Amsterdam, for the simple reason that, when this moment came, he wanted to catch her flat-footed, off her guard, without any preset response that could get in the way. He wanted just to scoop her up, so she wouldn't have time to think beyond the basic facts. She had been set up, and he was there to get her out of the line of fire—that would be enough for her to have to deal with; he didn't want to afford her the liberty for resentment or resistence or any other funny feminine motives for not doing precisely what she was told. Survival was going to be the issue. Cleverness would probably accomplish nothing more than getting her killed.

He went over to the wall with all the Penguin paperbacks and started looking through them, keeping his back to her and listening to make sure they were absolutely alone. The old lady usually left by around eleven-fifteen—he had seen her leave that first morning with what he presumed were the previous day's receipts in a brown canvas bank bag, and Janine had since confirmed it as part of the routine—but he wanted to be sure. He let his hand rest against the bookcase, as if that would help him to hear into the stockroom that could reasonably be assumed to be behind the heavy green curtains that covered a doorway cut through the wall at right angles to Amalia Brouwer's cash register. There were no sounds of boxes being moved around, no scraping of chairs, not even the tinkling of a radio. Nothing. If anyone was back there, they were either holding their breath or dead, and after a while the one amounted to the other, so there was no problem.

The Penguins didn't seem to be arranged in any particular order—in with a prose translation of the Anglo-Saxon elegies, *The Eustace Diamonds*, and volumes one and four of a collection of ghost stories was a copy of Conrad's *Under Western Eyes*. Guinness had tried to assign it for a course once, only to discover that it seemed to be completely out of print. He picked it off the shelf and turned around to look at Amalia, who was separated from him by a display stand full of French novels and who paid no attention to him whatsoever.

But that meant nothing. That was part of the decorum of bookstores the world over—nobody bothered you while you were browsing; you didn't exist unless you tried to steal something or had presented yourself to the counter and were ready to leave.

He allowed himself a nice leisurely stare—it didn't matter anymore whether she noticed or not, since in a few seconds he would become, for a while, the most important person in her life; and he felt the need to size her up, to settle on some mode of approach that might make all the difference as he tried to persuade her that the gray Opel parked at the mouth of the alley behind this building was her only vehicle to salvation.

And suddenly it occurred to Guinness that he felt sorry for her. She had been something of an abstraction up until that moment, but all at once she was quite real, a pretty girl sitting behind a counter while she read a magazine. He had seen a hundred girls just like her in his lifetime; they would come into his classes when he had been a college professor back in California and lean their tennis rackets against the legs of their chairs while they scribbled down in their spiral notebooks the facts of the English sonnet tradition or, more likely, wrote long letters to their boyfriends back home in Fresno. Amalia Brouwer wasn't so very much older, only two or three years, and she had that wonderful look of suppleness that seems to go with tanned skin and shoulder-length brown hair. She was up to her neck in trouble, the kind of trouble that could end her young life, although she hardly suspected it, and she wasn't really any more than a child. So far, for her, it had all been slogans and rushing around to cell meetings and heavy breathing in the name of the oppressed proletariat. There had been no chance for anything else; there hadn't been time.

He went up to the cash register, and, at last, she raised her eyes to him and smiled. It was a nice smile, although of course it didn't mean a thing, and he could see that her eyes were a moist brown and had the same oddly humorous quality as her father's, as if any moment she would break out into a laugh. He set the book down on the counter, and she turned it around to look at the price, and he reached inside his jacket to take out his billfold; he was already holding out a ten-florin note when she asked, in English, was there anything else?

"Yes. I wonder if you would have a copy of Maarten Huygen's *Counterespionage in the Netherlands*—I'd like the German edition."

You could watch the color drain away under the tan as her face hardened into a rigid mask. The cash drawer was already open, and she gripped its edge until her knuckles were white. It was nice to have caught someone so completely unprepared; it meant you had, for the moment, the home court advantage.

"Are you a policeman?" she asked, the words a quick jumble, as if forced out under pressure. She was really frightened, and her slender breast kept tightening the front of her cotton dress as she tried to catch her breath. You almost had the impression that this was the first time it had occurred to her that people went to jail for the sort of thing she had been up to.

Guinness smiled at her, but not in a way calculated to make anyone feel more at ease—it was a cruel smile, a display of malice and teeth.

"No, sweetheart, I'm not a policeman. I'm your guardian angel, come to save your goddamned silly little neck for you. You have a choice—you can come with me now, or you can go off with your friend with the white hair and end the evening buried face-down in a sandpit somewhere."

She simply glared at him. Her brown eyes had lost their look of amusement and now reflected nothing but the defiance of a hunted animal, cornered and hard pressed, but certain, at least, against whom she had to defend herself.

Well, Guinness hadn't really expected to be believed.

He put the ten-florin note back into his billfold and returned it to his inside jacket pocket, as if he had nothing else on his mind.

"By the way," he went on, "they got your boyfriend. Rênal is lying on the floor in your bedroom with the back of his head shot away. There's blood all over the place—I'm afraid your landlady's going to be furious."

"What are you talking about?"

"What do you mean, what am I talking about? He's dead. They went up to your apartment about forty-five minutes ago and blew him away. You don't believe me?—where do you think I picked up these?"

The passport and the fourteen-some-odd thousand francs were still in his left coat pocket. He took them out and dumped them on the counter, and Amalia Brouwer started, actually started, when she saw them. And then, very tentatively, with just the tip of her finger, she turned back the cover of the passport to look at the photograph on the inside of the second page. It was Rênal's right enough, with the seal of the Belgian Foreign Office embossed across the lower right-hand corner. It wasn't the sort of document a practical joker could pick up at your local novelty store.

"Then he is dead," she said, quite calmly—it was impossible not to feel a certain grudging respect for the way she was handling herself. "Either that, or he is under arrest. In any case, you could have been the one to kill him—I think, on the whole, that is the likelier explanation."

"Don't be an idiot. If I'd had him arrested, I'd arrest you too, and I'm manifestly not interested in doing that. And, if I'm not the police, why should I care about Jean Rênal enough to kill him? I didn't come all this way to fool with him."

"Then why did you come?"

He glanced at the front window. The lunchtime crowds were beginning to surge by, and Guinness studied their movements for a few seconds, trying to pick out any familiar faces. There weren't any, but how long could it take? Someone would be by soon enough, and all he would have to do was look in to see that Miss Brouwer was not alone, that she was keeping most unsatisfactory company and that steps would have to be taken. Guinness didn't want any steps taken—not now, not while it could still matter.

"Not here," he said, and took Amalia by the arm and began pulling her toward the green-curtained entrance to the back room. For a moment she resisted; she pulled away from him as if he were a common masher, some stranger taking a liberty. But Guinness discovered he had very little patience with balky young girls—he simply couldn't be bothered—so he dug his fingers into the soft flesh just above the inside of her elbow, where the median nerve rested against the bone, and when her eyes began to grow large with the pain he more or less dragged her along. She was no trouble at all.

The stockroom was cooler than the store. There were crates of books everywhere on the floor and two long workbenches on either side of the entrance, on which various posters and promotional mail were scattered. It was untidy and private, and you could probably scream your head off without being heard by anybody who wasn't immediately in the next room. Guinness pushed Amalia Brouwer over toward one of the two high stools that stood in front of either of the workbenches. When she was perched, she started rubbing her arm where he had held it, as if she wanted to make him feel ashamed of being such a brute, peering out at him suspiciously from underneath her scant eyebrows.

"Why did you come?"

Guinness grinned at her and sat down on the other stool, wondering why they all thought their precious dignity was so inviolate.

And then he told her—at least, he told her some of it. He rehearsed Flycatcher's record for her, the particular kind of bestiality with which he had made a name for himself, the fact that—her impressions to the contrary—the man had no allegiance to anything except money, and that there was hard evidence that she had been elected to take the fall on this particular occasion.

"Figure it for yourself. Rênal is dead. He's lying in your bedroom and you're scheduled to disappear today, to run off with Lover Boy to a life of indescribable happiness in the Workers' Paradise—that was the idea, wasn't it? And today was to be the big day?"

He knew he was right, had been right all along, from the way her eyes kept glancing off his face, as if she couldn't bear to look at him. He only wondered why he wasn't feeling more satisfaction with his victory.

"What do you imagine the police will make of it? A corpse in your boudoir and you've skipped out—what would you make of it? You're being set up, so why should they take the risk of leaving you alive?"

She could see the logic of it; that was obvious. She was smart enough for that. Her hands were curled in her lap and she was watching them closely, as if imagining that they too might somehow be brought to betray her. But the dream dies hard.

"I have nothing but your unsupported word that Jean is dead. A passport could be manufactured to order, I imagine—it proves nothing." She didn't even believe it herself.

"Then we'll just have to wait and see, won't we. What time are they supposed to come and fetch you?"

She wouldn't answer, of course; she merely shook her head and frowned.

"By the way—what name did he use with you? You needn't worry that you'll be betraying anything; it won't have been his real one. I shouldn't be surprised if it's been so long since he used that that he's forgotten it himself."

The question seemed to surprise her, making her look up from her hands and stare at him as if she were seeing him for the first time.

"Günner—Günner Borlund. He is Swedish."

"It may even be true."

For a long time they said very little to each other. They kept to their two stools, on opposite sides of the doorway, and Guinness occupied himself with a month-old copy of *Newsweek* that someone had left lying open on a stack of mailing envelopes. There was an article on the San Francisco Bay Area, where he had once lived, and he read it and looked at the color photographs and experienced something like a twinge of homesickness. He had liked it in California—aside from England, it was the only place he could imagine thinking of as home. Certainly Ohio wouldn't have qualified; he had been born there and was twenty-one before he ever got over the state line, but he remembered Columbus as a barren, forbidding, unhappy place and had never been back. In this life, if you were smart, you picked your hometowns for yourself.

Amalia Brouwer remained perfectly quiet. Guinness had taken Janine's shiny little automatic out of his belt and placed it on the counter next to him. He never even looked at it and hardly looked at her, but its mere presence seemed to be enough to keep her anchored in her place.

"He will telephone first," she said suddenly. "He will not come himself and he always telephones when he sends someone for me, so that I will know it is not a trap of some sort. I thought perhaps I should tell you. I should hate for you to imagine anything sinister." Her face was composed, but the faint timbre of contempt was unmistakable in her voice. Well, to hell with her.

"I promise not to jump out of my skin." He smiled, again not very nicely. "But before you go feeding him any little code words or otherwise indicating your distress, you might think to ask about Rênal. Just a piece of friendly advice—you do whatever you feel like."

And then he went back to his magazine. And again it was several minutes before either of them spoke.

"Why did you come?"

She looked at him with moist, unhappy eyes, almost writhing on her stool. And again, as in the instant before he first spoke to her, she managed to draw from him a brief spasm of pity—was there anything so terrible as doubt? When she knew for certain that she was betrayed, even then, she would be happier than she was at that moment, when she didn't know what she could trust herself to believe.

"Why have you come? Who are you that you should care, if you are not the police? Why could you not have left me alone?"

Well, yes. He supposed she would insist upon knowing. And, really, he couldn't think of any reason why she shouldn't know, except that it was the sort of disclosure Guinness couldn't help but shrink from making. It seemed almost a violation of privacy, but he supposed Amalia Brouwer had a right to so much of the truth as her own limitations could allow her to understand.

Guinness closed his magazine, wishing suddenly that this could have been simply another job, that he could have concerned himself with the relatively uncomplicated problems of effecting a murder, pure and simple, that he could have been spared these nice questions of credence and feeling. After all, when you killed someone at least you didn't have to persuade them that they were dead.

"I'm just a messenger boy," he said at last, his voice flat, as expressionless as he could make it. "For myself, I don't care anything about the matter. I was sent by someone else; he wants you gotten clear."

"Then who is this 'someone else?' "

"I've already told you, although probably you weren't listening. I come from Maarten Huygens—I trust you can still recall the name."

Guinness also had a daughter. He doubted he would ever see her again—she was almost as much of an abstraction to him as the little curly-haired Amalia had been to Emil Kätzner—but he hoped she might entertain a kinder memory of him than, apparently, the grown-up Amalia did of her father. Either that, or no memory at all—in the final count, that might be the best. But he hoped he wasn't hated. He hoped no one would ever see such an expression on his child's face at the mention of his name.

"Maarten Huygens never existed," she answered coldly, when finally she could bring herself to answer at all. "Maarten Huygens was a fiction, a bad dream, and when we all woke up we saw that there was nothing there but an empty space. So how could he have sent you?"

Guinness got off his stool—he discovered that his ass was beginning to hurt, so he slipped the automatic back inside the waistline of his trousers and stretched his legs, walking back and forth to the middle of the narrow little room. He didn't look at Amalia Brouwer's face anymore.

"Very well, have it your own way. But I met someone who remembers having been Maarten Huygens, who remembers you and would be just as happy if you could be kept alive. Do you remember your father at all? I've only met him twice in my life, but I should say he was the sort to leave an impression. He still has his red moustache."

"You might know that from a photograph—it proves nothing."

"No, I didn't get it from a photograph." He shook his head and smiled. "Did you ever see a photograph of your father? I doubt it. He was an East German agent, and a very good one. Before that he worked for the NKVD against the Nazis, and before that he fought against the Fascists in Spain. Like I said, he's very good—I don't imagine he's ever been dumb enough to leave any photographs behind him, do you?"

He would never know what she was going to say, because that was the moment the telephone chose to ring.

The conversation took place in French, which was not Guinness's strongest language. But he imagined he understood enough to know that she hadn't told "Günner" that she had a visitor. But you never knew, of course; the language itself might have been some sort of signal, and everybody always had just oodles of clever little code words they could work into almost any sentence to indicate they were in trouble—that sort of business was standard practice. And she had asked about Rênal. So you never knew.

"Did you understand?" she asked, setting the telephone receiver back down on its cradle. Guinness shook his head—he didn't see why he should feel under any compulsion to tell the truth.

"Not a word. What did he say?"

"Someone will be here in twenty minutes."

"What did he say about Rênal? I'm assuming you were bright enough not to take it simply on faith."

Amalia Brouwer regarded him with a kind of weary antagonism, and he knew he had won. She realized now that he hadn't been lying to her, and naturally she resented it—hadn't he robbed her of something? She would grudge him his triumph over her, but at least she would no longer proceed on any assumption that she knew who her friends were.

"Yes—yes, I was bright enough. Günner said that Jean was already there with them, that he had been brought in half an hour ago."

"Half an hour ago Jean was just beginning to come down with *rigor mortis.* Did you ask to talk to him?"

"No. I did not think of that."

"Just as well—your Günner might have smelled a rat. I don't suppose you're usually so wonderfully solicitous about your precious major."

It wasn't a very nice way to treat her—she stood next to the curtained doorway with her arms folded shelteringly over her breast, and she looked as if another word would knock her to the ground. She was thinking about Jean Rênal lying on her bedroom floor; Guinness had no idea what she might or might not have felt for him, but it was fairly clear that the contemplation of her own role in her sometime-lover's death perhaps wasn't the happiest train of thought that could have passed through her mind. Well, there was no harm in that. It wouldn't kill her if she lost some of her romantic illusions about the life into which Flycatcher had led her.

She closed her eyes, slowly twisting her head down and to the side in a manner that suggested something like real pain.

"Why can't you just leave me alone?" she asked again. There were tears in her voice and starting out from between her tightly shut eyelids. It was pitiful to watch and, as Guinness realized quickly enough, necessary to end—after all, Flycatcher's man would be there in less than twenty minutes.

"Not in the cards, Sweetheart. If I just leave you alone you'll end up just as dead as Jean, and we can't have that—your papa wouldn't like it. So come on. Pull yourself together. You can have a good cry over your lost innocence another time."

He took his handkerchief out of his trousers pocket and offered it to her, but she turned away from him. There was a box of kleenex on the stockroom counter—she didn't need him.

"Would I be permitted to go to the washroom and rinse off my face, or would you shoot me if I tried?"

"Go ahead—be my guest." He smiled at her with a contemptuous amusement he didn't feel. She wasn't going to pull a fast one now; she wasn't that stupid. And if detesting him was going to help her to keep from coming all unstuck again, that was all right too. Fortunately, it wasn't part of his task to be popular.

And she did come back, almost immediately. She had washed away all evidence of her recent emotional crisis and looked perfectly crisp and efficient again, as impersonal as a department-store mannequin. Guinness recalled the businesslike white cotton underwear he had found in the drawers of her bureau and decided that Amalia Brouwer probably wasn't nearly as tough as she thought she was, but it wouldn't hurt if she hung onto her sustaining myth perhaps just a little longer. Over the next few hours, she might really need to believe she was the iron maiden.

He told her what he wanted her to do when her lift showed up. It wasn't very complicated—all she had to manage was to sit out front by the cash register and let him have the work of convincing her that he wasn't just another customer.

"Just be sure that you make him come to you—will you know him?"

"No." She shook her head. "If it were going to be someone I would recognize, Günner would have said so."

"So much the better. Just sit so you're not facing the window directly—we wouldn't want him standing out in the street and waving at you. He'll come inside, and he'll close the door after himself, and then all you have to do is ignore him, just the way you would if he were somebody who's come in to check out the naked ladies on the magazine covers. Once he's inside, we've got him cold, but the farther he gets away from the door the better—we wouldn't want him to get any bright ideas."

"How do you know I will do as you ask? How can you be sure I won't signal him away?" It wasn't so much a question as a gesture of defiance. She stood in front of him, with her arms down at her sides, hating his guts, but they both knew she wasn't contemplating anything of the sort.

"How do I know you didn't signal Günner over the phone? I just have to hope you're not that stupid—besides, why would I bother with any of this, why wouldn't I just spirit you away now, if I didn't know I could make you believe me this way? I just have to count on that—if you want to know the truth, you'll do as I tell you for just a while longer. You don't have very much to lose, do you."

No, she didn't have very much to lose. Even she saw that. So she went out to the front and resumed her seat behind the cash register, bending her head down over the same magazine that she had been reading when he first came in. And Guinness waited out of sight behind the heavy green curtains, far enough away from them that not even the shadows cast by his legs would be visible underneath.

It was a long wait, but it was always a long wait when you had to stand perfectly still and count off the seconds like a schoolboy watching the clock through the last hour of the term. Actually it wasn't more than twelve or fourteen minutes before the little bell tinkled over the front door—it seemed almost that long before Guinness heard the same sound again, followed by the click of the lock catching as the door closed.

"Yes?"

He couldn't hear the man's reply, only a faint murmur of indistinguishable words, only enough to tell that it was, in fact, a man. Nothing more. Amalia Brouwer had spoken to him in English, which meant that she believed this was the right one.

"Yes."

There—she had said it again. That was Guinness's cue.

He stepped forward, sweeping the curtain aside with his right hand. In his left was the automatic. And the man whose voice had come to him as nothing more than a low rhythm of sound stood in front of the counter, his hands thrust deep into the pockets of a tan raincoat; he turned and looked at Guinness and then looked at the gun in Guinness's hand—it was impossible to say which surprised him more.

"You've got just the one chance," Guinness said quietly. "I want to see the palms of your hands, so bring them out where I can look at them and do it very slowly. I hate surprises."

15

He was a chubby, pop-eyed man of slightly more than average height, with curly dishwater-blond hair and greasy, yellowish skin. But if he wasn't very prepossessing, he also wasn't a hopeless fool—he brought his hands out of his pockets, empty and with the fingers spread. Guinness nodded and motioned him forward, pulling him through the curtained doorway, into the stockroom and out of sight of the street. They had things to discuss.

"You did that very well," he said, running his right hand over the man's pockets and along his ribcage as he felt for a weapon. There was a .45 Colt automatic in a shoulder holster—Guinness had never been able to understand how anyone could bear to walk around with a lump like that under his armpit, but there seemed to be something about shoulder rigs that appealed to some men's sense of *machismo*—he reached in under the raincoat and pulled it out, keeping the muzzle of his own pistol pressed hard against his prisoner's soft belly while he did it. For some reason fat men always lived in deadly fear of being gut-shot; just the merest threat of it settled them down wonderfully.

"I'm not an idiot, mister." Without moving his head a millimeter, the man looked down over the curve of his cheeks at the weapon in Guinness's left hand. "I know who you are, and I like breathin'."

"Good for you."

Amalia Brouwer was still standing with her back against

the green curtains, her hands lost somewhere behind the folds of her skirt. She didn't give the impression she was much enjoying the proceedings. Guinness held out the .45 to her and she stared at it blankly, as if she couldn't imagine the uses to which such a device could be put. Maybe she couldn't.

"Here, hold onto this."

In the end, the best she could manage was to bring one of her hands out from behind her skirt, extending it palm up. Guinness laid the huge weapon there, keeping hold of it as her fingers began to curl around the barrel and the trigger guard. She would accept possession of the thing and that was all; that much was obvious. She was a neutral—she wasn't going to point it at anybody.

Guinness had half-turned away from the other man. He kept his eyes on Amalia and he transferred the little nickel-plated automatic over to his right hand.

And then he took a quarter-step back with his left foot and, in a single smooth movement, twisted around counterclockwise at the waist and drove his left elbow into the man's midsection, just an inch or two below the breastbone. There was a short, painful-sounding gasp, and the man doubled over and crumpled to his knees, holding his stomach with both hands and pressing inward with his fingers, seemingly in an effort to keep it from tearing open.

After a moment, when he seemed unable any longer even to kneel, he brought one hand down to the floor to steady himself. Guinness waited perhaps a second and a half, while the arm began to accept some of the strain, and then swept it away with his foot. The man toppled over face first and, as soon as he was down, Guinness kicked him, hard, just under the right armpit. The sound he made as he lay there writhing on the cement floor was something between a sob and a deep, excruciating gurgle, terrible to hear.

"Have you got any twine?"

When there was no answer, Guinness turned around and found Amalia Brouwer staring at the man on the floor with a kind of appalled fascination. The .45 automatic was still cradled in her hand, but she seemed to have forgotten all about it; the only object in the universe was the man on the floor in front of her Guinness put his gun back inside the waistband of his trousers.

"Some twine? You know—string. Something like that. What's the matter, have you gone stony deaf? Get me some fucking twine, for Christ's sake!"

Finally, when she could tear her eyes away from the little drama of the man on the floor, she looked up at Guinness with an expression of dumb incomprehension. He reached over and took the .45 away from her, not out of any concern over her intentions but because she seemed ready to let it slip from her hand to the floor out of sheer absence of mind.

"My God," she said slowly, apparently still not quite able to comprehend what had happened. "Why would you . . . ?" The question simply trailed off into silence.

Guinness, by this time, had found the twine for himself—there were several spools of it in a drawer under one of the counters, along with a pair of scissors and a great quantity of mailing labels—and he was industriously tying his victim's hands together behind his back. There was little enough danger the man would try anything, but people always feel so much more helpless and vulnerable when they're lying face down on the floor with their hands tied.

"We were going to ask him a few questions, remember? Well—I just wanted to make sure we'd have his undivided attention. There now."

He stood up, taking the .45 from where it had been laying on a cardboard carton, and wiped off his hands on his trousers—first the left one, then the right, shifting the huge automatic back and forth between them. Then he stepped over to

Amalia and took her by the arm again, rather more gently this time, and led her over to where the man was trying to look up at them through large, terrified eyes. She was still speechless and followed along as meekly as a lamb. Guinness sat her down on another of the dozen or so book cartons in the tiny room, one where she would have a ringside seat to the proceedings, and then sat down himself on the floor, almost at her feet. He wasn't more than eighteen or twenty inches away from his nameless victim's face, and he cocked the hammer of the .45 and rested the muzzle casually against the man's thick neck, just below the corner of his jaw.

"Tell you what, pal—I'm going to ask you a couple of questions. I already know the answers, but the lady doesn't. If you tell us the truth, then everything will be fine, but if you try to lie to us, then I'm going to pull this trigger. I hope you believe me, pal, because I've used one of these mothers a couple of times before and they make a terrific mess. You believe me, pal, don't you? Hmmm?"

The man's face was badly bruised—Guinness wouldn't have been surprised if his nose was broken; there were thick tracks of blood streaming down from his nostrils—and he nodded painfully, trying not to move at all where the .45 pressed into the folds of his neck.

"Yeah. Yeah, I believe you."

And he did, too. Guinness glanced up at Amalia Brouwer, whose hands were folded together in her lap and whose slender body seemed coiled like a steel spring. She believed him so much that if he had fired at that moment she would have shot straight up through the ceiling. She was all primed for it.

"Okay, question number one: where's Rênal?"

"He's dead." The man's tongue came out perhaps a quarter of an inch and he made a brief stab at licking his lips, which were already so dry they almost looked cracked, but his tongue was just as dry, so it didn't seem to help. "They shot him. I wasn't even there—I didn't shoot him."

His eyes flickered up at Guinness, begging to be believed, and Guinness nodded, smiling.

"He was the lady's friend, pal, not mine. I really don't care whether you killed him or not. But try again. He's dead—*where* is he dead? I want to know where they left him, understand?"

"In the girl's apartment. Please, mister . . ."

But Guinness silenced him with a touch of the muzzle of the huge automatic.

"We're not finished, pal. I want you to tell the lady what they had in mind for her. Go ahead—don't be shy."

The man's eyes once again hunted for Guinness's face. Would he have to say it? Would he really have to say it? Yes—he would have to.

"We've got a farmhouse—it's away from everywhere, and one of the fields was turned over with a tiller just a couple of weeks ago. I was told to bury her out there."

Guinness glanced up at Amalia Brouwer and raised his eyebrows in a silent, half-mocking question. Was she satisfied? Would she believe him now? His answer was a barely suppressed shudder, as if she were already looking down into the damp, earthy-smelling grave.

"Now, one last question—who gave the order? I want her to hear his name." They waited, and the man tried once again to wet his lips, and then he shook his head.

"I don't know his name—if he has one. You know him, though. You've hunted him long enough."

"Is it Flycatcher?"

The man neither moved his head nor spoke, not for several seconds. He merely stared up into Guinness's face. And then, once more, his tongue passed over his dry lips.

"You know him, and he knows you. He don't scare easy, but you follow him around like a ghost. He hates you."

"Then it's Flycatcher."

Guinness put his thumb on the .45's hammer and let it down very slowly. He rose from the floor and looked around the room, as if searching for something. Then he pulled back the sleeve of his jacket and checked his watch.

"When will the old woman come back?" The question had been directed at Amalia, but she didn't seem to hear him. She sat on the cardboard carton, her hands still folded in her lap, seemingly lost in some private grief where she couldn't be reached by the sound of the human voice.

Had she loved Flycatcher? Or was she mourning for Jean Rênal, and for her part in his cruel, sordid end? Or was it for herself she mourned, for the believer in causes, for the child warrior who had been so happy to lose herself in the larger struggle? And now Flycatcher had been revealed as her worst enemy, and Rênal was dead, and the cause was nothing but the taste of ashes. Guinness was sorry, at that moment, that he couldn't have been Emil Kätzner. He was himself nothing but a common mercenary who had never believed in anything, who had never had an innocence to lose. Her father would have understood better and might have found something to say, some word of comfort—or, at least, of understanding—in this most terrible moment of her young life.

But he wasn't Emil Kätzner; he was only himself. So he put his hand on her shoulder and waited until she noticed and looked up into his face.

"The old woman, when will she come back?"

"She will not," she said, her brown eyes, so like her father's, swimming with tears. "I told her I would watch the store today so she could visit her sister—I did not want her here when the time came."

Guinness nodded. "Go get your coat and your handbag—it's time to go."

And while Amalia was gone, to fetch her things and perhaps to once more wash the sting from her face, Guinness crouched down beside the figure on the floor, who was still watching him with an intensity that hardly allowed for the taking of a breath.

He reached into the pocket of his jacket and took out a hard leather case, smaller than a pack of cigarettes—inside was a syringe, about the length and thickness of your little finger, and three tiny numbered vials of clear fluid. He filled the syringe out of the vial marked "2" and gave the plunger a slight push to force out the last bubble of air. Vial "2" was worth about five hours of deathlike sleep—you woke up with a crushing headache, but you woke up alive.

"What's that stuff?"

Guinness looked down at the puffy, frightened face and grinned rattily.

"You're taking a nap, my friend. A little snooze. When you wake up, if you're lucky enough to wake up before Flycatcher gets impatient and sends a couple of goons out looking for you, you'd be well advised to get yourself far, far away. He doesn't like screw-ups. Sleep tight."

He forced the needle in just where the trapezius muscle joins the neck. There was a little gurgling sound, and the body on the floor went perfectly slack. You couldn't even hear him breathe—Guinness pressed his thumb against the man's carotid artery just to be sure he was still alive; there was a heartbeat, but it was already very slow.

He noticed that the man's hands, which were still tied behind his back, were beginning to take on a reddish, puffy look—in another few hours they would probably be black. When he remembered the pair of scissors in the drawer where he had found the twine, he got up and fetched them and severed the bonds. Both arms immediately slipped to the floor with a thud.

When Amalia came back into the room, the first question she asked was, "Did you kill him?" She seemed to expect that he had.

"No, I just gave him something to put him to sleep. I'm glad the old lady is out of the way; she'd probably drop dead from shock if she saw him lying here like this. In a couple of hours he'll wake up and leave under his own power—no one will ever know he was even here."

Was it possible she was disappointed? She stood there, gazing down at the two of them as she clutched her large envelope-shaped pocketbook in both hands, her face an unreadable conflict of emotions. Perhaps she was expecting to exact some sort of revenge.

Guinness stepped over to the workbench and took the .45 automatic from where he had set it down while he was looking for the scissors; he held it out for her to see.

"He didn't shoot Rênal," he said quietly. "At least, not with this. Rênal was killed with something smaller, something on the order of a nine-millimeter, I would guess." He gestured toward the limp, almost corpselike shape at their feet and shook his head. "If you think it'd make you feel any better, go ahead. Take the gun, put the barrel in his mouth, and pull the trigger—you'll scatter his brains all over the room, but you won't have settled anything. It really never helps, take my word for it."

She looked at the weapon, and then at Guinness, and when it occurred to her that he wasn't kidding, her fingers tightened on the pocketbook and she shook her head, her lips soundlessly forming the word "no."

"Then can we go now? You've got a long drive ahead of you." Guinness led the way through the alley behind the bookstore, his hand closed over the nickle-plated automatic, which he had transferred to his jacket pocket. But there was no one unpleasant around—the police hadn't even ticketed Janine's car.

"Get in the back seat," he told her, speaking over his shoulder as his eyes worked over the sidewalks and the shop windows along either side of the alley and across the street.

"And stay down, where you can't be seen from the outside, until you hear different from me. I want to make perfectly sure we're not being followed before we pick up your driver."

"Where will I go?"

"Into Germany—to Düsseldorf. Someone will meet you there. I'm not sure what will happen then, not exactly sure, but they'll find a way to put you somewhere Flycatcher will never find you. If you don't do anything to attract attention to yourself, you'll be perfectly safe."

He heard the car door open behind him.

"Won't you be taking me?" she asked. He couldn't see her—his back was still turned—but he knew her hand was resting uncertainly on the window frame and she was thinking that this was her last moment of opportunity, that now, if she entered the car and went away with him, she had surrendered her freedom, possibly for the remainder of her life, and was entirely and irrevocably in his unfamiliar hands.

"No, I'll stay behind here. A woman I know will get you to Düsseldorf. You'll be safer with her than you would be with me. Too many people know me."

The door closed behind him and, in another moment, they were on their problematic way.

What lay heaviest on Guinness's mind was the consciousness that, by helping Amalia Brouwer to safety, he was putting Flycatcher out of his reach. All along, from the first moment, it had been a choice between the life of the one and—perhaps, if he got lucky—the final extinction of the other, but he was bound by his word to Emil Kätzner, who had known all along, he wouldn't have been surprised, that Flycatcher was behind his daughter's troubles and had kept his own counsel to tie Guinness even closer to him. After all, by the time Guinness had found out it had become impossible to turn back on what he had said he would do.

Which didn't mean that he wasn't entitled to regret it—just that Amalia Brouwer had to take precedence.

And so, when he was putting his questions to Flycatcher's errand boy, he hadn't even taken the trouble to ask, *Where is he?* He hadn't wanted to tempt himself. No, Amalia Brouwer came first, and if he saw her to safety it would have been too late anyway—Flycatcher would have had time to discover that his man was taken and he himself betrayed, and he would have been long gone.

That had been the way of it, all along. Guinness had continually found himself just a beat off the tempo. Always before it had been a matter of circumstance—Flycatcher had good people watching his back, and there wasn't much you could do about that—but now it was something Guinness had done, had chosen to do, to himself.

He just hoped that Amalia Brouwer somehow turned out to be worth it.

After a dozen or so blocks he let her come up for air. She sat directly behind him and he could see her in the rearview mirror, picking at her hair in that way women have when they imagine it has become disarranged.

"How did you meet him?" he asked suddenly, for no particular reason he could think of. Their eyes met through the mirror and, from the way hers narrowed, it was sufficiently clear she understood to whom he was referring.

"Günner? Through someone I had known in a political action committee. That was five months ago—he was authentic, you know? What you Americans call 'the real thing.' He asked me if I wanted something more than marching in anti-nuclear weapons demonstrations; he said it was possible to achieve more in a single afternoon than in all the rallies that have been staged since the beginning of time, if one simply had the courage. I thought he was a hero of the underground struggle—you should have seen the scars on his chest and thigh, great purplish things. He was no debating student."

"He got those scars in Mexico, running through the night in his pajamas, trying to keep his skin together. It didn't have anything to do with the Heroic Struggle for the Oppressed Masses; he's just a salesman of secrets whose business practices managed to make the wrong people angry. Not very many of us are heroes, not on either side, and your Günner is no Robin Hood. He does it for the money—anybody's money."

"Who shot him in Mexico? Was it the Americans?"

"It was me."

The .45 was still lying on the seat beside him; he picked it up and put it in Janine's glove compartment—she might have some use for it along the way, and he had a hell of a lot more faith in her capacities in that line than he had in Amalia Brouwer's. At least Janine didn't turn white when she found out her chauffeur wasn't a boy scout.

They drove back through the center of town in silence. It was just as well; Guinness was still busy with his rearview mirror, checking for excessively familiar cars in the street behind them, and he didn't want to talk to Amalia anyway. He had rather decided that he didn't like Amalia—she didn't strike him as the type who would get over her youth as quickly as one might have hoped. All that adolescent disapproval was beginning to get rather badly on his nerves.

It was nearly one-thirty, but the lunchtime traffic hadn't given any indication of an intention to slack off. Guinness took the car in a wide loop that ran over the Amstel, almost touching the railroad tracks, and then back down through some of the smaller streets near a star-shaped junction of canals called the Apollohal. Finally he was convinced. There were no bad guys on their trail. They were clean.

"Will I be meeting my father in Germany?" There was a certain ambiguous quality in her voice, as if she might have wanted to suggest that the encounter was something she would just as happily avoid.

They were driving along the length of one of the city's vast parks, the one that, looking down from Janine's bedroom window, was just visible as a line of treetops. Inside, along the walkways that threaded aimlessly through neatly clipped lawns, middle-aged couples, seeming to hold each other up, and young women with children made their uncaring way. Apparently there was a faint breath of wind because the leaves flickered on the poplar trees, but no one looked cold or reluctant to be out of doors. One had the sense that this world could be, on the whole, a very pleasant place if one simply had the wisdom not to tamper with it. But not everyone was so blessed.

"I shouldn't think so," Guinness answered, careful not to glance at his rearview mirror. "I shouldn't think that would be possible for him—at least he didn't mention it."

He stopped at a crosswalk to let a stream of festive-looking humanity pass in front of them. It was like a uniformed army, all the men with camera cases dangling from their shoulders and most of the women in short-sleeved blouses and tight, pastel-colored trousers—and an astonishing number of them were freshly sunburned on their arms and necks. They took forever, talking among themselves in loud voices that were almost inaudible inside the car and, in spite of their apparent cheerfulness, walking with the rolling, footsore gait of weary soldiers. Guinness and his passenger maintained a perfect silence as they went by.

"What is he like, my father?"

"I haven't any idea," Guinness was surprised into saying—he had thought, somehow, that the subject was closed, that Amalia Brouwer had wanted it to be closed; but apparently not. "Like I said, I've only met him twice. I doubt if I've spent a total of five hours in his presence, and I'd never heard his voice before three days ago."

"Was that here, in Amsterdam?"

"No—Munich. It wasn't possible for him to come here,

for reasons that had more to do with your safety than with his, so he asked me."

"And you came, all that way. Did he pay you?"

"No." Guinness shook his head, wondering why he was offended at the suggestion. "No, he didn't pay me."

He could feel the pressure of her hand on his backrest—she was leaning forward, and the tension in her slender body was something you experienced more than sensed.

"But if not for money, for what? You say you hardly know him, and yet you travel half the length of Europe and risk your life. How can he be a stranger if you have done all this simply because he asked you?"

"It was a favor, and you can owe a favor to a stranger. I owed him."

"What is his name? His real name, what is it?" She was peering at him through the rearview mirror, and Guinness didn't like the expression on her face. She was merely curious about a man who was merely interesting, and he found he was offended by that as well.

"I don't owe you anything," he snapped, his eyes narrowing to slits as he studied the road. "Certainly not that. His name is his business."

And that was where they left it. There were no more questions, and Guinness turned around and began his long, angular approach to Janine's apartment, where he would be rid of the burden of Amalia Brouwer's youth. She would be Janine's problem, and it was possible that Janine would be a better companion and courier, would find Emil Kätzner's child less of a burden to her attention.

Janine's building was one of five on that particular block, the second from the corner as Guinness drove past. And he did drive past; he went on for several more streets and then turned away and covered another two before doubling back and running parallel to the way he had come.

Partially it was a matter of habit—over the years stealth had become so ingrained in his character that he almost couldn't walk to the corner for a newspaper without checking the approaches. Wearisome, but it kept you alive.

He parked the car in a side street, where it would be invisible from any of Janine's windows or to anyone keeping watch from either the front entrance or the fire escape that ran down the back.

"Wait here," he said, his tone suggesting that inquiries would be resented. He got out and walked to the corner; Janine's building was a block down, but it was taller than those behind it and the balcony off her bedroom was in plain sight.

The glass doors leading out were shut.

16

In the summer I like to leave them open to the outside. It makes me feel less alone.

Apparently she was little afraid of burglars up there on the top floor, because she seemed to keep her balcony doors ajar even when she was gone—last night, at least, when she and Guinness had finally been able to come back and go to bed, the doors had stood wide open and he had no recollection of her going near them. And this morning, when he had left after breakfast, the curtains were restless with the gusting land breezes.

Even if she had closed them before leaving herself, she had been back now for a couple of hours. She would be waiting for him. She would have gone into her bedroom to pack a bag. She might even have decided to sit there on her vast bed, since the telephone was on her night stand. She had a long drive ahead of her and there had been little enough time for sleep the night before, so she might even have lain down, just to close her eyes for a little while.

After all, why shouldn't Janine conform to the pattern of her sex? Where else but in her bedroom—her sanctuary, the scene of her private reality—would she spend the time until he came to her with Amalia Brouwer and her marching orders?

And yet, the balcony doors were closed.

He should have known, of course. He should have foreseen this. The sense of being watched he had experienced that morning, which had disappeared almost as soon as he had left the museum, as soon as he had separated from Janine—they had followed her. They had figured out that, eventually, she could always lead them back to him, so they had left him to himself and followed her. He couldn't fault them since it was the obvious move. He had no one he could blame but himself. He was supposed to be so good at this business, the best there was—had he been fast asleep? He should have listened to his own instincts and seen this coming; he should have known.

Because it really was the obvious move. He was the Soldier, the celebrated killer of men. *Everyone has heard of the Soldier;* Janine had said it herself. His own gaudy reputation prevented anything like close surveillance—there were simply some men it was too dangerous to shadow; they had nasty tempers and eyes in the backs of their heads. Everyone has heard of the Soldier.

In the summer I like to leave them open to the outside. But they were closed—two flat sheets of glass, catching the early afternoon sun and throwing it down onto the street in patches of hard light. It hurt your eyes to look at them. They glittered like the windows of a hearse. *It makes me feel less alone.*

God, what had they done to her? Someone was up there; some stranger had closed the balcony doors to shut out whatever Janine had found to comfort her from beyond her balcony. She was not alone now. She had visitors.

Flycatcher didn't train his people to be particularly refined about how they did their work; he rather favored the sort who, as children, liked to set the cat's tail on fire and pull the wings from butterflies. And Flycatcher was supposed to be a frightened man these days—after all, the Soldier, that celebrated killer of men, was hot on his case—and frightened men are frequently undiscriminating in their cruelty.

So, quite possibly, Janine now had more than just one

reason to rejoice in her association with the Prince of Headsmen.

And then, of course, it could be nothing. Perhaps Janine had merely shut her windows because she knew she would be gone from home for several days—what could be more sensible than that? In all probability she was at that very moment in her kitchen, brewing up a thermos jug full of strong tea for the drive to Düsseldorf, threatened by nothing more sinister than a tendency of the hot water to splash when she poured it into her Delft china pot. It could be, as he was beginning to suspect more and more, that he needed that rest cure in London more than he realized, that his nerves were playing tricks on him, making him see in everything the oppression of his phantom enemies.

Except that he didn't believe it for a thin minute.

The buildings on that block were all about the same height, and close together. It was impossible to tell for certain from the ground, but probably their roofs didn't have any more pitch to them than would be required to let the rain run off, and certainly getting to them wouldn't involve overcoming anything more serious than a locked door. That part would be a walk.

He couldn't do it by himself—if there was more than just one, or at most two, goons in there with Janine, he would be a sitting duck. And there wasn't a soul to help except Amalia Brouwer. So that settled that; it would have to be Amalia Brouwer.

He went back to the car and took the keys out of the ignition to open the trunk, hoping to find a coil of rope. He was disappointed, of course; things were only that tidy in the movies—there wasn't even twenty feet of clothesline; there wasn't anything. Okay, so we do without.

"Listen," he said, sitting with Amalia Brouwer in the back seat of Janine's gray Opel, holding her wrist with just enough force to be sure he had her undivided attention. "I want you to do something. There's a building around the corner—I want you to go up to the apartment on the top floor and knock on the door. Just knock on the door, nothing else. There's a peephole, so stay where you can't be seen from the inside, and if anybody you don't know opens up, if you hear anybody's voice but mine, you run like the devil's after you, because he will be."

"Just knock? Is that all?"

"Just knock. I'll squire you around to the front entrance, and then I want you to wait outside in the sunshine for, say, fifteen minutes. There are five floors, so you can take your time going up the stairs—there's no elevator—and then, precisely twenty minutes after I've left you, not one second off in either direction, I want you to give a couple of good firm raps on that door. Use the butt of your fist and make it sound like you mean business. And for God's sake be on time—twenty minutes; don't be late and don't be early. Twenty minutes, on the tick. Got it?"

She looked at him out of her curiously soft eyes, the only inheritance Guinness found himself able to trace from Emil Kätzner, and her face tilted at an inquisitive angle as, apparently, she tried to read something from the tone of his voice and the way his fingers formed a tight, not-quite-painful fetter around her wrist. She was surprisingly calm, Guinness was happy to note; perhaps Amalia Brouwer would do after all.

"Is there anything wrong?"

Guinness smiled. "I don't know for sure, Sweetheart, but it wouldn't surprise me. It's a funny world."

He glanced down at the rather mannish watch she was wearing and saw that it had a second hand—that was something, anyway—and then let go of her wrist.

"Remember, twenty minutes. And for Christ's sake don't be noisy on the stairs."

She nodded, and Guinness took her big brown leather

pocketbook and dropped the car keys inside before giving it back to her.

"You'd better know now—if anything happens, and you end up making this trip by yourself, the man you want in Düsseldorf is Teddy MacKaye. He's a God-only-knows-what in the American consulate there, and you don't want to talk to anybody else. He's been briefed, so he knows you're coming. Tell him the Soldier sends his regrets but he was detained by other business. I hope to God you know how to drive."

She nodded, very serious about it all, and pulled the pocketbook up close against her side.

"*Will* I be going by myself?" she asked. Guinness could only shrug his shoulders, as if the question were of no particular importance.

"Could be. If somebody else opens the door, you just run. Don't be sentimental; don't wait around to see how things work out. These goons know what you look like and they're the worst enemies you've got in the world. You just run like blue blazes."

So they put their little plan into operation. Separating at the car, they converged on the front entrance of Janine's apartment building from opposite ends of the block—to the casual eye they were strangers, just a man inquiring the time from a woman he had never seen before—and that was how they began their countdown. Twenty minutes to go. No more, no less.

Guinness turned into the next doorway. He tried to keep from running up the stairwell, hoping all the time he wouldn't bump into anyone. He didn't want to be noticed—he had less than twenty minutes, now, and if a suspicious janitor or someone had tried to detain him it would have been hard cheese for them. He just couldn't have afforded the time it takes to explain anything to anyone, so he tried to act like he belonged there and not to make either more or less noise than one might expect from, say, the Fuller Brushman.

Predictably, the door to the roof was locked. The stairwell was an open affair, so if the residents of either of the two apartments on the fifth floor had opened their doors and looked out to see who was there they would have been able to catch a glimpse of his legs, from about the knees down, through the painted metal balustrade. Guinness tried to pick the lock as fast as he could—he didn't relish the prospect of shooting any inquisitive Dutch grandmothers, but tying people up with the drapery cords just takes too long.

Voilà! He was a genius, a credit to his profession. Twenty-three seconds and the latch tongue clicked back and the door yielded stiffly under his hand. A new world's record. Three minutes and fifty-seven seconds and he was on the roof.

The two buildings were flush up against each other—you couldn't have slipped a knife blade in between; all that separated them was a low retaining wall. The roof on both sides was composition, just gravel and tar.

Guinness sat down on the wall and took off his shoes. Walking around on that junk in his stocking feet wasn't going to be much of a thrill, but Janine's apartment was directly underneath now and he didn't want the bad guys to hear him through the ceiling. His shoes were the great thick-soled clodhoppers that she had found so frightfully amusing, and he wasn't sure quite what to do with them—he could hardly stuff them into his jacket pockets; they'd be no end of in the way. Finally he decided to leave them behind. If he was still alive in half an hour he could always come up and get them, and if he wasn't he wouldn't care how silly his corpse might look in stocking feet.

The roof was hot from the afternoon sun; it was like walking across a pancake griddle, except that a pancake griddle would at least have been smooth. Guinness had the pleasure of the gravel as well. He kept to the edge on the theory that it would be quieter than going directly across the center. The tar was sticky and clinging to his socks for dear life as he made his cautious way. All in all, it wasn't turning out to be a very pleasant experience.

When he had made it to the rear of the building and could look out over the edge to Janine's balcony, he thought for a couple of seconds that he might just faint dead away. Even just to the top of the parapet, which, praise be, was a nice, solid, flat, cement structure, was at least an eight-foot drop, without a thing in the world to hang onto except the top of the retaining wall. Guinness was just under six foot two, and he had to get down there without making a sound—and if he screwed up, or if the wind blew just the wrong way at the wrong moment, there was an unobstructed plunge of probably fifty feet to the sidewalk below. He didn't have any very clear idea of the chances of surviving a fifty-foot fall, but he didn't imagine they were spectacular. And it had looked so easy from the ground.

He checked his watch and, with a few seconds thrown in for heart failure, he had been on the roof for a shade over four minutes. He had twelve minutes left, and he had to think. God, the idea of falling scared the shit out of him—it always had; he hated high places. He wished to hell he hadn't struck on a line of work that was forever requiring him to play the human fly. It was very little to his taste.

The balcony was only three or four feet wider than the glass doors through which it was entered—if somebody was in Janine's bedroom, and if they happened to be standing anywhere near the middle, it wouldn't be much of a trick for them to catch sight of him. Probably he couldn't figure on more than about a foot of concealment. If they saw him he was dead meat. There wasn't anywhere to go; there wouldn't be any hiding places.

So he would have to stay as close to the edge as he could manage, coming down as noiselessly as possible on the parapet and clinging to the wall for dear life until he could lower himself to the balcony.

He reached down and tried to coat his hands a little with the roof tar, just enough to let him hold on a trifle better. God, what he wouldn't have given for seven or eight feet of rope—there was even a drainage pipe he could have tied it to, making everything easy—and all he had in that line was a silk necktie.

He let his legs dangle out over the edge, hoping no one would look up from the street and decide to report him as an attempted suicide (maybe that was actually what he was!), and then twisted around so that the top of the retaining wall was against his stomach. Then slowly, very slowly, he let himself down, feeling with his toes against the brickwork, hoping that some miracle would make the parapet a few inches higher for him. He was all the way over, with just his fingers hooked over the top of the wall, when, with the big toe of his left foot, he felt a flat, horizontal surface. Once, twice, three times he touched it, feeling for the outer edge—everything depended on not coming down on that edge and turning an ankle—and then, taking a gulp of air and holding it, he let himself fall.

Even with the top of the parapet under his feet, the sense that he would go right over and down to the sidewalk surged through him in great waves of panic, and he pressed himself to the wall, not daring to open his eyes.

And then he stepped down to the balcony, and it was over. He could hardly believe it. He felt like he hadn't drawn a breath in half an hour.

Janine's little automatic was in his back pocket. He took it out and snicked off the safety, holding it straight up and close to his body. He hadn't looked in through the curtains yet; he just kept his back to the wall, where he couldn't be seen from inside, trying to take up as little space as possible, and listened. There were cars down on the street—he could hear them plain enough—and the wind at five floors up made a dull hissing sound, but there was nothing from inside. He pushed back the sleeve of his jacket to look at his watch; he had seven minutes left before Amalia Brouwer started to pound on the front door.

There was no point in being subtle about it; if there was somebody in the bedroom, and he was looking in the right direction, he could see you just as easily even if you rose up out of the ground in a puff of smoke. So Guinness simply stepped out in front of the glass doors, crowded as far back against the parapet as he could to be out of the way of flying glass in case he should have to shoot.

Except for the body on the bed, there was nobody there.

You can expect a thing, you can tell yourself it's going to happen, and it can still manage to stop your heart. Guinness knew the rules, knew that in his profession people didn't bother about tying up their prisoners in neat little packages, all trussed and gagged so they could kick themselves loose in half an hour. In his league it was no longer a game, and the sanctity of human life wasn't very high on anybody's list of abstract moral values—he wasn't drawing any fine distinctions; he might well have done the same himself.

Still, somehow it hit him hard that they should have killed Janine.

Her face was turned slightly away from him, and the bed was on the other side of the unlit room, but even through the gauze curtains he could see that it was Janine and that she was dead. She had that abandoned look that the dead always seem to have, and Guinness felt the reproach. Alone in her bedroom, her slender little life gone, the victim of strangers—he should have found a way to have spared her this final indignity. He couldn't even tell her he was sorry.

The two glass doors were held together with a little latch; Guinness slipped one of his long, thin lockpicks between them and pushed it up until it popped loose from its slot. He entered the room without so much as a hinge squeaking.

The first thing that assaulted him was the smell. He couldn't remember anything like it, a peculiar compound of sweat and fear and something else he couldn't place, a kind of acrid stain in the air, something you could almost see. And then, of course, he understood.

Janine's sweater was half torn away and her skirt was bunched up around her waist, but somehow that was to be expected. Her mouth showed traces of blood at the corners, where she had fought against the gag. They had tied her to her bed—her feet were sticking out between the brass rails of the footboard, and on her face was an expression of agony such as even the dead are usually spared. She had suffered before they had finally gotten bored and one of them had pressed the muzzle of a small-bore pistol against her temple and put her out of her misery, and what she had suffered had had little enough to do with whatever sexual indignities she might have endured.

It was still lying on the floor, a small electric iron of the kind you could zip into its cloth traveling bag and take along in your suitcase. A homely little domestic item with which they had gone over the soles of her feet.

From the look of them, they had worked on her for a long time—God, it was a miracle they had even found it necessary to shoot her; it was a miracle, a grotesque joke, that anyone could go through all that and not have the good fortune to die of it. Guinness felt his heart beating against his ribs like a captured animal throwing itself wildly against the bars of its cage. She couldn't have been dead more than an hour.

Her eyes were still open. She seemed to be looking at

nothing but her own despair. *I tried,* she seemed to be saying to the wall. *I tried, but I couldn't stand it anymore.* Guinness brought down the lids with the first finger and the thumb of his right hand.

And then, quite suddenly, he no longer cared anything about his precious battle plan. In something like four minutes Amalia Brouwer was supposed to stand out in the hallway and knock, and that was supposed to provide the necessary moment of distraction that might give him a jump on whoever was waiting out there beyond Janine's bedroom door—oh yes, they had closed the bedroom door; possibly the smell bothered them.

But none of that seemed to matter anymore. Four minutes was simply too long to have to wait, and Guinness didn't care how many of Flycatcher's troops were sitting around in the kitchen drinking tea. He didn't care about having an edge; he just wanted to kill as many of them as possible before they could bring him down. To hell with Amalia Brouwer and her goddamned distraction. Somehow it simply wasn't going to wait any longer.

Just to redefine for himself the way it was supposed to feel in his hand, Guinness flexed his fingers around the butt of Janine's automatic—her silly little nickle-plated toy, which he had yet even to fire, so at least she would be getting that much of her own back. And then, with an angry, wordless, half-smothered challenge on his lips, he kicked open the bedroom door.

The man sitting at the breakfast table waited just an instant too long to reach for the Luger that was lying beside his coffee cup. He wasn't going to make it; he probably knew that, but he didn't have the presence of mind not to try. Guinness smiled at him as he pulled the trigger—he wouldn't have had it any other way. He shot him twice, not even hearing the report, only feeling the automatic twitch in his hand as two small red stains sprang up on the man's shirt-front.

He recognized him now—it was one of the men from the train. One of the Oregon schoolteachers, the tall one who had never had much to say for himself. So that was how they had known.

The schoolteacher was thrown back against his chair, pitching over onto the floor and leaving the Luger still lying on the table. Guinness had stopped paying attention as soon as he had fired, twisting around in a sharp, quick ducking motion as he turned to cover the rest of the room.

But there was no one else there, so there was no one left to kill. He had expected there would be more; he had expected that he would probably have caught a bullet by now—he had only hoped for enough time to take as many as he could with him into that good night—but suddenly he saw that he was alone, and the disappointment was almost painful. It was all over, almost before it had happened, and it wasn't fair. There had been only the one, and it wasn't fair.

But the one was still alive. Just barely, but still alive. Guinness knelt down beside him, hating him with a peculiar intimacy, as if they had been enemies forever. He picked him up by the lapel of his denim jacket and shook him exactly as if he had been a rag doll instead of a man.

"Oh, you son of a bitch," he crooned in his ear. "Don't you die on me. Don't you dare." But it was already too late. The light went out of the man's frightened, bewildered eyes, and in an instant he was beyond anyone's powers of vengeance.

But Guinness couldn't seem to let him go. He stayed crouched over him for a long time, unwilling to accept that the man was dead and their business was completed. He couldn't even bring himself to relinquish his hold on the denim jacket.

"Don't you die on me," he whispered. He was still half-heartedly trying to threaten the dead man back to life when he heard the knocking on the front door.

Three sharp raps. Guinness experienced a few wild seconds of hope before he remembered Amalia Brouwer and rose to let her in. He wasn't fast enough, however, to catch her before she knocked again—ten seconds, and three more short, insistent points of sound, like Morse code.

"Okay—I hear you." He pulled the doorknob toward himself and was initially surprised to see no one. And then he remembered his own instructions and, peeking around the edge of the frame, found Amalia Brouwer flattened against the outside wall. At least she knew enough to do as she was told.

"It's all right. Come in."

She said nothing, and as he closed the door behind her he found she was standing over the dead body that lay straddled over the backrest of a tipped-over chair, peering down into his face in a way that suggested she was trying to remember where she had seen him before.

"Was he another friend of yours?" he asked, perhaps not very nicely. His juices were still pumping pretty hard; he could feel the first surge of his anger still bottled up inside him and he found he really didn't much like anybody. Another time—if there was ever another time—he would be sure to apologize.

"No." She shook her head. "No, I have never seen him. Is he the one who killed Jean?"

"No, I don't think so. I've run into him once already this morning, and I don't imagine he could have been in two places at the same time."

And then she noticed the open bedroom door, and what was lying on the bed, and she uttered a little sound that was somewhere between a groan and a sob. Guinness was standing behind her, far enough off that he couldn't simply reach out and stop her, and the next thing he knew she was clinging to the edge of the door frame and her slender body was being shaken by episodes of choked weeping—it was quite impersonal; she had never set eyes on Janine, but who could have seen her like that without at least a spasm of pity and fear? Guinness didn't think any the less of her for it.

He took her by the shoulder and, very gently, turned her around to face him, to face away from the contents of Janine's bed.

"If you don't like it, don't look at it," he said quietly. He wasn't really being snide; at the moment it was the best advice he could think of. And immediately she began trying to compose herself—he could feel the tension in her arms as she forced herself back under control. And then it was done. Emil Kätzner's child looked up at him out of a face that was tear-stained but calm.

"Is that why you killed him?"

"Yes. That's why I killed him."

They stood facing each other for a moment, and then, when Guinness was sure she was all right, he went into the kitchen and found a steak knife in one of the drawers next to the sink.

Already he realized that he had been betrayed into a mistake, that the man watching him from the floor with dead eyes would have been more useful alive, but there was nothing he could do about that. His moment of wrath might end up costing him his life, but there was nothing he could do about that either. The die was cast.

He closed the bedroom door behind him and cut away the bathrobe belts and nylon stockings and strips of pillowcase they had used to bind Janine, and when he had released her he took her under the arms and pulled her poor mangled little body so that it lay straight on the bed. Then he rearranged her clothes so that they covered her again and folded the bedspread around her like a winding sheet. It was a perfectly meaningless gesture, of course—Guinness had never been able to bring himself to believe that it could matter to the dead how they were treated—but somehow it made him feel a little better. He couldn't have left her to be found like that by the police. She had been through enough as it was, poor little thing. He left the glass doors to the balcony open.

And then he went back out into the living room, where Amalia Brouwer was sitting on the edge of the sofa, facing slightly away from the dead man on the floor, apparently waiting for Guinness to come back and settle her destiny as well.

"You'll have to get to Düsseldorf by yourself," he said, sitting down beside her. "Our friend on the floor had a partner; they were like Mutt and Jeff, so I thought since I've killed the one I might as well kill the other. I'm going to try to kill all of them—every damned one of them."

"What of Günner? What am I to do if he pursues me?"

It wasn't a panicky question. She was a good kid; she just wanted to know whether there were any instructions about such a contingency. Guinness smiled at her and shook his head.

"Not to worry. Günner won't even give you a thought. Günner's going to be much too busy."

17

And so Amalia Brouwer was on her way. Guinness had waited with her until her nerves had settled a bit and then walked her back down to the car. She would sleep that night in Düsseldorf, under the protection of Teddy MacKaye. She was Teddy's problem now, and her own. And now Guinness was free of his promise to Emil Kätzner and had only Janine to think about—Janine and Flycatcher. Now he didn't have to choose anymore.

Because Flycatcher would wait for him now. He had known all along, from the very beginning; he had even managed to put his men on the train to Amsterdam, so he had known at least as early as Ernie Tuttle had known. Ernie seemed to have a snitch in his office, but that was his problem. All Guinness cared about was the fact that he seemed to have an appointment.

The other schoolteacher—why did he continue to think of him as a schoolteacher? the guy probably hadn't held a piece of chalk since high school—the one who had looked at Janine with such ravenous eyes in the Rijksmuseum hadn't been standing guard duty with his buddy in her apartment. And, in the general course of things, you didn't work over the soles of somebody's feet with a hot iron just for your own private amusement—you did it because you wanted something. They had followed Janine, followed her because they hadn't dared to follow Guinness, and the only thing they could have wanted from Janine was himself. Q.E.D. They had put her through all that—doubtless enjoying it, but they wouldn't have run the risks involved, they wouldn't have just picked on Janine, without a specific purpose—all that, just to find out where they could set up an ambush for the Soldier, the celebrated killer of men. And all because Flycatcher had finally decided that the cat-and-mouse game had gone on long enough.

And, of course, Janine had told them. How could she have kept from telling them? How much could mere flesh be asked to bear? No one, no one in the wide world, had the right to say a word against her.

But she had told them. They had shot her in the head; that was the seal on her confession. They never would have killed her if they hadn't believed her every word. So they would be waiting for him now at Aimé's apartment—to which, perhaps, Janine had hoped he would never have any reason to return.

After all, she knew he was coming to meet her. Had she told them that? No, he didn't think so—they had only left the one man behind, against the off-chance; there would be more of them waiting at Aimé's. No, she had kept faith and given him his chance to get away. That was like her.

Aimé, who slept next to her elderly boyfriend within sound of the sea, she might never come back to her apartment now. Sugar Daddy might marry her now and she could forget about her starvation diets and live to be a plump, respectable Dutch matron. She might never come back.

But Guinness would. He would walk right to the front door, with no tricks, and let them have him. It was the only way he could put himself within reach of Flycatcher, on Flycatcher's terms. It was what Flycatcher was hanging around for, and Guinness wouldn't have disappointed him for worlds.

Of course, they might do the smart thing, the thing Guinness would have done himself, and burn him down the second he stepped across the threshold. If all Flycatcher wanted was to be able to sleep easy at night, those would be the orders he would give, but Guinness had an intuition that that wasn't all Flycatcher wanted. It wasn't even the half of what he wanted.

You hunt a man for a long time, and you develop a sense of him. A feeling for his character, for the interior logic of his actions. And Flycatcher wasn't going to settle for a quick, safe bullet in the head—after all, Guinness wasn't Janine. Guinness had threatened him in a way that went considerably beyond the simple fear of death; Guinness had made him feel small and vulnerable. Guinness had frightened him and would have to pay, and the payment would have to be made in person, face to face, or Flycatcher would never get back his self-esteem, would never feel the same about anything again. It was too personal a matter between them to be left to subordinates.

Still, the odds were lousy. Guinness had to assume that he was reading Flycatcher right, who, after all, might just be frightened enough not to worry about his self-esteem, and he had to assume that he could somehow extricate himself from the trap that had been set for him, that he would somehow find a way of striking back. The chances of survival were negligible, and the chances of success weren't very much better. After all, people had tried for Flycatcher before—Guinness himself had tried—and the man was still alive. It didn't fill you with optimism.

But it had to be tried. Janine was lying tucked up in her bedspread with her feet nearly burnt off and a bullet in her brain, and she was there because of Raymond Guinness, whose name she had never even been allowed to know. If they had simply been working on a job together, a couple of paid government functionaries, that might have been something else, but Guinness had been in Amsterdam in the service of no master for whom Janine should have felt herself obliged to lay down her life; he had come on a personal matter, a favor for someone to whom he owed a purely private obligation. And Janine had died for that. She knew nothing of Emil Kätzner; she owed him nothing. She had died for Raymond Guinness—for the Soldier. And so his obligation was to her.

It wasn't much of a walk between the two women's apartments, not more than ten or twelve minutes at a good crisp pace. Guinness didn't hurry, however. It was a nice day, and he wanted to enjoy it. He wanted to keep in the sunshine and to bake the chill of Janine's bedroom out of his bones. He wanted to lose his anger, which had cost him enough already—now, if he made his score, it would have to be the hard way or not at all. Anger was just a nuisance; he wanted to clear his mind, to catch hold of the sense that the world had only begun for him since he had stepped back out into the light.

He took the long way, skirting the canal to give his eyes something to rest on besides the fifteen or twenty-some-odd feet of sidewalk directly in front of him. He liked to be able to smell the water, which was a greenish gray and half-covered with shadow from the embankment walls, and he liked the rough texture of the stone. He wondered whether there were any fish in these waters, or if they had all died off ages ago from the gasoline fumes.

He had the walkway pretty much to himself—it was an odd thing, but for some reason people didn't seem to like walking along the canalways. Perhaps because there was only the canal to see and they were more interested in the contents of shop windows. Or perhaps there was some other reason. He tried to imagine what it could be, but he couldn't.

Kätzner would have liked the shop-window idea, since he was a Marxist—or perhaps he had given up ascribing everything to the sovereign power of economics. Perhaps, by now, Kätzner too had lost interest in the motives of other people or had simply decided that they might be as inexplicable as his own. Under any circumstances, Guinness decided, he would stop worrying about why he seemed to be the only human being for thirty yards in any direction; the question of his own isolation was beginning to lose its charm.

The canal made a slight turn and suddenly, from where he was standing on the sidewalk, he could see Aimé's building. If there was a reception committee, and there didn't seem to be much doubt about that, they could see him too, and Guinness had made up his mind he was going to make his entrance nice and conspicuous. After all, he was just a poor frazzled assassin coming home to his borrowed digs after a hard day of plying his trade—why should he harbor any suspicions? Hell, he wasn't even carrying a gun.

That had been a hard choice, but Janine's little automatic now smelled rather conspicuously of gun powder and, unless they were just total buffoons, they would probably give it a sniff when they took it off him—he didn't want them forming any awkward conclusions. And he could hardly have commandeered the schoolteacher's Luger, since his pal might have wondered where the celebrated killer of men could have gotten it. So he would just have to grit his teeth and walk in there unarmed to take his whipping like a man. There wasn't any other practical way to manage it.

He had put his nose to the muzzle of that Luger himself and discovered that it hadn't been fired recently. So that meant that the other one, the short one with the reddish beard, the one who had eaten Janine up with his eyes, was the one who had pulled the trigger. That would be something to remember when the time came, but not now. Now was the time to be innocent and harmless.

The keys were already in his hand as he approached the outside door, but it was never left locked in the daytime. As he went up the stairs he tried to make his footsteps sound weary and unsuspecting—which, of course, amounted to nothing more than slow and noisy; it was hard work to keep from overplaying it—and as he approached the landing he kept his hand on the stairway bannister.

They had picked the lock, naturally, to let themselves in—and had left a nice big scratch on the brass while they were at it. Well, it didn't figure that the consummate professionals would be out doing this kind of routine legwork for anybody, not even for Flycatcher. He inserted his key and pushed the door open—he didn't find anybody at attention in the entranceway to point a gun at him, so he stepped inside, hoping that the clown who was lurking on the other side wouldn't collapse of heart failure.

Yes, the bedroom would be the right direction. They always wanted to sneak up behind you, and Guinness had no inclination to make it difficult for anybody. So he started back for the bedroom, swinging the door closed behind him. He had gotten about a step and a half when, out of the corner of his eye, he saw the shadow on the wall beside him—nothing dramatic, just a little darkening on the yellow paintwork. He saw the raised hand, and he waited for the blow, and he hoped the guy would know what he was doing and wouldn't kill him with his sheer incompetence. That was the problem with dealing with goons; the quality of their trade-craft could be so uneven.

He didn't really feel anything, but you never did. There

was just a kind of jolt, that might as easily have been coming up through the floor as from anywhere else, and then he could feel himself beginning to get very, very heavy.

He let himself drift, and by the time he had made it down on his knees the world was already beginning to turn a dull, smoky red. There wasn't any need to hit him again; he would be out quick enough, but the stupid bastard did anyway, and Guinness made himself a little promise that all overeager thugs would have their day of reckoning.

He was supporting himself on one arm now—the smoky red was darkening into black and his arm was getting weaker and weaker and finally buckled under him. He could see the floor coming up to smack him, and then it simply disappeared, just vanished, and he found himself drifting, drifting, drifting in the cold, comfortless, slate-gray waters of some soundless sea.

"I think you killed him—he's been out long enough. The boss isn't gonna like it if you've killed him."

Well, score one for the home team. Rumors to the contrary, Guinness had the distinct impression that he was not, in fact, dead. So—his reading had been right at least that far. And if he wasn't dead, then everything was still on track. He was unarmed and sprawled out on the carpet with the mother and father of all headaches, and doubtless these people planned for him to plug a hole in the ground before evening, but otherwise everything was just terrific.

Guinness hadn't yet decided whether or not to risk opening his eyes, but he knew that the speaker was kneeling down beside him on the bedroom floor, whither he had a dim recollection of having been dragged at some point in the festivities. He hadn't any clear idea of how long he had been out—or whether, in fact, he had ever really been all the way out at all—but he didn't see anything to be gained by appearing any livelier than he felt, which wasn't very. So he wasn't in any hurry to set anyone's mind at rest. Let them worry—these two could wait a little longer without permanent injury.

There were two of them. Precisely how he knew that he couldn't have said, but he knew. There was Red Beard, who was an acquaintance of long standing—and who apparently was the one who had hit him—and there was the other one, who seemed so solicitous of his well-being. Nobody else, just those two. Well, at any rate, two men weren't anything beyond the range of the possible.

"Come on, Soldier. No more playin' possum."

It was Red Beard's voice, familiar from the final few hours aboard the Munich-Amsterdam train and, of course, from this morning in the Rijksmuseum. The accent had broadened; the slight down-home twang was even more pronounced than it had been when he was playing the country cousin in front of Janine, but it was still he. Guinness opened one eye, and then the other, and saw him standing preternaturally tall directly next to his head.

"Come on, tough guy. George here's all worried about you, but I told him you was supposed to be a real hard-ass. Come on, rise an' shine."

Painter—that was his name. Guinness could remember it now. Jeff. *Pleased to meet you, ma'am.* Yes, it was all coming back to him now. And the other one, the one who was lying on Janine's living room floor with a pair of bullet holes in his chest, had been a Hal something. And now we had ourselves a George.

He made a little gasping sound and allowed one arm to stir weakly, as if he were groping his way out of the most profound unconsciousness. God, his head hurt him so bad he felt sick to his stomach, and he would have liked to throw up, if only for the dramatic effect, but he found that he wasn't quite that badly off—close, but still this side of emptying his guts all over the carpet.

He got another nudge in the ribs, this one probably hard enough to leave a mark, before he managed to pull himself over on his side and have a glance around. The light hurt his eyes, although he didn't suppose anyone had brought in any arc lamps just for his benefit; when he could bear to look he found George sitting over on the corner of the bed while Painter was still directly over him, smiling unpleasantly through his tangled beard.

"You look familiar," he was able to whisper. Painter nodded, and Guinness was now able to see that the smile was one of great personal satisfaction—our boy had nailed the Soldier, and he seemed to be under the impression that made him really hot stuff. George almost wasn't in the room with them.

"Yeah. I kinda thought you'd remember me. I was hopin' you would."

"Well, I do."

Guinness made a stab at looking like he wanted to get up, but he still felt heavy in the limbs so he allowed himself to slip back down to the carpet. The beginnings of an idea were forming in the back rooms of his mind—just a whisper so far, and he didn't want to rush it; these things came when they were ready. And, in the meanwhile, it wouldn't do any harm to play the pathetic casualty.

It was a good thing Painter was too busy savoring his triumph to be in much of a hurry. A smarter man, of course, would have hustled the body off while it was still weak and pliable, but Painter was having much too much fun playing Superman and wanted to take his time. Well, that was fine.

That was the sort of illusion it was well to foster. And besides, Guinness was even as yet feeling a trifle pasty around the edges and could use the time to convalesce.

Finally, however, he managed to struggle up into a sitting position, with his back against Aimé's chest of drawers. It wouldn't do to appear to be malingering. There was a taste of blood at the back of his throat, and he made a face and coughed up an ugly-looking clot of reddish-black phlegm. Painter seemed to think that was very funny.

"Could I have something to drink—some water? I feel like my tongue's crawled home to die."

"Sure thing, buddy." Painter glanced over at his partner, who still occupied the corner of the bed, and made an impatient little gesture, the way someone might summon a waiter. "George, get the man a great big glass of water—he's feelin' poorly."

What George made of all this was hard to say. He was smallish and spare and rather washed-out looking, as if the march between forty and fifty was proving to be over boringly familiar terrain, and he looked at both Guinness and his partner through the weary eyes of a man who had been taught the folly of taking any side but his own.

Nevertheless, he got up from the bed and dutifully padded into the kitchen, coming back in a few seconds with a tall cocktail glass full of water—there were even a couple of ice cubes in it, which Guinness fished out and held against the back of his head until they were too small to have any effect. He decided he would have to remember George in his will.

"You see how nice we treat you?" Painter asked, retiring to sit on the little velvet-covered stool in front of Aimé's vanity table. He was grinning like an ape, and the Luger in his right hand, a perfect match to the one that was still lying on the breakfast table in Janine's apartment, was pointing at nothing but air. He was so relaxed and confident that, had they been alone, Guinness might have felt tempted to jump him right that instant.

"The boss says you're real famous, almost like a movie star or somethin'. He told us to make sure you didn't get unhappy about nothin' or you might not come along with us to meet him, and that'd just very nearly break his heart—didn't he say that, George?"

He looked around for confirmation, but George kept his eyes on the floor, refusing to have anything to do with his partner's little joke. Painter, however, was undeterred. This was his big moment, it seemed, and he wasn't going to let it go to waste.

"That's what he said," he went on, treating Guinness to another display of his large, square teeth. "He told us we was supposed to be just like a couple o' girl scout den mothers at a weekend cookout and not let you so much as stub your toe, but you don't look like you're fixin' to be a lot of trouble. I think you'll be . . . Hey, man, what's the trouble?"

He reached over to catch hold of Guinness, who was beginning to collapse sideways down the chest of drawers, the half-empty glass of water spilling out of his clumsy grasp and onto the floor.

"I told you, you hit him too hard," George murmured from his station on the corner of Aimé's bed. "He's probably got a concussion or something—he'll probably die before we get him out to the Farm."

"Shut up, George," Painter snapped over his shoulder as he lifted up Guinness's eyelid with the tip of his thumb.

It was one of the crowning performances of Guinness's life; the man was staring directly into his pupil and he managed never to look at him. He merely stared off at some invisible object in the middle distance, drawing heavy, labored breaths while he let the whole right side of his body go as limp as wilted lettuce. With his tongue in between his back molars, he managed a few words in a thick, unintelligible slur—he really was doing it awfully well.

Painter bought it completely. Thrusting the Luger back in under his belt—the stupid bastard was so rattled he didn't even think to click on the safety—he reached around Guinness's back to pick him up under the arms.

"Come on, George," he whispered tensely. "Let's get him down to the car. Jesus, the fucker weighs a ton."

Of course, as soon as he had gotten Guinness to his feet, he realized his mistake. It was just too late to do anything about it. The timing was crucial—Guinness had let his arm come up until it rested across Painter's shoulders, who seemed to have settled upon a program of walking him along from behind. They weren't more than seven or eight feet from George, but George wasn't going to be any help. George hadn't seen the danger yet—you could tell from the unfocused look in his eyes and the way his arms were still dangling at his sides—and, besides, George's gun was in his shoulder holster. It would take him all week to get it out.

A step. Guinness allowed himself a single forward step with his left foot. After that it was easy—a quick counterclockwise twist with his upper body and he threw Painter over his hip, sweeping him around so that his legs seemed to go right straight up and out from under him and he hit the floor flat on his back with enough impact to take the breath right out of him. Guinness dropped down, planting his knee just an inch or two to one side of Painter's breastbone, and in a quick movement he had the Luger from his waistband. It was aimed and steady by the time George's hand had disappeared behind the lapel of his jacket.

"Not unless you feel lucky, pal." Still crouched over the man on the floor, Guinness might have been a hunting dog frozen on point. Except for his lips, nothing moved. Nothing, not even his eyes. "Your friend's a dead man, but you might have something to deal with—if you're not stupid."

Apparently he wasn't. George brought his hand out, slowly and empty.

"Okay—what now?"

"Now you take your coat off. Just use the tips of your fingers, pal, and don't hurry. That's a boy. Now unbuckle yourself from the whole damn rig."

When the shoulder holster, which held a small, elegant-looking baretta, was dumped in the middle of the floor, George was allowed to sit back down again on the corner of the bed and Guinness could turn his attention back to Painter, who was beginning to stir slightly as he tried to remember how to breathe. Painter wasn't any threat anymore. It would be a couple of minutes at least before he was alive to anything except his own physical agony, and Guinness was willing to wait. So he stood up and walked back across the room until he had his back to the opposite wall—he wasn't worried about a thing except keeping himself from getting splattered with the mess.

Finally Painter managed a wheezy groan and let his head drop to one side so that he was looking at Guinness, as if through the obscuring veil of his own pain. And, in the end, even that passed away a little, and he could see his Luger in Guinness's hand. His lips began forming some word, but Guinness only shook his head. Guinness didn't want to hear anything about it.

"You shouldn't have done it," he said quietly. "You should have left her alone."

He raised the Luger and fired.

A pistol shot is far less noisy than most people imagine. You always expect it to sound like the announcement of Armageddon, but actually, provided that you keep to well-made weapons of reasonably small caliber, the report isn't much more than a sharp crack, rather like the sound you might make stepping on a dry branch.

Of course, there are psychological factors involved; you blow a man's brains out in a quiet suburban bedroom and you have the impression you've made enough racket to wake the dead. Partly it's a question of acoustics, the fact of an enclosed space, and partly it's the surprise—somehow you don't imagine that anything could interrupt the domestic serenity of the room where a pretty girl is wont to take her repose. And partly, no doubt, it has something to do with the damage a bullet traveling in excess of eight hundred feet per second can do to the human cranium. Painter really didn't look very good lying there on his face with the blood pouring, simply pouring, out of the socket formerly occupied by his right eye, and the sight of him—or the sound of the explosion, or its suddenness, or all three in combination—seemed to be playing on poor George's nerves.

"Jesus."

It seemed to be all he could say, and he could only whisper that. He sat on the corner of the bed, visibly trembling, unable to take his eyes from the spot in the middle of the floor where his late partner had left the concerns of this weary world behind. Jesus. Whether the one word was a prayer or simply a muted exclamation was something impossible to tell.

So George watched the floor stain and Guinness, who regarded his business with Painter as finished and, anyway, had long since ceased finding anything interesting in the sight of corpses, watched George. Probably both of them were wondering if they had just beheld the future.

At last George was able to tear himself away, and he looked at Guinness with that species of abject, un-self-conscious fear with which we all consider the instrument of our annihilation. His mouth opened and he seemed to be trying to say something, but now no sound came out at all. It wasn't until the second attempt that he was able to frame his question—which wasn't even that so much as the confirmation of a fact.

"You knew, didn't you. You knew we were up here waiting for you."

"You guessed it."

Guinness smiled, and the poor man's face seemed to collapse, as if this were the final warrant of his helplessness. And Guinness felt sorry for him, and subtly ashamed because, after all, there were no victories over mortality and to be the object of dread was to presume to a kind of safety that rested on nothing but lies. They were the same clay, the two of them, and the fact that Guinness now held the gun hardly meant he had assumed the nimbus.

"I want Flycatcher, George." The sentence, although spoken softly enough, cut the silence like a knife blade parting taut silk. "Frankly, it doesn't matter to me whether I kill you or not—I'll leave that up to you. Tell me where to find your boss, and how many of his playmates he has with him and how they're deployed, and as far as I'm concerned you can take a walk."

Poor George, he didn't seem to know what to believe. Possibly it just seemed too easy. He shifted uncomfortably in his seat and stared down at his hands as if he had never seen them before. Possibly he wondered if it wasn't a con, and if he might not end up on the floor next to Painter if he said anything. Possibly he thought to play for time—after all, it was better to be alive for five minutes than for only thirty seconds.

"How do I know you won't just kill me anyway?"

Guinness smiled again. It was a reasonable question, and he never minded a reasonable question. It was even a good sign, an indication that perhaps the intelligence of self-interest would prevail at last.

"I won't because I won't have to—come on, George, you know who I am. I don't kill anybody without a reason; that kind of thing is the mark of the amateur. You'll tell me the truth because you'll have to, because if you lie to me there's nowhere in the world you can run where I won't find you. I don't close accounts on people until they're dead."

With just the merest shrug of his shoulders, with no more than that, he conveyed the depth of his scorn for any attempt to evade the impersonal harshness of his wrath. He was the Soldier, the celebrated killer of men. He was the Angel of Death.

"Think it over, George. And don't let any lingering traces of team spirit cloud your judgment. You'll have to tell me everything—you don't want Flycatcher after you too. Right now the only hope you have is that I come up winners. He'll know you sold him out because all the rest of them are dead, and he isn't any more forgiving than I am."

18

The houses along the road out of Amsterdam seemed conspicuous for their lack of privacy. None of them appeared to have any curtains in their front windows, unless one used that word to describe the intricate and almost transparent panels of lace that were tied back at the sides—at any rate, there was nothing to interfere with an unobstructed view directly into the living room, which was invariably spotless, a cozy little interior world of gleaming hardwood floors and arrangements of flowers on dark, polished tables. Perhaps that was the idea; perhaps all those Dutch country housewives understood their parlor windows as a medium for displaying the blamelessness of their lives.

It was hot. Guinness cranked down the window of his car—well, George's car—to let in as much of a breeze as he could make going fifty miles an hour over a single thin strip of faded asphalt that seemed to wind around like a tapeworm as it felt its precarious way along the narrow ridge of ground between the flat, marshy farmland on the one side and the sea on the other. The late afternoon sunlight was yellow and heavy. Even the trees seemed to be sweating. In the last five minutes the only other car he had seen was a bright red tour bus scurrying back to town so no one would be late for dinner.

"We'll just walk down together to where you've parked," he had told George, smiling benevolently, "and we'll sit side by side on the front seat while I turn the ignition switch—you'll have to forgive me, but I'm the cautious type; I had a bad experience in that line once, and I worry about booby traps. And then I'll let you off somewhere and you can make whatever arrangements you like for getting out of the country. I hope you haven't been spinning me yarns, pal."

George had shaken his head and frowned. No, George was the sensible type who wanted to live in obscurity to a ripe old age.

"Don't worry. I just worked for the guy; we were never joined at the hip. I haven't got any ambitions to become a high-priority item with you—I've seen what that's like."

It seemed that George had been another one of the ones in Mexico. He hadn't happened to be in the house that particular night, but he had seen the consequences and had been brooding about them, apparently, ever since. He was a realist, was George. He figured Flycatcher was beginning to look like a bad investment.

"You killed Olsen and Sweeney down there, and then yesterday Lind gets found in an alley, and now you've killed Painter and Dietrich. No thanks. I don't want to retire that way." He shook his head again, looking sadly down at the carpet in Aimé's narrow little hallway, his hand resting on the doorknob. "No thanks. You can have him. He's all yours."

The impression was that working for Flycatcher hadn't been a very rewarding and fun-filled experience over the past several months, which was nice to hear. Apparently he had nearly bled to death after the Battle of Puerto Vallarta, and the gunshot wound to the chest had messed him up pretty badly. There had been perforce a long convalescence, and he had come out of it a changed man. He had discovered what it was to live on a steady diet of fear, and the judgment seemed to be that it hadn't improved either his disposition or his professional performance. George didn't seem the chatty type, but on this particular subject he was able to screw himself up to a certain laconic eloquence.

"He's gotten nastier. He was never much of a charmer, but it's out of hand now. And he spends more time on looking out for you than on anything else—it's no good when the boss's always watching over his shoulder; it's bad for morale. We've always been a high-turnover operation, and he can't attract the talent anymore. These days it's all screwballs like this guy Painter. Dietrich wasn't a bad guy, though. Strictly a coat holder, but not a bad guy."

"What do you want, an apology?"

No, he didn't want an apology. Perhaps he just wanted Guinness to know that not everybody in Flycatcher's organization would immediately think about extracting information with a hot iron.

But Guinness didn't want to hear about that. He didn't want to know what role George might or might not have played in Janine's peculiarly sordid death—after all, he was letting the guy go and he didn't want to regret it—and George was smart enough to maintain a discreet silence on the point.

But for the rest he had been communicative enough, which was hardly surprising since his life depended on it. Flycatcher was waiting in an isolated farmhouse about a hundred twenty miles from Amsterdam. It had the further advantage of being on perfectly flat land, so anyone sneaking up on the place would have his work cut out for him, and the German border wasn't more than a half hour's drive away. He had five men with him—no dogs this time, only men; apparently he had learned his lesson—and the men were equipped with automatic rifles. George said that it had been months since Flycatcher had gone anywhere without such a bodyguard; even when he had ventured into the city to pay his amorous little visits to Amalia Brouwer, the goon squad would be parked out in the street, glowering at the passers-by, tossing cigarette butts out of the car windows while they waited for him to finish. It must have been fun for everyone.

And what about now? Was he sitting in his bedroom, staring at his packed suitcases and waiting for it to be over? Was he thinking how much easier he would rest when he had seen Raymond Guinness with the brains leaking out through the back of his head? Guinness couldn't help but wonder what sort of death had been planned for him, what would have seemed humiliating and painful enough to make amends—and he wondered if, in the solitude of his private reflections, Flycatcher didn't understand perfectly well that it wasn't going to be that easy, that no one was going to bring him his heart's gall all trussed up in a neat little package, like a waxed-paper bag of jelly doughnuts, that this had long ago ceased to be a quarrel that could possibly involve anyone except themselves.

Guinness was glad that he had a nice long drive ahead of him and glad of the opportunity for being alone before this final confrontation. He might not have been as ready if Flycatcher had been waiting just around the corner or on the other side of the city. It had already been a harrowing day and it was a long way from over; already he felt burnt out, as if he hadn't had a moment's peace since the day he was born, and it was hard to care about living through even the next quarter of a minute, let alone all the hours and hours that separated him from any quiet of mind—and that was a dangerous way to feel, because it made you careless and could get you killed.

But he had a little time now to compose himself, and, taking advantage of it, he discovered with something like relief that at least the anger was gone. That was good—he would kill Flycatcher; somehow or other, he would manage that. He still wanted Flycatcher's death more than his own life, but in the ensuing war of nerves, their contest of blood and dishonor, anger would have been just something in the way. The victory would go to the dispassionate, even if he didn't live to enjoy it.

Guinness hadn't had anything to eat since breakfast—God, he couldn't even remember breakfast—so, in the first little town that turned up, he pulled into one of the parking spaces with which the picturesque old central square had been painted over and found himself the Dutch equivalent of a sandwich shop.

Actually, it was closer to a British pub, a sort of cross between a tavern and what the Americans euphemistically called a "family restaurant." The main staple of business seemed to be drinks of various kinds—most of the dark little cellarlike room was filled with circular tables at which spruce clerks and farmers in heavy, mudstained boots and black trousers sat moodily over glasses of brown beer—but there was a kitchen, and they would make you up a plate of any one of a half-dozen different things if you asked them. It wasn't Burger King, but it wasn't a den of iniquity either.

The woman behind the bar was a chubby, fortyish blonde who looked like she knew everything there was to know about the tactful defense of her ass when the closing-time crowd began to get a little rowdy. She smiled at Guinness and seemed startled when he spoke to her in English; they tried German and French and finally settled back on English, over which her command was less than perfect, and he managed to talk her around to a bag of sandwiches and a quart of what turned out to be very good lemonade.

On the other side of the square there was a men's clothing shop and what looked like a hardware store. Guinness stowed his provisions in the car and went across to see what he could come up with. A black windbreaker jacket cost him the equivalent of about thirty-five dollars, and he picked up a spool of picture-hanging wire, a pair of wire cutters, a roll of electrical tape, and a nice heavy rigid fisherman's knife with a four-inch blade for about another twenty at the hardware store. The clerk gave him rather a peculiar look as he sorted out Guinness's purchases, but he didn't say anything, possibly only because of the language gulf.

He sat in the car eating one of the sandwiches, which was filled with mustard and thick slices of some extremely spicy variety of lunchmeat, and drinking from the quart jar of lemonade and feeling a lot better. Food always had a calming effect, but it wasn't simply the tranquilization of the vagus nerve. All the way from Amsterdam he had been thinking about Flycatcher's Palace Guard, about the problem of laying siege in open country to a farmhouse guarded by five armed men. All he would have to balance those deplorable odds was the element of surprise, and he really doubted that Flycatcher would be much surprised. Flycatcher and his army of five—shoot one of them and they still had you outnumbered five to one; shoot one of them and you lose surprise. Guns were noisy, and Flycatcher wasn't some tame little citizen who would assume it was simply a car backfiring.

Guinness had the Luger and George's little baretta, which on the whole he preferred, locked in the glove compartment. They would have their uses later on, but, at least to begin with, he would need something subtler. And now he had a knife and a spool of wire, which improved things enormously; probably, at that moment, a particularly reckless bookie might have offered a wager at something as low as two or three to one of his surviving on into the next morning, so things were looking up.

"About four miles outside of a little burg called Tulp, there's a dirt road that forks off the highway—you can't miss it; just this side there's a stone pylon, about seven feet high, with a brass plaque. I stopped to read it once, but it's in

Dutch; I think it's some sort of war memorial. Anyway, another three miles on that dirt road and you pull up in front of the house—they can see you coming, plain as day, for the last three-quarters of a mile."

George had been right, you couldn't miss it; but Guinness didn't turn off onto the narrow dirt road that branched to the right about a hundred yards beyond the pylon commemorating some obscure tragedy of July 20, 1944. He didn't really imagine that George had expected him to.

He continued on for another couple of miles, until he found a spot where it was possible to take the car off the road. There was a crossover, a place where sections of drainage pipe had been placed in the ditches that ran along either side and then covered over with dirt, probably so that farm machinery could be moved from one side of the highway to the other. Guinness bumped along over the unplowed rim of the field until he could pull up behind a stand of trees that would shield him from the eyes of passers-by.

He put on the black windbreaker—in a few hours it would begin to get dark, and he wouldn't care to be any more visible than necessary—and threaded his belt through the leather loop of the knife scabbard. The guns went into the pockets of the windbreaker; carrying both of them was a trifle awkward, but there was nothing for it since they were slightly different calibers and therefore he wouldn't be able to pirate the Luger's ammunition for the baretta. They would both have to come.

He made a heavy loop with the picture-hanging wire, just large enough to be a comfortable fit when he slipped his hand through, and then ran off about two and a half feet and made another loop at the other end. He wrapped the loops with the electrical tape so there wouldn't be any chance of his cutting his fingers on the wire, and he had himself a very serviceable garrote. He wound the thing up into a loose coil and put it in the back pocket of his trousers. He was ready now, there was nothing else he could do. So he hid the car keys under the carpet and started out on his hike. He figured, what with following the contour of the land to keep himself hidden, that he probably had a good five miles ahead of him.

It wasn't going to be an easy five miles, either. The land was plowed, which made it troublesome to walk over, and the only cover came from the rows of trees that had been planted with the apparent motive of marking off one farmer's field from another. There were also irrigation ditches, but they were usually only about three feet deep—it was with something less than enthusiasm that Guinness considered he would probably end up making the final several hundred yards of his approach crawling through them on his hands and knees. Well, it was better than driving up in style to get your head blown off.

Time, he decided, was probably not much of a factor. He wouldn't be working against the clock because, after all, Flycatcher was waiting for his troops to come back with their illustrious prisoner, and they couldn't have any idea when Guinness would be returning to his borrowed apartment—they didn't even know what he was doing in Amsterdam.

Of course, it would have been a long time since Flycatcher had figured out that Amalia Brouwer wasn't going to show up. Had he connected Guinness with that affair yet? Would he have gotten nervous enough to send one of his boys around to the bookstore to see what had happened, and would they have found that fat slob still sleeping like a baby on the stockroom floor? They'd make the connection fast enough then. Guinness wished to hell he had done the professional thing and killed the greasy bastard when he had had the chance; now, when they finally managed to wake him up, he would be eager enough to spill his bloated guts. It had been a mistake, a moment of weakness. An unwillingness to pay the full price in blood.

Still, it was perfectly possible the guy would have snapped out of it on his own before they found him, and doubtless he would have been smart enough to know that it was not an occasion to hang around. So Flycatcher might not have tied Guinness in yet with his other troubles—he might assume that Amalia had simply been arrested, and he would have no reason to worry then because he wouldn't have told her about his little rustic hideaway. Flycatcher was many things before he was that dense.

It was his pattern to leave the end games of his little intrigues to underlings, while he waited at a safe distance to see how everything turned out. It was his strength and his weakness—if an operation went sour, he wasn't there to get captured or killed; at the same time, however, he wasn't there to keep his people on track, to give that vital word that might prevent the whole shebang from blowing up in their faces at the odd unexpected little snag.

Flycatcher had survived a long time in a high-risk business, but there had been costs. If he had been in Amsterdam this afternoon, he most probably could have ensured Guinness's death, but he hadn't been, and his troops, who seemed a lackluster enough collection, had had to fall back on their own limited resources of guile. And now he waited, out of contact with his men—a fair share of whom were already either disaffected or dead—and unsure of his position. Maybe this time his own caution would form the noose that hanged him.

Guinness just hoped the son of a bitch didn't get an attack of nerves and skip out over the border into Germany. It seemed little enough to ask.

It was already after five o'clock, but the summer sun was

still hot. Guinness could feel it pressing down on his shoulders like a weight; he had a vivid impression he might simply simmer to death inside his black windbreaker before Flycatcher ever had a chance at him, and that wouldn't be fair. He tried to stick to the trees, but there was hardly enough shade to matter. It took him close to two hours to get within sight of the farmhouse.

There were men out right enough. Guinness threw himself down into an irrigation ditch, coating his trousers with mud in the process, and looked over the edge through a thin little fringe of marsh grass. About two hundred yards away, sitting on a patch of high ground, there was visible a male figure—with the sun behind him, he was little more than a silhouette—with what one assumed was a rifle across his knees. He meditatively smoked a cigarette. No one else was in sight, but Guinness assumed Flycatcher wasn't relying on a single guard. Probably, in another quadrant of the perimeter, another man was sitting with a rifle over his knees.

The tactical problem, of course, was that the guy had his back to the farmhouse, which was probably two hundred to two hundred fifty yards behind him. This was reasonable enough—after all, he wouldn't be watching out for an attack from that direction—but it made things damned inconvenient. It meant that Guinness would have to slip in close enough to the house to be out of the guard's peripheral vision and still contrive somehow not to get spotted by anyone who, out of sheer boredom perhaps, might happen to be glancing out a window. And George hadn't been kidding—the surrounding countryside was almost as flat as a billiard table. There had to be easier ways to make a living.

The evening breeze had begun to stir, so at least there would be a little covering noise. With a reptilian slither, he began making his clumsy way down along the bottom of the ditch, hoping to get a little more parallel with the house before he risked showing himself on higher ground.

The irrigation ditches traced their way around the borders of the rectangular fields, each of which was probably about seventy yards by forty, making rather a more orderly pattern than the usual patchwork quilt one sees from the windows of airplanes. There was no going straight across from one side to the other because, unfortunately, all the fields had been cleared at some time in the not-too-distant past and the only cover they provided consisted of strawlike stubble, about four inches high, which would probably make a terrific racket while it was cutting you to ribbons through your shirt. So the ditches were it—you had to crawl along through the half-dried mud and then do a right-angle turn when you were behind your quarry. Guinness hadn't made a hundred yards before he thought he would die of exhaustion.

And the worst part of it was that, while he was trying to keep his ass down so no one could see him, he couldn't see them. He couldn't see anything, really, except the sides of his goddamned ditch; Flycatcher could have been standing directly over him, grinning maniacally as he lined up the muzzle of an AK-47 with Guinness's left ear. It was almost more than flesh could bear.

Every thirty or forty yards he would stop, rest for a few seconds, and hazard a quick peek up over the marsh grass—it was an absolute necessity, that furtive little check across the landscape; it was all that kept him from scaring himself to death with his own morbid imaginings. His thighs and upper arms, after a while, felt like they weighed a thousand pounds to the square inch, but there was always the thought that at any moment some goon might spot him, that the longer he was out there the more likely that was to happen, to keep him going. In a sense, fear and weariness canceled each other out.

It probably took him something like the better part of an hour to get directly behind his mark, who never stopped smoking cigarettes as he sat quietly on his fragment of raised ground near the intersection of two ditches—that was a piece of luck; Guinness would be able to get almost within arm's reach of him without having to rise up where he could be seen from the house.

The man's tranquility was amazing. It was obvious he expected simply to rest there, peacefully looking out over the barren fields that stretched away from him in a mud-stained grid, right up until someone came along to relieve him. The watch was obviously the merest formality. No one was going to try to sneak up on the place. No one would dare.

The last forty feet seemed to take forever. Guinness had taken the baretta out of his jacket pocket and was crawling along with it in his left hand, trying to keep it up out of the mud—if the guy turned around, he would have to shoot him; the game would be up then, but he wouldn't have any choice. He would have to shoot him. And then he would be stuck out there in the open, where Flycatcher and his boys could pick him off at their absolute leisure.

He could hear the little sucking sound of the mud every time he lifted his hand to move it. He could hear his breathing, which was even louder, and the pounding of his heart, and yet the guy didn't move. It was a miracle, an inexplicable mystery. Thirty feet, twenty, ten—Guinness could see the very weave of the heavy plaid coat (why would anyone wear a coat like that in the middle of summer?), and yet the broad back never turned and the automatic rifle remained flat across the man's lap, as inoffensive as a plank of wood.

Slowly, slowly, Guinness raised himself up to a low crouch. He was so close now he could smell the cigarette smoke as it drifted backward toward him in casual, trailing little puffs; it seemed impossible the man shouldn't be able to feel him through the back of his head. He slipped the baretta back into his jacket pocket and took out the garrote, pulling the wire tight to take the kinks out of it.

The classic method is to shape the wire into a wide loop you can pull tight by drawing your hands apart. It was really better that way, because if the thing went all the way around your victim's neck, there was less chance he could somehow slip free. Guinness simply waited, hardly daring to breathe as the man reached up to take the cigarette from between his lips. With his hands through the black-taped coils at either end, Guinness held the loop of wire delicately by his fingertips. For reasons he would have found impossible to explain, he waited until the man had exhaled the smoke from his lungs and had taken another breath before, with a quick little movement that was like a start, he slipped the loop over his head and pulled it tight.

19

It was a short, brutal struggle, made even more terrible by its very hopelessness. Guinness dragged the man down with him into the ditch, pulling for all he was worth at the handles of the garrote; he had expected a terrific fight, but Flycatcher's sentry seemed to have no thought for anything except trying somehow to claw the wire away from his throat—he hardly seemed to recognize that Guinness was there.

And, finally, he was quiet. Guinness kept the tension up until his arms ached, just to be sure, and when he released his hold there was the ghastly mechanical sound of air escaping out through the windpipe of a corpse. It was all over within perhaps two and a half or three minutes.

The man's face was several shades darker than normal—almost like a sunburn except purplish rather than red—and there was a thin trickle of blood from his left ear. His eyes were wide and staring and his tongue, which looked like it had pushed its way out of his mouth of his own accord, seemed at least twice normal size. All around his throat were the deep clawmarks left by his fingernails as he had tried to get free. One didn't imagine that it had been a very nice way to die.

They lay side by side in the ditch, the dead man and the living, while Guinness tried to catch his breath and still the wild beating of his heart. He felt almost strangled himself.

It was only then, after some semblance of calm had returned to him, that he realized how tired he was. He felt almost as if he could have curled up next to that corpse, right there in a muddy ditch, and gone to sleep. He felt spent—there was simply no other way to describe it.

There was a line of trees perhaps three hundred yards farther on—in fact, it was something more than a line; it seemed to be the margin of the cleared ground, beyond which there was a thick, shrub-clogged wilderness. He would have to get to that and make his way down past the farmhouse if he was to have any hope of bagging the man who, unquestionably, was guarding the road. Three hundred yards. Three hundred yards of crawling along on his hands and knees like a lizard. It hardly seemed physically possible.

And then, as he tried to roll a little off his right arm, which was beginning to feel slightly tingly from lack of circulation, he found his hand resting on his dead companion's shoulder. He could feel the coarse texture of the plaid jacket under his fingers.

Well, why the hell not? The farmhouse was nearly as far distant as the line of trees, and from three hundred yards a man is simply a blob on the horizon. Anyone looking that way would see what he expected to see, a man in a plaid jacket, with a rifle slung over his shoulder, walking toward the woods to answer the call of nature. He would know who the man was—he wouldn't need to strain himself by checking too closely. It was worth a try.

Still lying flat in the ditch, he worked the jacket over the man's shoulders and down his arms. It wasn't a very pleasant operation, but finally he managed to get the thing free and to slip his own left arm into the sleeve. He stood up to finish putting it on; it was much too big through the chest and perhaps an inch too short, but no one was going to notice at three hundred yards.

There was a nearly empty pack of cigarettes in the right

pocket, Camel filters. At the urging of his second wife, Guinness had quit smoking; she had said she had no intention of ending up as a middle-aged widow clerking in an insurance company, so he could just damn well take a few reasonable precautions with his health. But Louise had been dead for nearly four years now, the victim of her husband's past, a past she had known nothing about. And the man who lay with his face nestled in the mud had been a chain smoker—there were cigarette butts and smudges of powdery gray ash all around where he had been sitting—so Guinness shook out one of the Camel filters and stuck it in the corner of his mouth, lighting it from the book of paper matches that had been inside the cellophane wrapper. Anything to improve the disguise—and, considering the immediate alternatives, dying of lung cancer didn't seem like such a terrible destiny.

He picked up the rifle—it was nice to have a rifle for a change; the best pistol in the world wasn't worth a damn at any distance that mattered—and started toward the cover of the woods. No one took a shot at him, no one even showed his face. So far, at least, his luck seemed to be holding.

There was something oddly comforting about the presence of trees. You seemed somehow to make less noise walking. You had the illusion that you might even be invisible. Guinness tried to keep at least sixty or seventy feet inside the woods; he even took off the plaid jacket and left it rolled up behind a rock on the assumption that he would be harder to spot in the black windbreaker—after all, hunters wore bright plaids so that other hunters wouldn't have any trouble distinguishing them from the background, but the rules were a little different that particular afternoon. He decided he would have another cigarette and lit it with the still-glowing remnant of his first.

It was almost twilight, and the trees made long slanting shadows across the dark ground and their leaves clattered together in the rising wind. In an hour, or perhaps a little longer, it would be dark; the sun would simply go out, like a candle someone snuffs between his fingers, and the only source of light for as far as the eye could see would be the windows of Flycatcher's farmhouse.

In the darkness even the familiar becomes strange. Numbers have no advantage then—or, at least, not as much. The darkness would be in Guinness's favor.

Provided he could pick off enough of Flycatcher's bodyguard before they realized they were under siege.

That was the whole scope of the problem; there were five of them left, if you counted Flycatcher himself—and why shouldn't you count Flycatcher?—and there was one of Raymond Guinness. And he had the hour or so until sundown to whittle away at the odds.

The border of the woods tended to slant in rather drastically as you got more toward the front of the farmhouse. Guinness could see now that the property was wedge-shaped; the back part, where he had come in, and across half of which he had had to travel on all fours before he killed the first guard, was the thick end, and the front narrowed until it was nothing but the dirt road that led out to the highway.

The front was uncultivated—there were patches of sparse grass, but no one would have mistaken it for a lawn. Some past set of tenants, apparently, had been using it as a dumping ground. There were several empty cardboard barrels lying around and three or four pieces of derelict farm equipment—a set of tiller blades sat rusting in the sun about a third of the way between the woods and the farmhouse, and, farther down and near the road, lay an old-fashioned mowing machine, its saw-toothed blade sticking up in the air like the battle standard of some aboriginal chieftain.

The second guard, a thickset, hardened-looking young man with tarnished blond hair, stood leaning against the tiller carriage with his arms folded across his chest as he stared sullenly down to where the dirt road made a turn into the trees and disappeared.

Guinness watched him for several minutes. He sat behind a bush at the edge of the tree line and watched him, precisely as a naturalist might have watched some interesting and wary species of wildlife. He wondered what the hell the guy was brooding about, or if perhaps that wasn't simply the ingrained turn of his countenance, the little sweetheart. He also wondered how he was going to get close enough to him to kill him, since there were no longer any irrigation ditches to crawl through. He decided that probably he wasn't.

No more than about sixty feet separated them; it would have been the easiest thing imaginable to take him off with the rifle, which seemed a nicely balanced article and fired a 308 high-velocity cartridge that could be counted on to do a very complete job on anyone. But that still left the odds at four to one.

He had more or less made up his mind to wait until the fellow's relief came along and then try to nail them both—he would hold his fire until the new man was in place, get him first, and then get Blondie on his way back in to the farmhouse, preferably while his back was still turned and before he had a chance even to figure out that something was wrong, and to hell with playing fair—when Blondie, all on his own, started heading toward the woods, holding his rifle across its barrel in one huge hand. So that was what had been worrying him—he needed to take a leak.

There wasn't anything to do but wait. Guinness couldn't have moved without being seen, since the guy seemed intent on hitting the bushes at a spot only about twenty-five feet to the left of him. He really was a big brute, dressed up like a lumberjack in heavy lace-up boots and faded jeans and a dark checked Pendleton shirt with the sleeves rolled up over his heavy, matted forearms and the tail hanging out all the way around. Guinness was just as glad there was so little chance of his being called upon to wrestle him to death; the really massive ones always made him wonder if he would be able to take them all by himself or if he might not have to use a club.

He let him get about ten feet inside the tree line, where, at least, they would be out of easy sight of the house, before he stood up.

"Just keep walking," he said quietly, only just loud enough for his voice to carry the short distance between them, as he brought up the automatic rifle. "A bad move gets you cut in half."

There was only an instant in which the big man hesitated—he turned his head, saw the weapon that was pointed at him, and did as he was told. When they were far enough into the woods, Guinness told him to stop, and he did that too. He was still holding his own rifle in his right hand.

"Set it down. Do it gently—bend at the knees and put it down on the ground. That's a boy."

They were only about seven or eight feet apart now. Guinness's prisoner was still standing sideways; he turned his head toward him, and there was an unpleasant glitter in his eyes, whether of anger or fear or something quite different it was impossible to say.

"I must take a piss," he said, in a marked accent—German, or Dutch, or perhaps even Scandinavian; at any rate, Northern European—that contrasted strangely with the colloquial vulgarity of the sentence itself.

"Who's stopping you? I'll just stand here making notes."

The man stepped around a quarter turn, so that his back was to Guinness, and brought his hands around in front of him as if to undo his fly. God, Guinness thought, how he hated amateur productions—the guy was so obvious it was painful.

Just to be sure his rifle wouldn't go off by itself from the jolt, he clicked the little safety catch up with his thumb as he stepped forward. And then, with a quick circular motion of his hands, he swung it around, catching the big goon just behind the left ear with the stock. The concussion was surprisingly loud, exactly as if he had struck the trunk of a tree rather than a man's head. Blondie pitched straight forward and fell to the ground at full length—he never even twitched; you might have supposed he had been chopped down.

Both his hands were still tight against his stomach as he lay there. Guinness knelt down, pressing his knee into the center of the man's spine, and, one at a time, pulled his arms away from his body. Sure enough, when the right hand came into view he found it dragged along with it a shiny pistol—shaped like an automatic but really just a standard double-action, with a barrel no longer than the handle—the trigger guard still threaded around the thick first finger.

"Nice try, pal."

He turned the body over and was surprised to see the eyes still open, still with their glittering expression. He wondered if the guy had really thought it might work, if he had really believed Guinness hadn't spotted the pistol's outline under his shirt, or if he simply hadn't cared. Some of them, they wanted to make everything into a grandstand play—they just didn't know when to give up, or didn't care.

Guinness took his fishing knife out of its scabbard, set the point between the fourth and fifth ribs, just to the left of the sternum, and, holding it steady in his right hand, struck down on the butt with the heel of his left. Blondie convulsed slightly when the blade went into his heart, as if a current of electricity had passed through him, and then he was still again. It was only a formality; he had been dead from the moment he started fishing around under his shirt for that silly little gun.

Guinness withdrew the knife—somehow they always went in easier than they came out—wiped it off on the dead man's shirt, and put it back in its scabbard. The whole day, it seemed, had been filled with corpses, and he was sick of killing. Six people dead since the morning, four of them by his hand, and there was no end in sight. The world was being turned into a charnel house, a battleground littered with bodies; they would all murder each other until no one was left and they were all stretched out to rot in the sun. And then, when the crows had finally picked their bones clean . . .

What? Little bunnies, flicking their cottontails over endless clover patches? No predators, no more carnage? No more pointless savagery? The gods smiled on cruelty and left its victims to extinction. That was the morality of nature, simply to be one of the survivors.

So he would try to survive. There were four left, and he would try to kill all four, since that was to be the price of survival, and he wouldn't kid himself anymore with fictions of revenge. He couldn't settle up for Janine; there wasn't anything he could do that would make anything right again for her, because she was one of the dead.

But he would kill Flycatcher. To see Flycatcher dead was worth anything, anything at all. Just let him kill Flycatcher, and he would consent to lay down on the ground beside him and they could rot away together.

Three minutes later he was back at the edge of the woods, at a spot about seventy yards from the front door where the tree line had veered in sharply enough to put him at about a forty-five degree angle to the house. He had an unobstructed line of fire; nobody could leave the farmhouse from that direction without his having a clear shot at them. He had even found a log—not a fallen tree, something more on the order of a utility pole, about a foot thick at the base—that for some reason had simply been discarded there and that would make a dandy brace for the rifle.

He would use Blondie's—after using the other on the big lummox's skull, he no longer trusted it to be absolutely in perfect shape, but he had the clips from both weapons, and each of them contained about twenty rounds. It was enough. There were only four men left, which was hardly an army. Sufficient firepower was the least of his worries.

The operation had by now resolved itself into two separate tactical problems. The first one, to further reduce the odds down to, say, two to one, was fairly simple—it wasn't going to be forever before two more of Flycatcher's bodyguard would be sent out to relieve the two who, at that precise moment, were lying flat on their backs at various points around the property, getting used to their permanent retirement. There was no way of saying what the drill was, but the second watch would be along directly, if only to find out where the hell their friends were; and when they came out the front door, Guinness was all set to blow them away. That part was going to be easy.

The other part, however, was what to do about the cars. The little covered port, in which two dark blue vehicles of considerable size but indeterminable make were parked side by side, was on the other side of the farmhouse. Guinness could only just see the front bumpers shining redly in the last of the late afternoon sun. He had observed no back door when he had been crawling around at the far end of the property, and, since it seemed unreasonable to suppose that a dwelling would have only a front entrance, he concluded that the house could be entered or left from the carport.

It was a difficulty—how was he going to keep Flycatcher

from simply bolting to his presumably armor-plated chariot and taking off, as he had in Mexico?

Two to one, in the pitch black of night, was something you could work with, but you had to disable the cars. You haven't set much of a trap if, once you've sprung it, your mouse still has a hole he can wriggle through.

And this wasn't Mexico—you couldn't simply torch the damn things, even if somehow you could get close enough to try. There were fire brigades, and watchful neighbors who might notice the bonfire, and there were police. No, you had to keep this a private party; you wanted no official interference. So you had to hit upon something a little more tactful.

Guinness didn't like it, but he supposed, really, there was no other way. So once he had taken out the second pair of guards, once he had declared himself, he would simply have to head down toward the very narrow end of the cleared property, where he could find a covered spot that looked straight up the road, and wait there in the hope of disabling the car as it came toward him. He could try for the tires, or spray the engine and see if he couldn't tear something up under the hood, but he still didn't like it. It was just too chancy—however, he couldn't think of anything better.

At a few minutes before eight, in the final moments of the twilight, two men came out through the front door of the farmhouse. They had rifles slung from their shoulders and they let the screen door bang closed behind them, so they weren't expecting trouble. The lights inside the house were already on and they stood there on the porch, simply stood there, as one of them lit a cigarette. It was like a shooting gallery.

Should he wait and let them get a little farther from the door? It would be nice if he could discourage Flycatcher from retrieving the rifles, since there wasn't any point in his having more weaponry than necessary. No, the precise number of rounds of ammunition wasn't going to be a big factor—better to be sure of these two, to take them out while they were being so cooperative and standing so still and so close together.

Guinness chose the one closer to his side of the door for first honors. There wasn't any particular reason for it, except for the fact that he was a slightly less perfect target because he was facing toward his companion and was thus more in profile. Better to leave the easier one till second; he wouldn't have as much time with him.

He had never, of course, fired this particular rifle and had no idea for what distance it was sighted in—or even if they had bothered to sight it in at all. That was something else he would find out.

He chose a spot just under his man's left armpit, found it in the sights, took in a breath, let it out halfway, held it, and squeezed the trigger. At first the guy didn't even move, and then, quite suddenly, he simply fell down, exactly as if his whole body had gone slack all at once. When they fall like that, they're dead.

Number Two didn't move either, apparently slow to understand what had happened, and Guinness pressed the little switch to convert from single-fire to automatic. He had no idea how many rounds he let off in the one quick little burst; there was just a blur of sound, and Number Two started jerking around like a dancing marionette. The impact had thrown him back, and he hit against the screen door with a crash that even Guinness could hear. He was dead too, or he would die quickly enough. In either case, Guinness didn't waste another thought on him but slipped quietly back into the trees—it wouldn't take a genius to figure out where the shots had come from, and he didn't particularly want to be right on the spot if somebody inside the farmhouse decided he wanted to shoot back.

Once under the cover of the woods, he ran for all he was worth, trying to make the two hundred fifty-some-odd yards to where the trees closed around the narrow dirt road before he heard the sounds of a car starting behind him. There was no other escape for Flycatcher—he had to come that way and it was the obvious thing for him to do. Guinness simply ran, desperate to make the distance before Flycatcher pulled himself together enough to see his chance—unless the man was a fool he would know he had to make a break for it, and he wouldn't try it on foot, not with Guinness lurking around out in the darkness, so it would be the car; there just wasn't anything else for him to do.

When he had gone what he judged to be far enough, Guinness thought there was a fair chance he might pass out. He sank to his knees and then, when that didn't seem enough, just fell over on his face and lay there, waiting to catch his breath. He noticed that his face stung and discovered that he had apparently been cut across his nose and his right cheek by a treebranch, but he was so tired he couldn't bring himself to care. He was forty-one years old and it had been a long day, and, obviously, he was getting out of shape. He just wasn't up to these mad dashes anymore; he should confine himself to drawing-room assassinations, where a retreat down the fire escape would be about as strenuous as things ever got.

He got back up on his feet and looked around for a spot with a good clear view of the road, one where the car, when it came, would be heading straight for him, and when he found it he detached the half-empty box clip from his rifle and replaced it with the full one—you couldn't know; having twenty rounds all at once might make all the difference.

He lay there waiting, flat on his stomach between a couple of bushes. In the course of only a few minutes the last lurid rays of the sun had been extinguished and the sky had turned to an almost perfect black. The only light anywhere was from the farmhouse, which still seemed to blaze from its front windows. Apparently Flycatcher wasn't going to worry about the electricity bill—he had other problems; he would just leave things as they stood.

Eventually his breathing returned to normal, and Guinness tried to listen for the sound of the car. There were birds in the trees over his head, and apparently he had disturbed their repose with his arrival because they were only just now beginning to settle down again. But there was nothing else. He waited, straining to hear the dull throb of an engine, but there were only the birds and a faint whisper of wind stirring the branches above him. The lights continued to burn from the farmhouse windows, and the night was as quiet and still as an untroubled conscience.

How long did he wait? Ten—fifteen minutes? And Flycatcher didn't come. There was no sign of life or movement; Guinness might have been alone on the planet. And then the farmhouse lights fell dark.

20

So Flycatcher remembered Mexico too. What did he imagine, that Guinness was lurking behind the carport door, ready to burn him down the second he set foot outside? Something like that, apparently. Anyway, he wasn't going to get caught in the same trap twice. Such was the blindness of memory.

To test the proverb, Guinness held his hand up. Well, yes, he could just see it—a dim outline perhaps a foot in front of his eyes. Everything else had simply vanished. He might as well have been blind. There wasn't even a moon.

Through concentration of effort, he was gradually able to distinguish the shapes of tree trunks, not as themselves but as alternating bands of more and less opaque blackness. That, however, seemed to be the absolute limit.

So, darkness. He wondered which of them it favored more—himself, presumably, since it negated the possibility of coordinated action. There were just the two of them now. Or, if you trusted George's figures and cared to count Flycatcher's one remaining bodyguard, there were just the three of them. Guinness decided he had better not count out the bodyguard.

He tried to see things with Flycatcher's eyes, which, presumably, were as blind at that moment as his own. Flycatcher would know everything now—that the trap in Amsterdam hadn't held; that all four of his outside men were dead; that, except for the one that was left, he was alone.

And he would know it was Guinness waiting for him. Nothing would be hidden from him now.

Would he be tired of running? Was that, perhaps, the reason why his car had remained where it was, why he had apparently decided to forego escape? Was it caution or merely weariness? Well, they were both tired then, he of running and Guinness of chasing. They would let this be the end of it. It was time to stop this nonsense, and either live or die.

At about that moment he became aware of a faint crackling sound, no more than a texture of noise over the silence, something you almost couldn't be sure you were hearing at all. But, as he listened, resting the palms of his hands on the ground in a perfectly unconscious effort to focus its blurred impression, he knew it was out there. There was something—someone.

Two, or one? No, one. One man, somewhere behind him, the moldering debris of fallen leaves and dead grass crackling slightly under his feet. He was moving very slowly, with almost painful care because he hadn't found what he was looking for and didn't want it to find him. Guinness stood up, not even moving his feet, trying to gauge the distance. Whoever he was, he was close, but not close enough, not close enough to try anything. Not yet.

He had left the rifle lying on the ground, and now he took the baretta from his pocket. This would be work at close quarters; the rifle would only get in the way and he didn't want something for which he would need both hands. The baretta would be like simply pointing a finger. With as little noise as he could manage, he began working his way farther back into the covering woods. Somehow he felt certain that this new presence was seeking him out along the border of the trees. When he felt he was far enough inside, he dropped down to squat on his heels and wait.

It seemed forever. Perhaps he really had only imagined the sound—perhaps his mind was playing tricks on him and he should just lie down for a little snooze. What he wouldn't have given, suddenly, for a quiet twenty minutes of sleep; twenty minutes and doubtless he would wake up with his head wonderfully clear again. Except that, of course, the chances were he would wake up dead. Because he hadn't imagined anything. Because there was a man coming through the woods, with the object of killing him.

Because by then, of course, he had seen the guy. He wasn't so much a visible shape as merely a hint of movement, something vague that moved from one spot to another and then was gone. But he was there.

They weren't more than twenty-five feet apart. Guiness was quite sure the man hadn't spotted him—he was too wary; he was still searching, still feeling his way. It was eerie to be so close to him and yet unseen. It was like being invisible; it introduced into Guinness's mind a brief moment of doubt concerning his own bodily existence. But that passed. They were both of them real enough.

He weighed the baretta in his hand and then decided that, no, it wasn't the time to be firing off guns. After all, he had no absolute guarantee that this man was so utterly alone—it might be what Flycatcher was waiting for, the sound of a shot to tell him where to send a wide stream of automatic-rifle fire from some safe distance. It would be the sort of thing that would occur to Flycatcher, although it seemed unlikely that he would have confided the plan to his subordinate. No, this wasn't the moment. He put the pistol back into his jacket pocket and waited, his back flush against the trunk of a large tree, with nothing separating him from the dim shape of his hunter but a diminishing emptiness. Twenty-five feet. Now less. Now still less.

And it wasn't Flycatcher. Guinness was one of the few

American operatives who had ever seen Flycatcher in the flesh, and this wasn't him. The shape, for that was all it was, was too broad. And shorter—Flycatcher was a tall man, taller even than Guinness, who was six-two. And he moved wrong. There was none of Flycatcher's innate grace. This was someone else.

Guinness knew what he had to do, but somehow he couldn't seem to make up his mind to do it. Just push off and rush the guy, hitting him like a football tackle before he had a chance to know where he was. And then a few quick, disabling blows, followed by whatever means of homicide happened to be ready at hand. The distance was nothing—it would be over in an instant, and yet, for several seconds, he couldn't bring himself to move.

He didn't know this guy, didn't have any reason to kill him except for the obvious one. The poor slob wanted to murder him, but the inclination was perfectly impersonal—it was merely his job, hardly the sort of thing you could hold against him. It was an unhappy coincidence that they both happened to be in that line of work, nothing more. Guinness didn't want to kill him; he just wanted him to disappear, to leave him alone so he could go on with the work of killing Flycatcher, but it wasn't to be. It was all he could do to restrain himself from opening his mouth and uttering an apology, right there in the black of night. What a shock that would have been to everybody's weak nerves.

At the last possible moment, when he was sure that the man would see him in another few seconds, he made his charge. He pushed away from the tree like a racer from his starting blocks and, as his target began turning around to see what the stir was, caught him just above the waist, driving his shoulder into the solar plexus. There was a sharp gasp, a kind of muted bark, and then the bushes rustling as they went down together, but nothing anyone else would have heard even fifty feet away.

It was all done by feel—Guinness found the jaw with his one hand and brought the other fist down like a hammer-blow to the throat, not enough to kill but certainly enough to give the gentleman something else to occupy his attention while Guinness searched for the gun.

It was like wrestling with an octopus—arms flailing about wildly in an effort to do . . . what? Push his attacker away? Fight back? Or just get to the choking pain in his throat so he could hold himself tight where he was hurting? But in his right hand, apparently forgotten, was a small revolver. Guinness grabbed it around the cylinder—the thing can't fire if the cylinder can't turn—and twisted it loose with a snap that he assumed was the man's finger breaking.

And then, throwing the revolver away with a quick little spasm of movement, he simply started swinging, hitting at the man's face and neck with his clenched hands, like a maniac. There was no resistance after the first few blows, but Guinness kept on until he had to stop, until his knuckles felt like they were breaking, until he couldn't bear to keep his hand closed. And then he stopped.

The man was out cold—there was no fight in him, no strength in his body. But he was alive. Guinness put his ear down close to his mouth and could hear his breathing. That had to stop.

It was a simple enough procedure to smother someone; you simply pinched off the nostrils while you covered the mouth with the heel of your hand—it was called "Burking," after a certain Burke who had been hanged in Edinburgh in 1829 because people objected to the manner in which he procured unmarked bodies for sale to the medical school there. The procedure was even simpler when your victim was unconscious. Aside from a little writhing around, this one hardly struggled at all. Guinness waited until his thumb could no longer find a pulse as it pressed against the carotid artery, and then he waited a little longer, and then he let go. Once again, he had been a shining success. Once again, he had graced the world with another corpse to lie unburied in the darkness. It was a marvelous achievement.

There is no one so hardened, not even Raymond Guinness, the celebrated killer of men—at least, no one who is not actually and clinically insane—that he never experiences a moment of remorse for the actions of his life. Guinness had his store of haunting memories, the faces of the men he had killed, faces he would carry with him down into the obscurity of his grave, but he believed that this one, this mere shape beside him here in the darkness, might be one of the ones . . .

But there was time for that later. Tomorrow or the next day, if he should chance to live so long, he could indulge his private conscience; he could enjoy the luxury of his black thoughts, when there was less chance they might get him killed. But for the moment there was no time—he was still at hazard, he forced himself to remember; he had other business.

Because, of course, Flycatcher had read his mind. Flycatcher had known that Guinness would come running down to this place, where the trees closed in around the only road out; he had known that Guinness would wait there for the car to come. Flycatcher had understood the logic of the thing, had seen through Guinness's eyes. It reminded you that you were not dealing with an amateur. It reminded you that you couldn't trust anything, not even your own instincts, because the intimacy that had grown up between hunter and hunted had opened up the mind of each to the other.

God, his knuckles were killing him. In a tentative way he

felt them with his fingertips, and they were sore to the touch. Especially the left hand. They felt about twice normal size, but that was probably just an illusion. Already he found it nearly impossible to make a fist; in another hour both his hands might be perfectly useless.

What would Flycatcher expect him to do now? Where would he be? He knew where Guinness was, at least at that precise moment. Flycatcher could be anywhere. Guinness felt himself to labor under some intangible disadvantage.

But the conditions of the struggle hadn't really changed. Flycatcher wouldn't simply shinny out a back window and take off into the covering darkness—he had had plenty of opportunity to do that. Apparently he had it in mind to stay, to finally have it out and, one way or another, rid himself of Guinness's intolerable presence. He would stick around.

But where? Was he out prowling around somewhere, looking for Guinness while Guinness looked for him? No, it would be too great a risk—he would send out his last remaining thug, probably realizing that his private army was simply something in the way, but he wouldn't go himself. Flycatcher was a strategist, not a hunter; he would realize that in an equal combat he was no match for Guinness. He would not venture out into the darkness. He would try to keep the odds in his favor.

So, once again, we came down to the farmhouse and to the two cars in the little open garage.

And he had to find Flycatcher. He had to know exactly where he was and fast, while he could still bend his fingers enough to pull a trigger. Because now, it seemed, there was a time limit.

Guinness found the spot where he had left his rifle and sat down on the soft ground, cradling the stock across his knees. He didn't have a plan now—he didn't really know what he should do. If he waited where he was, there was a good chance Flycatcher would be on top of him before very long—after all, there weren't any *guarantees* he would sit quietly in the front parlor and wait on Guinness's pleasure; in his present state of mind, whatever that might be, he might just decide he had little enough to lose from a little recklessness.

And if Guinness went back up toward the farmhouse he opened up Flycatcher's avenue of escape. It seemed a choice between imponderables.

And, of course, Flycatcher was as aware of the alternatives as he was. They were each waiting to see which way the other would jump—and Guinness was at the disadvantage of being committed to a particular course of action; Flycatcher could choose either to fight or to run, but Guinness could only fight. He was bound, Flycatcher was free.

Or maybe not. Maybe there was no choice for Flycatcher now but to make his stand. Maybe he was sick of running. How was Guinness supposed to know? He didn't have a window into the man's soul.

But he knew this much, that had it been under any terms possible he would have walked away from the whole sordid business. At that moment he didn't give a damn what happened to Flycatcher; he felt like disappearing, taking his savings out of the bank and retiring to a beach resort in Central America while he waited for some thug with a grievance to find him out and put him out of his misery. He was bone weary and disgusted with the terms of his existence and couldn't manage the slightest shred of belief that it would make any difference at all who killed whom this night. It just didn't seem very important.

Which was fine, of course, except that he really was, in fact, committed. There might be a momentary comfort in imagining the possibility of chucking it, but that wasn't really something he had any choice about. Too many people had died—it didn't matter how they had died, whether he had killed them or whether someone else had; Janine was just one more among the others—and together they seemed to have a right to insist that he play it out to the very end.

It isn't your show anymore, they seemed to announce with their silent voices. *It's ours now—you made it ours, and you don't get to call it off.*

Guinness discovered that he could no longer make a fist. His hands really were swelling up, both of them. The left one, his good one, was much the worse—he must have broken something.

And then, for no particular reason, he glanced up and saw that the farmhouse lights had just come back on again.

And then, of course, everything was made clear to him.

In the pitch black, it took Guinness something like five minutes to find that damned mowing machine again. It had been standing not twenty feet from the road, right in plain view, but that had been in daylight and daylight had been quite another matter. Guinness stayed by the road, squatting down every ten or twelve feet until he spotted the ragged outline of the mower blade against the light from the farmhouse. Fortunately, he was well outside its reach, so, unless Flycatcher had a searchlight up there he wasn't telling anybody about, there was little enough chance of being seen.

The blade was hinged at the bottom, so you could pick it up when you weren't using it and keep it out of the way, and the hinge piece was held together with an ordinary cotter fastened with a pin. Guinness unhooked the wire that kept the blade erect, eased the blade down to the ground, and took out the cotter. That was the easy part—the fucking blade was about nine feet long and probably weighed around a hundred twenty pounds, and Guinness, with one hand probably broken and both of them tender and blown up like bladders, had to drag it out onto the road, which somehow, by the time he got it there, seemed a hell of a lot farther away than twenty feet. And all this had to be done without making a sound.

When he finally got it there, and after he had sat for a while with his hands tucked up into his armpits, rocking back and forth and feeling sorry for himself, he found a couple of pieces of abandoned two-by-four and propped the blade so that its huge teeth were sticking up at about a forty-five-degree angle. It would do.

And then, with his little trap set, Guinness picked up his rifle from where he had leaned it against the mowing machine and headed back into the cover of the treeline.

It took him about forty minutes to work his way up through the woods until he reached a point directly opposite the farmhouse—he knew perfectly well that Flycatcher was expecting him, and he couldn't be absolutely sure the dear boy wasn't planning an ambush. But apparently all his elaborate precautions were quite pointless; Flycatcher didn't spring out at him from behind a clump of bushes, and he wasn't greeted anywhere by a hail of automatic-weapons fire. Apparently Flycatcher just wanted to parley—and to get him away from the road.

Because, of course, that was supposed to be the whole idea. After all, Flycatcher wasn't an idiot. He had sent out his last boy, probably without much expectation of success, and had sat back waiting for the pistol shot that never came. And after a while, in the threatening silence, he had decided that now he was absolutely alone, so he had turned on the farmhouse lights so Guinness would know where he was—where he was, at least, at that precise moment. They would have a little conversation, you see, and try to arrive at an understanding by which they could both leave the property alive.

Guinness didn't believe it for a minute and didn't imagine Flycatcher did either. It was just a ruse, a means of shifting the conditions of conflict. But, for their own separate reasons, they might each be willing to maintain the fiction, at least for a little while.

So he waited, crouched behind a tree, far enough away from the edge of the cleared land so that there was no chance of his being seen from the farmhouse. He waited with the rifle cradled in his hands, just on the off-chance that Flycatcher might be dumb enough to show himself at a window. He crouched in the darkness and waited for the final act.

"GUINNESS?"

He found he had actually started at the sound—he had been expecting it, but somehow it had come as a total surprise. He remained quiet and waited.

"GUINNESS, ARE YOU OUT THERE?"

Needless to say, no human outlines appeared framed in any of the windows—well, he really hadn't thought any would. Flycatcher was probably pressed up against a wall, clutching a rifle against his chest in just the way Guinness was. Anyway, he was inside the house—there wasn't going to be any ambush.

It occurred to Guinness then, as something of a shock, that the bastard knew his name. But, after all, there wasn't anything to be shocked about. It was the sort of thing that could be found out, and Flycatcher would want to know.

"I HEAR YOU, FLYCATCHER—SPEAK YOUR PIECE."

Was Flycatcher surprised to have gotten an answer? Maybe so—at any rate, it was several seconds before he spoke again.

"GUINNESS? NAME YOUR TERMS." There was a short pause, but he wasn't waiting for an answer—maybe he only needed to catch his breath. "I'M SICK OF THIS. JUST TELL ME WHAT YOU WANT AND YOU'VE GOT IT—NO TRICKS."

Really, it was hysterically funny. Guinness didn't even try not to laugh; he hoped Flycatcher could hear him. After all this, to suggest there was any way they could keep from going to extremes—really, if Flycatcher could imagine that, it was too droll. But he really didn't suppose Flycatcher imagined anything of the kind.

"NO DEALS. YOU'RE A CORPSE, PAL. COME OUT OR STAY WHERE YOU ARE—YOU SUIT YOURSELF. BUT EITHER WAY I KILL YOU. COUNT ON IT—YOU'RE ALREADY A DEAD MAN."

It was a long speech to be shouted across maybe twenty-five yards, and he didn't suppose Flycatcher even hung around to hear the end of it. Probably he was already on his way, but that, of course, had been the whole idea—on both sides.

Guinness stood up and stepped out into the clearing. He was no longer worried that anyone would shoot at him; it hardly even crossed his mind. The light from inside was still streaming through the farmhouse windows, and he kept his rifle at the ready, but it hardly seemed to make any difference. His left hand was so swollen and tender by then that he could hardly bear to curl his fingers around the wooden stock. Perhaps, if it came to it, he wouldn't be able to pull the trigger. He was no longer sure, even of that.

But no one fired at him. The farmhouse was already empty. He had not taken half-a-dozen steps before he heard the engine of a car roaring into life; Flycatcher was in a great hurry to get away.

Almost right up to the final moment it went exactly as Guinness had expected. The dark blue Mercedes jumped out onto the road almost as if it had been kicked; Flycatcher must have had the accelerator right down to the floor, because the back wheels were shooting up great plumes of dust that hung gloomily in the yellowish light. A good guess was that the car was up to seventy before it had gone much over a hundred feet. The noise was deafening.

And Flycatcher was running blind. He wouldn't have any desire to turn himself into a target, so he relied on the light from the farmhouse for as long as he dared. Perhaps a hundred fifty yards before the night would close over him—the road began to turn there, and the trees were right up against you; after a hundred fifty yards you had to turn on your headlights and hope you were out of effective range, because you had to be able to see where you were going.

But by then it was too late. Or perhaps Flycatcher never even saw the mower blade. If he did, it was probably too late even to get his foot to the brake pedal. At any rate, watching the thing happen from a distance of about three hundred yards, Guinness didn't have any sense that the Mercedes had tried to slow itself. It must have been going at close to ninety miles an hour at impact.

There was an explosion—the front tires blowing, presumably—swallowed up immediately in a chaos of sound. It was ghastly—a piercing squeal as the car went into a skid, the sound of tearing metal, a heavy rolling, another explosion, but this time like the muttering of thunder in the restless heat of a summer night. It was beginning to burn, and the flames parted the darkness like a curtain, opening to you what had happened.

The Mercedes was off the road, lying on its side against the trees, burning. In that first instant it was almost completely engulfed in the lurid fire—the mower blade must have been kicked up underneath and ruptured the gas tank.

Guinness began to run toward it. He dropped his rifle and simply started to run. This was beyond anything he had expected, beyond anything he had intended. He had to get there while there was still time.

In a matter of minutes the fire would catch the trees

enough to be visible out on the highway. Someone would see and call in, and trucks would come to see what was the matter and contain the blaze. In twenty minutes, certainly no more, there would be people everywhere, and eventually they would find the other bodies and realize that something terrible had happened, something they would never understand. Guinness knew that, and he knew that by then he would be long gone, but before then he had to get Flycatcher out of that car—he couldn't simply let him burn to death.

But he needn't have worried. Flycatcher had been thrown clear. He was lying in the road, perhaps thirty feet from the burning car—close enough, certainly, to feel its heat—but in a few moments he would be beyond danger from anything mortal.

Because when he had been thrown out—or had tried to get out—the car must have gone over on him. He was simply smashed, smashed like a china figurine that had fallen to the floor. He would never get up again; that he was alive at all was a cruel joke.

Guinness knelt down beside him and took the limp hand in both of his, trying to find a pulse. He was surprised when the fingers closed around the ball of his thumb and the eyes opened and looked into his face. Somehow, by some miracle, Flycatcher was still conscious. There was still some flicker of life in his ravaged, sunken face, a face much older than the one Guinness had first seen in the lobby of a motel in South Carolina. Of course, he was dying now—that might have been it.

His lips moved, as if he wanted to say something, but Guinness couldn't hear him over the muffled roar from the fire and bent down until he was almost touching the dying man's shattered chest that jerked and quivered painfully as it tried to catch and hold a breath of air.

"Is it enough for you?"

The question was nothing more than a whisper, but Guinness was reasonably sure that was what he had said.

"Are you quite satisfied now?"

Whatever answer Guinness would have made, he never had the chance. Almost as soon as Flycatcher had spoken, the convulsed breathing was stilled. The face took on the immobility of a stone mask, and he was gone.

21

Guinness had been in Düsseldorf for three days, and already it was beginning to itch like crazy under the cast on his left hand.

"Take it easy," the Company doctor had said. "Just make sure you exercise the fingers for twenty minutes every day and you should regain about ninety-five percent full function—at forty-one, you're getting off lucky."

Well, he wasn't complaining. After all, the trade didn't absolutely demand that he be a fast-draw artist. He was alive, which was more than could be said for a lot of people.

And Amalia Brouwer, it seemed, was going to America.

At Guinness's insistence, they were giving her the full treatment, the sort of thing usually reserved only for high-level defectors, which, God knew, she wasn't. They would manufacture her a new identity, a full history of documentation, and they would set her up somewhere—she seemed to have taken a fancy to the idea of California, so presumably they would put her down there—and they would keep a loose watch on her for the first year, just to be sure she didn't run afoul of anything she shouldn't. It was all perfectly unnecessary, as Guinness had had pointed out to him more than once—after all, Flycatcher was dead, and who the hell else would take the slightest interest in a Dutch bookstore clerk?—but he wanted it impressed upon her that this was to be a radical break with her former life, that people were willing to go to a lot of trouble to wipe the slate clean for her. Maybe then there was a chance she'd be smart enough to keep out of mischief.

And Flycatcher really was dead. Guinness had brought back the collection of passports—there had been five of them, all in different names, even one of the bright red numbers reserved for officers in the KGB—and the wallet he had lifted from the inside pocket of a dark brown sport jacket that had already grown stiff with blood in the heat from the burning Mercedes. He had been received as something of a hero when he presented himself to Teddy MacKaye at the operations desk at the Düsseldorf consulate. His clothes were dirty and he probably smelled bad, and his hand was blown up to the approximate size of a baseball glove, but the man who had closed the file on Flycatcher was entitled to a little extra consideration. And if he wanted some little chit of a girl treated like the biggest catch since Rudolf Hess, then so be it.

"Do you really think he was KGB?" MacKaye had asked. Guinness, whose hand was soaking in a bucket of ice water, had shaken his head. No, he didn't think so—he didn't think Flycatcher had ever really worked for anybody but himself. And MacKaye had nodded, having received the definitive opinion on the subject. For a while there, Guinness wouldn't have been surprised to have had his opinions solicited on the origins of Stonehenge; for a while, he was treated like a cross between Captain Marvel and the Oracle of Delphi.

Of course, they weren't quite as happy with him when they found out about all those unexplained homicides over which the Dutch police were scratching their heads. Eleven dead bodies in a little under thirty-six hours were deemed to be just a trifle more than such a small country could comfortably absorb, but since none of the victims had been the sort of people anyone could care about—just a little whore, a

Belgian traitor, and a crowd of foreign criminals—no one really minded very much. Flycatcher was dead, that was the main thing, and the rest they would let pass.

In the end, the Dutch authorities decided that they must have come in on the tail end of some sort of gang war. They ran ballistics tests on all the guns involved and found that several of them were linked with other crimes, and, since the carnage had ended as abruptly as it had begun, they were inclined to let the matter drop. At least, that was the official story; what they really believed was something impossible to know.

"It was a pity about Janine," Ernie had said when they had a chance to talk with comparative safety over the consulate phone lines. "Did you get a chance to know her at all? She was a hell of a girl."

"No, I didn't get to know her very well." It was only a casual reference—Janine was a white chip on Ernie's poker table, and people died every day. Oddly, Ernie was much more upset about Rênal. Everybody, it seemed, was upset about Rênal. It made you wonder what they had had going for them.

And that was okay with Guinness. He couldn't have cared less about him, but he was much more willing to talk about Rênal than about Janine. He discovered that Janine was on his mind a good deal, and that they weren't very happy reflections. When the debriefings were over, he would go to London for a long vacation while he waited for his hand to mend, and he would think about Janine while he was there too. And maybe, finally, he would get her out of his system. Certainly he didn't want to talk to anyone about her, and especially not to Ernie. It was none of Ernie's business.

And for the time being, until Amalia Brouwer was shipped off to the New World, he hung around the consulate offices, avoiding casual conversations and trying not to let the way the secretaries looked at him get on his nerves—he knew it wasn't anything personal, that like everyone else they had heard the stories, but it made him feel like Jack the Ripper. In the afternoons teams of intelligence analysts asked him all sorts of stupid questions, the answers to which were picked up by the tape recorder they thought they had concealed so cleverly under the table, and in the evenings he would take long walks through town, trying not to make it too hard on the guys who had been assigned to follow him. That was standard procedure after someone has been through a very rough mission and knows more than makes people feel quite comfortable, and he didn't take that personally either.

And the rest of the time he spent in the apartment they had assigned him—it was full of microphones too; they even had one concealed behind a heating grid in the bathroom. He kept busy reading *Middlemarch.* Other men had booze, or heroin, or the treasured fidelity of their wives. Guinness had *Middlemarch.* He would lie in bed until eleven-thirty in the morning, drinking tea and reading. It was a way to pass the time.

And when he was sick of reading, and they had run out of questions, and his feet hurt, he could always divert himself with pondering over what had been so terribly important that eleven people had had to die for it.

He had long ago learned to live with the fact that he wasn't a very nice person—he didn't ask anyone to approve of him; he hardly even approved of himself. At the moment he was the Company's official Golden Boy. He had killed Flycatcher and everyone was very happy about that, so the carnage that had led up to such an aggreeable outcome was passed over in ostentatious silence. If he had problems dealing with his own attenuated moral sense, that was entirely his own affair. Nobody was interested. Nobody but Guinness, it seemed, cared about the victims of the late massacre.

Well—that wasn't quite true. They had cared about Rênal. In fact, Ernie had been reasonably pushed out of shape with him until he had been assured that someone else besides the celebrated killer of men had pulled that particular trigger. Then it was all right, and Guinness was returned to everyone's good graces. But they had, in fact, cared about Rênal. They were sorry he had died, and one suspected this had little enough to do with his purely personal charms. They had wanted him alive for some reason of their own. One wondered what it could have been.

Of course, Guinness was reconciled to the fact that he would never find out. It was the curse of everyone in the profession—you never got to find out. You had your little piece of the puzzle, and you never got to see the rest of it and so never knew whether anything you had done ever made any difference. You were isolated from the consequences of your actions.

But they had wanted Rênal to defect. And the only possible conclusion to be drawn was that he was some sort of a plant—either that or a decoy.

It was a familiar tactic. You stuff some poor clown full of misinformation, you grind it into him like corn into a goose, and then you arrange for him to get caught. The enemy thinks they have a prize and everybody's happy, with the possible and unimportant exception of the goose. It was the sort of thing that was done all the time.

And Flycatcher, of course, had made such a roaring big deal out of the whole operation—could it have been that he knew Rênal was something less than the genuine article? Maybe he was Flycatcher's decoy; maybe Flycatcher had another line into NATO and was drawing attention away from it by allowing Rênal to so pointedly display his disloyalty.

Were they all, perhaps without realizing it, playing the

same dreary little game? NATO wants Rênal to defect because he's their plant, and Flycatcher wants the same thing because he's his decoy? Did NATO know about Flycatcher's real source? With Flycatcher's death, it all became somewhat academic, but one couldn't help wondering.

And what about Kätzner? Had he turned out to be somebody's patsy too? Poor Kätzner. Guinness didn't like to think about Kätzner, didn't like to think that the colonel had finally ended up as the cat's-paw of his disdained superiors, but still, it seemed entirely possible.

"I know no details. I simply saw her name on one sheet of an operations report, and, believe me, it was not possible to inquire further."

That was what he had said. Had it been arranged that he should see that single sheet of paper? Had his people had their own reasons for closing Flycatcher's game down? They must have known about Kätzner's daughter; it was the sort of thing intelligence agencies made a point of knowing. Could they have set Kätzner up? Was that to be his reward for a lifetime in the service of the Revolution?

But Kätzner had never been one to think in terms of rewards or revenge or justice. Perhaps he had known he was being used and simply hadn't cared—that also would have been like him. For Kätzner there was only the Cosmic Joke, and the only rectitude lay in knowing when to play the fool and when to laugh.

But Guinness didn't like to think about Kätzner. He had no desire to spend his middle years as a student of such ironies. There were certain parts of the puzzle he thought perhaps it might be better that he didn't see.

Wheels within wheels within wheels. They took everything away from you—your moral dignity, even your sense of voluntary action. And all of it, probably, didn't mean a fucking thing.

So he tried not to think about it. He tried to concentrate on *Middlemarch.* He would be like Mr. Casaubon and spend his time pondering over Dagon the Fish God. He would go over to London in a few days and spend hours and hours in the Tate, looking at the Turners. He hadn't spent any real time in London in ten years—it would be interesting to see how much things had changed.

But he would be going by himself. Just like the first time, over twenty years ago, when he had come off a freighter with a letter of acceptance from the graduate program in English at the University of London and an ineradicable conviction that the world was his personal property. At twenty-one, most of us are dumb enough to believe almost anything.

He had friends in London, people who might still remember him from the old days, but he didn't suppose he would look any of them up. He would keep to himself, trying to attract as little attention as possible, and he would go to the Tate and look at the pretty pictures. He would give his old acquaintances a break, since there seemed to be so little recent evidence that being on intimate terms with Raymond Guinness was conducive to a long and fulfilled life. He would catch up on his sleep and try to put on a few pounds and play the tourist. He would leave it at that.

He might even be finished with *Middlemarch* by then, which would be just as well because he wasn't enjoying it very much. And maybe, after a week or so, he would be able to get this cast off his hand before it drove him crazy. Just the last two joints of his fingers were sticking out—he could barely touch the tips of his first finger and thumb together—so he was eating a lot of sandwiches and other junk that he could manage with just the right hand. But the itching was the big thing; it was destined to end with his smashing the bloody cast into powder himself because the skin was still too tender for him to get a pencil or something underneath to scratch the inside of his palm. The doctor said at least another week, but, all in all, it was gradually making Guinness pretty irritable and men had killed for a great deal less.

He would give it another four days and then he would just have to see. Ninety-five percent of full function—what the hell did that mean anyway?

But it was only the third day, after all, and Amalia Brouwer was going off to America. In forty-eight hours she would be sitting in an apartment in Los Angeles, nerving herself up to go down to Bullock's to replenish that dreary underwear collection of hers. Guinness wondered if perhaps he shouldn't say something to her about it, if perhaps it wouldn't be the sagest piece of advice he could give her under the circumstances: *Go buy yourself some mint-green see-through panties, Sweetheart, and see about starting life all over again.*

But he probably wouldn't say anything at all like that. He might be *in loco parentis,* but he was hardly the person to advise anyone about the conduct of their lives.

He had seen her only once since his arrival, for about fifteen minutes while he was waiting for the doctor to come and paste his hand back together. She had wanted to know how things had turned out.

"As you see," he had said, with a slight shrug that suggested he would regard the answer as self-evident. "I'm here. That should tell you something."

"Then Günner is dead?"

"Yes. Lots of people are dead—why should Günner be any exception?"

She took the news perfectly calmly, as if she were listening to reports of the football scores. She didn't ask any of the customary questions, so perhaps this particular lover had failed to touch her heart. Perhaps they all had; she struck Guinness as a cold little fish, which might turn out to be just as well for her.

So they had sat together in one of the empty offices at the consulate, with nothing further to say to one another. He was tired; the only thing that had kept him awake during the long drive from Holland was the throbbing in his hand, and even that sensation was beginning to lose itself in a general feeling of spiritual numbness. He wished to hell she would go away, but she stayed, sitting quietly with her hands folded, like a Victorian maiden paying a courtesy call on her senile old aunt. We sit with the wounded Soldier until the doctor comes—he seemed to find himself the victim of her sense of social duty.

He discovered he was unable to make up his mind about Amalia Brouwer. She was like her father, without the humanizing irony. And it had cost too much to have her sitting there beside him on the green Naugahyde sofa, but that was hardly something for which he could blame her. Those were decisions that, one way or another, he had made himself.

No, he didn't imagine he would ever warm to her very much. It mattered very little, however, since he was unlikely ever to see her again. She was going to California. In fact, the plane left that very afternoon.

And she was waiting for him in the consulate lobby, her brand-new raspberry Samsonite suitcase parked over by a wall. It was rather an odd color, but he chose to interpret it as a hopeful sign—she had decided, apparently, to enjoy a conspicuous existence, just like the rest of the human race.

And she smiled when she saw him, as if somehow he had become her only friend on this earth. Well, and perhaps he had. Someone had taken her out to buy a new summer dress—he had heard from Teddy MacKaye that she was afraid to leave the building on her own—and she looked very pretty. If she didn't blow it, she would do all right for herself in her new life.

"I am on my way to become a capitalist princess," she said, smiling to indicate that it was a joke she was making. "Perhaps I shall end by marrying a millionaire."

Guinness made a sound that passed in polite circles for laughter and wondered how Amalia Brouwer had come to be gifted with this strange capacity to make him feel uneasy, as if she were always dancing carelessly at the mouth of the abyss.

"You look very nice," he said. "Have they arranged everything for you?"

He tried to smile, but he kept seeing the expression on Janine's dead face. *I tried, Soldier. I tried, but I couldn't stand it anymore.* He couldn't smile, and Amalia Brouwer had no right to make jokes.

"Yes. They have arranged everything."

"Then go. Be happy, stay out of trouble. And when you get there, remember what the ticket cost. Janine, Günner, a lot of other people you never saw or heard of. You weren't responsible—I'm responsible—but you were involved. California is a long way away. Remember what the ticket cost."

For a moment he thought she was going to cry—so perhaps she wasn't quite made out of ice after all. But she didn't. She simply looked up at him as if she expected somehow he would exonerate and forgive her. As if the burden of guilt were somehow hers instead of all his own. He reached down and took her hand; it was very small, and somehow nerveless, as if it were merely an object attached to her body.

"Nobody blames you, kid. Live your life, and make the most of your second chance. There won't be a third."

"I know that. I feel as if I am abandoning my whole past."

"You are—you're lucky."

"I know that too."

So it might be all right after all, and the toaster salesman might have a chance for an unruffled existence, when it came his turn. It seemed possible, at least.

"My father—will I ever see him?"

Guinness shook his head, sorry for her now because now it was more than mere curiosity that had prompted her question. Perhaps she felt the need of some new mooring as she drifted away from all the old ones. Perhaps a little of her gratitude extended to the man who had once been Maarten Huygens.

"Forget about your father. He would prefer, I think, to be forgotten; he knows he could never bring anything but more trouble down on you now. Forget all of us, forget we ever existed. Remember everything else, but forget us."

And then some faceless consulate employee, someone Guinness had never seen before, came along and ushered Amalia Brouwer out to a waiting car. She turned around once as he led her away, and Guinness smiled, at last, and waved goodbye. He was glad he had decided not to tell her—she would have enough of that sort of freight to carry through life.

And then she was gone. Emil Kätzner's little girl, who would now be swallowed up in the anonymous mass, to be subjected to nothing more terrible than the ordinary tragedies of ordinary life. For her, at least, there would be no dried blood spattered over the wallpaper.

"You'll never guess who they found shot to death in his hotel room," Ernie had said, as if he were posing a riddle. "In Munich, and the very next day after you left—Emil Kätzner. Can you believe it?"

It was one of those times when Guinness was glad most of his conversations with Ernie Tuttle were conducted over the phone. It was possible to lie to your friends over the phone; they couldn't see your face.

"Why shouldn't I believe it? Did you think I'd killed him?"

"No, man. The idea never even crossed my mind. He killed himself, apparently; they tell me the gun was still in his hand. I just thought it was an interesting coincidence, you going rushing off to Amsterdam with blood in your eye on the very same day a hard case like Kätzner decides to end it all—did you know, his own people didn't even know he was in town; his blowing his brains out seems to have been as much of a surprise to them as to everybody else. Of course, you wouldn't have a clue about any of this, now would you."

"Not a clue, Ernie."

Not a clue—except that this last action of Emil Kätzner's life had all the resolute clarity of a stage drama. It was classical tragedy, Oedipus gouging out his eyes in self-inflicted retribution. It had that kind of grand and pitiless logic. The poor bastard.

"We must bear the consequences of the ways we have chosen for ourselves," he had said. *"There is very little point in pretending to be the victims of circumstance, because what is that but the sum of what we have done with our lives?"* The poor bastard.

Had he been meant to see that sheet of paper with his child's name on it? Had they hoodwinked him into betraying the loyalty of a lifetime, into taking his own life because he couldn't support the tension between his duty to the child of his middle age and to the cause of his passionate and romantic youth? Or had he known what they were doing, and had his suicide been simply a gesture of defiance, a refusal to be robbed of his integrity?

To know when to play the fool and when to laugh.

Well, those were his secrets, not Guinness's. They would

remain his secrets. They were no one else's. Guinness had played his part, had stood in the lobby of the American consulate and watched the sole survivor leave for the 6:04 flight to New York on her way to the beaches of the California coast line, that last perimeter of the Western world. Let her lose herself in some harmless oblivion where mortal gestures are as incomprehensible as the language of a vanished race.

He waited until the door had clicked shut behind her, and then he turned on his heel and retreated back to Teddy MacKaye's office. He would be leaving himself tomorrow afternoon, and Teddy had said something about making the rounds together before Guinness pushed off. Teddy wasn't a bad sort. *Middlemarch* could wait a little longer.